FENGRIFFEN &
OTHER GOTHIC TALES

FENGRIFFEN &
OTHER GOTHIC TALES

DAVID CASE

Edited with an Introduction by
STEPHEN JONES

Afterword by
KIM NEWMAN

VALANCOURT BOOKS

Published by Valancourt Books, Richmond, Virginia
http://www.valancourtbooks.com

ISBN 978-1-943910-07-6
Also available as an electronic book.

All Valancourt Books publications are printed on acid free paper that meets all ANSI standards for archival quality paper.

Set in Dante MT

Contents

Introduction

I FIRST MET DAVID CASE in October 1979. I was attending the Fifth World Fantasy Convention in Providence, Rhode Island. It was my fourth successive World Fantasy, and I was still overawed by both the convention and just how different America was from Britain in the 1970s.

And so it was that I found myself on the Saturday afternoon sitting with a group of authors in the bar of the Biltmore Plaza Hotel and experiencing with fellow Brit Peter Tremayne (Peter Berresford Ellis) the previously unknown delights of free hot food and copious cuts of cheese served during the "Happy Hour". (Back in those days, Peter was a well-known horror writer, long before he became world-famous as the author of the popular "Sister Fidelma" mysteries.)

Anyway, we were enjoying a few beers and good conversation when Ramsey Campbell returned from the bar with a man I had never seen before wearing a fisherman's cap. A big man. An outdoors-type of man.

"Do you know who *this* is?" Ramsey asked me, almost in awe, indicating his impressive-looking companion. "Er . . . no," I replied. Everyone around the table held equally blank looks.

"This is *David Case*," he said. I could tell by the note of awe in Ramsey's voice that this was someone I should take notice of. But, to tell the truth, I was still none the wiser.

While Ramsey introduced David and his English wife, Valerie, around the table, I wracked my brains trying to remember where I had come across his name before.

It turned out that David and his wife had come into town to buy some supplies and had stopped into one of his favorite bars for a drink. He had no idea that the World Fantasy Convention was being held in the same hotel that weekend or that, even more bizarrely, his current editor—the late, great James Turner of Arkham House —was also in attendance.

While all these pleasantries were going on, I was desperately sifting through my beer-impaired memory for where I had heard of David before—and then I had it! Herbert van Thal's legendary, if not to say infamous, *The Pan Book of Horror Stories*.

During the early 1970s I had read a number of David's stories in that annual anthology series. Not only did some of them take up more pages in the book than almost all the other contributions combined, but the quality of the writing was noticeably superior to much of the misogynistic and sadistic dross that van Thal was using in the series around that time. What I did not know at the time was that a number of these stories and novellas had been culled from David's first two collections of horror stories.

Following our very pleasant meeting in the Biltmore bar in Providence, I kept an eye out for more of David's work and was rewarded a couple of years later by his Egyptian novel, *The Third Grave* (1981), published by the venerable Arkham House imprint with illustrations by Stephen E. Fabian.

In fact, David was busy writing in various genres, and he has reputedly produced more than three hundred books, ranging from softcore porn to popular westerns, under at least seventeen pseudonyms. His 1975 western, *Plumb Drillin'*, was optioned as a movie project for Steve McQueen before the actor's untimely death in 1980, and David's work has been adapted for film twice.

Since my first meeting with him back in Providence, I had heard that David had been travelling around Europe, spending much of his time in Greece and Spain. I was therefore surprised to learn from Ramsey Campbell (there's that man again!) that David had settled in London, less than half-an-hour's journey from where I lived.

We eventually renewed our acquaintance, and over the next couple of decades I was able to publish a number of his stories in my anthologies, bringing several of his classic tales back into print for a whole new generation of readers.

Despite hailing from upstate New York, David Case has always had an affinity for the Gothic, going back to his very first collection, the now-fabulously rare (and expensive!) *The Cell: Three Tales of Horror*, published by Hill & Wang (US) and Macdonald & Co. (UK) in 1969. However, it was with the title novella of this present collection—originally published in *Fengriffen and Other Stories* by Macdonald in

1971, and as a stand-alone volume entitled *Fengriffen: A Chilling Tale* by Hill & Wang the same year—that he truly embraced the themes and atmosphere of the classic Gothic novel.

Two years after its first publication, *Fengriffen* was filmed by British company Amicus Productions as —*And Now the Screaming Starts!* (1973). At the time Amicus was a rival to Hammer Films, and veteran director Roy Ward Baker created a handsomely mounted melodrama involving an ancient curse, vengeful spirits and an unconvincing crawling hand (left over from Amicus' *Dr. Terror's House of Horror* almost a decade earlier).

Filmed on a low budget around Windsor, a town on the outskirts of London, the impressive cast included such renowned British actors as Peter Cushing, Herbert Lom, Patrick Magee, Stephanie Beacham, Ian Ogilvy and Guy Rolfe, along with early roles for Frank Finlay and Michael Elphick.

Pan Books published a paperback film tie-in with a suitably gory cover.

Almost three decades after the first appearance of *Fengriffen*, David returned to his Gothic roots again with the short stories "The Foreign Bride" and "Anachrona" in a new collection, *Brotherly Love & Other Tales of Trust and Knowledge*. Published in 1999 with a superb dust-jacket painting by Les Edwards and an Introduction by Ramsey Campbell, the publisher unfortunately turned out to be less than honest (or competent—the cover reads *Brotherly Love & Other Tales of Faith and Knowledge*!) and fled the country not long afterwards, consigning the book to relative obscurity.

"The Dead End" is almost a short novel in itself. Originally published in *The Cell* and reprinted in the thirteenth volume of *The Pan Book of Horror Stories* (1972), its antecedent is that greatest of all Gothic novels, Mary W. Shelley's *Frankenstein; or, The Modern Prometheus* (1818; revised 1831).

More recently, David Case's career as a horror writer has received a welcome resurrection. In 2010 I put together *Pelican Cay & Other Disquieting Tales* for PS Publishing to celebrate the author's stint at being a Guest of Honour that year at the World Horror Convention held in Brighton, England. The collection took its title from David's powerful zombie novella, which was nominated for a World Fantasy Award in 2001.

Meanwhile, Centipede Press has recently produced a major retrospective of the author's fiction in its *Masters of the Weird Tale* series, edited by S. T. Joshi, and now Valancourt Books is issuing new compilations of David Case's work in attractive, affordable editions.

David's meticulous attention to detail has always set his writing apart from much of the literature labeled as "horror", which can only be applauded in a genre that all too often sacrifices both substance and style for cheap effect.

David Case is a true original and, as with his previous collections, this present volume showcases that individuality in every story. These Gothic tales combine the psychological with the supernatural to dazzle the reader with their author's precise command of language, setting, and character.

Stephen Jones
London
September 2015

Fengriffen

M Y FIRST IMPRESSION OF FENGRIFFEN HOUSE was skeletal. I saw it from the carriage, rising against a stormy sundown like the blackened bones of some monstrous beast—not the fragile, bleached bones of decaying man, but the massive, arched columns of a primordial saurian who had wandered to this desolate moor and there lay down and died, perhaps of loneliness, long ages before. The spires and towers loomed up in sharp silhouette and the structure squatted beneath, sunken but not cowed, crouched ready to spring, so that the house seemed to exist on two planes at the same time —massive and slender, bulky and light, gross and fragile. It was a building that had aged through a series of architectural blunders, and it was awesome.

Our approach was from the east, by a twisted trail through the hills. The agony of sunset formed a backdrop to the house. The sky swirled darkly above a fringe of blood-red etching on a low and tempestuous evening. The turrets were aglow and the tallest trees caught the final slanting rays of cloud-filtered sunlight, while the world below was already drenched in the gloom of night.

I am a man of science, seldom affected by moods and not much given to fanciful thought. And yet as I gazed upon this remarkable construction, I sensed a pervading evil, an adumbration of unholy darkness. For a long minute I continued to stare, before I was able to smile at myself for my irrational sensations and lean forward to the driver.

He did not wait for my question.

"Aye, this be Fengriffen," he said.

He cracked his whip. I leaned back again. The wind was in the trees, playing a leitmotif behind the horses' clattering hooves. Perhaps it was the chill in the air that caused me to shiver.

The carriage swung around and halted before the front entrance, an archway of stone set with massive wooden doors—doors capable of admitting giants, doors worthy of a drawbridge, doors to stand fast against armies and defy the rush of dragons. A man feels his insignificance while approaching such portals. The driver brought my bag, leaving the horses, who were eager to move on to the stables, to suffer the habit of obedience and paw restlessly at the turf. As we drew near, the doors opened silently. A servant, bent and deformed with time, took my hat and stick and relieved the driver of my bag. The driver returned to his carriage and I passed through the arch and into the house.

"You will be Doctor Pope?" the servant said.

"I am."

"The master is waiting in the library. If you will follow me, sir?"

He ushered me through paneled hallways of such dimension that the corners were shrouded in darkness, and rapped lightly upon a door. A voice called, "Enter." The servant opened the door and stood back. I went into an impressive room of oak and leather and mellow candlelight. Charles Fengriffen walked across the room and extended his hand.

"Ah, Doctor Pope. It was kind of you to come so quickly. I am indebted."

His grip was firm and dry. He was a tall, lean man with aristocratic features and sufficient graciousness to keep arrogance from taking control. Yet beneath this surface lurked something of strained emotion—a hint of desperation behind his eyes. I was scarcely surprised at this, for he had not summoned me from London without reason.

"I trust your journey was comfortable?"

"Quite so."

"And not, I hope, in vain."

His eyes held mine for a moment, then shifted restlessly. It was natural that he should experience some degree of nervousness at this meeting; natural that he should have qualms and doubts concerning a practitioner of an infant science, not regarding the urgency of his summons. I had long grown accustomed to such reactions—resigned to them, I might say, for they so often prevented effective results.

"I hope not, sir."

"Yes," he said. He looked about the room with a vague expression; came to himself again and offered me a seat by the fire; sat opposite, then immediately rose again and crossed to the mantel. He returned with a decanter and, without inquiring whether I wished to drink, poured me a brandy. I sipped and found it excellent.

"I expected you are tired and hungry," he said. "Perhaps, before we talk . . ."

"I am more curious than tired."

"Curious?"

"Curiosity is necessary in my field."

Fengriffen nodded.

"How did you come to hear of me, sir?"

"The village doctor recommended you. Doctor Whittle. A good man, well able to mend a broken bone, but unversed in modern techniques of . . . of——"

"Psychology."

"Ah, yes. Psychology. Yes. Doctor Whittle has heard of your studies at Leipzig and your subsequent success, and suggested I enlist your services."

"That is rare. Few provincial practitioners have faith in my science. Few, indeed, have knowledge of it."

"As I say, Whittle is a good man who recognizes his limitations."

"And the problem?"

Fengriffen gestured meaninglessly.

"A matter of psychology, certainly?"

"I am not sure, sir. A matter in which I am helpless—in which I desperately need help. It is my hope that you may provide it. You will not find me ungrateful——"

I held my hand up, palm toward him. It is never good to speak of financial reward in these things.

"Your message mentioned your wife . . ."

"Yes. That is so."

"And something is troubling her?"

He nodded, looked down at his hands, then raised his eyes and stared directly at me. "I fear she is losing her sanity," he said.

This was more overt than I had come to expect. We regarded one another for some moments before he shuddered slightly and looked away.

"What causes you to believe this?" I asked.

"There are certain symptoms . . . certain changes in her attitude toward me, alterations in her physical appearance, a disinclination toward all the things which she formerly found interesting. It has the appearance of declining affection, and yet I am positive it is more than that. We were very much in love, you see." He seemed to be repeating this sentence to himself, pondering over its significance or mourning his loss. I waited silently.

"And since her pregnancy, these changes have become more rapid, more apparent."

"That is often normal with pregnancy."

"These are not normal changes, I assure you of that. My wife seems to despise me, almost to fear me. I have often found her staring at me with unconcealed loathing. And, too, I have seen her gazing at herself—at her swollen stomach, you understand—with an inhuman grimace. I fear she does not want my child. If it were a case of not loving me, that is one thing. But there seems no reason, no justification, and I must fear that her mind has conjured up some falsehood . . ."

"Sir, you must realize . . . I am a doctor and a psychologist. I am not a counselor upon marriage."

"Yes, yes. I am aware of that. Perhaps it will appear to you that my wife no longer loves me. Perhaps, objectively, it must appear that way. But I know Catherine—I knew her, we were very happy. Her actions are inexplicable to me. If you can fathom this mystery . . . find, if not a cure, at least some reason behind it . . ."

"I will do what I can."

"I can ask no more."

"Does your wife know why I am here?"

"She knows you are a doctor. I have not informed her of your . . . your field of study. Do you wish to speak with her?"

"In due course. Not directly. She will dine with us?"

"As you think best."

"Yes. It is often better to observe a person before inquiring into the anamnesis of the illness. It makes it easier to form an unprejudiced opinion, you see. If I might be shown to my rooms, now . . ."

"Yes, of course."

He sprang up and drew the bell cord. I finished my brandy and rose. Fengriffen was about to say something further, then hesitated as the door opened and a maid appeared.

"Ah, Mrs. Lune. Will you show Doctor Pope to his rooms now."

"Very well, sir," she said.

I followed her from the library.

Fengriffen's eyes followed me.

Mrs. Lune was an elderly woman with a firm jaw, the sort of servant who attaches herself to a household early in life and remains in their service a lifetime. She preceded me up the wide staircase with a proprietorial stride, thrusting the candlestick like a weapon before us—an ineffective weapon pitted against the black shadows of this vast edifice, washing a meager and transient path along which we trod. But Mrs. Lune had no need of illumination, for she must have known this house completely, stone and nail, through her long years of service. At the top of the stairs we turned down a hallway or gallery lined with numerous portraits, presumably the Fengriffen family, all done in dark and somber tone and attitude. I lagged somewhat behind her, interested in the family resemblance that ran through this ancestral chain. Heredity and inherited traits are, naturally enough, very interesting to me and I believe them as valid as environment in the understanding of a personality, believe that a physical resemblance may well offer a hint of further and deeper inheritance; for a man whose bloodlines are potent enough to pass on appearance will naturally pass on the less obvious aspects of his person to some degree.

Mrs. Lune, finding that I had dropped back, paused and turned, offering the light to my direction. The stern Fengriffen faces glared at me from the wall, surrounded by massive gilt frames that bore at the bottom the names and dates of the portrayed individuals. They seemed to progress in chronological order, beginning at the head of the staircase. I moved down the line, glancing at the dates and noticing that the canvases became less antiquated, if no less grim, as I advanced. They were spaced at regular intervals, as if the purpose were to form a family tree or chart that was easy to decipher, rather than a gallery of artistic interest. So regular, indeed, was the layout that when I came to a break it impressed itself sharply upon the optical sense.

I looked beyond, and saw that the paintings continued again. Only one was missing. The wall at this point was slightly lighter in a rectangle the size of the frames, as if the missing picture had but recently been removed. The fact nudged my curiosity.

"There seems to be a missing ancestor," I remarked.

"Yes, sir," Mrs. Lune said, and quickly added, "Your room is just here, sir."

"Who might this be?"

She appeared not to hear me, but moved off, opened a door leading from the opposite side of the gallery, and stood back waiting for me to enter. Instead I walked past and observed the next portrait, finding it to be the penultimate one. It was Peter Fengriffen. The last portrait was of Charles Fengriffen himself. He looked remarkably like his father on canvas—more so, indeed, than he looked in the flesh, for his picture had the lifeless and stiff attitude common to all the portraits. By the simplest logical deduction, it was apparent that the absent picture, being the antepenultimate, had been of Charles Fengriffen's grandfather.

"What has happened to the missing portrait?" I asked.

"I wouldn't know, sir," said Mrs. Lune, and immediately my curiosity moved past idle musing, for it hardly seemed possible that this woman would fail to know such a simple fact concerning the house she managed.

"Perhaps it has been removed for restoration?"

"That might well be, sir," she said.

She would obviously say no more. I shrugged and moved past her into the chambers assigned to me. Mrs. Lune entered behind me and proceeded to bustle about making preparations that had already been seen to. The fire had been laid, the candles lighted, the heavy curtains drawn, and the bed turned down. Mrs. Lune scurried about, poking at the wood and patting the bedclothes, adjusting the curtains an imperceptible fraction, moving a candlestick a trifle.

"Will that be all, sir?" she asked when everything was to her satisfaction.

"Yes, this is fine."

She moved to the door, then hesitated.

"Yes, Mrs. Lune?"

"You are a doctor, sir?"

"I am."

"You'll forgive my asking? Are you here to see about the mistress?"

Genuine concern played upon her countenance. I wondered what she had noticed of Catherine Fengriffen's disorder—if, indeed, there was a disorder. Charles Fengriffen had thus far been vague, and I debated whether I should attempt to elicit further details from this woman.

"I intend to speak with her, yes," I said.

"You won't be . . . forgive me, sir, but you won't be cutting into her, will you?"

"Cutting?" I repeated, not sure of her meaning.

"You won't be cutting into her body, will you, sir?"

"Good heavens, no. I'm not a surgeon."

"No, I meant . . . well, boring holes into her skull or anything devilish like that?"

"Trepanning?" I asked, incredulously.

"If that's how it's called."

"Wherever did you get such an idea?"

"Well, I've heard tell of such, sir."

"Here? At the house?"

"Oh, no sir. No, in olden times."

"Very old, I should think. My good woman, that was a prehistoric remedy for letting out evil spirits."

"Yes, sir," she said. She wasn't at all surprised at the information.

"I assure you, I will perform no physical operations of any nature. I am a . . . a different type of doctor."

Mrs. Lune peered at me. The candle she held cast oblong shadows upward over her face, and her eyes glinted from the darkness of the sockets.

"It's not a doctor as is needed here," she said.

"Whatever do you mean?"

"Oh, sir, it's not for me to say," Mrs. Lune replied.

She left the room, closing the door behind her. She closed it rather quickly. I stared at the oak panels for a moment, pondering upon this remarkable conversation. Then I turned to the room. My bag had been brought up and there was hot water in the basin. I began to dress for dinner.

*

Catherine Fengriffen greeted me civilly enough, but with a coolness that seemed more than normal reticence at meeting a stranger ... a coolness that was all the more surprising in that she gazed full upon my face for an inordinate length of time. It was impossible to judge the emotions that she experienced during this appraisal, whether curiosity or malice or scorn or possibly even friendship. I found it difficult to return this equivocal observation. At length she turned away and stared at her husband in a similar manner. I regarded her thus, in profile, finding her a strikingly beautiful woman. And yet when she had looked at me, I had not been aware of that beauty. It existed in the superficial structure of her countenance, but dimmed in her expression. She was younger than her husband. Quite young, in fact. But even in her youth there lurked a paradox. Her complexion was smooth, clear, free of wrinkles, yet she was strained and drawn. Her carriage was erect and graceful, yet one had the impression that she bore a heavy weight upon her shoulders. Her eyes were bright, but it was the brightness of sunlight filtered through an overcast sky. The cords of her neck were prominent as her head turned. She kept her hands clenched at her sides. She was swollen with child, her condition more advanced than I had expected, but she lacked the glow and bloom of pregnancy that normally adds so greatly to a woman's appearance and personality. She stared at Fengriffen every bit as long as she had stared at me, as if he, too, were a stranger, and I had ample time to study her features. I decided that despite the tenseness, none of the more overt signs of mental disturbance lurked there.

Quite unexpectedly, she turned back to me.

"You have journeyed from London?" she asked.

I told her that was so.

"A tedious journey," she said, and her tone implied that my travel had been wasted, that the journey had been more useless than tiring.

Then we went into the dining room.

It was a spacious chamber with an Adam ceiling and a trestle table of polished oak, at which we were seated some distance apart. Jacob, the old fellow who had admitted me upon my arrival, served us from the sideboard. He was attentive and efficient, if somewhat slowed by age, as he shuffled along the considerable length of the table, serving us in turn. The food was abundant, and the claret superb, but the conversation added nothing to the gracious atmosphere. I made a few idle comments concerning my journey. Fengriffen spoke of his horses without the passion of a true horseman. We discussed, very briefly, the differences we had found in life on the continent. Catherine said nothing. At one point, while we were talking of Italy, her eyes lighted and she assumed an attitude of interest, but this lasted for only a moment before she lapsed once more into a morose and disinterested expression. I found her behavior peculiar, but not outstandingly so . . . more preoccupied than disturbed.

Presently, partly through lingering curiosity but also in an attempt to keep the feeble and faltering intercourse going, I said, "I took notice of the gallery upstairs. It seems a very complete history of the Fengriffens."

Catherine looked up sharply, and Charles occupied himself with his goblet.

"I didn't count them," I continued. "How far back does the representation go?"

Fengriffen thought for a moment.

"Twelve generations," he said.

"A long time."

"Something of a family tradition. I've had my own portrait added. Perhaps you noticed."

"I did, indeed. There is a distinct physical resemblance running through the series. Unusually so."

He nodded.

"I can't say I approve of portraits in such a stilted manner, but I didn't wish to break the continuity."

Catherine had been staring at me once again.

"I find the resemblance rather disturbing," she said.

"Indeed? In what way?"

"It may be all well and good to have an ancient family and be proud of one's bloodlines, but surely a man should be an individual—should be more than another link in a chain of deceased humanity?"

"Every man who ever lived is that," I told her. "That, at least. He may be more, in his own right."

"I express myself badly," Catherine said.

Fengriffen turned his goblet about, cupped in both hands, swirling the wine.

"I mean to say—if such a strong physical resemblance is inherited, does it not follow that other traits will be passed on as well? The bad as well as the good?"

"Catherine . . ." Fengriffen said, and paused.

"Not necessarily," I said.

She smiled. It was an inordinately bitter smile.

"I bow to superior knowledge," she said.

"I do know something of heredity . . ." I began.

"I'm sure you do, Doctor. I'm really not interested."

Fengriffen turned toward her and was about to speak, but I thought it better to discontinue this line of conversation; I interrupted by saying, "Twelve generations, you said? Is the gallery complete for that time?"

He turned slowly back toward me, his lips still parted in preparation for speech, and nodded.

"I noticed one space that was vacant. I expect that picture has been removed for cleaning or restoration?"

"That is correct. It has been sent away to be repaired. There was a slight accident, actually. One of the servants . . . carrying a candelabrum . . . stumbled . . . you undoubtedly noticed how dark it is in the gallery in the evening . . . stumbled and fell against the painting. The candlestick was forced against the canvas with violence and tore the fabric. It was necessary to have it removed."

"Ah, I wondered."

"Why should you wonder?" Catherine inquired.

"Such is my nature. Which ancestor was it, may I ask?"

"My grandfather," Charles said.

"Henry Fengriffen," said Catherine, as though mouthing an anathema.

Charles scowled.

"I suppose Mrs. Lune was the culprit? It seems her domain."

"Yes," Fengriffen said. "Yes, I believe Lune was the one. I don't really recall. An accident, hardly worth remembering, of course."

"Will it be returned soon?"

"Why, I don't really know. I haven't thought. Why do you ask?"

"I take an interest in such work. A layman's interest. I should be interested in inspecting the quality of the restoration."

"Jacob, clear these away," Fengriffen said, gesturing at the remains of our dinner.

"It was rather badly damaged," Catherine said to me. "I shouldn't be surprised if it is beyond repair."

And she smiled again, the same bitter smile turned upon her husband this time, while Jacob hovered between them, bent over at his task, for all the world like some Gothic gargoyle sprung living from the wall.

Catherine excused herself as soon as the meal was finished. Fengriffen and I retired to the library for coffee and brandy. The wind was rattling the windows ominously, but the fire was burning and the room was pleasant. Fengriffen stood silently at the window, hands clasped behind his back, until Jacob entered with a silver tray and began to pour the coffee.

"Well, Jacob?" Fengriffen asked, without turning around. "What do your joints say? Are we in for a storm?"

"Not tonight, sir. Only been aching a bit through the day. Maybe in two or three days."

"They can say what they like about this modern weather prediction, there's nothing as accurate as old Jacob's joints," Fengriffen said.

Jacob seemed enormously pleased at such praise for the corporal barometer of his bones. He was almost smiling openly as he shuffled from the room. Fengriffen left the window and sat opposite me, his long legs extended in a relaxed posture, his face composed, his hands clasped before his breast. He looked almost too much at ease.

"Well, you have seen my wife," he began.

I nodded.

"Did her behavior not strike you as . . . as not normal?"

"A trifle distant, perhaps."

"Ah, but of course, you did not know her before. You have no means of gauging the depth of her change. She was warm and loving, the antithesis of what she is now."

"But a change of that nature hardly implies insanity."

His head was slightly forward, and he regarded me from the tops of his eyes, rather like a practitioner of the gentle art warily circling a formidable antagonist. Here again was the difficulty in my profession. I was employed to find truth, yet he dreaded truth; I was instructed to correlate facts, yet he withheld those facts. There would be more to this case than studying Catherine; it would be necessary to relate those studies to her husband—to judge her mental state objectively, and then to comprehend how that state appeared to Fengriffen's subjective perception. I had little doubt I could discover the dichotomous truth. My doubt was whether those truths would be the solution.

"Oh, I know," Fengriffen said. "You believe she has merely ceased to love me."

Merely? It seemed a curious word.

I said, "If she has ceased to love you, there will be reasons for that, too. But my task is to unravel the wandering paths of the mental process, to untangle the web of disorder. With understanding, often comes cure. But that is all I can do. I cannot persuade her to love you if she does not . . ."

"Nor would I expect it."

"It might well be necessary for you to change."

He shook his head. I was not sure what he meant to negate by this gesture. A brief silence followed. Fengriffen leaned forward to poke unnecessarily at the fire, shifting the flaming logs. The reflection danced curious patterns across his cheekbones. I sipped my brandy and coffee and waited. He took a cigar from his pocket and offered me one, and we made something of a ritual of clipping the end and lighting up. A light grey haze arose between us. We looked at one another through this smoke.

"You won't make a hasty judgment?" he asked. "You will speak with Catherine?"

"Of course."

"Alone, I expect?"

"Eventually. But first I should like to listen to you, to form a background upon which to judge. Tell me how you met, how you came to love and marry."

"You think that will be relevant?"

"Anything may be relevant. Who can say? At some point, some

occurrence—or, more likely, series of events—your wife's attitude altered. It is possible to reason back from the fact to the cause, but I believe it more effective to look first for that cause, and apply it to the effect. It may not be difficult. I can stand apart and look objectively upon events in a way that an involved person cannot."

Fengriffen nodded.

"Whether knowing the cause will enable us to change the effect, of course, is a different matter."

Once again his head nodded.

"Tell me as it comes to mind."

Fengriffen drew on his cigar and settled back. His eyes were closed. After a few moments he began to speak . . .

"I was born here at the house. My mother died while I was yet a child, so I remember her only in the barest snatches of recollection, more a mood than an image. I spent my childhood and youth in these surroundings, and I believe, according to the standard judgments, that it was a happy time. That is, I recall more pleasantness than otherwise, more happiness than grief, and the normal pangs of adolescence were mild. But I did not know Catherine in those days, and can see no possible connection. Well, those years passed, as years tend to do. I became a young man. Happiness, to a man, is not the constant that it is in childhood, and I decided I must see something of life. I arranged for rooms in London. My father had no objections to this, indeed thought it a fine idea, and provided me with adequate income. So I ventured, for the first time, away from my home.

"I was instantly charmed by an urbane existence. I was, I fear, something of a wastrel, spending my time in the pursuit of pleasure and wallowing in the charm of degradation. I realized all this at the time, of course, although I now understand it in a different light. But I might describe myself—might have even at the time —as a gentlemanly rogue or a philanderer or perhaps a mild libertine. I had the typical realizations of a young man and, even more typically, thought them unique unto myself, never dreaming that I was merely experiencing the same perceptions that all men do."

He paused.

"I expect this is the sort of thing you had in mind?" he asked me without the slightest trace of embarrassment. I was taken by his natural and direct approach to self-analysis, and nodded.

"Yes. Continue."

"I drank rather too heavily, and gambled considerably, although never exceeding my means or getting into debt or difficulty. There was always some sober part of my mind to hold the reins on abandon. Still, it was a wild life. It was London in a vintage year. Many the sunrise did I see through bloodshot eyes and hazy perception, many the turn of a card upon which I wagered recklessly, believing love a living entity that stood at my shoulder, many the theater I attended, playing my own little romantic role before the stage amidst an audience all of whom believed themselves to play the lead. And yes, there were women of dubious virtue, as well."

Fengriffen smiled slightly.

"Catherine knew of those women before we married," he said, anticipating a question that I wouldn't have asked.

"It was while I resided in London that I first made her acquaintance, actually. This was—let me see—it must have been seven or eight years after I first arrived there. My original intention had been to spend a year, two at the most, and then return home. But one tends to fall into a track of existence. Time passed quickly, the year was over before I knew it, two and three years passed at a stretch. Similarity of events grants fleet wings to the passage of time . . . reduces the constant of time's value. I was ensnared. I have no doubts, in retrospect, that I was infinitely bored by my meaningless life . . . so bored that my senses were numbed and I could not perceive my boredom through my stupor. So, like Hector around the gates of Troy, I was dragged behind the chariot of monotony.

"Then I met Catherine. I was immediately struck by her beauty, but at the time I was interested in less permanent arrangements than marriage, and it was apparent that Catherine was not the sort of woman who . . . you understand? We became friends, and there was great affection between us, but nothing more . . . nothing spoken, at least, although I expect the seeds of love were sown long before they were acknowledged. Catherine knew the sort of life I was leading and did not castigate me for it; viewed it with, if anything, an amused tolerance."

He drew on his cigar, as though using it to paragraph his speech, and I watched the long white ash advance up the cylinder, sending tentacles into the leaf.

"And then, quite unexpectedly, my father died.

"I was left in possession of these estates, and with a sense of filial failure. I had not seen my father in several years and animadverted upon my neglect. It brought a sense of reality back into my life, however. I had inherited responsibility. I suddenly understood how jaded I had become with my wild life, and knew it was time to return home.

"I did so. But I had not been here a month before loneliness and celibacy began to interfere with my happiness. I determined to find a wife, and Catherine sprang instantly to mind. She was talented, charming, graceful, and beautiful—all that a man could desire. Her financial means were limited, but her family was old and of excellent lineage. Money meant little to me, I found myself possessed of far more than I should ever need."

He gestured vaguely at our gracious surroundings with the hand that held the fine Armagnac.

"I believe it meant little to Catherine as well . . . that money could never enter into her decisions. I loved her and flattered myself that she loved me in return. Perhaps that was my error. I pray to God it wasn't. Although the alternative . . . it may have some bearing . . ."

Fengriffen's face clouded darkly for a moment as he twisted his thoughts in silence.

"But I ramble. In any event, I loved her. It was curious how I suddenly realized this love—realized that what I had believed to be friendship had been forged in a false image, that my emotions toward her were an anamorphosis which, when viewed correctly, ceased to be deformed by my perception. It was love revealed, and I longed for her. I journeyed to London immediately and proposed marriage. Catherine accepted me without the slightest hesitation, with a smile and an amused, tolerant glance, as though she had expected my proposal and had been awaiting it patiently. Perhaps my intentions had been more obvious to her than to myself. At any rate, we wed in London, as soon as it could be arranged, and left directly for our honeymoon on the continent.

"It was a time of extreme happiness. More. It was bliss and ecstasy. I had not the slightest doubt I had married wisely and

well ... married, I might say, to perfection. Catherine proved all I
could have desired, and more. My love increased beyond restric-
tion, beyond limitation, beyond the capacity of thought. And she
responded to my love in the same manner, until we were linked
together by bonds greater than either emotion or ratiocination,
greater than the sum of both. We traveled through France and
Italy at a leisurely pace, stopping when it struck our fancy and
taking several months longer than we had intended. We shared
the pleasures of new discoveries without need of words, with our
own communication—a smile, the tender pressure of a hand, a
glance—sufficient to send a deluge of feeling cascading between
our minds and hearts. We needed no one else, avoided other people
for the most part, sought private experience and beauty and found
it everywhere—found it in the caress of a Mediterranean breeze,
the color of a cloud, the eternity of a shapeless lump of rock. We
ventured to the museums and appreciated the subtle touch of the
old masters; then the wind would stir Catherine's hair along her
neck and all the talent and glory of Rubens or Botticelli was as
nothing to her splendor. She was the brilliance in the chiaroscuro
of life. She was mystery understood, reflecting love with an albedo
to shame the moon into darkness ... Ah, but why attempt to
express a thing you have not known? You understand? We were in
love without boundaries."

Fengriffen leaned toward me.

"And then, eventually, it was necessary to return to manage my
estates. Had I known, I would have forsaken all. I would willingly
have lived as a peasant on some rocky precipice, a shepherd in some
rustic cabin, a fisherman on a stormy sea. But I did not know. Damn
me, I could not have known. And so we returned.

"And that was when the change began."

His voice hardened and his face tightened. The ash dropped
from his cigar, unheeded, fragmenting against his well-polished
boot.

"I can place it to the second, you see."

I raised my eyebrows. He failed to see my gesture, for his eyes
were turned inward. He was looking at the past, recorded in his
mind, lurking and lingering in the shadows—cowled shapes,
silently waiting for the moment when defenses are down and they

may rush out to deal a savage wound. The recollections of regret, those parasites that torment their host and rage like dragons through the brain. I felt less objective than befits my profession.

"It was the very moment when she first looked upon Fengriffen House," he said, at length. "You have seen the house. It is impressive and, somehow, eerie. Even I, who spent all my childhood roaming through these grounds and rooms, often feel a strange mood pervading the walls themselves. Yet it is a house, no more. The mood stems from the mind. God knows it was the farthest thing from my thoughts on the evening I brought my bride home—an evening rather like this one, in fact. The sky was flaming and the house was framed against the sunset. We were in an open carriage, winding through the hills, as I looked fondly at my bride, wishing to witness her first reaction to her home, hoping she would be pleased. I knew, of course, the exact point where the road turned past a shoulder of barren land and left the view unhindered. Our carriage made the turn. Suddenly Catherine stiffened and shuddered. Her lips parted and she gave an involuntary gasp. I believed she had taken a chill, so I drew her to me, felt her trembling, asked what was wrong. She would not answer me. She continued to stare toward the house with an expression difficult to describe . . . an impression of foreboding, perhaps. But, whatever had caused it, it was from that moment that the change began."

Fengriffen leaned back again, his senses once more in the present, emerged from the forest of recall.

"I see," I told him. "And I do not see. Has she ever told you what it was she felt upon first sighting the house?"

"Never. I do not believe she knows herself. It was a feeling, unique but intangible."

"Intangible. Yes, I felt something of that myself."

"There are legends, of course," he said with a gesture of depreciation. "What ancient home is without its ghosts, its haunts and superstitions? I pay them no mind, certainly. The servants believe them, I expect. And I fear Catherine has come to believe them as well. But at the time when she first saw the house, she could not have known of the legends, which seems to make them an after-effect, irrelevant; a symptom rather than a cause."

"What are these legends?"

"They are nonsense. I shan't waste your time with them—cannot, in truth, recall the details myself. The point is, from that very instant, and without any connection, Catherine began to draw away from me. She became reticent and silent; took long solitary walks and spent hours alone in her room, or here, locked in the library. Books had never seemed to interest her very much before, and the obvious assumption was that she no longer wished to be with me. All the pleasures we had shared ceased to exist. I tried, at first, to ignore the change—to force myself to think it the normal way in which a marriage settles after the first passion, after the romance of the honeymoon has become a daily pattern of necessity. But I could deceive myself only so long. Eventually I had to admit that her love had changed, to attempt to find the reasons. Catherine would not speak of it, however. I asked her, begged her to tell me what was wrong. She would not even admit to a change. I told her we could go away again if that would please her—told her that we could leave instantly, retracing the paths where we had found such happiness, that her love was all that mattered to me, that I would gladly have dressed in rags and torn a living from the soil with naked hands as long as that love existed. She merely shook her head, rather sadly, and—the only time she came close to admitting the change—said that it was too late, that the past could never be recaptured. Then she left me, standing helpless and hopeless, seeking desperately for some hint or clue amidst my grief. I could only hope that time, that greatest of all healers, would undo the unknown damage. But time did not heal. Time served against me. By the time we knew Catherine was with child, the change had become so pronounced that it was apparent even to the servants that something was wrong. I have heard them discussing it amongst themselves. Can you imagine, sir, the agony of overhearing such intercourse? My wife will no longer even admit me to her room. I have done nothing, to my knowledge, to offend her—am willing to make any sacrifice at her slightest whim. And she refuses even sacrifice. I am desperate, sir."

And it was a desperate and beseeching glance he turned upon me, waiting for me to speak. I wished I could have found words of encouragement, but it was too early, I knew too little. The simplest answer seemed the most likely—that she no longer loved him, that his own fancy had contrived this sudden change, protecting his emotions by inventing the balm of hope.

"You have told me everything?" I asked.

He nodded, slowly.

"You have no idea as to the cause?"

"None. Catherine has mentioned the legends, and has made it clear that she despises this house, but that seems to bear no relation to her feelings toward me. I have offered to take her from here, but she has refused."

"The legends. Yes. Well, they could have affected her in this manner, one supposes. If she has that turn of mind—has connected you with the house and all the hatred and fears that have developed in relation to it."

"If only it were that simple . . ."

"No, Fengriffen. Not simple. It would scarcely be a rational judgment, but it could be a deep connection, difficult to sever."

"I understand that, sir. But I fear certain possibilities more than I fear irrational connections within her mind. It is selfish, of course. But love is a selfish thing—necessarily so, since it is reflection. But other possibilities . . . what I mean is . . . I have mentioned, I believe, Catherine's financial circumstances when we met. Is it possible she wed me for wealth, loved me superficially in the gaiety of London and the brief happiness abroad, and then found her feelings too shallow to cope with life in this secluded place? That she began to regret her marriage and then, when she became pregnant, saw the child as a hindrance to escape, saw her route to freedom blocked by her swollen womb?"

"Is that what you believe?"

He started to reply, then clamped his lips together and said through clenched teeth, "No, damn it. No."

"If it is so, there is little I can do."

"You can find the truth. I must know."

I nodded. I felt very sorry for this man.

"I will speak with your wife tomorrow," I said.

"And, waiting, I will know how Aegeus felt, waiting on that rocky coast for his son to return—praying that you will raise a white sail, sir . . ."

But I feared it would be black.

*

That night I found sleep elusive. Hypnos is a fleeting god when the mind is aroused, and Fengriffen's tale had moved me to feeling. I sat at the window, smoking a pipe and looking across the moonlit moors. The landscape was silent and awesome, blocked in patterns of silver and black. Thoughts ran at random through my brain. I was not seeking a solution—knew there could be no more than conjecture, as yet—but the thoughts had a will of their own, tempting me with vague urgings, telling me at one moment that it was obvious she did not love him, at the next that there was some mystery far deeper to be disclosed. I recalled Mrs. Lune's curious comments, remembered the missing portrait and Catherine's bitter smile, thought of the strange chill that had moved me when I first saw the house. Yet I made no effort at correlating these factors. They moved at a level beneath the surface of ratiocination, while my controlled thoughts were superficial. I looked at the moors and I smoked. When my pipe burned out I filled a second, lighted it, tamped it down carefully, and fired it again until it was burning evenly and the smoke was cool. Tobacco is an ally of contentment, and I told myself I must be content with the cheerful blaze still in the grate and the wind howling ineffectively outside, shaking the trees in a fury but unable to get to me—indeed, defeating its purpose as in rage it sucked the draught up the chimney and caused my fire to burn more freely. I was able to judge the force of that wind by regarding the shadows beneath the trees. The filigreed moonlight shifted and blurred, laying silver tapestries beneath the limbs. It was hypnotic. I lost awareness of time as I studied the moving shadows. My second pipe went out. I pulled thoughtlessly at the mouthpiece. My eyes grew heavy. Then, gradually, I found myself looking at a different shadow. I must have observed it for some time before I realized it was more than the wind snatching the trees. For this shape had advanced beyond the trees, bringing a shadow of its own; it moved near to the house and then paused. I snapped to alertness. I stared at this dark form and had the grotesque impression that, whatever it was, it was staring back at me. A finger of ice tapped up the articulation of my backbone, leaving me rigid in its wake.

And then the shape was gone.

I leaned closer to the window, but there was nothing there.

If it had been, it was gone.

A jest of deceptive perception, I told myself.

Then from the trees came the unearthly howl of a dog—a sudden, rising sound that ceased as abruptly as it had begun, in a way no dog willfully terminates its cry.

A dog, I told myself. No more.

But strange, formless doubts accompanied me to my bed that night . . .

I found Catherine walking in the gardens.

It was early and a damp mist clung to her, so that she appeared to drift over the ground. I had to quicken my stride to overtake her. She did not seem aware of my approach, but gazed abstractedly off into the distance. Yet when I spoke, she was not startled. She seemed to have been expecting me. She nodded and I fell into step beside her. She was wrapped in a tweed cloak and wore stout walking shoes, yet her manner implied more than a sensible stroll before breakfast. We moved on for a short distance without speaking. Then we came to a shattered stump from which the fallen trunk still angled to the earth, and Catherine sat upon it.

"Why have you come here, Doctor?" she asked.

"Your husband summoned me."

"Is my husband ill?" She smiled slightly.

I found a loose tongue of bark, and pulled a strip from the dead tree. The wood beneath had not yet begun to rot.

"Charles believes me insane," she said.

"Not insane, no. Unhappy."

"And can you treat unhappiness? Is there some arcane herb to cure it? Some unguent or liniment to make me content? Some leech to draw sadness from the soul?"

"You are unhappy, then?"

"Surely you don't ask me to diagnose my own sickness?"

"I ask you to talk with me."

"Of what?"

"Whatever you choose."

"Of unhappiness?"

"If you like."

She shrugged. I shredded the strip of bark and let the fragments drift away on the mist. The sun was rising now, distorted by the dampness and applying a pastel wash to the landscape. Catherine was silent for a time. She seemed indifferent to her surroundings, to me, even to her own sensations. Then she shrugged a second time, and looked up at me.

"What is the harm?" she asked. "What is the good, certainly, but what harm in speaking? You are right. Charles is right. I am immensely unhappy. It is no one's fault, not even my own. I am accursed."

I looked at her rather more sharply than I had intended.

"A fanciful word? Perhaps. Or do you think it an expression selected by an infected mind?"

"Words are symbols. No more."

"Yes," she said. "Yes, there are far worse things than words."

"Will you tell me?"

She began to tell her tale . . .

"I love Charles with all my heart," she said. "But what is the heart? It beats so many times a day, it stops. So it is with love. My heart still beats and I still love. Sooner or later . . . rather sooner, I fancy, it will stop. But I love my husband and I pity him. I know the agony my behavior must cause him. The very fact of your presence here is proof of his pain. And yet I am helpless to avoid it. My love is not lessened, but my responses are. Responses are not governed by that pounding organ; reactions are not carried through the blood-stream. I cannot tell Charles of my feelings. Confession is impossible for me. I feel as an unfaithful woman must feel . . . a woman who continues to be devoted to her husband and yet is driven by some prepotent whim into infidelity."

She shook her head.

"No, I have not been unfaithful," she said. "Not in the common sense of such words. But here again we have symbols, and I have been unfaithful in a far more terrible way than words can encompass. Words that I can use. Infidelity is a living entity within this house, an organism dwelling in the walls themselves. The instant I first looked upon these wretched towers and spires, these ghastly rocks rising from the desolate moors . . . You, sir, have seen this place. Did you not feel the evil?"

I did not reply.

"Ah! Blind men of science. I know no science, and therefore wear no blinders. Truth cannot penetrate the shell of false knowledge which foolish men have erected in the name of progress. But I am not hindered by this. When this house first came into view, I shivered. I felt a shaft of cold enter my body. Charles drew me to him, inquired as to my trembling. And what could I tell him? It was a feeling, the symbols were inadequate. Or are feelings symbols, as well?"

"Perhaps they indicate."

"Yes. Well, this feeling indicated. If only I had known what it indicated, I would never have entered the house. But I did not know. I told myself I was being ridiculous, and I passed through those loathsome portals. Inside, with the fires laid and the candles burning, it was momentarily better. For a while I became more cheerful, and thought of my fear as irrational and absurd; tried to believe I had, as Charles suggested, merely taken a chill. Then the other indicators began to appear. Mrs. Lune kept regarding me with eyes of pure and simple pity, looked at me as one might some piteously malformed infant or some innocent prisoner unjustly doomed to the gallows. This threw my husband into gloom. He shot Mrs. Lune a fierce glance which I was not supposed to notice, and she left. He sat brooding, his chin lowered to his chest. It was the first time I had ever seen Charles other than gay and cheerful, and I inquired about his mood. When he glanced up at me, for an instant, I saw something in his expression which might well have been fear. But he, as I had been, was unable to express his feelings. He said he was merely tired after our journey, and suggested that we retire . . ."

Catherine paused. I had taken my tobacco pouch out, and begged permission to smoke. She granted it. I dropped the dark, dry tobacco carefully into the bowl, leveled it with my thumb, lighted it, and added a grey haze to the heavy air. The mist was sinking low now and the sky was lightening. Clouds hung like sheepskins against an El Greco heaven.

"I had been given a separate room," she said. "I did not wish a room apart from my husband, but modesty is a powerful restraining force. I found it impossible to speak of such desires . . . do not know how it is that I am able to speak thus to you, sir . . ."

"I am a doctor."

"A curious sort of doctor, I imagine ... to listen to events as if they were symptoms."

"There are certain new methods——"

She raised her slender hand.

"No matter. It is nothing to me. But I am speaking ... shall I continue?"

I nodded, the pipe in my teeth.

"That first night Charles slept in my room, and all was well but for the nagging memory of my feelings. But in the morning, alone at my toilet, I once again experienced that dread chill. It enveloped me. It was much greater than it had been in the carriage, and different ... did not seem to originate from within, but to be an external circumstance. It was as if the atmosphere were closing in to crush and freeze my body. For long and terrible moments I was helpless in the grasp of this sensation. I could neither move nor speak. But I determined to struggle against it, told myself it was an irrational foreboding, nothing more. I forced myself—it took great effort, sir—I forced myself to rise from the table and move to the window, willing my limbs to obey, my muscles to function, as one moves through deep water. Feeling as if I would soon suffocate, I threw the window open wide and stood gasping for air. Gradually the feeling began to subside. I could feel it, a physical thing, being drawn from me toward the window. The cocoon of cold slipped from my flesh, the curtains quivered, and then I was left trembling, gazing out across the bleak moors. I concentrated on the view, to keep my mind from other tracks. The moors were— they are—beautiful. Stark and hard and lonely, but tranquil and peaceful as well. A sense of eternity is engraved in the rugged tournure. Some of this peace reached out for me, and I determined that I would grow to love this land as much as did my husband. I hung suspended in the balance between this desire and the fear of—of whatever caused my fear ..."

"Ah, but this is meaningless to you—to one who has not experienced the sensation."

"No, not meaningless. Somewhere there is a key, if we can find it ... a Rosetta Stone to unlock the mystery, to decipher the language of the mind."

"It is not within my mind, sir."

I chose not to comment on this point at the moment. I wished her to continue. But she stood up, drawing her cloak around her as the wind tossed her golden hair in wild disarray.

"Come, let us walk," she said.

I nodded.

"I will show you the place where I walked that morning . . . my first morning at Fengriffen House; where I strolled in solitude, attempting to let the peacefulness seep into me, determined to be at ease and grow accustomed to my new home . . ."

I followed her around the fallen tree.

"An ill-advised attempt," she added.

We followed an all but nonexistent path, overgrown and broken, which wound from the gardens across a field of gorse and heather and thorn. I walked slightly behind Catherine. She had a determined stride and erect carriage, and moved rather more quickly than is normal for a woman in her condition. The mist had been torn now, scattered and drawn to the sky, and the clouds were increasing and darkening, dividing and joining, drawing slender and then breaking apart like monocellular creatures in an act of reproduction. And they were reproducing. The sky had become overcast, only a few wedges of blue were visible, and the gaps were closing. I wondered, vaguely, how Jacob's joints were reacting. The field ended in a ragged line of trees, the limbs and trunks tortured into grotesque angles by the wind, the ground beneath mottled with filtered sunlight. Catherine headed for this woodland. The ground was more broken here. I moved to her side and offered my arm, but she did not take notice.

She moved directly into the trees. Large rocks were entangled in the roots on either side, but Catherine followed a narrow opening, passing through shadows and shafts of light, certain of her bearings.

Suddenly she stopped, gesturing with one hand.

I moved past her, and found myself in a graveyard.

It startled me for some reason. Catherine was staring at me, smiling. It was not a pleasant smile. Her hand was still extended in the gesture toward the tombstones, slabs of granite and marble sunken into the earth, ancient and discolored as the decaying teeth of dragons. They seemed to signify rot and corruption. They were not well cared for, and there was no apparent order in the arrangement of the graves ... Gravity and time were working their ways upon this place.

"This is where my walk brought me," Catherine said. "I sought peace and tranquility, and fate guided me to these forsaken tombs ... this place of memory and sadness, where my husband's ancestors are interred and where some day my earthly remains will be left to molder. Not a pleasant thought, Doctor. Not the conversation you might expect from a young woman with child. But I have no fear of death now; I would welcome it if it truly brings oblivion. At that time, I did not have such thoughts. I saw it as an omen, however. It frightened me, yet something kept me from fleeing. I wandered among these odious monuments to Thanatos as though my steps were preordained. I glanced at the stones, but moved on ..."

As Catherine spoke, she advanced into the graveyard.

"See, here is the grave of Charles's father. It is quite recent, the stone has not yet sunk into the earth. The coffin will still be intact. Perhaps the corpse will not yet have rotted, perhaps strips of flesh will still hang from the bones. How long does corruption take, Doctor?"

Despite the grisly aspects of her subject, her voice was detached and calm. She continued to move past the headstones. I noticed how deeply her stout walking shoes pressed into the dark earth, and had a ghastly image of some force drawing her down toward the graves, reaching up through the earth to grasp at her ankles. Or was the force above, pressing down upon her sagging shoulders? I wished to persuade her to leave this morbid place, and strode after her.

Suddenly she halted.

"And here is the sepulcher of Charles's grandfather," she said. "The monument remaining to a man who governed and ruled and ... It is no more than rough-cut stone, you see? Not the only thing he left to his descendants ..."

It was an arched slab of granite, set with a brass plate. The weeds had begun to overgrow the stone, but the inscription was still decipherable. Henry Fengriffen had lived to a ripe age. The rectangular outline of the grave had settled at a lower level than the surrounding soil, and seemed darker within the grave's boundaries. Catherine stepped directly onto this lowered patch and passed her hand across the dome of the tombstone. Her face contorted with an expression of loathing—an expression far too intense to signify hatred or fear, but rather as her countenance might have reacted had she been looking at the contents of the opened coffin itself. I stared at her, fascinated, remembering that it was Henry Fengriffen's portrait that had met with an accident.

"Catherine . . ." I said softly.

She did not notice my voice. She turned and leaned against the stone, the black earth oozing at her feet.

"Something drew me to this very tombstone," she said. "I knew nothing of the legend then. And yet I passed the others with scarcely a glance, directed to this particular grave by some magnetism of the senses. Everything was clouded, I saw only the stone. Around it the world was hazy, but this rock stood out, illuminated in my vision. I approached from this side . . ."

Her calm was gone now. Her eyes were wide, turned toward me but not seeing me.

"Suddenly, from behind the tombstone, a face rushed up at me! A hideous face with hollow eyes and a red smear running upward from the corner of the mouth to the cheekbone . . . a smear the color of blood, as though he had been tearing into raw flesh. I staggered back and cried out. Never have I known such horror. I did not believe it a human form, but thought it some fiend, perhaps a ghoul feeding upon the corpses. I tried to rip my eyes from this manifestation of evil, but they were held rigid in their sockets; wished to escape into unconsciousness, but could not faint; wished to scream, but found my vocal cords bound in a knot. This face turned upon me. The eyes glowed from the shadows, the mouth twisted in a leer, showing blackened teeth—teeth like these tombstones, wide spaced and rotting. For an eternity we looked at one another, and then, abruptly, he had vanished into the trees. His figure was tall and gaunt, swathed in rags of fur and leather. I could hear his passage through the undergrowth. Then all was silent. I was unable to move. I was petrified. Time had no meaning, even my heart was frozen. I stood that way for God knows how long, and then suddenly my reflexes returned, my muscles melted into obedience, and I fled back to the house.

"From that moment, all hopes of ever finding peace at this place were shattered . . . I left the mortal remains of my hopes to molder in this graveyard . . ."

Catherine laughed.

Despite myself, I looked at the trees behind the stone. She saw my glance, and laughed harder, leaning back until she was actually seated upon the headstone.

"Well, Doctor? What does your learning tell us?"

"This apparition—" I began.

"Oh, it was no apparition. The creature exists. It is even human, one supposes."

"You know this?"

She nodded.

"I have seen it since," she said.

"Then surely it is some wretched man dwelling in these woods. A poacher, perhaps. A hermit . . ."

"But, Doctor . . . you assume too quickly. Often, I have found, doctors are prone to that blunder. But I knew it was real, even then. When I reached the house I went to my room and lay for several hours in cold dread. Eventually, I summoned my strength and went downstairs. Charles was in the library. I told him what had happened, and watched his jaws tighten, watched the skin grow white across his cheekbones. I asked if he knew who the creature was, and at first he did not reply. I could read his thoughts, knew he was trying to decide what to tell me. Finally, he said that the man was a gamekeeper, and that I need not be afraid. Yet even as he said this, I could see the fear which enveloped him. I sat beside him and took his hand. It was cold. But he would tell me no more.

"A woman of curious disposition I have always been, but it was far more than curious speculation which drove me to discover the secret of this mysterious and hideous man. I sensed that in some way he was inextricably bound to my fate.

"I summoned Mrs. Lune to my room. That good woman arrived, and I managed to assume an appearance of calm, to keep emotion from my voice and merely mention that I had seen this man on my walk and did she have any idea who he might be. At the moment I described the red mark on his face, Mrs. Lune's kind, solid face dissolved. She was near to tears. She said she would rather not speak of it. I insisted, forcing my voice to a sternness and annoyance I did not feel.

" 'The woodsman,' Mrs. Lune said.

" 'But who is he? Is he a servant?'

"She shook her head and muttered something to herself.

" 'Then why is he on my husband's lands?' I demanded.

"Mrs. Lune's shoulders quivered. I asked the question again, crossly, wishing in no way to cause her anxiety or pain but feeling that I must know the truth.

"She said, 'I don't rightly know. Really I don't. I've heard tell as he's inherited the right to live in the woods . . . in a cabin . . . where his father lived before . . .'

" 'But why should this be?'

"Mrs. Lune wrung her hands together and said, 'Some injustice . . . in the past. I've heard it spoken of. Something that the master's grandfather did which wasn't . . . which hadn't ought to have been done. And then he wrote it in his will that they had the right to live on these lands always . . .'

" 'What was this injustice?'

" 'I can't say, madam.'

" 'Come, tell me.'

" 'I cannot. I don't know. God help me, I don't. Please, madam . . . that's all as I've heard whispered . . .'

"And despite both coaxing and threatening, I could learn nothing more from Mrs. Lune."

"She seems a superstitious woman," I said. "Surely you have not let such talk disturb you? These people believe in legends and tales . . ."

Catherine shook her head.

"Disturbed," she said. "Yes, it disturbed me. But here again, you do not know. I was determined to know what this legend was. I had to know. I dismissed Lune, much to her relief, pondered over what little I knew and decided that I would ask Charles when he came to my room that night—more than ask, I intended to demand the truth. It was compulsive. I had to know how this legend and that odious creature affected me. I believed that with knowledge I would be able to defend myself against this influx of dread and fear, this feeling of absolute despair. I still feel that had I been fore-warned . . . No, that is untrue. It was already too late."

The wind was rising with the sun. It toyed with the gnarled trees and shifted the slender shadows along the aging monoliths. Somewhere distant a small animal scurried through the undergrowth; a solitary bird was describing an arc high above. Perhaps the rodent scurried because it, too, saw this gliding hunger against the clouds. I noticed these things, for I had succeeded in putting my emotions aside, lis-tening to Catherine objectively so that external events and appear-ances were magnified in my perception—so that my senses rushed in to fill the void where emotion should have reigned. I was aware of her voice, not in relation to my sensations, but played against a natural background. The heavy scent of rich earth, mingling with the heavy air; the flickering play of light and shade; the ponderous motion of laden clouds—all these assumed a reality beyond the nat-ural and formed the set upon which Catherine's monologue was enacted.

"Charles did not come to my room," she said. "I have found that when my husband is disturbed or worried, he seeks physical effort. He has always been that way. I expect it is a good way to be. He drives his body to fatigue, and releases his mind. Well, he was dis-turbed that day. He spent the afternoon and early evening riding with the hounds, following a mad course at breakneck speed and allowing no moments for thought. I waited for him to return. Sev-eral times I saw him in the distance, leaping the stiles or thundering at full gallop across the fields. When he returned the horse was lath-ered to a frenzy, and Charles was exhausted. He trifled with dinner and then retired to his own room. I was forced to do the same. I lay tossing restlessly in my own bed, disappointed and impatient, but hardly angry. I am a passionate woman, but not irrational; my pas-sion is not aroused before my husband expresses desire. And such were my sleepless thoughts that it was not passion which caused me to wish my husband were at my side. I speak of desire because . . . well, because——"

"Because?"

Catherine shrugged.

"It is a basic function of mankind," I said.

"It is more than that. Never mind. Let me continue . . ."

I could not help but wonder at the significance of this reference to physical need, but chose not to press the issue. She was talking freely, and I did not dare tempt her mind from the track.

"Inevitably, my thoughts turned to the woodsman. I saw his face, haunting me. I closed my eyes and found the vision even stronger when trapped behind the lids. All the details were there, more graphic in my mind than when I had actually looked at him in the flesh. Once again I saw that frightful visage rise up from behind the tombstone; saw that birthmark so much like blood from a grisly feast, those blasted, shattered stumps within his mouth, and the inhuman eyes turn toward me. I could not drive the image from my feverish brain. I could think of nothing else. For hours I lay there, drenched with cold perspiration and staring at the ceiling while seeing the woodsman . . .

"At long last, I felt sleep begin to creep over me. I tried to accept it. My mind dimmed, then snapped awake once more. Objects in the room seemed to draw toward me, swelling out of all proportion, and then recede into darkness. Gradually I sank into a state of torpor. The mind can bear just so much turmoil, and then it erects the protective barrier of insensibility. Values cease to have meaning, a diaphorous slumber stands sentry over sanity . . .

"And then it came.

"It was the same feeling I had felt in the morning, but magnified a hundred times. It was far more than a rushing of air, closing of the atmosphere. There was a sound at the window, the curtains billowed inward, and then the thing raged within the room, swirling in the corners, blindly seeking and assembling. It gathered above my bed. It descended upon me . . . a touch of air so heavy and so cold that it had substance. It wrapped itself about my body like a living thing, holding my limbs motionless and piercing my breast until my heart itself was impaled. I could not move, I could not cry out. My eyes were open wide, I was fully awake but totally helpless in this supernatural grip.

"I cannot say how long I endured this frozen embrace. It seemed hours, perhaps it was minutes, but for this time I was captive, a prisoner of forces beyond comprehension. And then, finally, it seeped from me. I could feel the pressure lessen, the chill grow faint, the rushing sound abate gradually until it was gone, and I screamed . . .

"I screamed again and again, mad with terror and awakening the household. I was no longer held fast, and yet I could not move . . . my own fear had taken over the function of deadening my limbs.

"Charles was the first to enter.

"He stood in the doorway, wild-eyed, his hair disheveled, holding a pistol. His noble head swung from side to side as he sought a target. Mrs. Lune appeared behind him, one hand clasped at her throat. Her throat writhed like a snake beneath her fingers. 'The curse, the curse . . .' she babbled, over and over, until Charles pushed her roughly aside and closed the door.

"He came to the bed, attempting to conceal the pistol beneath his dressing gown. He sat beside me, took my hand, and looked into my eyes. I knew how much effort was necessary for him to appear calm. He stroked my hair and spoke softly, and I told him of what had occurred, my words falling out in mad confusion and disorder. He attempted to quiet me, told me I must have been dreaming, while I clung to him and begged him not to leave me alone. Eventually I managed to gain some semblance of control. More for Charles's sake than my own—all peace of mind had fled from me forever in those timeless moments, in the grasp of intangible talons—I let him believe he had convinced me . . . let him think it had been a nightmare.

"And yet, even then, we both knew better."

Catherine pressed her toe into the damp earth, leaving a sharp impression at which she gazed with interest.

"And yet—" I said, and my voice stumbled at some obstacle in my mouth. "And yet it must have been a dream."

Catherine raised a look of disdain and scorn.

"A dream caused by your disturbed and feverish state of mind."

"Of course," she said. "A dream. Can you cure me of a dream, man of science?"

"If we can find the root of the dream. Dreams may appear

reality. The line of demarcation is fine, and when the mind is intoxi-
cated with emotion . . ."

"But it was no dream," she said. "It was real. That was the first
time, but not the only time. Many times since have I felt that frozen
touch. And one time, Charles came again to my room . . . but no
matter."

She leaned toward me.

"I am wrong to mock your ignorance," she said. "I know you
wish to help me. But I know, too, that you cannot help me. No
living man can."

Her eyes burned; windows on the inferno that was melting her
mind.

"One more thing I will tell you," she said.

I waited.

"The next day, I went into the woods and sought out the woodsman . . ."

"Yes, I went alone into the middle of the forest and I sought that
base mockery of all that is human . . . sought him and found him."

She grimaced.

I regarded her incredulously, appalled.

"It was not courage, or bravery," she said. "I had no choice. It
was compulsion. I went alone and unarmed along the overgrown
trail without the slightest doubt in my mind that I would find him.
It was a certainty. I walked straight to his wretched hovel without
a single mistake, although I had never been in those woods before
and there were many trails intersecting. He lived in the middle,
where it is thickest and darkest. I came to a clearing, and there was
the man's cabin. I stood in the trees for perhaps half an hour, gazing
at the ill-kept structure. It did not appear real—far less real than
the experience you believe to be a dream. I felt no fear at this point.
My legs rebelled and for a time refused to carry me forward, but
my mind felt nothing of this. At length, I walked into the clearing
and approached the door. It was open. The woodsman was within,
crouched over a filthy pot suspended over the fire. His brutish dog
was beside him. Both man and beast looked at me; neither appeared
surprised at my appearance in the doorway. The dog raised his lip
but made no sound. The man did not speak. His demeanor was not

so repulsive, somehow, in his own foul den. I felt something akin to pity.

"I told him I wished to speak with him.

"He did not reply. He lifted a wooden spoon and stirred the odious contents of his pot. I entered and stood beside him. The contents of the pot bubbled and cast fetid fumes from the greasy surface. Foul odors rose, too, from his unwashed body and filthy rags. I felt nauseous and dizzy, but determined. I sat—actually sat—upon the bare floor beside him and asked him of the legend. It seems impossible, and yet at the time it was natural; it was necessary. He seemed to debate, if such a mind is capable of abstract thought, and then, still turning the spoon sluggishly through his ghastly stew, he began to speak.

"He told me, in coarse language and crude accents, of the legend and the curse . . ."

Catherine lowered her voice, but raised her eyes.

"And there I came to know my fate."

A long silence—a silence befitting our sepulchral surroundings—followed these words. No animals darted through the undergrowth now; the bird of prey had dropped toward the horizon and taken the sound of the wind with him. It was so still that I fancied I might be able to hear the vermicular scavengers that bloated and gorged, performed their necrophagous task beneath our feet. I shuddered at the thought.

Catherine continued to stare at me, judging my reaction.

"And the legend?" I whispered.

She shook her head.

"Of that, I will say no more. It faults my husband's ancestors, and makes a jest of innocence. It is a tale of flagitiousness which I cannot repeat."

She rose from the tombstone and the wind returned suddenly to gather her golden hair and pluck at her cloak.

"I am tired now. I have said enough."

"I will walk back with you."

"As you wish."

She turned. For an instant I believed she intended to address the tombstone or the grave, but then she turned once more and brushed past me. She walked quickly. I overtook her and once again she ignored my arm. We passed through the trees and out into the open field. The stables were at the far end, and the house towered above and beyond. Catherine headed toward the house, paralleling the gardens by this direct route. Fengriffen appeared, walking toward the stables, but if he noticed us he gave no sign. He walked with a preoccupied air. Catherine glanced at him, then looked away.

"Well, have I incriminated myself?" she asked.

"I don't understand."

She turned, stopping so abruptly that we nearly collided; gripped my arm and looked, intensely and searchingly, into my face.

"Am I mad?" she asked.

It was rhetorical. Catherine did not think so.

I knew not what to think.

I went up to my room, but the moment the door was closed behind me I was taken with a restlessness, an urge to action or motion. I filled one of my briars and tried to channel this feeling into contemplation to piece together what I had learned and discover, in theory at least, how a dream and a rustic woodsman and a legend of wickedness could combine to the sum of Catherine's disturbed state, could result in loss of love for her husband, who seemed in no way responsible. But the evidence was not sufficient, and I felt positive that I had not been given all the relevant details by either Fengriffen or his wife. That is a grave difficulty in my profession, for people place hope without placing trust. Despite my efforts, I was unable to forge my restlessness into rational force.

I stood up and wandered to the window.

The next logical step, I believed, was to discover what this legend consisted of. It had obviously affected Catherine tragically, although it was impossible to know whether that effect had been due to the content of the legend itself, or to the peculiar method by which it had been revealed to her. From my window, looking past the far wing of the house, I could see the stables. Fengriffen was still there, talking to the groom, and I contemplated asking him what this legend was. But he denied belief in superstition, dismissed such things with impatience, and would not understand how a thing need not be true to be valid. If he were to reveal the legend to me, it would surely be modified by his own beliefs and would scarcely be the same tale that Catherine had heard. Who involved in this could be objective? For I would need, at the very least, objectivity.

And at the very best?

The woodsman.

I glanced up at the sky, wondering if the impending storm would hold off long enough for a visit to that hovel in the woods —perhaps hoping for black and swollen clouds, for I did not relish the thought. I had to scoff at my own timidity, to tell myself that Catherine had ventured there before me, alone and unprotected. I turned my gaze toward those woods. The sky was low with unbroken clouds, but I refused to allow myself that excuse. It was in the woods I must seek the clue.

I donned a heavy cape of Scottish wool and changed my light stick for a heavy cudgel I had purchased in the Swiss Alps. As my hand closed upon the thick shaft, I felt a touch of irony in the fact that a man of science should take heart and comfort from a length of carved hardwood. Yet such is man, and to say that a man knows himself is to say that he has looked into a bottomless chasm and claimed discovery . . .

Fengriffen was watching while the groom saddled his horse. He was immaculate in finely tailored riding clothing, absent-mindedly slapping his crop against a gleaming booth. My path took me past the stables, and I paused. He walked toward me, still snapping the crop.

"You have spoken with my wife?"

"Yes. We talked."

"Have you learned anything?"

"Things, yes. It is necessary to connect them."

"To separate the truth from the absurdities, you mean?"

"No. That is not what I meant."

He looked speculatively at me.

"Then you have nothing to report?"

"Not as yet."

"I see. Well. And where are you going now?"

"A walk. I often walk while I think."

"Will you ride with me instead?"

"I think not. A solitary stroll is more conducive to contemplation."

"As you wish."

I started to turn away.

"I expect Catherine told you a great deal of nonsense?"

I turned back without replying.

"I mean to say . . . you cannot take all she says these days at face value."

"I will make the evaluations," I told him.

For a moment I thought he was going to make a sharp rejoinder. Then he shrugged rather elegantly.

"Of course," he said.

I crossed the field on a tangent to the course Catherine had led me over earlier, coming to the trees somewhat to the south of the graveyard. When I was in the shadows I paused and looked back. Fengriffen was watching me. I had the impression that he had watched me all the time it took to transverse the rolling ground. It was hard to be sure at that distance, but he appeared to be scowling. The groom was behind him, holding the horse patiently. Fengriffen turned away then and swung gracefully into the saddle. The horse took two steps sideways, rearing slightly, and then they were off at a gallop. The groom looked after them, scratching his unruly hair and pushing his cloth cap to the back of his head. He waited until Fengriffen had turned his mount sharply around the side of the house, then moved into the darkness of the stables.

I moved into the woods.

The wood, although wild and overgrown, was not large. I anticipated little difficulty in locating the woodsman's dwelling. There were numerous trails, slender paths where the growth had been beaten down by the passage of animals, and I followed the largest of these. Occasionally I looked up through the twisted limbs to judge the position of the sun by the brightness of the clouds, thus attempting to keep some semblance of direction. The deeper I penetrated into this forest, the thicker the trees became, and the lower limbs caught at my shoulders and hindered my progress con-

siderably. These trees were somewhat protected from the bellow-
ing wind. They were formed more symmetrically than the twisted
arbors of the periphery, and stood taller as they contested with their
neighbors for the favors of the sun. It was a contest for survival, one
which all had not won, for withered dwarfs, lifeless and dry, clung
to their neighbors, wrapping tormented roots and boughs tena-
ciously about the healthy bowls, drawn to the flowing sap . . . arboreal mendicants in a kingdom that gave no alms. Several times I was
forced to squeeze past these misshapen forms where they leaned
over the path, and once a dead limb cracked sharply at a slight pressure from my elbow. It was not difficult to think of this forest as a
physical manifestation of a twisted mind, for I have trod through
mental labyrinths just as I wandered through those trees, seeking
the darkest spot in the deepest and most secretive seclusion.

The earth became damper, almost swampy. The mud sucked
at my boots, reluctant to release my feet. It became exceedingly
unpleasant, and in annoyance I used my stick to batter at the tenacious creepers and vines; I caught myself doing this and, chuckling
at such unguided rage, paused to light a pipe and allow my nerves
to relax. Then I pressed on more slowly through the fuscous forest,
and came abruptly upon the cabin.

It was a structure of rough grey stone and splintered wood, badly
in need of repair. A thin ribbon of smoke arose from the jagged
chimney, coiling upward for a few feet, then taken by the wind
and torn to shreds. I stared at the hovel for some moments before
I became aware of the woodsman. He was seated in front of the
door, directly in my line of vision, yet so well was his figure suited
to the surroundings that I had failed to notice him until he moved.
He raised his head to regard me. His countenance was terrible
to behold. The birthmark—for such the blood-image proved to
be—stretched in a wedge of vascular tissue from the corner of his
mouth to his temple, and his greasy hair fell in matted twists over
his brow. I was repulsed by his appearance, yet his features were not
without intelligence—not the intelligence of civilized man, but the
animal wile and suspicion of one who lives alone with nature.

He did not move at my approach, but his mouth opened, the
long wolfish jaw dropping to reveal tobacco-stained teeth. Beside
him stirred an object that I had taken to be a pile of rags. It proved to

be his dog, a mangy creature of skin and bone; this brute regarded me in exactly the same manner as his master.

I moved to within a few feet of this bestial pair, and leaned on my stick.

"I wish to have a word with you," I said.

He nodded. The dog moved toward him, slinking, and he placed a gnarled hand on its neck.

"Will you grant me a few moments?"

He blinked. Perhaps he was unaccustomed to a civil approach, or perhaps unused to human relations in any form.

"I've not done nothing," he said.

"I did not imply that you had."

His discolored fingers moved nervously through the animal's stiff pelt.

"This here be my home," he said. He nodded his head, as though affirming the words to himself. "Ain't no one as can deny me my land. I can't be sent from here." He slowly closed one eye and cocked his head so that the cords stood out in his stringy neck. "It's all written out proper."

"I have no wish to send you away, my good man."

"Did ye come from the manor, then?"

I nodded.

"From Fengriffen?"

I nodded again.

He turned to the dog and made a curious sound deep in his throat, whereupon the brute lifted a ragged ear. The dog's teeth were every bit as foul as the man's.

"I am a doctor," I said.

Something akin to interest sparked in his eyes.

"The mistress will be poorly, then?" he asked.

I ignored the query. "I understand that the mistress spoke with you some time ago."

"Oh, aye."

"I would like to know what you spoke of."

He shook his head. His expression was sullen and stubborn, but modified. It was as if he took pleasure from the mood.

"Will you tell me?"

"Nay."

"But why not?"

"Ain't no reason I got to. This here be my home. No reason to talk less I like."

"But surely there can be no harm in it."

He shook his head again.

I contemplated offering this wretched creature money but decided against it, feeling certain that he could be bribed into speaking but that what he said would lose all validity if he spoke purely for emolument, that he would tell me anything that came into his dubious mind and take some perverse pleasure in the deceit.

"And yet, you spoke willingly enough to the mistress."

"Not the same. Not the same at all. I had to tell the mistress as I did."

"Had to?"

"Was a duty."

"But you won't tell me?"

"No reason."

I stared at him, trying to trace the meanderings of his thought process, wondering if his refusal was merely a characteristic perversity or something more motivated.

I said, "The mistress is ill. I believe you may be able to assist in curing her by revealing what your conversation was concerned with."

He looked incredulous. His odious face registered amazement for an instant, and then pleasure.

"Cure her?" he asked. "Cure her?"

His laughter was fiendish and inhuman. It seemed impossible that such sound could be formed on living vocal cords, resonated in a human skull. It vibrated and undulated, then broke off in a fit of coughing that racked his emaciated form.

He spat upon the ground and peered at this mucoid blob with interest, studied it as some arcane sorcerer seeking knowledge in the entrails of a sacrifice. I shuddered with revulsion. When he looked up again, no trace of amusement marked the passage of his laughter.

Then, without another word, he rose and entered his hovel. The dog crept after him, slinking like a reptile, and the door swung

closed on broken hinges. I was left standing alone, my hands
clenching my stick. From within came a repetition of that hideous
laughter. Once more it ended with uncontrolled coughing. I was
filled with a mad, irrational desire to bring my cudgel violently
against the man's gruesome mouth, to still that abominable sound.
And what use would that have been? Was I, too, sinking into the
strange mood that tormented this estate? Or was my loathing for
this creature directed by some instinct deeper than the rational,
passed down through the eons of time, some fear that recognized
pure evil and caused a physical reaction, some racial memory, long
forgotten in the conscious mind, lying dormant until an hour of
need?

I turned and plunged into the forest, too tense for proper consideration.

It was not difficult to imagine the effect the woodsman had had on
Catherine, both at his sudden appearance in the graveyard and on
her visit to his dwelling. Indeed, I found it hard to keep his image
from springing into my own mind in all the odious detail, and it
had obviously been far more terrible for her, with her mind already
stimulated by fear and resting precariously on the balance of sanity.
What was more difficult was judging why he had been reluctant to
speak to me—had, in fact, displayed all the overt signs of a guilty
conscience. Did he, in fact, have some dark secret to conceal, or was
his silent suspicion no more than a constant state of mind? I could
not decide with any sense of certainty. But one thing I did decide.

I was determined to know the legend.

In the morning, I asked Fengriffen if I might have the use of a
carriage for the day.

"Certainly," he said. "But why, may I ask?"

"I wish to go into the village."

He frowned. "Wouldn't your time be spent to better advantage
here?"

"I have decided it will be advisable to have a word or two with
the village doctor."

His frown darkened. "Old Whittle? I've already informed you
that by his own admission he is powerless in this matter."

"I think it might prove wise to speak to him. I must gather

facts from different points of view before I can sift them together. Whittle may well have noticed symptoms which were meaningless to his frame of reference, but might be of value to me."

Fengriffen nodded, slowly. "As you wish. Will you require a coachman?"

"I will drive myself."

He nodded. "I'll arrange for a carriage to be readied," he said. He started to move off, then paused. "Did your walk yesterday stimulate any theories?" he asked, peering rather sharply at me.

"It's too early to judge."

"You went into the woods, did you not?"

"Yes, in point of fact, I did."

"You didn't encounter anyone there, by any chance?"

Something in his tone set my senses rasping.

"Why do you ask?" I said, carefully and casually.

"Oh, nothing. Some difficulty with a poacher. Nothing of importance."

He turned then, his shoulders high and square.

"It was just an idle thought," he said.

I did not press the point.

I sent my card into Doctor Whittle's office, and he admitted me immediately. He was a man of considerable age, with snow-white hair but a spark of youthful interest in his eyes. His office was a pleasant room, tinged with the lingering odors of tobacco and coffee and books—pleasant without pretense to luxury. We shook hands. His grip was firm and he inclined his head in a gesture that was deferential but in no way servile. I liked the man instantly; recognized qualities that would make him worthy no matter what his chosen profession.

"I wish to thank you for your recommendation," I told him. "It is a compliment."

"Ah, on the contrary," he replied. "It is a compliment to myself, to be able to. I have read something of your studies and work—all I have been able to, in fact. My regret is that I am too advanced in years to pursue this new science myself."

He offered me a seat and sat opposite, his desk between us and the window behind him. I could see the dull red gables and chimney pots of the village and in the distance a few sheep dotted on the hill. A tranquil and pastoral view, seen across the shoulder of a tranquil and practical man. It struck me as strange that in such a setting I had come to seek the clue to a disrupted and tormented mind.

"Yes," he said. "I am fascinated by these new theories and approaches . . . but you have come about Catherine Fengriffen, of course?"

"I have."

He spread his hands. "I fear I will be unable to help you, Doctor Pope. I treated her to the best of my limited ability, without results. At the first I expected she was in the initial stages of brain fever and recommended the usual treatment, relaxation and fresh air. But it is far deeper than a physical disorder of the brain. The mind, perhaps. But that is not my field."

"Yet the mind and the body are inextricably connected. Either can affect the other. If I might ask you a few questions, first concerning the general state of her health?"

"Certainly. But as far as I can determine, her health . . . her physical state . . . is satisfactory. I have given her a thorough examination and can find no symptoms of any malady known to me. She is listless. She has no interest in life. And what may be more to the point, she does not appear to desire to regain her interest, seems quite content to sink into torpor and lethargy. Although I can recognize these attitudes, I can find no reason for them." He paused, frowning slightly. "I have the impression," he added, "that she does not find her condition a mystery . . . that she believes she knows what has caused this Laodicean state and, furthermore, believes it chronic and incurable. But that is only my passing impression, Doctor. I could not vouch for it. The acedia is present, but by what reasons I am helpless to discover."

I nodded. This much I had already discerned.

"If you have any specific questions?" he asked.

"Not concerning her health, no. I do, however, wish to make a certain inquiry. Perhaps you will know the answer . . . perhaps you will be surprised at the question, as well, but I believe it may have some bearing." I paused. I was suddenly almost reluctant to take this line of inquiry farther; I examined my own feelings and found myself disturbed, as if I were moving into a field where I did not belong, intruding where I could do no good. This was a unique and, considering my science, an adverse mood. Yet it persisted, despite my realization—proof of the fact that more than awareness is necessary to subjugate emotion. The good doctor was waiting, obviously curious at my sudden hesitation, and I forced myself to trespass beyond the boundaries of unfounded dominions.

"Are you acquainted with the Legend of Fengriffen, Doctor?" I asked. He seemed momentarily startled. His bright eyes blinked, the reaction of a wise bird. "The legend concerning the woodsman?" I added.

Doctor Whittle nodded slowly.

"I believe there may be some obscure connection between this legend and her state of mind, you see. That the knowledge has affected her in some manner."

"She knows the tale, then?"

"Yes."

"Charles asked me not to mention it in her presence. Not that I would have, of course. But perhaps he, too, saw that she might be susceptible to it?"

"I believe so. But she has heard it. She is possessed of an imaginative mind. If not superstitious, at least fertile and able to be easily stimulated. In many ways, this fecundity of consciousness is a blessing; in other ways, as in the case in point, it can be a curse. But it may well be of great help to me if I, too, know the legend."

Once more he nodded.

"Well, it is not so much a legend," he said. "It is, in fact, truth. A terrible tale, but true. I know, Doctor, for I was there. The curse, certainly, is nonsense, but the tale itself is nightmarish. I can fully understand how knowledge of this crime could have affected a young woman; I will freely admit that it affected me to a certain extent, caused me to spend many a sleepless night as, despite my efforts to resist it, the gruesome details assumed a place in my mind . . ."

He paused, withdrew a rosewood snuffbox from his waistcoat, and offered it to me, tapping the box. I partook of a pinch—overdid it, in fact, and sneezed, but was too engrossed in this conversation to let such an impropriety bother me. He placed the box on the

desk and spent some moments squaring it with the corner, as if this
regularity were of enormous importance.

"It was long ago," he said. He moved the box another millimeter.
"I was but a young man, in my first year of practice, and perhaps I
would not have been so troubled had I been more experienced in
the agonies of accident and illness. It is hard to say. I have never
spoken of it, you see . . . only speak of it now because I understand
the necessity, and because you are a man of science. And yet,
through all these years, the interest—is that the word, I wonder?
Are terrible things always of lasting interest?—the memory, at least,
persists in vivid and graphic detail. I recall the sounds and the scents
and the colors which at the time were carved so deeply into my
perception. I recall, too, my own emotions—indefinable, because
they were interwoven and mingled, but with something of horror
and something of outrage and a great deal of physical nausea. Still,
you will want facts, not impressions . . ."

"Impressions, too, may be valuable. Tell me all you can recall,
both of fact and feeling."

"I recall everything," he said. The snuffbox was lined up perfectly
with the corner of the desk now, and he suddenly tapped it with
his forefinger, causing it to spin across the polished surface. It slid
toward the edge, and he stopped it under his hand with a startlingly
violent motion, as if he were swatting some loathsome insect.

"It is not a pleasant tale," he said, with an understatement that
did not match his expression.

Then he told me the story . . .

"It was in the time of Charles's grandfather, Henry Fengriffen," he
began. "I was, as I have told you, in my first year of practice, and was
called in a professional capacity just after the event. But I had better
tell it in chronological order, to avoid confusion and also because,
even now, I find it difficult to be objective, to avoid stressing certain
aspects out of proper proportion. Since that time I have had a great
deal of acquaintance with violence, but this was my first involve-
ment with the evil of which man is capable—and still, I believe, the
most gruesome. Like a man's first love, a man's first cognition of
evil remains imprinted upon his soul. Thus . . . It will be necessary
to tell you something of Henry Fengriffen first.

"He was a strange man, this Fengriffen, a man of sharply changing moods. Not a brooder, but a man of impetuous action and insufferable arrogance, for the most part . . . a debauched man, I might say. And yet there was this acute definition in his attitudes; that is, he would, commit some base act and, moments afterward, suffer enormous regrets and do his best to undo the damage he had done. Of course, that was not always possible. He did not seem to realize this; he seemed to believe that a gift of money was all that was required to atone for debased and wicked actions. Despite his regrets, he found it constitutionally impossible to offer apology. Perhaps he never saw the faintest possibility of lowering himself in such a manner and truly believed that money purchased absolution and respect; more likely, he did not condescend to desire respect, but merely wished to absolve himself in his own mind. Oh, he possessed virtues as well. He was extremely generous and absolutely loyal to those he had befriended, was truly admired and esteemed by all whom he had not injured. And in justice to the man, I must say that it was far easier to be debauched in those days. Henry dearly loved to play the squire, galloping madly through the fields of his tenants and drinking heavily with his companions, journeying to the cities and seaports to wench and game and carouse with a savage abandon. I cannot imagine the depths of depravity to which he sank on these bouts of libation, nor do I care to. I know he often fell in with the foulest sort of fellow, the scum of the docks, professional pugilists, purveyors of women and chronic tosspots—God knows what else. Perhaps he absorbed the wickedness from these wretched creatures; perhaps his own inclinations were magnified by their presence; perhaps he was helplessly drawn to them by the gravity of evil. I do not know if I say this in excuse for the man, or merely because it is how I remember him. Yet I also remember that he gave lavishly to the poor, that he arranged many times to supply me with medicines and to pay my fees for treating the unfortunate; that he financed the renovation of the church although he was a professed atheist; that although I was appalled at his way of life, I could not help but recognize his charm. Not an easy man to judge harshly—a man, in fact, whom I would have thought inherently good, beneath his vulgar exterior, had it not been for the affair of which I am speaking.

"Now. Fengriffen had at that time a young gamekeeper living in a cabin in the woods. Silas, his name was. He was a local lad—I had often seen him in the village. He seemed a pleasant youth, well set up and rather handsome, lean and powerful and attractive despite his crude leather clothing and cloth cap, and a large and unsightly birthmark on his cheek. Not intelligent, of course—surely not educated—but none the less a fine example of sinewy health and unspoiled nature. The young girls of his class were all attracted to him, would greet him with blushes and lowered eyes as he strode down the street. He could, I suppose, have taken his choice of any of them, and eventually, when he was perhaps twenty-five years of age, he took a bride from the village. Her name was Sarah. She was barely seventeen, a virgin of unblemished beauty. It was first love for both of them. They were married in the village, and on the wedding night Silas brought his bride back to his rustic cabin, thinking it proper to consummate the marriage in the place where they would undoubtedly have lived the rest of their natural lives in concord and happiness. Would have, I say, for this is where the foul deed occurred . . ."

Doctor Whittle had begun to toy with the snuffbox again, staring down at it intently, as though the rosewood were a crystal revealing the past.

"Henry Fengriffen heard of the wedding, and of the bride's virginal qualities. Normally, that would have meant no more than a crude conversation or coarse joke with his cronies, but fate played a cruel hand at this point. For he was riotously drunk, at the tail end of a three-day binge, and alcohol had destroyed what judgment he possessed . . . left a vacuum to be filled by lust. He decided to view the bride, decided it was his feudal right, perhaps. His cronies were in accord, as usual, always willing to make sport. So they mounted at the house and thundered off across the fields and into the woods, ignoring the dangers of galloping through the trees, setting the forest vibrating with their foul-mouthed shouts and raucous laughter. It seems incredible that they did not suffer at least one injury on that mad gallop—an injury which might well have proved a blessing by preventing a far worse event. But the devil guided their horses, and they arrived at the cabin. I firmly believe that at this point no harm was intended; that it was no more than a drunken jest. Who knows? At any rate, they dismounted and came to the door just as the couple were bedding. Fengriffen beat loudly upon the entrance, shouting demands for entry, until at length Silas opened the door and peered out suspiciously.

" 'I have come to view the bride,' Fengriffen roared.

" 'She is abed, master,' Silas said.

" 'All the better then, my man,' said Fengriffen, and he pushed the gamekeeper roughly aside and strode into the cabin. His cohorts trailed in behind him, amidst laughter and gaiety. Several had brought bottles of wine, which they passed around, drinking from the necks and spilling the liquid down their chins and chests. You may imagine the feelings that overwhelmed poor Silas at this intrusion. His bride pulled the coarse covers up to her throat, staring in wide-eyed dismay, and her fright added to Fengriffen's pleasure. He was well acquainted with women of easy virtue, of course, but virgins were not so well known to him.

"He grasped the covers and pulled them roughly away, leaving the pitiful woman naked and cringing upon the cot while Silas looked on in helpless rage and frustration. Fengriffen's companions all crowded around, joking and drinking and slapping each other on the back. Silas was trembling violently. His eyes rolled about madly, his fists clenched and his teeth sank into his lower lip.

"Some wit said, 'Been many the year since old Fengriffen has sighted a virgin, eh lads?' and they all thought this enormously humorous. They roared with laughter, and Fengriffen determined to have his own jest.

"He turned to Silas and asked, 'Have you taken her yet?'

" 'No, master.'

" 'Then I claim my right to break her!'

" 'No!' Silas shouted, advancing.

"Their eyes locked. Fengriffen swore, afterward, that up to that very instant he had no intention of actually committing this act, that until then it had been no more than an amusement. I believe him in this. But he was a strange man. The moment his servant denied him the right, he felt an overpowering compulsion to take it. They stared at one another, their wills locked along the visual path. Neither would yield. The others became silent, fascinated now. If Silas had been a weak man . . . but he wasn't. A servant, but a man in his own right, and he placed himself between Fengriffen and the bed, his powerful arms folded across his chest.

"Possibly, even then, Fengriffen would have heeded words of reason, would have yielded to pleading. But Silas had no words of persuasion; he could not have spoken in such terms to his master. Fengriffen stepped forward, and Silas acted in the only way known to him—like a threatened animal.

"He seized Fengriffen by the shoulders and threw him violently to the floor. His eyes were blazing, his broad chest heaved with hatred, and he drooled from the mouth. He stood over Fengriffen in a threatening manner, and Fengriffen shouted for assistance, suddenly terrified by his servant's black rage, thrown into a fury by the attack. His companions hesitated for an instant, stunned by the scene, and then they obeyed Fengriffen's command and seized Silas.

"Silas struggled with preternatural strength, knocking several to the floor. I treated their wounds, I know the unbelievable extent of the damage he inflicted upon them. But they were too many, and in the end Silas was subdued and held securely.

"Held, Doctor, and forced to watch, while Henry Fengriffen raped his virgin bride."

Whittle paused.

"Not a pretty tale," I said.

He looked at me rather sadly.

"There is worse to come," he said.

When Fengriffen had had his way with her, he stepped back from the bed and bowed sardonically to his disobedient servant; with a gesture he offered the ruined bride to her husband. He was satisfied that he had justly punished the man's insubordination. Silas was still held by the others, having ceased to struggle while Fengriffen abused his bride, but now he fought again, foaming at the mouth and uttering bestial snarls. Sarah was hysterical, sobbing and moaning, scarcely able to breathe. Her eyes rolled. And then she saw the axe which leaned against the wall, close by the bed. It was a heavy-headed tool which Silas used not only to chop wood but to dispatch animals caught in his traps, and there was a dark stain of dried blood on the metal. She stared at this for a moment, until the import registered, and then she seized it quite suddenly and dragged it to the bed. She had not the strength left to lift it, but dragged it across the floor and then up onto the cot. Before anyone, except Silas, had ascertained her purpose, she drew the edge across her throat—held the head in both hands and worked it back and forth like a blunt saw. The poor woman could not face life after her debasement. Not with sanity.

"The men released their grip on Silas at this, not thinking of the consequences, for they were taken aback by this action they had not bargained on; for all the flagitiousness of their deed, they still regarded it as no more than a humorous episode to be retold amidst ribald laughter at the fireside, just as they might have recalled dallying with a woman of the streets in carnal frolic or, perhaps more to the point, remembered some particularly violent end to a hunt. They did not actually think of a gamekeeper or his wife as human beings, you see.

"Silas tore free of their loosened grasp and fell to his knees beside the bed. No one sought to restrain him now. Sarah was babbling incoherently as Silas gently withdrew the axe from her hands. The wound was not fatal. She hadn't the strength to press deeply enough to sever the jugular vein. But the flesh was broken and torn in a jagged line, and blood streamed down her naked body in rivulets which mingled with the previous blood of her ruination.

"Silas stared at her for an instant, moaning deep within his breast—moaning in his very heart, which ceased to beat for that instant and then commenced again, drumming the burden of torment through his arteries. He sprang up, his blood pounding, and spun around, swinging the axe in a wide and vicious arc at Fengriffen's head. Fengriffen raised his arm to ward off the blow and the edge caught him a glancing cut across the shoulder. He fell against the wall and Silas stepped after him, raising the weapon to dash his brains asunder. But once again he was seized by Fengriffen's cohorts; once again he struggled with berserk rage, only to succumb to the weight of numbers, struggled with even greater vigor, so that they were forced to land several heavy blows on his head before he could be subdued.

"Fengriffen arose, holding his shoulder. He was insane with anger. His arrogant pride could not encompass an attack of this nature, and he was aroused far beyond the bounds of convention; no matter his guilt, he could not tolerate equality. Silas, although semi-conscious, still retained a firm grip upon the axe handle with his right hand, and in that instant Fengriffen saw what form his revenge must take.

"He commanded his companions to drag Silas outside. They did so as he kicked and bucked spasmodically between them. His head hung down, he was dazed, but still he would not yield. Fengriffen followed, directing them to force his gamekeeper to the woodpile which stood beside the cabin. There was a chopping block beside the wood, and Fengriffen pointed to it with a quivering finger. His friends hesitated at this, not realizing his intentions and wanting no part of murder, but Fengriffen ranted and howled with such fierce domination that eventually they obeyed. They bent Silas to his knees before the chopping block.

"Fengriffen sent one of his men to the well for a bucket of cold water while he took off his coat and rolled up his sleeves. He was sweating, his eyes were inflamed, blood ran from the gash in his shoulder. But he ignored the pain. His rage at being wounded far outweighed the pain of the wound. The man returned with a bucket. Fengriffen seized it and placed it beside the chopping block.

"Then he gave a further command. When his companions saw he intended less than murder, they were no longer reluctant, for they were men of his temperament and inclination, and understood intolerance. Two of them grasped Silas's right arm and forced it upon the block. The wiry hand writhed like a pale squid in the moonlight.

"'You have raised your hand against your master twice in this night!' roared Fengriffen. 'It shall not happen again!'

"He took up the axe and positioned himself to the side of the chopping block.

"'Will you beg mercy?' he demanded.

"Silas turned his head to the side, looked up at Fengriffen with one eye, in profile, and spat out a foul oath.

"'Then take justice!' Fengriffen said between his teeth, and he swung the axe over and down.

"The edge dropped across Silas's hand at the knuckles and buried itself into the wood with a dull clunk. The severed fingers flew up like splinters, spinning in the air. The index finger curled up like a wood chip, striking Silas in the face. Four separate streams of blood spewed across the chopping block. Silas's body leaped convulsively, but he made no sound. His eye was still turned upon Fengriffen. Fengriffen stepped back and nodded to his men, who thrust the dismembered hand into the bucket of icy water. Then they all moved away.

"Silas knelt there, his head resting on the block now and his right arm in the bucket. The cold liquid numbed the bloody stumps and kept the fire from rushing up his arm. He did not move, did not dare withdraw his hand from the icy anesthetic. The gentlemen stood around him, silent. They were abruptly stricken by the awareness of their fiendish crime. Fengriffen was pale and perspiring as he slid his coat back on. Suddenly they all wished nothing more than to flee from that terrible scene.

"They moved, still in silence, to where their horses were tied, unfastened them, and began to mount. Then Silas moved. They all paused. Fengriffen had one foot in the stirrup and halted, frozen in place, looking back over his shoulder. He saw Silas's left hand begin to grope like some sightless animal over the ground; one by one, Silas found his severed fingers and gathered them into his hand. Then he wrapped his left forearm around the bucket, cradling it to his chest, and with his right hand still immersed, stood up. He raised his face to Fengriffen. The moonlight struck full upon his countenance as he drew his mutilated limb from the merciful water and pointed the gory stump, a blunt and solitary finger of accusation, at Fengriffen.

"The cold had stopped the rush of blood, but sluggish drops crept down his forearm and dropped heavily to the earth. The agony, as air replaced liquid on that open wound, must have been almighty, and yet no pain showed in that bleached face.

"And he mouthed the curse . . .

"A curse that has fathered legend, a curse which must have come from his soul, for that rustic tongue knew no words of anathema. His arm extended, he made his vow: swore that the monstrous spirit evoked in the blood of this night would know no rest until it had known vengeance, and that the next virgin bride of Fengriffen House would taste the horror of violation.

"His voice held them in unbreakable bonds of frozen steel. No one moved. Even the horses stood still as statues, showing wide white eyes. At last, Silas pressed the gruesome remains of his hand back into the bucket, and turning, staggered to the cabin. The blood which had run down his arm left a trail in his wake. The moonlight plunged darkly into these drops of blood, and dark terror plunged into Fengriffen's heart . . ."

Well, as I say, Fengriffen was a man whose moods changed quickly, and the curse had acted as a catalyst upon his emotions. He became instantly sober and overflowing with remorse. Despite his wound, he galloped all the way to the village to summon me, and burst into my rooms, demanding haste. I wished to treat his shoulder first, for it was a rather nasty gash—I did not at that point understand what had occurred in the woods. But he would not allow treatment; he cursed me most foully for suggesting it and between his verbal abuse told me in fragmented phrases—phrases which were all the more vivid for being disjointed—what had happened. Later I was to hear the tale in a more restrained manner and be able to piece together all the details, but at the time I received impressions rather than facts, impressions which came from his tone of voice as much as his words, from his wild eyes as much as from his broken speech. And you can imagine what those impressions were like.

"Fengriffen rode back with me. We lathered our horses and sent stones clattering beneath their hooves in a mad dash such as I have never made before or since. He had inspired me with his own sense of speed—he was the sort of man who is capable of transmitting such emotions and desires to another. But when he had led me to the cabin, he would go no farther, could not face his crime again. He turned back and I went on through the last few trees and into the clearing. The first thing I saw was the chopping block, with the axe still buried in the surface. I turned my eyes away from this, dismounted, and entered the house.

"Silas was kneeling beside the bed. The bucket was on the floor beside him and his hand was in the water. His left arm cradled his bride. As I approached he turned his head, as on a swivel, to look at me. God knows how or why he had retained consciousness, but he had. He recognized me, seemed perfectly aware of his surroundings, rational and coherent. He had lost a great amount of blood, and the bucket was filled with shredding ribbons of congealed grume, but the water had preserved his life. Better it had not.

"Silas refused to let me attend to his hand until I had seen to Sarah's superficial wound; he gnashed his teeth at me like a cornered beast when I hesitated. She was babbling and her eyes were clouded. The flesh was torn at her throat, but it was not serious— not that torn flesh. There was a far deeper wound beyond her throat, for her mind was gone. In those moments of agony and terror she had been reduced to a madwoman. Silas continued to hold her to his breast as I treated her injury. His fist was clenched against her shoulder. As I tilted her chin back, she slipped slightly in his arm, and as he caught at her, his hand opened.

"And his fingers fell out.

"All four severed fingers dropped into Sarah's lap, and we all looked down at them. If there had been any hope of restoring her sanity, it fled at that instant. She emitted an inhuman howl, a sound which no human should have made. Not the sound of human emotion, but a meaningless cry, the automatic response of a mind from which comprehension has ebbed. It is a sound which still vibrates in my ears, on nights of solitary silence ... vibrates from within, where it is stored, woven into the fabric of mind ..."

Doctor Whittle walked to the window and stood looking out, his hands clasped behind his back beneath his coattails. He seemed to have aged, but perhaps that was because I could no longer see the bright intelligence of his eyes. I assumed that his tale was finished, and was about to speak when he turned back to me.

"Well," he said. "The rest is anticlimax. Silas lived. Sarah lived. Henry Fengriffen's regret knew no bounds. He wished to make restitution, but Silas would accept nothing, refused money and food and wine, all the material possessions with which Fengriffen settled his debts. This drove through Fengriffen a frustration, a spit of helplessness on which he revolved over the fire of guilt. He became desperate to atone for his crime—in his own eyes, of course. But when he sent wine, it was poured into the ground;

when he sent food, it was left to the wild animals or to decay; when he sent money, it was scattered among the trees. For Silas believed that retribution would come in a different manner.

"He continued to live in the cabin, tearing a meager existence from the woods and nursing his wife. She had changed from a beautiful and healthy young bride into a thing of horror with scarred throat, a hag in rags, frothing at the mouth and wild of eye, thin as a skeleton, with long talons and filthy habits. An odious mockery of woman. Several times she ran away, or perhaps wandered off, and Silas was forced to search for her on the moors and bring her back by force.

"And still he loved her.

"He seemed to realize that her insanity had no bearing on justice, and continued to cohabit with her as a husband. Eventually, years after, I was astounded to hear that she had given birth to a son. I ventured to the cabin, more, I must confess, through curiosity than duty. The child was a robust enough lad, but marred by the hereditary birthmark which Silas possessed—larger than Silas's and more hideous, like a web of blood. Sarah had become the most wretched creature imaginable, scarcely human—a grotesque caricature of a madonna, clutching the squalling infant to her sunken torso. Silas, too, seemed to have become somewhat deranged; he was far more incoherent than his rough accent warranted. But with great effort I came to understand that he had at last accepted a gift from Fengriffen. For Henry had never desisted in his efforts, and upon hearing of the child's birth he saw his opportunity to present a gift which Silas could neither return nor refuse. He never assumed that Silas would have children, quite naturally, because of Sarah's condition. Now that it was an accomplished fact, he made a small alteration in his will—small enough, you will think—to the effect that Silas and his descendants were granted the eternal right to reside in the woodlands of the Fengriffen estates. He had probably expected Silas to refuse this right in theory while remaining there in fact, since there was nowhere else for him to go, and that the true value of his recompense would go in time to the child. However, such was not the case. Silas seemed inordinately pleased with the rights granted to his child. At first I took this as a sign that his hatred had lessened over the years or that he had let the past slip in his senile brain until its importance diminished, for he had refused gifts of far greater value. Such, however, was not the case.

"While he was telling me of this, he took the child upon his lap and let it make a plaything of the gnarled stump of his hand. The child began to laugh with glee as its tiny fingers explored the grottoes and crevices of that gruesome toy, and Silas's eyes lighted with fatherly pride—and with something more—upon his offspring.

"He was pleased, you see, because he knew his son would be able to remain there to witness the revenge. And so, it would appear, he has . . ."

Doctor Whittle raised his eyebrows.

"Silas's child, then, is the woodsman who dwells there now?"

"He is. Both Sarah and Silas lived well into old age, lived long past self-sufficiency and depended on the child to feed them, while all the time, over all those years, Silas instilled the rotten seeds of hatred into the boy, warping his mind until he knew only visions of vengeance. They died, within a few weeks of one another, some few years past now. But the son has remained."

"This explains a great deal, Doctor," I told him.

"Will it be of value?"

"I hope so. It is obviously the root of the damage, and must be plowed from her mind."

I stood up, extending my hand.

"You were most kind to afford me so much of your time," I said. "Perhaps we shall meet again."

"If you are staying at the house," he said.

"Ah, of course. You will deliver the child . . ."

"Yes. As I have most children in the village during these long years."

"When is the child due?"

"Oh, quite soon. Within the week, perhaps."

I nodded thoughtfully. Whittle was a man in whom one could place the utmost confidence, and I said, "I have an idea that the birth may well prove a turning point—that the cares of motherhood and child love may bring her mind back from the dark course it has taken. It will leave her less time to brood. We are men of science, Doctor. We do not countenance the power of the supernatural. But Catherine Fengriffen is a woman, and by believing in the curse, she has given that curse a power to affect her . . . has invested in a nonexistent concept, you see."

"Then let us pray that the new interests of motherhood will dull that power," Whittle said.

"Yes," I said, but I had long since subjugated prayer to insight. Still, one hopes.

I drove slowly back from the village, pondering upon Henry Fengriffen's crime in relation to Catherine, trying to superimpose my mind upon hers and understand what the full effect had been when, in those distasteful surroundings, she had heard the tale from the child of Silas and Sarah—the child who had been sired and reared with but one purpose in mind, guided toward one goal, instructed only in the one dual emotion—hatred and revenge. Even Doctor Whittle, who had not been involved directly, had found it impossible to be objective while recalling the events of that terrible night. How much more frightful had the telling been as the words fell from the woodsman's lips, as Catherine looked into those brutish features, and watched the twitchings of that mobile birthmark which ran from his lips? Yet however disturbed and troubled she must have been, had the tale been enough, in itself, to force her to her present condition? Was she irrational enough to blame her husband for the sins of his forebear? Or was there something more, something that Doctor Whittle did not know? It seemed likely. Catherine did not have the symptoms of one whose mind had snapped under stress and emotion. She was still aware of the proper proportion of her life, and even if she believed the curse and lived in constant terror, awaiting God knows what frightful vengeance, that alone would not account for her negative reaction; it might have caused a positive state of nervous fear, but not her decline into resigned indifference. I was baffled by this paradox, and felt certain that some essential fact had eluded me, or been deliberately kept from me. My first task, then, was to discover the truth.

I left the carriage at the stables. The stable lad was looking up at the dark clouds, his young face creased prematurely with his frown.

"Will it rain in the night?" I asked.

"Well, I've never known it to hold off so long once that the clouds are black as this," he said, waving his greasy cap at the ominous heavens. "It's right peculiar. Old Jacob says t'won't come down 'til 'morrow, though. Never know old Jacob be wrong nor neither. Right peculiar. Makes a fellow wonder what's a' waitin' fer."

I smiled at this personification of the impending storm. The lad jammed his cap back on, pulling it well down so that a few strands of matted hair stuck out at right angles from beneath the band. He began to unfasten the harness with the deft motions of experience, still glancing upward, suspicious of those looming clouds.

"Don't much fancy weather o' this sort, neither," he said. "With the sky low and the air all heavy and wet, like. Sort o' the same as bein' in a cell an' not havin' air to breathe proper. Ain't right, somehow. Makes the 'orses fussy, an' all. Whilst they's bein' groomed ye can feel 'em all shaky under yer 'ands, and all the night ye can hear 'em a-pawin' at the ground, an' snortin' like pigs. 'Orses got plenty o' sense, mostly. Ain't very long on wits, 'orses, but they 'as plenty o' cunnin'. They can tell when t' weather ain't as it oughts to be."

He started to say something more, then clamped his mouth shut and shrugged, rather embarrassed at having spoken at such length or, perhaps, at having voiced an opinion. He grinned foolishly and turned away.

I walked on to the house.

Catherine did not dine with us that evening. She was staying in bed as her time drew near. Neither Fengriffen nor I had much appetite, so the meal was quick and quiet. We adjourned to the library, and after coffee had been brought in and Jacob had departed, I told Fengriffen that I knew of the curse.

His eyes were sardonic as he depreciated my statement with a quick gesture of intolerance. This annoyed me, and I gestured in turn, causing his aristocratic eyebrows to lift in surprise.

"What is a curse?" he said. He leaned toward me, his brow furrowed in chevrons of irritation. "Words, no more. Superstition. Balderdash. I did not summon a priest to exorcise my home, I summoned a doctor."

"It is a doctor to whom you speak, sir."

"But, in all truth . . ."

"It is not a matter of truth, but of belief. If your wife believes in this curse, what does truth matter? The mind is capable of conjuring its own truths."

"You mystify me, Doctor."

"Ah, but it is you who have added to the mystery. You have not revealed all that you know. Perhaps you have told me all you deem relevant, but you are wrong in your selections. You knew that your wife visited the woodsman?"

His frown shifted crosswise, corrugating his forehead, and his face darkened.

"I know that she compromised herself by going, alone, to his hovel, yes. That is the wrong of it, not some absurd vow of revenge."

"You judge her harshly."

"But with justice!"

"Ah yes. The Fengriffen justice. The justice your grandfather inflicted upon his gamekeeper?"

His eyes glowed, and for a moment I thought he was about to strike me. His hands clenched on the arms of the chair and his frame tensed and trembled. I leaned toward him, ready for what action he might take. My anger at that moment was as great as his. We were both on the edges of our seats, our faces close together and our eyes fighting a skirmish over the intervening distance. In his countenance I saw the inherited attitudes of his grandfather, saw the descendant of that unjust man struggle in the grip of his heredity. Then he relaxed. He slumped back in his chair, his face averted and turned slightly from me. He became absolutely still. From his posture he might have been asleep, but I knew that he was waiting for me to speak, waiting for whatever hope or insight I might give him. He was a man born to violent emotions, but he had managed to subdue them, and my own anger faded.

I spoke softly.

"My science is in its infancy. Less. No more than a zygote in the field of knowledge. I have never claimed to understand the workings of the mind, but I have often looked upon the symptoms, and believe me, they can be awesome. Some day, when the spark which has fertilized this unborn science has caused it to emerge and mature—some day, in the distant future, it may be possible to trace the functions of thought through the convolutions of the brain and up the articulation of the spinal cord. But as yet we are less than mice in a maze, and the mind is the greatest of all mazes. Then, sir, if we do grope our blind way through the labyrinth, who knows what mental minotaur may lurk at the center? I am no Theseus. I have no ball of twine to guide me, and make no false claims. I may only treat the symptoms from the entrance to these devious corridors. If that is not enough . . ."

"It is enough," he whispered.

"Then believe me. Your wife's illness is connected with the curse."

"Damn the woodsman!" he said. But there was no anger in the condemnation. He was quite calm now, his face the color of ash. "Can he really be responsible for my wife's behavior? Can she have truly heeded that creature's words?"

"Responsible? Only insofar as he revealed the past, and certainly she believed him, for it was true. The responsibility must lie with your grandfather's actions, and your wife's willingness to assume beyond the facts."

"I cannot understand these things," Fengriffen said. "It seems we are discussing some form of black magic, some dark art of a former age." He did not speak sarcastically now, but with genuine bewilderment.

"You are confusing a science we do not fully comprehend with vague notions of sorcery or witchcraft. You deny the curse—and rightly so, for yourself. But you cannot deny the effect it has had upon your wife. To cure her, we must deal with this curse, seek to disprove it, demonstrate the error of her thinking and show her the truth which is obvious to us."

Fengriffen nodded slowly.

"Perhaps we may begin now," I said. "Tell me—your father, did he, too, deny the curse?"

"Certainly. If he ever so much as thought of it. We are not a family of idiots."

"And your mother."

"Of course."

"Tell me something of your mother."

"But what possible bearing can this have?"

"I cannot profess to know, unless you tell me."

"This is absurd. I do not know what miracle I had hoped you to perform, Doctor, do not understand what curious methods you studied in Leipzig, but——"

"First and foremost, I learned that without confidence I am powerless."

"I must continue to place faith in you, I expect. My last forlorn hopes, eh? Well, what of my mother?"

"Who was she?"

"A noble lady of great distinction," he said with some degree of pride. "Slightly older than my father. I told you she passed away while I was but a child, and I cannot remember much about her, cannot differentiate between what I recall and what I was subsequently told. She was a widow . . ."

"A widow?"

"Yes. The widow of my father's greatest friend. There had long been mutual admiration between them, apparently, and after her period of mourning—during which my father aided her greatly in the handling of her affairs—it was quite natural that this respect and affection blossomed into love. Not the romance of youth, you understand, but the deep bonds of mature feeling. And thus——"

"And thus," I interrupted, "when your mother first came to Fengriffen House, she did not come as a virgin bride."

Fengriffen blinked.

"Of course not. A widow . . ."

He paused, regarding me with a strange expression. Yes, Charles knew the form the curse had taken. This was not the way to disprove it, and for some time we were silent.

Jacob knocked and entered, cleared the coffee cups away, and asked if we required anything further. Fengriffen dismissed him with a wave of the hand and he left, limping more noticeably than before. The time of storm was approaching, to the discomfort of his old bones.

"Well?" Fengriffen asked.

"Shall we try a different approach?"

"As you like."

"When was it that your wife destroyed the portrait of Henry Fengriffen?"

He did not appear surprised at the question. "Has she admitted that to you?"

"It was obvious."

"Yes, I expect it was. It is difficult to tell a stranger, even a doctor, of such things. I should have, of course, for it was a milestone in her decline.

"It was some months ago, at the time her behavior became noticeably worse." He paused for a moment. "It was, in fact, the very day when Doctor Whittle informed us that she was with child. He told us both together, smiling at the opportunity to bring us such good news. I was delighted, of course. I turned to my wife. Catherine had become pale, disturbed, visibly shaken. Her reaction was inconceivable, for we had discussed the possibility of children and she had been as desirous as I. I was dumbfounded, reached out to take her hand, whereupon she rose and left the room without a word. It was extremely embarrassing. Poor old Whittle looked absolutely confused. He had come as a messenger of joyful revelation, and been treated as a harbinger of gloom. I smoothed it over as best I could, making some feeble excuse for her. Of course, that was before her state of mind had changed so greatly that I confided in him. He accepted my excuses graciously, and departed. I went to Catherine's room. The door was barred, there was no sound within. I did not knock, but retired to my own room, and to bed. I could not sleep. I pondered her reactions and the hours passed tediously as I gravitated between annoyance and concern.

"I was still awake, although drowsy, when I heard Catherine pass in the hall. I recognized her step. In those early days of our marriage, I recognized everything connected with my beloved. I thought she was coming to my room, and waited hopefully. But the steps passed, moved on down the hallway. I rose and went to the door, thinking perhaps she was walking in her sleep. As I looked out, I heard a low exclamation, a wordless utterance, and saw that she had paused in the gallery. I was transfixed. She stood there, a wild thing in her flowing nightgown, staring at the portrait, and as I watched, she suddenly slashed at the picture with a letter opener she kept in her room. Again and again she slashed at the canvas with quick, desperate strokes, muttering and groaning as she tore it apart.

"I did not attempt to stop her, for I was too stunned to move. When the task of destruction was ended and the ruined canvas hung down in ragged strips, Catherine stepped back, gathering her gown around her as though taken by a chill. Her bosom heaved, she drew her head back. Suddenly she seemed to become aware of the letter opener, and threw it violently from her hand as if it were unclean . . . as if it had become soiled by contact with the portrait.

"She came back down the hallway, saw me suddenly as she drew near, but passed without a word. Her face was twisted with malice, with hatred . . . with God knows what. It was not the face of the woman I loved."

Fengriffen shuddered.

"God, it was dreadful," he said.

"And did you not connect this destruction with the curse?"

"I connected it with madness," he whispered, and lowered his head.

Then, simultaneously, we became aware of Catherine's presence at the doorway.

Fengriffen's head snapped up from his chest, alarmed at her presence and at his own previous statement. Catherine was very pale, swaying on unsteady legs, yet her expression was collected and calm. She looked at her husband, then looked at me, and a grimace vaguely akin to a smile caused her lips to rise at the corners. It was a terrible twisting of the mouth, unrelated to the placid expression in her eyes, the grotesquely deformed offspring of laughter and the ancestor of the rictus of rigor mortis. I could not face that play of feature, and looked away.

Fengriffen sprang to his feet.

"Cathy! You should not be here!"

"Oh? And where should I be?"

Fengriffen advanced toward her, took two strides and then faltered as if at some invisible barrier, stopped and stared helplessly across the intervening space where unknown emotion had erected a frontier, where the border guards of their disturbed relationship refused to let him pass. His shoulders quivered. Catherine looked beyond him, and caught my eyes again.

"So you have heard the curse," she said.

I nodded.

"And scoffed at such nonsense?"

I shook my head slowly. "Few things are nonsense," I said. "Nothing voiced in the agony of a broken heart can be nonsense."

"There you are wrong," she said. "Is he not wrong, Charles? Accusation can be nonsense."

And she gestured, as though it were unimportant.

Fengriffen turned to look at me, seeking an ally. I did not know what to say; what could I possibly say in the presence of both of them together? His eyes slid back toward his wife, but she was still looking at me.

"And you are wrong, also, about the curse," she said. "You have not understood the meaning, have looked beyond the obvious and found something less foreign to your understanding, less difficult to countenance in your learned system of validity. No, Doctor. The curse is not driving me insane, any more than the crime was insanity. Do you not see that? The poor woman went mad as a result of the crime, just as I fear I will go mad as a result of the revenge. But that is an after effect, no more. The vengeance chooses a far more terrible form than mere madness . . ."

In truth, I saw nothing of madness in her appearance at that moment, heard nothing of insanity in the voice which delivered the abstruse message. I wished her to continue, for I sensed she was about to reveal what she took for truth. But her face clouded then, and she turned, biting her lip, and rushed from the room. Her motion broke the spell which had held Fengriffen, and he moved after her, shouting for Mrs. Lune. That good woman appeared, scurrying down the hallway and intercepting Catherine at the foot of the staircase. Mrs. Lune was as pale as Catherine as she took her arm. Catherine leaned heavily against her and Lune assisted her up the stairs, whispering words meant to be soothing, but losing the calming effect in the troubled tone.

Fengriffen stood at the foot of the staircase, his arms swinging about as though he struggled against bondage; he gazed up at the departing forms until they had vanished, then turned to me.

"What can she mean?" he asked.

I did not reply, for I did not know. But there was something else which I desired to know, which I needed to know. I took his arm and led him back into the library. He kept shaking his head from side to side, dazed or puzzled, continuing to do so even after he had resumed his seat. I stood before him, waiting to engage his eyes, but he refused to look at me. His head still rotated, heavy-lidded, swinging across and below my line of vision. I placed my fist against my hip, pushing my coat back. There are little tricks of convenience which one learns. I drew my watch from my waistcoat and glanced at it, then let it dangle on the chain. His eyes fastened upon this pendulum as the gold gathered the firelight, and his head stopped moving.

"You have not told me all," I said. "Still you persist in denying me the facts."

"I have, sir," he said. "I have told you everything that can be of importance."

"You have, at some degree of inconvenience to myself, and considerable expense, brought me from London——"

"Expense means nothing to me!" he snapped.

"Nor to me."

"If you would prefer payment in advance, I shall be glad to issue a check at this very moment."

"You miss the point, sir. Money is little, and does not much concern me. But I cannot approve of waste, and you are wasting my time, hindering what little abilities I may have brought here with me."

The watch revolved. His eyes were fastened upon it, pinned to the darting shafts of reflection like butterflies on a mat. His eyebrows moved like wings, but his eyes were secured, looking into that little golden world, gazing into a dimension in which his suffering had no reality. In that moment, he would have willingly plunged bodily into this minute world of shifting brilliance where his mind had already fled, where his consciousness rode smoothly down the bands of light and slipped off, painlessly, into the mellow shadows. I caused the watch to swing farther and faster, and he frowned in visual pursuit, disturbed at this changing pattern, troubled as the spinning dimension changed to the lateral.

And then I clapped my hand over the watch.

Fengriffen blinked back to reality.

I slipped the watch into my waistcoat again. I had no desire to mesmerize the man; I had brought him to the borderline and snapped him abruptly back, and it had served the purpose. He looked into my face now. All traces of aristocracy had vanished from his features. He ground his teeth and his eyes rolled, but he was aware of his own existence.

"You have omitted at least one point of importance," I said. "Through guilt, or pride, you have been silent. Your wife spoke of accusation. You have accused her of something, is it not so? Something which you have kept from me? Something relating to her behavior?"

Fengriffen nodded.

Now we would have truth.

"Yes," he whispered. "Yes, I omitted one thing. I omitted it from my own thoughts, as well, you see . . . from my voluntary thoughts. I cannot keep it from my dreams, nor keep it from stealing suddenly into my mind when control is relaxed—stealing like some vicious footpad from the dark alley where it hides, to strike a savage wound, again and again, opening the old scar tissue with another dreadful gash. Injuries to the body, Doctor, are simple things. They are mortal, or they heal. Not so these scars on the soul. They, too, can be mortal, but they do not kill. They, too, can heal, but the scar tissue is weak and can be opened again at the slightest touch of memory; opened as painfully each time, these gory wounds which do not bleed, these violent blows which do not bring unconsciousness, these lethal strokes which send a poisoned spear deep into the heart and fester without death. Yes, Doctor. I omitted it . . ."

He stood up, brushed past me, and moved to the mantelpiece, where he poured a large tumbler of brandy with shaking hand. The decanter clattered against the rim of his glass and a few drops spilled, unheeded, onto the carpet. He raised the glass to his lips with a sudden movement, as though he would drain it at one gulp. But he took a small sip only, the glass rattling on his teeth, before turning toward me.

"You are right," he said. "Perhaps the solution lies in this omission. Perhaps a doctor is not required. It would be so simple a solution, you see, and yet so terrible to admit. Pride? Ah yes, pride. And pain. Doctor, you must swear you will never repeat what I am about to tell you . . ."

"I am a doctor, sir."

"Forgive me," he said, lowering his head. "I scarcely know what I am saying. Give me a moment."

His downcast eyes were looking into the amber liquid in his glass. He swirled the glass, watching the liquid lap at the rim— watching the liquid, but seeing something else reflected in those dark depths; seeing some memory trapped in the moving mirror, a memory he wished to drown there, but which was capable of surviving beneath the surface until, in an unguarded moment, it would rise, twisting and bloated, like some monster from the deepest fathoms rising to the surface to devour the fragile vessels of happiness.

For long minutes he stared into the liquid looking glass; then suddenly he raised it, and this time he drained the contents—this time he drank those reflections, shuddering as they sank into his belly.

And there, too, they survived . . .

Fengriffen set the empty glass down and leaned against the mantle-piece, passing a hand across his brow. I knew that he would speak softly, and moved closer to him, on a tangent, so that he would not be distracted by the motion.

"One evening," he said, "some eight or nine months ago, I returned unexpectedly from town. I cannot recall just when this was, in days, but it was before her symptoms had become so pronounced—before we were aware of her pregnancy, that is, although it must have been within a week or two of the conception. Well, I had been in town on business, and planned to stop the night, but the business was settled more quickly than I had expected, and I found myself able to return by the last train. I had left my carriage in the village, and proceeded home as soon as I had detrained. The house was in darkness when I arrived. I awoke the stable lad, of necessity, but saw no reason to disturb Jacob and let myself into the house. I went directly upstairs. It was necessary to pass my wife's room on the way to my own, as it still is, and I moved as quietly as possible to avoid awakening her as I passed the door. Just as I had advanced that far, I heard a sound which caused me to pause. It came from Catherine's room, a faint murmur which could have been whispered conversation or inarticulate mumbling. I could not tell. I was not suspicious, and believed her to be dreaming or experiencing a nightmare; I wondered if I should wake her. It was quite late. As I paused, debating, I heard these sounds increase. I said I was not suspicious, but suddenly a cold fear enveloped me as the sounds became more distinct. I advanced silently and listened at her door—a shameful act, I realize, but perhaps you can understand the torment of such a moment, the impulsive desire to know the truth, the manner in which jealousy may affect honor and judgment and cause one to act in a fashion unsuitable to a gentleman. But enough of such excuses. I advanced shamelessly to her door and placed my ear against the panels.

"And then I knew the sounds, Doctor.

"They were the noises of love."

Fengriffen's face was dark and stormy and he looked directly at me now, his eyes smoldering with feelings even deeper than the molten jade of jealousy.

"The noises of love, Doctor," he repeated.

"Sounds with which I was well acquainted. Pantings and stirrings and soft moans, murmurs and sighs and the metallic protest of the bedsprings. And they were not recognized objectively, for I was aware of my wife's own voice emitting these nonverbal but expressive—oh so expressive—intonations. When one lives as a husband to a woman, he learns to recognize the peculiarities of her oestral frenzy, the pitch and cadence of her passion, the rhythm unique to the woman he loves. And in that manner these sounds were transmitted to my brain, the sibilants piercing the gutturals bludgeoning, the timbre vibrating with shattering effect.

"I stood, my mouth gaping open—forced open, as though to provide an exit for the rage and jealousy which welled up to proportions too great to be contained within my breast. And then those emotions escaped me, in the form of a strangling cry, and I rushed at the door in a blind rage. It was barred. I battered against it with my fists and kicked with my feet. At the violence of my attack, the noises within Catherine's room ceased abruptly. The door held and I stepped back, as a terrible hush fell over the house. Into this silence my agony expanded. The silence seemed worse than the sounds. I threw myself at the door once more, and this time it yielded and flew open. The lock was torn from the frame and fragments of wood hung dangling across the entrance, the door itself swung back and crashed against the wall. It was a stout door and a strong lock, but in that instant my strength had been supernatural. Nothing organic and fashioned by human craft could have stood against me. But the explosive effort had drained my momentum, and I staggered against the splintered frame for support, and looked into the room while those jagged shards swayed up and down before me; looked past those broken sticks and saw a scene which burned itself into my mind.

"Catherine was sitting up in bed. She was naked. The bedclothes were disarranged and trailed onto the floor. She turned her face toward me, mouth open and eyes glazed, and for a moment she appeared not to recognize me—appeared unaware of where she was, or who she was. Her white flesh glistened with perspiration, her hair was disheveled, and she had raised one slender hand to her throat. I noticed the pulse beating in the hollow of her neck and the way her bosom rose as she inhaled heavily; noticed, in vivid detail, all these aspects of her appearance, and then, looking beyond her, saw that the window was open. The shutters had been thrown wide, and the curtains were drawn outward, as with the passage of some departing form—carried after somebody, in the rush of flight. Even as I looked, these curtains slid back into the room.

"I was at the window in three strides, but the night was black. Perhaps it is fitting that this night was black, black as the tomb of love, black as the crypt of respect, untouched by the moon which had lighted other times. I looked out, but could see nothing; I turned back to Catherine, and as I did so, I became aware of a stench pervading the room and assaulting my nostrils—a strange and moldering odor of decay, as might have been left by a man who has traveled on foot through the rotting autumnal forest. This odor coiled sharply up my nasal passages, agitating and causing me to choke and gag. I fought against revulsion and moved back toward the bed. The heavy scent faded as fresh air poured into the room, and my nostrils stopped tingling. Catherine had not moved, other than to turn her head as she watched me cross the room, but her eyes had brightened. There is a certain way in which her eyes begin to shine at such moments—a light from within, piercing the clouded lenses like sunlight as an overcast sky begins to break. I observed this change. My raging emotions had frozen into objective calm, as though feeling had solidified into a protective barrier of ice before my brain, and it was from behind this defensive wall that I looked at Catherine.

"She is my wife, Doctor. I have loved her, and I have seen, in blissful moments, how she appears when the physical act of love has been completed. And that, Doctor, is just how she appeared at that moment.

"This is exactly how she appeared . . ."

Fengriffen stopped speaking and spread his hands in a shrug that did not signify indifference.

"I accused her of infidelity, of course. There was . . . is . . . no doubt of it. I did not accuse her at the moment, could not bring myself to utter a solitary syllable, but went to my room where I lived through the most terrible night of my life. But in the morning I accused her. What would any man have done? She did not deny the charge, did not even comment upon it, but gazed at me as though I were incomprehensible—as though she did not understand my words. But there was nothing she could have said, at any rate. The results of my accusation?" He smiled sadly. "It was as if I had been in the wrong, Doctor. Since that night I have been refused admission to her bedroom, exactly as though I had wronged her."

Fengriffen left the fireplace and walked along the side of the room; he turned at the corner and passed slowly along the bookcases. I saw the tightness of his clenched jaw cause his cheeks to harden in ridges, and he struck his fist into the open palm of his other hand several times, but without force.

"If she has been unfaithful . . ." I said.

He stared at me.

"Have you not driven her farther away? Surely your own behavior has been altered by the belief?"

"No, no! Doctor, I am willing to forgive her. I have told her so. I will forgive her anything, if forgiveness will regain her love, for I love her beyond recrimination, beyond jealousy, beyond even pride. She will not allow forgiveness, will not listen to my words, does not care. She does not wish my forgiveness, Doctor, for she despises me."

"A woman's reaction to her own guilt—" I began.

"Guilt be damned! Find out why she ceased to love me. Tell me what to do. It was shortly after that terrible night that the initial signs of pregnancy appeared. I hoped that it would bring us closer. You know that it had the opposite effect. My child and heir will be born, Doctor, but to what situation? Cure her of this madness before the child arrives, for the love of God!"

And he confronted me with such an expression of dumb agony and bewildered pain that I looked away from his face. When I looked up, Fengriffen had left the room.

I sat alone in the light of the fading fire, turning the possibilities over in my mind and attempting to shape insight into the framework of facts. I was not at all convinced that Catherine had been unfaithful to her husband; I found his whole painful tale rather unlikely, too vivid and too obviously contorted by his own fears and feelings. On the other hand, I felt that he had at last told me the truth as he saw it, and that something out of the ordinary had taken place in Catherine's bedroom. Fengriffen's supposition was the most logical and simplest; it was strengthened by Catherine's refusal to deny the fact, and by her spurning of his proffered forgiveness, and yet I could not think her subsequent behavior in line with this solution, could not, somehow, see her as a woman who would admit another man to her own bedroom and commit adultery within her husband's home. If she truly no longer loved him, there was nothing I could do and nothing I should attempt to do, for dying love is without the range of science. But she had told me that she loved him, and I believed her. She had also told me she had not been unfaithful, granting me the denial that she kept from Charles. It created a paradox and forced a new approach, a new alternative. Ah, there was an alternative, and it had been gradually taking form in my thoughts— a figment of the mind that I had never before encountered but had studied as a classic aberration, and that could have accounted for her behavior. It was a frightful, malignant disarrangement of reality, unfounded and uncommon, a fixation from a darker age that should not have survived the light of reason, but that had found fertile ground in Catherine's mind when, inflamed and distorted by the woodsman's terrible tale, she had returned to this house. But dreadful as it was, it could be treated and cured, once I had discovered how she came to formulate such a concept. That would be the problem. Where had this hallucination seized her? Where had she acquired the germ of the idea?

Contemplating this, I gazed idly about the room, looking into the long wedges of shadow at the corners, at the orange embers of the fire, and the volumes that lined the walls . . .

I paused.

Fengriffen had mentioned that Catherine spent long hours alone in this room. At the time that fact had assumed no importance, beyond her obvious desire for solitude, but I saw it now in a different aspect, felt with a sudden certainty that the answer lurked somewhere amongst the collected knowledge on these shelves. I did not know what book it would prove to be, but was positive that one of these ancient volumes held the secret, was certain that Catherine, in bewilderment and distress, had turned to these books, seeking a name for her turmoil. And as surely as one may turn to learned works for knowledge, so may one turn to books for evil, without desiring evil, guided by frustration and doubt. The image was vivid. I could see the poor woman, caught up in feverish fear, driven to these books in a desperate attempt to understand what she believed was happening.

I rose from my chair and moved along the shelves, drawing several volumes out at random. The backs were free of dust, but the tops had eluded Mrs. Lune's diligence and carried mantles of flaky grey undisturbed through the years. I glanced at the titles and found that the library was stocked at random, with volumes on diverse subjects in no particular order but in every field of knowledge.

On the second circuit, I found the book I sought.

I knew, even before I pulled it from the shelf, that it was what I sought; knew, also, that it was the worst it could have been; drew it down and saw that the top was without its coat of dust, and that Catherine had delved into it more than once.

The book was *Malleus Maleficarum*.

It was the illustrated Paris edition of 1497, that wicked classic that had given rise to the Inquisition, that sinister work of demonology that had caused torture and torment beyond reckoning and crystallized the black fears of superstition into hysteria. Now once again, in an age when it should have lost its terrible power, it had struck at Catherine's bewildered mind.

I carried the book to the table, conscious of the weight and the scent of old leather and of something more—perhaps the evil that pervades those pages; carried it with my arms outstretched, subconsciously keeping the foul object away from my body, and placed it down on the binding. I ran my hand across the pages, and let the book fall open where it would, let the binding bend where it had most recently and most often been folded.

It dropped open in the second part.

I looked at the page, knowing beforehand what the subject would be.

Incubus.

Sexual relations with demons.

That was the subject . . .

I did not trouble to read those lines that had devoured Catherine's reason, but closed the book quickly, as though it were a Pandora's box from which evil spirits and monstrous devils would fly at me—intangible and without substance, yet able to create concrete destruction. I returned the book to the shelves, and found that the hair upon the base of my skull had risen, as I realized what infernal torment the poor woman had been put through. Despite the hour, I felt I must speak with Catherine without delay, and summoned Mrs. Lune without informing Fengriffen. Mrs. Lune was reluctant to disturb the mistress; she hemmed and hawed and offered excuses until at last I convinced her of the urgency and she led me dubiously up to Catherine's room.

Catherine was awake in bed, the covers mounded over her swollen stomach and her eyes alert in an anguished face. She seemed surprised at my entrance. Mrs. Lune hovered by the door, nervous and uncertain.

"I must speak with you," I said.

Catherine frowned.

"I told him—" Mrs. Lune began.

"It is all right. You may go."

Mrs. Lune looked relieved; she departed, leaving the door ajar.

Her footsteps echoed down the hall. I moved to the side of the bed
and sat on a chair, leaned forward and spoke with urgent demand.

"You must tell me what you believe to be true, madam. For the
sake of your sanity and your unborn child. I am a doctor. You must
remember that, and think nothing of embarrassment or shame."

"Shame? What do I care for shame? There is nothing you can do,
you waste your time here."

"I can listen."

She smiled grimly. "I know more of this matter than you, Doctor,
with all your science and learning. I know from experience."

"Then, perhaps, I shall learn from you."

She looked startled at this. "Do you know what has happened to
me?"

"I know what you think has happened."

"Have you heard of such things?"

I nodded.

"Very well, then. I shall tell you, Doctor. You will not believe me,
but you shall hear the truth."

She smiled again.

Then she spoke.

"I resisted. You must believe that, Doctor. I resisted with all my
strength, but resistance was useless. It was not a physical thing, you
understand. It was my will which faltered and yielded. What it was
or how it was possible, I do not know. I have searched the books in
the library and found certain terms and names which may apply,
and yet they are no more than the names of superstition and witchcraft and sorcery, of self-deceit and ignorance. This was none of
those. It was real. If I am mad, then madness followed the reality. If
it was a dream, then dreams are real. And if any ordeal could have
been more terrible, then the human mind cannot conceive of it.

"It came in the night, Doctor. It came, whatever it was, each
night that I slept alone. The prelude was that feeling of stifling
weight and cold, and each time it came it was heavier and colder;
each night it seemed to have greater substance. Instead of a chill
in the air, it became a form of coldness which moved in from the
window and lay beside me and, at length, covered me. What is a
spirit, a shade, a ghost? No more than a shape of temperature?

"I lay in silence as this presence came to me, and whimpered with fear at its touch; willed it to be gone and struggled—for weeks I struggled—against it. But each night my struggles were less. It did not hurt me. There was no pain, and even the cold was not unpleasant, but the sensation was so horrible, so inhuman, that I felt myself being dragged into a different dimension, a different plane of existence, a different sphere of reality. And I knew, with overwhelming self-hatred and loathing, that I would eventually be sucked away. Perhaps my will was weakened because I knew it was futile, but that does not matter—what does a night, a week, a month matter, when the result must inexorably be the same?

"And so I surrendered.

"The thing took solid form. As it solidified it emitted a hideous odor of brimstone and rot, and the cold lessened; the molecules of the air compressed until I could see the shape of this thing. It was wavering and transparent, but it had form. It whirled in the air above me, and then it descended upon me. I had no energy left. My thighs parted. I felt the clammy caress and closed my eyes, for I did not wish to see it; pressed it away with my hands, listlessly, and found my arms passing through it with sluggishness, as though through a heavy liquid. The odor caused my brain to spin, thick and fermented and foul the fumes passed into my mind. And then this being took me.

"I felt it enter my body.

"I felt it tremble and heard an unearthly moan, as though a great wind had risen within the confines of my room—or perhaps within my body itself. It moved. I moved with it. God help me, I could not keep myself from joining in that terrible coupling. I do not know how long it took, but finally I felt the thing complete the act, felt the hideous emission within me.

"Then it drew away, whining, from my body. It swirled above me for a time, and then departed. The curtains moved with its passage, and I was alone again, trembling and quivering and—ah, how do words describe such feelings? What more can I say?

"After that, the being returned every night. I no longer offered even token resistance, my power had been destroyed by the spiritual burden deposited in me. I waited for its coming with loathing and horror and yet, terrible to say, with expectation. The sensations of the act were not unpleasant. I was dazed. But I awaited it, and each night it came to me. I had become the mistress of this being, and each night I awaited its pleasure. I joined into the act with this thing of horror, and sank to the depths of evil.

"Then, one night, it failed to come.

"That night I knew the terrible fate it had brought to me, knew that its mission was ended and that it would come no more."

Catherine's eyes were wild, and that bitter smile played grotesquely over her lips.

"And so I have told you," she said. "Now perhaps you may tell me something, Doctor?"

I said nothing.

"You have read *Malleus Maleficarum?*"

"And *Dictionnaire Infernal* and *Alexicacon* and a dozen more, yes."

"And what is your opinion on the much-debated subject, Doctor?"

"What is that?"

"Can incubi reproduce in the body of mortal woman?"

She looked down at her enlarged belly and her face twisted into hatred.

"I live in dread of bearing the demon's child," she whispered.

And it was with cold horror that I left her room . . .

I spent a considerable portion of that night in deliberation, wondering whether I should reveal the true nature of Catherine's fantasy to her husband. It was not easy to decide upon the best course. Fengriffen would surely be relieved to find that he had not been made a cuckold, but he was not a man of any great tolerance or understanding and it was difficult to forecast what his reactions would be when he discovered the fiendish delusion under which his wife's sanity sagged. Finally, however, I decided that it would be best to tell him, that my own work, in banishing this monstrous shape from Catherine's mind would be made easier by Fengriffen's knowledge. But I did not wish to discuss the matter in the library, where the conversation must necessarily be flavored by our previous discourse; did not wish to speak anywhere in the house. It was such a dark subject that I felt it could be managed far better in the open air by daylight. Thus I waited until we had breakfasted, and asked Charles if he would ride with me.

He shot me an inquisitive glance, but made no comment, nodded his acquiescence. I went to my room to change into clothes suitable for riding, and when I came down again there were two horses saddled and waiting in the forecourt. Fengriffen was holding the reins of his big bay hunter and looking up at the sky. The stable lad held my horse, a rather smallish and placid-looking gelding that suited me perfectly.

"It'll rain today," Fengriffen said.

"Has Jacob pronounced upon it?"

He nodded and swung easily into the saddle.

"Well, we needn't ride far," I said.

Fengriffen nodded again, his face grave. The lad gave me a leg up and stood back, pushing his cap up in that gesture of habit he possessed, and watching as we set off. Fengriffen was a fine horseman and rode naturally, without thought for the motions, leaving his mind open to concepts and continuing to glance up at the sky from time to time. For my part, I was still turning over possibilities, wondering if I had made a mistake in my decision and how best to convey my meaning in layman's terms that he could grasp; wanting him to comprehend objectively, so that he would understand without shock or repulsion, the dark forces that held Catherine.

We rode side by side, the hoofbeats dull on the heavy earth, following the tournure of the rising land and skirting the trees. Fengriffen's height and the height of his big bay combined to give me a feeling of relative smallness beside him, made him seem somehow larger than life as I looked sideways and saw his lean form silhouetted against the overcast sky—larger in the way that an elongated El Greco is larger, and grim as a Goya. We moved the horses at a walk for some half hour, until the house was no longer visible around the turning of the forest's contour; then he reined in suddenly and looked at me down his nose, from that great height, placing his hand against my horse's bridle as though he did not trust my ability to halt the beast. His nostrils flared and his steed pawed the ground restlessly.

"Well?" he asked.

"Let us dismount."

We did so. Fengriffen secured the horses loosely to the limb of the nearest tree. An outcrop of grey stone jutted from the woods at this point, a wedge of rock through which gnarled oaks twined their twisted ascent and probed and burrowed with sigmoidal roots between the stones. I sat upon the rocks. Fengriffen placed one foot beside me and leaned over, his elbow on his knee. Dismounted, he still seemed disproportionately angular. The horses eyed us with patience, but Fengriffen was not patient.

"Well?" he asked again.

"There is an abnormality in your wife's mind," I began, carefully choosing my words. His lips moved, and I held one hand up.

"Wait. Don't interrupt me yet. Hear me out before you speak. It is abnormal, but hardly insane. However, if allowed to persist, there is every danger that it may cause insanity. It is a belief which was quite common in former times—in the Middle Ages. But it is not common now, and the uniqueness in itself makes it far more dangerous. It is connected with the curse, but I do not believe it was caused by the curse, nor by knowledge of the curse. Rather was her mind ripe to seek the curse as a method of self-inflicted punishment. I believe that your wife is suffering guilt for some reason—some act of which I do not know, and doubt she knows herself—and that this feeling of guilt was inflamed and magnified by her credulity concerning the woodsman's tale. The connection has taken the form of a dream, or nightmare, which recurred for a time, and which was of a quality that made it appear real, made differentiation between nightmare and reality impossible to her."

"Dreams? How can dreams do this?"

"Because to Catherine they are not dreams. They are real. They are far more real than whatever has caused her guilt, for her mind has failed to countenance that—has blocked it from her consciousness as a protective measure. But this must be the starting point. If I am able to delve beneath her conscious memory and discover the reason for her guilt, I may be able to deal with it. It might well be a long and tedious process."

Fengriffen took his pipe and tobacco pouch out and began to stuff the mixture into the bowl with great concentration.

"Could this guilt be rooted in infidelity?"

"It could. But not, I think, on the instance you are referring to. Then again, it could have any of a hundred other motivations."

"And these dreams?" he asked. He stuck a phosphorus match and applied the flame to his pipe. "What is the nature of her dreams?"

"Sexual."

Fengriffen scowled, not with anger but rather with the effort to understand; scowled with the pipestem clamped in his teeth and ribbons of smoke rising above him.

"You should understand that sexual guilt need not have a sexual cause," I told him.

He said nothing.

"Do you know what an incubus is?"

Fengriffen nodded slowly, took the pipe from his mouth. "A demon or devil which seeks intercourse with mortals, is it not?"

"That, and more."

"But that is an absurdity."

"To you and me. Not to Catherine. You have, in your library, a volume which deals with such things—deals not as science would deal, but with all the evil belief of an unenlightened age and superstitious faith. Your wife had read this volume. It is easy to believe that what one reads in print is fact. Catherine could not admit that her dreams were dreams, could not face the fact that she was experiencing dreams of sexual content. She sought an answer, and found it in the wicked teachings of that infamous book at a time when her mind was already disturbed by knowledge of the curse. In conjunction, they formed a cycle. The dreams became increasingly real as her mind inflamed, and her mind was driven farther from reality as these dreams intruded more and more."

"But why should she have had these erotic dreams?"

"There again is the unknown guilt. It could be something from her past, some long forgotten event of childhood. Or it could stem from a simple need, a failure on your part to satisfy her carnal urges adequately. I think this rather more than likely, in fact. But, and this I must stress, the very nature of her dreams, the very fact she was unable to admit that they were dreams, proves her innocence."

Fengriffen raised his eyebrows.

"The lascivious do not become deranged over nocturnal eroticism. They enjoy it, as a substitute for their desires. It is the person who attempts to repress these sensations and emotions who becomes disturbed. The dread of the sleeping representation of the sexual act increases in proportion to the degree of repression. In one with a predisposition to instability, severe repression of erotic desires can lead to fantasies which pass beyond the realm of sleep and persevere into the waking hours. You understand? Your wife cannot believe that she has erotic dreams, and so turns to the curse which began in a sexual crime, and to what she has read of supernatural concepts, as an explanation. She came to believe that a demon was visiting her."

"This surely is madness."

"For ages it was the accepted explanation. Even the word 'nightmare' comes from this idea. 'Mare' was the Old English for demon, you know. I told you the belief is uncommon in our day, but hardly inconceivable."

Fengriffen shifted his foot upon the rocks. "And the night of which I told you? The night I broke into her room? Is it truly possible that what I believed to be infidelity was really no more than a dream?"

"Possible and, indeed, probable."

He breathed a sigh of dubious relief. The wind had risen, and played through the horses' manes. The sky seemed ever darker. The scent of rain was heavy on the air.

"And you will remain here? Remain as long as necessary?"

"Of course. She does not despise you, she despises herself. She keeps you from her, not for lack of love, but to keep her husband from soiling himself with a woman who has cohabited with a demon. Catherine believes herself unclean and unworthy."

Again he shifted his foot, tapping his riding crop against the ankle. "But a cure is possible?"

"I believe so."

"And you will remain here? Remain as long as necessary?"

Fengriffen seemed to have acquired a new confidence in me following my relevation, and in turn I lost my reticence and doubt about confiding in him—made, I fear, the error of thinking he saw his wife's illness in the same way as I, and understood all the connotations.

"I shall stay at least until your child is born," I told him. "It may not be necessary after that. The very fact of normal birth and motherhood may be the greatest cure—may cause her to effect her own cure, within her own mind."

"I don't see . . . normal?"

Fengriffen frowned, and I realized he had not followed our conversation to the same conclusions that plagued his wife; that perhaps it would have been better if he did not. But now he began to understand. He began to see the terrible fear that gripped his wife's sanity in the fetid talons of dread. His face changed. His frown gave way to incredulity for an instant, and then turned to horror. He stared at me with hatred, for I had released this evil that flitted and flew through his mind, evil that was beyond his power to rationally dismiss. His countenance became terrible to behold. The muscles writhed beneath the tautly drawn skin in a dozen vermiculate twitchings.

"She believes that?" he whispered.

"She fears that."

"That in her womb she bears a demon's child?"

"Her aberration—" I began, feeling an appalling sense of helplessness as I looked into his face, looked beyond his features and into the depths of his emotion.

But Fengriffen was no longer listening to me.

This was the brittle ice of emotion, and it crackled perilously beneath the burden of distress.

Fengriffen stamped his foot.

Turf sprang up around his polished boot. He slammed one fist into the other hand with a sharp crack, and at that very instant the drums of thunder began to roll across the heavens. It was as if the gods themselves shared the man's agony. The sky blackened, echoing the dark sentiments of his countenance, as the clouds altered without changing place, rolled ponderously over to present the darker side of this arched ceiling. Through the darkness ran a hook of lightning. It split the blackness, and Fengriffen's eyes gathered in the momentary illumination, reflecting their own dark light. The first drops of rain descended, slow and heavy as lost hope, while the mournful wind dipped down to toss Fengriffen's hair in wild disarray. He tossed his head back and the hair fell over his brow. He looked less than a man—and more. He looked an idol carved by pagan hands, a colossus fashioned from veined marble and set with obsidian eyes that glowed and revealed the furnace blazing within the cavern of his skull.

Another wave of thunder beat above us.

"You speak of curses!" he said. His voice was hollow, its timbre forged in a chest cavity where the heart had diminished and left a void. "Far better infidelity than this! Far better madness to idiocy! Madness to loss of all reason, to the slobbering depths of mindlessness!"

His head swiveled back toward the direction we had come from, toward the house. He raised his hand and his lips moved without sound. I do not know what malediction he mouthed in that moment, but know it was terrible indeed.

Then he moved to his horse in two huge strides, jerked the reins free, and mounted with a suddenness that caused the brute to shy and stumble; kicked his heels savagely into the animal's sides and blasted off at full gallop, spraying the turf behind him. A clot of muck struck me on the forehead. I wiped it away with the back of my hand and looked after him, shielding my eyes against the angled rain. Something of his agony came to me in sympathetic vibrations, and I felt a great weight suck at me, felt my boots sink into the softening ground, as though gravity had singled me out to test its prowess and drag me down into the underworld. For some minutes I stood there, motionless, long after Fengriffen had vanished into the storm. Then my horse whinnied. The sound brought me back to time.

I mounted and rode after him.

The storm was absolute.

I could not see more than a few feet before me, and even those feet were a shifting haze. I was forced to let the horse have his head and return us with animal instincts, while I cursed myself for a blunderer, castigated myself for having assumed that Fengriffen could possibly have accepted such knowledge with rational objectivity. The horse did not blunder, did not need vision or intelligence, but headed unerringly toward the stables. And what use, I asked myself, is the mind to mankind? Man would survive without conscious thought—would survive more surely and more efficiently devoid of that useless by-product of the brain that causes the suffering unique to homo sapiens, that makes man, alone of all creatures, torment and destroy himself, as I was tormenting myself at that moment and as Fengriffen was doing on a level beyond words. The mind is the descendant of the thumb and the vocal cord, and a malformed child it has always been, a mistake of evolution with the unique ability to bring its own extinction. So my own mind told me, as the horse moved on and the rain stabbed through my clothing in a hundred places.

The beast's hooves rattled suddenly, and I knew we had come into the courtyard. Lightning forked down and I saw the house rush at me, then diminish, as illumination played its optical jest. I kept my head down and my shoulders hunched, waiting until we had entered the shelter of the stables before I looked up.

Fengriffen's horse was there, lathered and dripping. The young lad was unsaddling the animal, and glanced up at my entrance.

"Where is your master?" I asked as I slid from the saddle, loosing a halo of water from my sodden hair.

"Don't know, sir. He seemed in a rare state. Happen he was vexed with the rain, but he leaped from his horse and ran off without a word for me. Took the spade with himself, and all. Peculiar, I'd say."

"The spade?"

"Aye. The one which I uses for muckin' out the stalls. Can't see what he wants with that."

He took the reins from me.

"Did he head toward the house?"

"Couldn't say, sir."

I looked toward the entrance. The rain lashed across. But I could be no wetter than I was, and wrapping my cloak about me, I walked out and started for the house. A light bobbled before me. A moment later the light was a lantern, and old Jacob was peering up at me from his shrunken stature, his face cowled in a rain hood.

"Is the master with you, sir?" he asked.

"He has just left the stables."

Jacob looked about meaninglessly in the impenetrable rain.

"The mistress's time has come," he said. "We have sent to the village for Doctor Whittle, and Mrs. Lune sent me to fetch the master."

"You didn't pass him on your way from the house?"

"No, sir. I wouldn't have come on if I had."

"Where could he have gone?" I asked, and no sooner were the words voiced than with a dreadful conviction I knew where Fengriffen was; knew that when he had turned toward the house and mouthed those silent words, they had not been directed at Catherine, nor at the house.

I seized the lantern from Jacob without a word of explanation, knowing he must think me mad as I plunged off into the storm, wondering where madness did lie as I hurried toward the graveyard.

The rain was alternating now.

For an instant it would lift, as wind and cloud toyed with one another, and then it would fall again in a curtain as dense as a cataract. Against this liquid tapestry my lantern's feeble beam bounced back, illuminating no more than a yard before me, serving more to blind me in the rebounding glare than to light my path. I slipped and slid in the mud, and several times came close to falling; bumped suddenly against some solid object, giving my shin a nasty rap; saw in a momentary flash of lightning that I had banged into an ancient sundial in the gardens, overgrown with slimy moss. It seemed a curious object to encounter on this sunless day, seemed to offer mute testimonial of brighter times. I passed around it, brushed through some shrubbery, caught a glimpse of the fallen tree upon which Catherine had seated herself, and then began to cross the field. Each time the lightning ran across the sky I could see the line of trees before me; each time they were a bit taller, a bit nearer, and I plodded on doggedly, placing one foot before the other and not thinking of time or distance or discomfort, until at last I was within the forest.

The trees offered a certain amount of shelter, but did not increase the visibility, for the lessening of the rain was more than made up for by the gloomy shadows that clung to the ground in the darkness and then threw sudden trestles across the lightning's flash. I held the lantern up and peered uncertainly ahead. I had been there but once, and was unsure of my directions, uncertain at what point I had entered the arboreal perimeter. I advanced a few feet and paused again. The forest seemed different under the onslaught of this deluge. The bows sagged and the rain battered at leaf and limb. I had no idea which way to go.

And then my blood froze.

I heard the sound of the spade.

It was a sodden sound in the heavy earth, and following each thud came a low, coarse grunt of exertion. I moved toward this noise like a sleepwalker, a zombie, a nyctophobe cast into night. The lantern was before me, throwing moths of light that darted through the timber and then vanished in the greater flare of the heavenly currents. I was frightened and I was fascinated. I moved on toward that sound until, without warning, I stepped past a tree and stood at the edge of the graveyard.

Just then another jagged stroke split the sky.

Blinding light blocked the shattered cubes of tombstones and sent white tentacles over the sunken graves. I looked upon Fengriffen . . .

He was bent over his grandfather's grave.

As the light ran down his profile, dividing him into carnal chiaroscuro, he appeared but half a man. His head was down, he did not notice the lantern that quivered in my hand. He was intent upon his task. He stooped farther and lifted. A pile of black earth slid from the spade and ran down the mound behind him. He stooped again as the illumination faded. The darkness dropped between us and my lantern could not reach him. I stood, as rooted to the spot as the tombstones themselves. I heard the spade again, and again, and then another electric tongue tasted the sky and he was thrown into view once more. The mound was higher; he had diminished as he sank lower into the opening grave. As he heaved up, his face turned toward me, blinded in the glare. His lips were squared back from his teeth, and the teeth ivory geometries. His eyes streamed tears of anguish that mingled with the rain, and his nostrils flared like a hunting beast, scenting its prey. The powerful shoulders bunched with muscle. He lifted and, mercifully for my eyes, the spade fell again. It was through this darkness that I heard the hollow clunk of spade against the coffin. I closed my eyes. If lightning flashed again, I did not wish to see. There came a brittle sound of shattering wood, rotten with damp age, and then a ripping sound, as of one tearing at a coffin with his naked hands.

He cried out.

He cried in words that fit no language, sounds that symbolized emotions so deeply buried that words had never been conceived to signify their meaning, so dark that they had never been recognized by the conscious mind or the rational tongue.

I heard other sounds from that opened grave.

I could bear no more.

I retreated, staggering and stumbling, to the edge of the woods and sheltered as best I could beneath the spreading arms of an oak and did not think.

Fengriffen came out of the trees a few yards to my right. The storm had ceased. It had ended abruptly some time before. I did not know how long before, or how long I had been sitting beneath that tree. A few drops continued to fall infrequently; the forest dripped and splattered. Across the field the house glistened and the courtyard gleamed. I stood up as he walked past. He seemed dazed and bewildered, and carried his hands clawed at his sides. The fingernails were torn and bloody from ripping at the wood—what else they had rent asunder, I did not wish to know. I moved toward him, my joints stiff with damp and my muscles protesting the long, motionless vigil, and he turned without surprise, peered at me without recognition.

I spoke his name.

"What? Yes? What?" he said, syllables without meaning.

"Come back to the house."

"What? Oh, you."

I took his arm.

"You," he said.

"Come to the house."

"Yes. All right."

"The doctor has been summoned."

"What? Why?"

"Your wife . . ."

"Oh. Yes. I see. Yes, I had better be there."

His eyes shifted over me, darting and rolling and blinking. When I turned him toward the house, he did not resist; I retained my hold on his arm and felt him gradually relax, until he was striding out in a normal manner. We were halfway across the field when it occurred to me that I had left the lantern beneath the tree. I did not bother to return for it. What, after all, is a lantern?

Doctor Whittle's carriage was at the door. I wondered, vaguely, whether he had come through that blinding torrent or sufficient time had lapsed since the storm abated. Jacob ran out to meet us. He was excited and rather pleased, and informed us that Whittle was already with Catherine. Fengriffen nodded, his face changing from uneasiness to concern. I felt as if I could see his distressing thoughts—the thoughts I had sown—running from his mind as the rivulets of water slunk around the flagstones at our feet; dropping from his heart as the final heavy blobs were wrung from the voided clouds. Sunlight had pierced the sky, the day had brightened, and Fengriffen's foul deed in the graveyard had served to dissipate his raging energies, had left him calm and reasonable, allowing his thoughts to return to his wife and child. It had scarcely been a therapy one could prescribe, but it had worked, and perhaps it had been for the best, for there was no telling what alternative measures he might have chosen.

We entered the house.

The servants were scurrying about in preparation. Whittle's voice called out some instructions from above. Fengriffen and I went into the library and found that Jacob had coffee waiting and the fire alight. The wind was sucking flakes of flame up the chimney. Fengriffen smoked furiously, alternating between cigar and pipe as though he could not determine which offered more tranquility. He felt the normal nervousness that an expectant father feels, and it was magnified, no doubt, by his hope that the birth would effect a cure and return his wife to him. He tried to sit, but leapt up again each time, after a few seconds, and paced about the room. After several attempts at distracting him with conversation, I, too, sank into silence amidst my tobacco fumes. From time to time I looked at my watch. It seemed to be taking a long time, although I had no professional experience of such things. Fengriffen, however, never so much as glanced at his time piece as the afternoon wore on. He became, if anything, more calm, did not pace as much, and spent some time at the window, looking out into the gardens with composed features and motionless hands. There was a bird singing in the nearest tree; singing, no doubt, because the rain had brought the worms out.

At last came the cry of a child.

Fengriffen was at the window as it sounded. His shoulders stiffened, and for a moment he did not move. Then he spun about and sprang to the door. I followed into the hallway in time to see him take the stairs three at a bound and rush down the corridor upstairs. His excitement proved contagious, and I followed at only slightly less speed, arriving at the top of the staircase as Mrs. Lune emerged from Catherine's room. Her face was white. Fengriffen had to check his dash to avoid colliding with her, and she made no attempt to move from his way.

"A son," she said. "A fine son."

But there was something wrong with the way she said it. Her tone caused Fengriffen to stare at her for a moment, before he moved past. Doctor Whittle appeared at the doorway, standing directly in the entrance, as if he would bar access. He shot me a meaningful glance over Fengriffen's shoulder—almost, I thought, an imploring glance—as Fengriffen looked past him and into the room, looked from the doorway, as he had looked on that other fateful occasion.

And looked at a scene even more terrible.

I moved to his side and shared this sight. Whittle still looked at me. Catherine was in bed with her child.

It was *her* child.

She held it in the tender arms of a mother, but her face was turned away as if she could not bear to look. Fengriffen looked. He was rigid beside me, and I felt myself stiffen and grow cold as my nerve impulses stumbled at the gaps.

The baby bore the blood-red mark upon its cheek.

Fengriffen gnashed his teeth. Fengriffen clenched his hands. Fengriffen swayed for a moment, then regained his balance and took one step into the room. Doctor Whittle, moving backward, remained between him and the bed, and I advanced to his side. I thought we might be forced to overpower him—to attempt to subdue him—and Whittle thought the same. But Fengriffen took only the one step forward.

"Accursed harlot," he whispered, so softly that Catherine could not have heard him.

He turned the eyes of a cornered beast upon Whittle.

"Is it possible?" he asked.

Whittle peered at him.

"Could her fears have caused the child to be marked in this manner? Could shock or fright have cursed my child with the mark of the woodsman?"

The doctor looked away, embarrassed. His eyes turned to the bed, dropped. He did not know where to look within that room. Catherine whimpered, keeping her face to the wall. Mrs. Lune was at the doorway, her albescent face set with tearful eyes and quivering lips. Fengriffen turned to me, grasped my collar in his torn hands. Minute details swell in times of stress, and I noticed that he had not troubled to wash the caked blood from his fingers; noticed as those very fingers twisted savagely in my garments, forcing me up and back.

"Tell me! Is such a thing conceivable?"

"I do not know," I said.

"Within the realm of science . . . within knowledge of man . . . is it possible?"

Froth flecked his lips, but his voice was controlled and calm. He might have been Socrates asking an absurd question to reveal the nature of truth; Diogenes, holding up the twin lanterns of his eyes above an honest man—or he might have been benighted Heracles, wallowing in the Augean filth. I tried to shrug, but my shoulders were held fast in his powerful grip, and the effort brought his hands closer to my throat.

"Perhaps," I said.

"Perhaps?"

"Science is not a cul-de-sac."

His hand tightened even more. I feared he would throttle me. I clamped my own hands upon his wrists, attempting to loosen his hold, but his strength was superhuman—supernatural, even—and my fingers closed over corded bars of steel. I felt the power run down his forearms and flow into torque at my breast, felt that very power run into my own body in a charged current of pure fear, as those fingers, still bloody from rending a coffin, tightened and twisted. I cried out. Whittle saw my distress. He laid his hand upon Fengriffen's shoulder to restrain him, and that hand virtually leaped away, as Fengriffen's trapezius muscles exploded along the line of his shoulders. Fengriffen reared up until his form seemed hardly human as it towered above me, around me. He drew my face to his. His eyes seemed to expand to preternatural dimensions into which I would be dragged.

"Have you ever known it to happen?" he whispered, with the pulse beating at his throat and spittle at the corners of his mouth.

"Please—" I gasped.

He blinked. The pressure lessened. Despite the physical discomfort he was inflicting upon me, it was not an attack—no more does a drowning man in a dark sea attack the driftwood whose buoyancy is salvation—his eyes were beseeching, his voice pleading. He had not realized the menace in his embrace, but had realized one thing only—that there was one possibility to which he might cling, one floating hope to keep him from the depths, one answer he must seek. But I could not bring that answer to my lips. Never have I felt so helpless, never have I so regretted what little knowledge I may have. I wished with all my heart to voice the lie; wished to deceive this pitiful creature and with my deception give him peace. But there, across the room, was the child. There, upon the child's face, flowed the hereditary stigma of another man. There, in the poor infant's chromosomes, lurked the genes of a different and baser lineage waiting to develop. What greater evil to give him hope now, knowing that hope would mutate to suspicion; suspicion would undergo the lethal catalyst of observation, and become certainty; that certainty would be more terrible by far when, magnified by time, it filled the empty vessel where hope had dwelt.

My lips parted, but the words faltered at the barrier of my throat.

"You—have—never—known—it—to—happen?" Fengriffen demanded.

His voice mesmerized me. Slowly I shook my head, just once, from side to side, knowing that I was cursing this woman across the room as surely as the woodsman ever had, yet unable to do otherwise. Fengriffen deserved the truth. He watched my head rotate through the gesture of negation as he might have watched a cobra rear back to strike, fascinated by the venomous fangs of denial, pierced by the poison of knowledge, paralyzed by the toxic truth that ran through his veins.

Slowly his hands unclenched.

He pushed me from him with open palms, sending me spinning against the wall. His efforts had reopened his wounds. A smear of blood marked my linen. His eyes fastened upon this, widened. He raised his hands before his face, fingers hooked, flesh shredded, staring at them with disbelief, with incredulity, staring as he might have stared at some alien objects that had attached themselves as parasites upon the ends of his arms.

"Why, I had forgotten that," he said, in amazement.

He shook his head.

He turned toward his wife.

"For that," he whispered, staring at her.

Catherine looked at him then, for the first time since he had entered the room. She jerked spasmodically. A solitary teardrop ran unheeded down her cheek. Her eyes were wide receptacles, gathering the shaft of loathing he hurled at her, and she held the child closer to her breast; held it, not protectively, but as a shield against his hatred.

Fengriffen held his hands up for her to see.

"For you have I torn my ancestor from his grave!" he cried.

And then he was gone.

The echo of his cry howled in the room, and his footfalls were heavy on the stairs. The echo died. The downstairs door banged as its great weight closed.

I looked at Doctor Whittle. Doctor Whittle looked at me.

Mrs. Lune came into the room. She was moaning. Her hands were clasped at her breast. She passed us, moving to the bed, and I forced my eyes from our gaze of mutual horror—ah, is horror synallagmatic?—and followed her. I felt I must do something, and it was a greater feeling than that inspired by professional obligation. I leaned over the bed.

"Catherine?"

"Leave me," she said.

Her voice was rational, but there ran a quake beneath the surface, an undercurrent beginning to stir.

"Please hear me."

"Leave me. It is my child. No matter what else it may be, it is my child. Leave us alone."

"You must face the truth!" I said loudly, wishing to shock her, to bring that subterranean trembling safely out in an avalanche of tears. For despite the mark that proscribed her guilt, I still believed her—believed, that is, that she thought her fantasy was fact, that in subconsciously denying the truth she had fashioned a delusion far more terrible than any fact could be.

She shook her head violently from side to side. Mrs. Lune perched on the edge of the bed and slipped one arm around her shoulders in futile comfort, shot a vicious glance at me, and then looked suggestively toward the doorway.

"The truth, Catherine!" I shouted. "For the sake of your sanity, and your child!"

"I know the truth!" she screamed. Spittle sprayed from her lips in the intensity of her conviction. The child's face crinkled, preparing for tears. Catherine raised her face, and madness danced in her eyes.

"It is true, true, true!"

She gasped and choked. Doctor Whittle tugged gently at my sleeve.

"Perhaps later," he said.

I nodded. Perhaps too late. I felt a great exhaustion drop over me and my shoulders sagged. Whittle was right. There was nothing I could do. I followed him to the door as Mrs. Lune drew Catherine tenderly to her bosom and stroked her hair. Whittle closed the door behind us and sighed, then led the way toward the stairs. I paused, for no reason, as we passed through the gallery, and just then came the muffled sound of Fengriffen's horse crossing the courtyard at a gallop—crossing the courtyard toward the woods.

Whittle and I sat in the library. The afternoon angles had slanted into evening, and now night spun a shroud for the window. Whittle was waiting for me to speak, looking at me in silence and thinking that I was delving into dark fields where strange blooms grew at night; thinking that I would pluck abstruse theory, like a mythical flower, from the fecund soil of science. Perhaps my demeanor was such as to give this impression, for I was staring intently at the window and my brow was creased. But I looked at a window, no more; I did not even penetrate the glass with my gaze. It was beyond theory. The fact seemed undeniable. What Catherine believed—that she had been visited by a demon lover—was absolute truth, for her. What that hideous birthmark signified was absolute truth for me. The two truths existed on different levels, dual dimensions that could not be joined. Whether or not that absolved her of guilt was not a question for science, nor one I would wish to answer.

It was one her husband must answer, however.

God help him.

Presently Whittle broke the silence.

"It couldn't be possible, I suppose?" he asked in weary tones.

"What's that?"

"It couldn't be possible that she might have marked her child through fright?"

"An old wives' tale. In accepted theory it is impossible. In fact? Well, that is more to your experience than mine. Can you offer him hope? Have you ever known a child to be marked in that way?"

"No," he said, and sighed. "And yet it seems incredible that she could have allowed the woodsman to . . . to . . . that she could have taken that creature from the woods into her room and submitted to . . . incredible."

"But she didn't," I said. "On the level of her own awareness, she did not. Whoever it was—the woodsman, we must suppose—who crept through her window in the night, she truly believes to be the incubus which her unbalanced mind has summoned."

"God help the poor woman," Whittle said. "And God help poor Charles. Can she be cured of this madness? Will he have tolerance enough to judge her innocent in intent, if not in deed? He is not a tolerant man. You know, of course, where he has gone?"

"I fear so."

Whittle had his snuffbox out, had placed it on the ornate Regency table and was squaring it with the corner.

"You have known him for years, Doctor," I said. "Is he a man who will kill?"

Whittle shrugged.

Revenge begets revenge.

"He is a Fengriffen," said the doctor.

Into the silence that followed walked Mrs. Lune. She was clutching a Bible in her hand, and her eyes were rubescent in the wake of tears. She crossed the room with a determined stride and stood over me.

"The mistress is sleeping now," she said.

"Good," I replied, although I had no idea whether it was particularly good or not, for the footsteps of merciful Hypnos are dogged by his son; Morpheus stalks without pity through the gentle glades of slumber.

"Please, sir . . . may I have a word?"

"Certainly."

She clutched the Bible tighter, clutched it as a preacher grips the rostrum when about to hurl his theology like a gauntlet before the congregation.

"I know as you're a doctor, and trying to do what's right; but sir, if I may say so, there are things you don't understand as well as some. If I may speak my mind, and no offense, sir. The poor mistress has . . . I mean, there are things . . ."

"I am conversant with the details of the curse," I said, to help her out and hurry it on.

Mrs. Lune nibbled her lip.

"You see, sir, if you could convince the master that it is true . . . that the poor mistress is innocent . . ."

"I will not deceive him," I told her rather firmly. I did not want her to continue, for it was pointless. "I will do my best to instill tolerance and understanding in Fengriffen, but I cannot serve him duplicity."

Mrs. Lune looked toward Doctor Whittle.

"I'm sorry," he said.

Mrs. Lune knew few words. The thought was in her head, and she struggled for expression, casting her eyes about the walls as though to take, by osmosis, the needed vocabulary from the learned volumes on the shelves.

Her mouth opened.

And a piercing shriek reverberated through the house.

I started and Doctor Whittle started and Mrs. Lune, her mouth still open, trembled spasmodically. That scream had not come from her. I leaped up and dashed into the hallway, as a second cry sounded—less shrill, as agony replaced shock. The scream came tumbling down the stairs, turning over and over as it fell headlong and came to a sudden crashing halt against my eardrums. I rushed up the stairs, moving against that descending sound as against a river current, feeling that I swam upstream in the soundwaves.

A third cry did not come.

It was only Whittle's footsteps behind me that punctuated the silence as I threw open Catherine's door.

Catherine was alone in her bed.

The child was gone.

The room was cold.

Unbelievably cold, colder than air should be, and despite this chill a foul odor billowed about, an odor so heavy that it seemed to be visible. I crossed the room and threw the shutters closed. The fetid stench caused me to gag, and for a moment I leaned against the sill for support, shaking my head to clear the lingering fumes before I turned to Catherine.

"The baby," she said. "It has taken my baby."

I sat on the edge of the bed and took her hand. Her flesh was molded from melting ice. She began to babble indistinctly. Whittle stopped in the doorway, recoiling at the olfaction of decay.

"Who has taken the child?" I asked.

Catherine grimaced and contorted. I could see the flesh creep convulsively on her arm, as if the skin were not fastened to the bone.

"Was it the woodsman?"

She stared at me without comprehension.

"Who took the child?" I repeated.

"He took it. He."

"Who, for God's sake?"

"The father," she moaned.

I took her by the shoulders and shook her. Her hair slipped over her forehead and her neck swayed back and forth. She did not resist, but seemed to welcome the violent motion, and began to throw herself about. I stopped shaking her, but she continued to jerk rigorously and her head banged against the headboards so that

I was forced to restrain her movements. She trembled under my hands.

I forced a penetrating sharpness into my voice, and threw the words down through the clouds that hung over her mind.

"The woodsman," I said. "The woodsman took the child. The woodsman is the father. It has been the woodsman all along. You have enchanted yourself into fantasy. The woodsman! The woodsman! It was a man, a living man, no more!"

But Catherine did not hear me.

Beneath those clouds, her mind had turned in upon itself. Like a wounded shark, twisting to devour its own flesh, she tore at the weave of her sanity.

"The woodsman!" I shouted.

"The father," she said. "My baby. His baby. The father. He came for his child. He has taken the baby. Gone, gone, gone. Where, where, where?"

"Catherine!"

Her eyes were suddenly lucid.

She frowned.

"Where?" she asked. "I wonder where they have gone?"

And the shutters came down again. She cringed and twitched and babbled. I sighed and stood up. Mrs. Lune appeared, trembling as violently as Catherine, and approached the bed warily, Bible held before her.

"Stay with her," I said.

Mrs. Lune turned her old eyes upon me. They mirrored a belief I could never dispel. Perhaps it was better that way. She cradled Catherine in her arms.

"Poor innocent," she said.

In the hall, Whittle took my arm.

"For God's sake, what caused that odor?" he asked.

"I don't know. An unwashed body, steeped in the muck and slime of rotting vegetation, befouling itself of filthy habit—what else could it be?"

He shook his head. "I have dealt with the corruption of death, undiscovered behind closed doors for weeks; have amputated limbs so festered with rotten pus that the flesh separated at the touch. But never have I encountered such a stench. To think that a creature wrapped in that odor has been with Catherine . . ."

He shuddered.

"It must have been the woodsman, come for his child as the climax of revenge."

"What can we do?" Whittle asked.

We moved toward the stairs through the dark arch of the gallery.

"Where do you suppose he will take the child? To his cabin? Or will he do worse? What action can we predict for that debased mind?"

We had started down the stairs.

"I doubt the child is in immediate danger, other than possible exposure. We must recover it as soon as possible. But I doubt the woodsman will deliberately injure it. It is, after all, his own son. He would have no reason to wish it harm; will, more than likely, wish to keep the child, as the incarnation of his fulfilled vengeance."

"Exposure is danger enough," Whittle said. "Pray that he maintains enough human sense or animal instinct to keep the child warmly wrapped. But Doctor Pope, there is another danger we must consider." He turned to face me at the foot of the stairs. "Fengriffen has gone for the woodsman," he said. "If he is waiting there now, in his state of mind, who knows what he might do? We must make haste, must pursue the woodsman and overtake him before he returns to where Fengriffen waits, and avert . . . avert God knows what act . . ."

I nodded agreement. I knew well what Fengriffen was capable of when blind rage and agony possessed him, had seen him in the graveyard, and felt the strength of his limbs in the bedroom. It was an innocent baby, but it bore the hated mark of Catherine's shame, and it was well that we should hasten.

We headed for the door, and suddenly Whittle stopped. He winced and closed his eyes. The sound of Catherine's incoherent babbling had pursued us. It was warped, a mutation of human sound, mangled and twisted out of shape as it passed through closed doors, through the floor, through the dense stone of the house itself; elongated as it slid through grain, compressed as it seeped through rock, bent upon itself as it turned the corners and shattered as it dropped through space. It was a sound to climb the backbone with feathery touch and run like morbid plague through the blood.

It was a sound that Whittle had heard before.

He did not have to tell me. I knew.

The sound that Sarah had made, as she lay defiled, and Silas's severed fingers fell upon her lap.

We paused just outside the massive door, with the vast house towering like a monolith above us. I took a deep breath of the air, welcoming the untainted freshness, and noticed that Whittle did the same. We both turned toward the stables, but with second thought I stopped him.

"It may well be wiser to follow on foot," I said. "He has only a brief start, and must carry the child. There will be delay while horses are saddled, and it will be more difficult to follow his tracks from the saddle."

Whittle nodded.

We reversed direction to take up the trail in the muddy earth beneath Catherine's window; we had moved only a few strides when hoofbeats clanked on the flagstones, and Fengriffen loomed up in the darkness, very still and straight upon his horse. He did not notice us until I called his name, then he halted and dismounted, letting the reins trail free to the ground. The horse stood very still.

"It is done," Fengriffen said.

His rage was gone, he was very calm.

"What have you done, Charles?" Doctor Whittle asked, in the tones of the confessional.

"Done? I have done murder. What else?"

He shrugged.

"What else?" he repeated, and from inside his cloak he drew a revolver, looked at it as if he were pondering the function of such an instrument. The revolver looked very large, very hard, very real. He stared at it and his wrist turned, slowly, until the weapon was directed at his face. I attempted to seize him, but he stepped back, shaking his head.

"No, no. Don't worry. I shall not take my own life," he said. "I was merely looking into the barrel, you see, wondering how it looked to the woodsman in his final moment of life. It is most curious. Have you any idea how large this little black hole appears? It is so much more than a rifled bore through a cylinder of metal. It is a tear in the stuff of space and time; a black hole in creation; a bottomless shaft which can suck a man's soul down, down . . . down to whatever other dimensions may exist. Or may not. Most curious, indeed. And the woodsman looked into this chasm, and he smiled. I find that peculiar, to smile into a rent in the universe. Don't you think that peculiar, gentlemen? His dog snarled and cringed, but the woodsman smiled, and I shot him dead. I shot him directly in that odious blemish which has destroyed my life, so that the blood flowed out and covered it. And still he smiled. He was dead, but the smile was set on his lips. He will carry that smile to the grave.

"And then, gentlemen, I stood there for a long time. There was an axe in the corner—perhaps the same axe which my grandfather used—and I stood there for a long time and wondered if I should use the axe to remove his smile. But, in the end, I did not . . ."

Fengriffen smiled placidly.

"I'm rather pleased that I didn't, you know. It would have served little purpose."

"And the child?" Whittle whispered.

Fengriffen reversed the gun in his hand and passed it to me. I slipped it into my pocket.

"I am no barbarian," he said. "I could not harm an innocent child. My wife must leave, and take her child, as soon as she is able, of course. But I bear no malice toward the infant."

"But where is the child?" Whittle asked. It was a desperate query, for he had already seen the anachronism of our suppositions.

"Where? I don't understand you, Doctor."

"Did not——"

I silenced Whittle with a gesture.

"How long has it been since . . . since you killed him?"

Fengriffen looked confused.

"I have no idea," he said. "How long has passed since I left the house? I rode directly to his cabin. What difference can it make?"

Whittle and I regarded one another.

"What is there that I fail to understand?" Fengriffen asked, swinging his head between us.

There was a great deal we failed to understand.

Words were not necessary.

Whittle and I moved to the corner of the house, moved side by side, coupled by the same emotion, while Fengriffen looked after us in bewilderment. The earth was soaked with the storm. Our boots left deep indentations in our wake—deep and unavoidable. We rounded the corner and stood beneath Catherine's window. It was not a great drop. It would have been a simple matter for an agile man to jump from that height onto the soft earth.

Then we looked at the ground.

There were no prints.

There were no prints but our own.

No man had dropped from that window . . .

"Could she . . . could Catherine have destroyed the child in some manner?" Whittle whispered in horror.

"I do not know. I know nothing."

Fengriffen came around the corner of the house and stared dumbly at us. We stared at the ground, and as we stood there the wind rose again. It was above us, in the highest trees, and yet in its passing came a wave of unearthly cold, damp cold, as of the moldering grave. The gnarled oaks moaned, and from a great distance came the forlorn howl of a dog. The wind passed in a moment, and was gone . . . gone, God knows where, scattered and lifted and freed. I looked out across those moors, and shivered. The dog stopped howling. Only Catherine's mad laughter came to replace the wind, echoing through the fabric of that accursed house.

Anachrona

IT CHANCED THAT IN THE YEAR 17— three young scholars were riding to Vienna from the east. They were Percival, Clement, and Leonidas, the best of friends, who read the classics and dabbled in the sciences together at university. Now, the spring break, they had a mind to see Steinhem's fabulous automaton, The Contented Man, so much talked on and admired this season. Educated and curious and of vivid imagination, such a scientific phenomenon interested them. As they rode abreast, engaged in lively and learned discourse, they slowly closed the distance on a solitary rider following the same road.

For some time they had been aware of him. The land was rolling, verdant, and dotted with white spring blooms and they would see him for a while, then he would be blocked from view by a fold in the terrain, only to appear once more. He was tall and solidly built and wore a long black cloak and a wide-brimmed hat. He carried no weapon they could discern, but this was a civilised age and their own swords were ornamental.

At times they closed on him rapidly, then he would seem to move ahead faster, while maintaining the same gait. He rode with a certain lack of grace, as if well enough acquainted with horses but untutored in the finer points of horsemanship.

At intervals, this man dismounted and stood beside the road, his face turned up and the brim of his hat tipped back, as if looking for a hint of rain. At other times he reined in and, without dismounting, affected the same posture, sitting perfectly still on the docile animal.

When they had nearly overtaken him, he turned his mount from the road and dismounted once again. They saw he moved stiffly, as if he had been too long in the saddle. His horse stood loose-reined and obedient and he inclined his face up in the peculiar attitude they had noted. He was staring directly at the noonday sun, expressionless and unblinking. This seemed so unique that the three students reined in.

"Oh, I say, sir— You will harm your eyes!" Percival cautioned. "You should look through smoked glass—"

The stranger ignored this well-meant advice, or failed to hear it. The young men were perplexed. Was he perhaps in a trance or suffering some disorder? They looked more closely and, for a time, believed him to be blind, for his eyes were dull and closed. But then they saw it was not so, for those grey eyes opened and began to stir in their sockets, becoming animated.

Was it their duty to intervene? But they were of a philosophical nature, not given to action or physical decision, and they simply sat on their horses and stared at him as the stranger continued his remarkable scan of the sun.

Presently, he shifted his stance and lowered his head. He had still not blinked nor were his eyes watering. They had thought those eyes were grey, but now they appeared yellow, almost golden, as if they had gathered the celestial light and retained it. They knew it was strange that the colour should alter and that he could gaze at the sun without tears, but anatomy was not one of their studies.

Now the stranger became aware of his audience for the first time. He remained impassive although his shoulders lifted in a shrug. "It . . . exhilarates me," he said.

"It cannot be healthful," Clement murmured.

To this he made no reply. He had piqued their curiosity and, having halted, it seemed awkward to simply ride on again. Leonidas queried, "Do you go to Vienna, sir?"

"I do. I wish to see Steinhem's creation," he replied, distinct but not discourteous.

"Ah! We too are bound there," Clement said. "Will you ride with us?"

"I must set my own pace, and will not delay you," he answered. "I am failing, I fear—"

"Ailing, sir?" Percival expressed concern.

"If you choose," said the stranger. "I can travel only a short distance and must stop to recover my spirits. You must please yourselves, dear sirs."

He swung back into the saddle much more actively than he had dismounted and they rode off apace. The scholars sought to draw him into converse; he was neither friendly nor unfriendly and replied without commitment. They introduced themselves; he seemed not to feel obliged to do the same. The students spoke of Copernicus and Galileo and how and if the heavens revolved, debated the Greatness of Frederick and the principles of Kant and the Anabasis of Xenophon. The stranger took no part and showed interest only when they speculated on Steinhem's automaton, but then only listened and put forth no views. For a time they kept company. He rode methodically and, after a mile or two, began to lag behind.

His eyes were once more dull and grey.

The youths exchanged glances and wondered if they should stay for him. But they were eager to proceed and he seemed not to need their company or assistance and had not proved a conversationalist. They carried on, glancing back occasionally and seeing his face was again turned up, his hat pushed back. They marveled at this. Percival suggested the man was in need of a leach and Leonidas was of the opinion he had contracted a virulence and Clement avowed he was undernourished.

They carried on and in due course came to a wayside inn. It was past noonday now and they took venison and ate at a crude table in the forecourt. With mouthfuls of meat and malt, they manifested Platonic ideals to impress the buxom serving wench who actually thought them weak and wan.

As they dined and discoursed, they saw the stranger proceeding down the road. It seemed he would ride on past, and almost did, but then turned in as if as an afterthought. He greeted them with a nod and summoned the ostler, giving instructions for the care of his horse. The beast was led off to the stables and the scholars naturally expected the stranger to join them. But he stood for a time quite motionless. Then it occurred to them that perhaps he had scant funds and Percival called an invitation. The man hesitated, then joined them at the table, removing his hat courteously. His face was remarkably angular and faceted; he appeared a gentleman of good breeding who had grown jaded and world weary, yet there were no lines or wrinkles as one might expect, no runic creases to show he smiled or frowned.

He declined the offer of food and drink; pressed to take at least a goblet, he did so but held it cradled in his hand and was not seen to drink.

"Have you traveled far?" Clement asked.

"Yes, far and long," the stranger replied. It seemed he would not be specific. It was evident he welcomed the company of learned men, yet suffered some strange lassitude that caused his mind to wander and falter. When he began to speak again, his movements were those of an expressive fellow, yet delivered mechanically and not at all random or vivacious.

"In France, I sought out Lavoisier and learned of combustion and chemical reaction, but that had no bearing on my quest," he told them and they listened. "In Bologna, I met with Calvani and found myself intrigued by animal magnetism; it was more promising, but had not aided my research—"

Then he gestured, shrugged, and fell silent.

The students were deeply impressed by a man who had conversed with such legends of their age. When he ceased to speak, they felt obliged to make their own knowledge known and they spoke in turn, as the stranger attended, smiling faintly and inclining his head at intervals. It could not be ascertained if they impressed him in their turn.

They knew of Huygens and Newton, of pendulums and gravity; far, far away, Benjamin Franklin flew a kite and discerned things positive and negative, but of him they had not yet heard. They were familiar with Hippocrates and Harvey and knew that the blood circulated, yet believed it should be let from the veins to balance the bodily humours. They were aware of Hobbes and primal psychology, but Freud was not yet born, nor his father, and the workings of the mind were a mystery. They lauded the logic of Descartes—at which the stranger was heard to murmur, *Cogito, ergo sum*," with a most diffident smile.

Had they sparked this strange man's interest; could they draw him out?

"And you, sir," said Leonidas. "In your travels and tuition, which thinker do you most admire?"

He replied instantly.

"Anachrona."

The scholars blinked as one at this unexpected suggestion and looked to see if he was mocking them.

"But surely he is discredited," Percival protested.

"A mere alchemist," muttered Clement.

"False science and medieval wizardry," Leonidas objected.

"You have not read him then?" asked the stranger.

"His theories are bizarre and, in any event, his books are banned by the Church and burned," Percival stated.

"As was he, the heretic . . ."

"At the stake . . ."

"In crueler times," added the enlightened Clement.

"Yes, that is so," agreed the stranger sadly. "I recall . . ." His voice trailed off. They looked at him in a combination of suspicion and alarm, for his eyes had begun to flicker as if a reel unfolded behind them, bands of light and shadow rolling vertically. For some minutes he was lost in thought, as blind as Sampson in Gaza, absorbed within his own skull. Gradually the reeling slowed and ceased and he regarded them once more.

"You were about to say, sir? You recall—?" Percival spoke.

"Yes . . . what I recall . . . from studying his work, to be sure," he quickly amended.

"Naturally," said Leonidas.

"Does some of his cant still survive, then? I believed it destroyed, and he with it," Clement put forth.

"Still? No, no. There is none. It was long ago that I looked into the finds of Anachrona, and learned not enough . . ."

The students waited to be told more, beguiled by such arcane and abstruse studies, although knowing them as chimera.

But the stranger said no more.

They lingered over their lunch, but there was little further discussion and when it came time to ride on the stranger was not inclined to join them, nor did they request it. They resented the likelihood that he had taunted their learning and scorned their pretensions. To put forth the name of an alchemist when dealing with scholars was an outrage; to then fall silent and offer no attempt to justify his selection was a scandal. They felt he had mocked them and it left them disturbed and subdued. Far quieter than was their wont, they pressed on through the fading day and, at dusk, came to the gates of Vienna. They took rooms at an inn and arranged to view The Contented Man in the early morning.

They talked little before they retired and spoke not at all of the stranger.

Steinhem's mechanical man, although not as amazing as they had hoped, was cleverly constructed and well worth the visit. They were the only audience at this unfashionable hour and the attendant who ushered them in moved like an automaton himself, groggy with slumber. The Contented Man was seated in a large chair of intricately carved wood, which made them wonder if it was not self-contained but had its works housed in the solid frame on which it rested.

Inanimate upon their arrival, it was nevertheless quite lifelike. The face and hands were of soft clay, skilfully contrived. The fingers were jointed, the eyelids and jaw hinged. The machine wore a dressing robe of velvet, a knitted nightcap with a tassel, and Turkish slippers that curled up. In one hand it held a porcelain pipe.

The students strolled about, observing this creation from all angles, their hands clasped behind their backs and their faces thoughtful, much like surgeons diagnosing the plague or skeptics wary of hypochondria. Then they positioned themselves before it again and signalled to the attendant who went behind and made adjustments. Chains and linkages could be heard to run within.

The automaton then took on vivacity.

Its eyes slowly opened and shut and its head turned from side to side. The movements were smooth and nearly silent. It did this for a time, like a living thing limbering up. Then one hand lifted the pipe to its lips. There was a ticking, well oiled and muted. Its lips pulled on the pipestem and a wisp of smoke drifted from the bowl. It was all quite marvellous.

The automaton lowered the pipe again and its jaw levered open. A whirr of sound came as templates and disks engaged and taut strings were plucked. It spoke in a flat, hissing voice.

"Such is contentment," said the automaton.

Then it became lifeless again. The attendant worked the key and recoiled the springs. The scholars stayed for a second performance, but it was the same as the first. They had hoped the automaton would be more versatile and do more, perhaps even ride and walk. But they were mildly satisfied.

*

It was still early in the day. They took lunch and then, having no taste for the fleshpots of Vienna, or at least not admitting to such, they headed back as they had come. The day was not as pleasant as the one before. The sky was heavily overcast and there was a chill wind from the north. It grew progressively colder and darker and a storm threatened.

Drawing their cloaks about them, they speculated on what future marvels of clockwork might in time be fashioned and how Steinhem's work might be improved, perhaps aided by the power of steam. As it got still colder and heavy drops of rain began to fall, they regretted not having stayed in the city. But they were loath to turn back and pressed on, thinking to find shelter and lodging in the wayside inn where they had lunched the previous day—in the company of a man who neither ate nor drank and may well have mocked them.

And then they came upon that man.

They noticed his horse first, saddled and bridled and grazing unattended some distance from the road. Then they saw the black-cloaked stranger reclining on the ground, braced on one side. They walked their mounts up. He seemed benumbed and only half conscious as he sprawled in the gathering gloom, unsheltered from the dark deluge descending. They halted and dismounted. He gazed up at them. His eyes were opaque but a glint of interest could be seen, like a single spark still burning in a blackened ember.

"Are you not well, sir?" Clement solicitously inquired.

"Has your horse thrown you?" Leonidas asked.

"You are drenched and must be frozen," said Percival. He offered his brandy flask, but the fallen stranger refused it with a feeble gesture.

"I have told you there is a fault in me," he said. His voice was weak. "My energy drains with dispatch and I must wait until I may . . ."

All three students were about to suggest finding shelter, but he waved an impatient hand.

"But tell me, pray— You have seen Steinhem's automaton?" he rasped with an urgency that seemed strange under the circumstances when such a trifle should be irrelevant.

"Indeed, we have—" Clement assured him.

"It was rather intriguing." Leonidas shrugged, for they did not choose to seem fascinated by the invention which, after all, was a mere curiosity.

"Tell me of it," the stranger implored.

With each of them supplying a few descriptive phrases and moderating dismissal, they jointly explained what had been less than fabulous. With every word, the face of the fallen stranger grew sadder and more disillusioned.

"It is but clockwork, then?" he sighed.

"Why, what else?" Percival countered.

"Ahhh, I had thought . . . hoped . . . perhaps elektron," said the stranger, and looked sharply at them.

The scholars, not unversed in Greek, were perplexed.

"Amber?" translated Leonidas. "Why, no. It was clay and metal and . . ."

"No, no. Not that," the stranger interrupted.

"But surely the word means amber—?" Leonidas, sure of his languages, insisted.

The stranger nodded. "That is the Greek word, yes. It was used differently by Anachrona . . . an adjunctive meaning, not yet coined in our tongue. I had aspired that Steinhem . . . but you are sure? If only— Amber yields a certain pulse, a flux; it has an attraction when rubbed, you see. The ancient Greeks . . . it was known to them, but never tapped. Refined by Anachrona, it . . . but Steinhem's automaton is clockwork, you say. It was foolish to hope that he had discovered the source . . ."

"Ahhh, yes, your reading of the alchemist—"

"He was far more!" the stranger said.

"You delude yourself, my good man," Percival said, still smarting a bit from the mockery he perceived.

"Whatever bizarre ideas you have acquired from looking into forbidden books—" Clement put in.

"More than his books," said the stranger. It was not exactly anger in his expression as he stared up at them, it was more akin to aggravation tinged by disappointment. Schoolmasters had looked at them in this way when they gave the wrong reply. Then he truly astounded them.

"I was his . . . his student . . ."

"But, sir . . . he has been dead for . . ."

"Yes, and died cursing the benighted fools who killed him!" the stranger cried. His dull eyes began to reel again, but this time he continued to speak. He was rambling with a fever, they thought, yet his words were clear.

"His carriage was erect, his voice strong, even to the end. He bowed not and knew no forgiveness. With the flesh smoldering on his bones, he defied them. But what is flesh, eh? The body is supported by a skeleton, the brain is held by a skull . . . where are the bones of the soul?"

The students looked at the stranger and they looked at one another. What crazed rambling was this? He spoke with such bitterness he seemed to be salivating, yet his lips were dry.

"The pyre was fired by his own books, you know; his collected wisdom flaming at his feet! I believe he regretted that loss more than his life. It remains . . . vivid to me . . ."

"You have had a vision, sir," Clement suggested.

"It was revealed in a dream?" Percival asked.

"A revelation," muttered Leonidas, and the scholars were not at ease with such things.

The stranger's eyes ignored them, reeling and inverting, but he spoke again.

"The smoke rose in black plumes and the pungency of charred flesh was heavy. He looked at me, as I stood amidst the howling crowd. He saw me clearly, but showed no reproach—for it was he who had instilled in me humility and composure. Three times I made to walk away, to deny him thrice—as did that other disciple so long before—for, yes, I was the disciple of Anachrona who died for his beliefs."

His upturned face was contorted, grimacing. The students' lips moved as one, silently calculating impossible years; this stranger seemed of middle age, no more. Yet they hung upon his words as if mesmerized.

"His last words were, 'Fools, fools . . . why am I born before my time?' and with that his noble head dropped and he died. Somehow his death freed me of the inhibitions with which his living eyes had pinioned me. With the master gone, only his writings remained. I sought to salvage what I could of the smoldering, blackened pages. The crowd believed me in a frenzy or a fever and tried to draw me back from the flames. They could not. In fear and superstition they fell away, for they could not control me nor the incandescent pyre hinder me. But it was too late. The pages crumbled to ash in my hands and the knowledge was lost."

He grew calmer now, and quieter, and, the vision unfolded, his eyes no longer flickered and reeled.

"It was long ago," he sighed. "Time has brought dissolution and claimed its due."

The youths waited to make sure he had ended.

Percival managed to say it first.

"But to have been attendant at his execution, you must be—?"

"Yes, I have been long," said the stranger. "Lived long, if you choose; Descartes may have had it so."

He lay back seemingly resigned.

But at that very instant the clouds sundered and a fan of sunlight fell upon the earth. The wet, white ground flowers glistened and the grass gleamed. The light advanced towards them and the stranger turned to face it. It was slow in reaching his face and he spoke once again.

"Well, there is little point in seeing a clockwork toy, it seems. I thank you, gentlemen, for saving me the remainder of a fruitless journey." It was a dismissal. They stepped back in obfuscation. The stranger waited for the light with those strange eyes that drank from the sun. Baffled and bewildered, the scholars thought him a liar, or a madman. For they were as learned as any in this year 17—.

The Foreign Bride

IT WAS A STRANGE AND DESOLATE PLACE to which he brought his
bride, a place riddled with suspicion and superstition whence he
alone had ever travelled far. He was lord of the manor, such as it was,
a massive, grim house of stone looming over the fields in which his
tenant farmers eked out a meagre existence. His name was Xavier.
He was well enough liked, not familiar, certainly, but just in his
dealings and more generous than he needed to be; a better man,
they said, than his father before him. He never begrudged a cadger
of tobacco when he rode by and was accepted as one of them, of
the land, although of a standing so elevated it was like a different
dimension to the peasants.

Occasionally, he went abroad.

It might as well have been to Xanadu to the local minds; they
thought him bold and daring to take such adventures on himself,
leaving the comforts of his home—comforts by comparison to
their own rude hovels, to be sure—to venture to the beyond.

In the big house, he lived all but alone, without servants but
for the local woman who saw to his needs. Marisa stayed at the
great house, and with her child. She, too, although of local stock,
was thought different. She was raven dark and of a fiery nature
in contrast with the dour, brooding, solemn ways of local wives.
Too, her child had been born out of wedlock, the father unknown.
For that, Marisa would have been scorned and castigated by the
scandalised and moral townsfolk, but the lord had taken her on
as help—perhaps out of charity, perhaps simply to prove himself
above their mean-minded ways—or perhaps for other reasons,
hinted at, seldom spoken.

Marisa had been with child, not yet delivered, when first she went
to live at the manor. Months were calculated. The child was born
and christened Ivan, a proud name not often used by the peasant
stock from which she had sprung. Xavier looked fondly upon the
child; hushed rumours were spread, but cautiously; he was lord of
the manor, different from them, with a code alien to their senses.

The paternal possibilities were more cause for a knowing wink and a leer than had some farmer's son been deemed responsible. A number of years passed, each like the last. Marisa and the child stayed on. Had they been of a different class, perhaps the lord might have made her his wife, but naturally that could never be. Such a union would have scandalised the serfs far more than illegitimacy. They were nevertheless surprised when, from one of his journeys abroad, he brought back with him a bride.

None more surprised than Marisa.

Catherine contrasted with Marisa, fair and voluptuous, no more attractive or intelligent, but better born, you see, in a time and place when such things signified. The bride from afar was placid and docile and kind tempered. She had won Xavier with her good humour and nature as much as her physical charms, as if, unknowingly, he sought a bride the opposite of his housekeeper. Then, too, in the courts of foreign lands, his outlook may have altered; hers was unchanged; he spoke her language well enough, she little of his and less of the coarse dialect of his tenants and peasants.

Cold could not describe the chill with which Marisa greeted the new mistress, nor fire the fever in her eyes. Catherine was not oblivious to this mood, but indifferent. She was out of place; it was natural for Marisa to resent another woman to serve; perhaps in this strange land all servants were surly.

She noticed that Marisa looked with resentment on Xavier, as well—and thought her husband kind for tolerating such an attitude from a common housekeeper, and one with a bastard child besides.

She was not unhappy, though ill at ease, in this place of dark hardwood forests and rocky domes, seemingly bleached of colour and devoid of the gay music and discourse of learned men. Yet she loved Xavier dearly and would be with him wherever, true to her wedding vows.

Her life was uneventful; it suited her well enough. She was tolerant of boredom. Xavier had few books—she had read them all—she took long, solitary walks through the harsh hills and along the swift-flowing stream. To reach the stream directly, she would have needed to cross through the graveyard, but this she would not do. Catherine thought it wrong to tread on graves. Skirting that morbid burial ground, she could be seen from town, and often was. Once she was seen by Marisa, as she stepped from the village shop laden with spiced sausage and crusty loaves. Her dark eyes narrowed.

Was it then the idea took root?

"Is she banished from hallowed ground, then?" Marisa put forth to all around her. "Dare she not step on sanctified soil, yet is compelled to pass close to a place of the dead?" The sowing had begun; Marisa was to plant ideas just as the dead had gone into the ground.

One day the foreign bride came innocently upon her husband and the servant in heated converse. She had not meant to eavesdrop and her knowledge of the language was, in any event, rudimentary, so that she caught only snatches of speech while remarking the bitter tone.

"Why, Master—why have you done this—betrayal—what of me and of our—?"

Xavier spoke sternly.

"The boy! The boy!" she persevered. "Have we offended, my lord? What of Ivan? What will become—?"

Again Xavier interrupted, more harshly, yet not unkindly, as if simply stifling words he did not wish to hear, without malice but firmly, to she who spoke so beseechingly.

How very strange, thought Catherine, *that a domestic should dare address her master so impassionedly! Shall I ever understand such foreign fashions?* But of it she thought little; it could have nothing to do with her. She treated Marisa civilly, but often remarked the smoldering hatred in those dark and fathomless eyes and was given to wonder why?

She wondered why her mare bolted one day, too. It was normally a gentle brute and Catherine rode well. But on this occasion as she rode beside her husband the animal was frisky; as they broke into a trot and she posted in the saddle, the mare abruptly snorted and reared and thundered off. Taken unawares, Catherine might well have been thrown and injured herself grievously. But she tightened her thighs and remained in the saddle without undue difficulty, not troubled, perhaps even exhilarated by the sudden burst of energy and speed in the clockwork routine of her days. Xavier, white-faced with panic, kicked on in pursuit, but Catherine had brought the

mare under control herself and was sitting undisturbed when he
galloped up. The animal had calmed; a burr was found beneath the
saddle cloth, not an unlikely event in this dusty and thorny land.
Freed of that spur, her mount was placid once more.

But for a time it had been foaming at the muzzle and wild in the
rolled-back eyes—and animals are well known to have senses and
instincts unknown to man and many panic when evil is astride, as
Marisa was to point out to those who had seen.

In recent years, Marisa had stayed much in the manor, coming to
the village only for the shopping and then insolent and haughty,
treating the shopkeepers and those she passed in the streets with
unconcealed disdain. Living in the great house, she had come to see
herself as above these folk she had known all her days, although but
a servant with bastard child.

But now Xavier had brought back his foreign bride, Marisa came
more frequently to town, and with a changed manner. Often she
stopped at the crude inn for a rough goblet and gossip. The towns-
people had mildly resented her previous airs, but in their humble
way had understood. She was of them still, and more so now, and
they forgave her foolishness and felt a certain sympathy, perhaps
pity, for Marisa with the coming of Catherine. For her part, she
seemed to regret her former aloofness and wished to ingratiate
herself. They saw, too, that she who had never before manifested
the trappings of worship, now constantly wore a large crucifix at
her throat. Often she would finger it, cautiously, as if she feared it
hot to the touch. Subdued and somehow wary, even furtive, she
would toy with the talisman as she spoke.

Often she spoke of the foreign bride.

"She is not of us," Marisa would complain, at her place by the
hewn counter, rather than the benches where the local wives
would take a draught. "She has brought her alien ways and who
can say where it may lead?"

They would regard her and maybe nod. Yet the bride had done
them no wrong and even had the grace to smile as she rode through
with the master and they had no cause to hate her—although they
knew that Marisa was right, and understood the emotions of envy
and jealousy and loss.

Marisa was dogged; she sowed her crop daily now.

"Pale as a wraith, she is, her lips are red, her cheeks glow with a health that is not holy. Ah, she has captivated the master, it is plain. It is as if she is a witch, a sorceress, an enchantress, bewitching the poor master . . ."

Although she spoke from spite, those people were not far evolved from the primal terrors; her words made them nervous.

"Even her name is unnatural! Catherine!" she would spit it out as something vile. "He calls her Cathy. Who has ever heard such a name? It is not Christian—it is like blasphemy on one's lips!"

And, indeed, they did have difficulty in winding their tongues around such strange syllables.

"Why has she never entered the church, then?" put forth Marisa on a day of turbulent wind and ponderous clouds churning through a pewter sky. Catherine was not of their religion, to be sure, but the fact was easily passed over; it had no significance to those who knew only one binding theology. Marisa had drunk more than usual this day. She leaned at her confidants like an anarchist conspiring in an attic. "Can it be she does not dare? Eh? Might the icons not reverse themselves in her presence, shunning her, turning to face the walls? Would she then be revealed for what she is, eh? A witch cannot worship; a demon knows no devotion; the sacrament would spring from her lips!"

How uneasy such talk made them!

Yet it was but the raving of a scorned woman, they had no cause to hate the foreign bride.

Then the deaths began.

Young Otto vanished first.

A plump and friendly child, he had been playing beside the swift stream not far from his home. His mother looked out from the unglazed window from time to time, without concern; no wolf had been seen for a decade. Summoned home for the crust and cheese of his lunch, he did not come. His mother went to fetch him and he was no longer there. Close-knit, the villagers turned out in the search. The pool in which the stream drained was dragged by nets, the nearby woods explored, to no avail. The wailings of his mother climbed to the clouds; even at the distant great house they could be heard. In time the search was abandoned and it was assumed Otto had been taken by a beast, although there were no signs. Such things were no longer common, but not unknown. His parents, mere peasants, could offer no reward; with grim stoicism it was accepted and life went on.

Otto was not yet found when Horace, son of the baker, disappeared.

The baker was a man of relative means; the search went farther and they looked longer than they had for Otto, alarmed greatly now and bearing crude arms—spades and scythes and lighted brands. They found the child impaled on the angled limb of a gnarled and withered tree, his limp body hanging like bunting on a maypole. His throat had been opened; corruption had already begun. The wife of the baker cried out her grief and fell into the arms of the mother of Otto, who was taken by a seizure, fearing her own son had been thus fated. There was no doctor to examine the body. As lord of the manor, Xavier acted as coroner, but unqualified and untrained. He found the task distasteful. Had it been the work of a wild animal? The blood had been let, the flesh untouched, the body hoisted. It was strange and disquieting. Xavier could bring no verdict.

The little body was taken to the graveyard.

In going to bury Horace, Otto was found.

In the graveyard, where they had not thought to look in seeking the living, with Horace in his box but not yet in his grave, they found the body of Otto, sunk down as though pressed into the soft loam, half buried in the humus, his body deflated and drained of substance. His throat was opened, his juices sapped. He lay as an empty skin, seeping on his own down into the earth of the graveyard. Around the small corpse the grass had sprung up verdantly, nourished by his blood.

Fear was as tangible as if it walked among them like a stranger new come to the town. Life had ever been hard and grim here, but its reality had been known in all factors. Now eyes rolled and talk was hushed.

"What has brought this curse upon us?"

And, to this, Marisa replied, "What has changed?"

"Never have we been so cursed before, through all time," she put to them. "What has changed? She has come!" And she cast a look towards the great house and shuddered through all her form.

They saw the truth of it; all else was the same, but the foreign bride was among them. Yet none dared broach this to the lord, for believing in mystery and the unknown, they still knew it had no place in the science of their age. What words could be spoken? they sighed; there was nothing to be done; they must only keep their children safe at home and wait, unable to act—unless the blood-letter should be found in the act!

And at those words, whether from her own lips or another's, Marisa was seen to tremble and sway and moan, her eyes closed and her fists clenched, so that for a time they believed her in the throes of a fit.

The children were under the watchful eyes of parents; no further victim offered itself. Marisa stayed more at home. She brooded long, and pondered deeply—and looked at Catherine often. She kept close watch on Ivan, too, for like the others, he was not allowed to roam—and like his mother, he now wore a cross at his throat. Marisa had stressed the urgency of that precaution to the townsfolk. But crosses of precious metal were not readily obtain-able and the priest was loath to bless those made by hand, and of mere wood, when they fetched them to the church—that church that the foreign bride had never entered and where, Marisa vowed, the holy water would boil in the font and blister her pale flesh in the steam.

Marisa seemed under a great burden in these days and turned violently from side to side, as if facing a decision to the left, another to the right—as if those decisions were dogs that fought over her like a bone.

Once she saw Catherine talking to the boy, in the high vaulted chamber of the entrance. She was quite casual and friendly, her blonde head to one side as she sought to understand his words, a slight smile on her so red lips. Ivan chattered away vivaciously, at ease with the foreign lady. But how should she know she was his ruin? Catherine would make a fine mother, in time, Marisa saw, and her face clouded in anticipation of the wrong she would do unknowingly to Ivan, should she replace the firstborn with a son—a sturdy, fair-haired, legitimate heir.

With this, Marisa stopped her constant turning from side to side and looked straight ahead.

Catherine was quite fond of the servant's lively child and looked forward to having her own sons and daughters, hers and Xavier's. If it was to be so. She liked all children. She had been spared the gruesome details of the recent misfortune and knew only that two peasant youths had died in novel circumstances. It troubled her but only with passing sympathy, as a horse mistreated or a dog unjustly whipped. She was not without charity, but they were not of her experience.

It was unlikely it should be her who found the third child dead, and that she should know him.

That thought actually came to her mind, the unlikeliness of it, before the horror stepped in.

Xavier was away, seeing to the details of the further reaches of his holdings and Catherine, on her customary walk, following her habitual routine and route, stepped from the path to gather flowers as she was often seen to do—and came upon the body in the thorn and the ground flower.

That was when she thought it unlikely.

Then she saw it was Ivan and thought, too, that he was only sleeping, for he looked peaceful enough. He lay on his back, his face tilted down, his chin on his breast. He no longer wore the metal cross, but she failed to notice that, for to Catherine it was no more than a bauble, an ornament, of no value beyond the intrinsic. She spoke softly to him. She stepped around him in growing alarm. His eyes were open; his chest did not rise and fall; was he in a trance?

She sank to her knees beside him. On his face was a look more of surprise than of terror, nor had his body been savaged as the others had—but Catherine knew nothing of that, shielded from the grim details and, in truth, her discovery was brutal enough. She leaned over him like a parent to a cradle, to see if life still ran in his veins. But nothing ran in those empty vessels. As she gently raised his shoulders, his head lolled back and she gasped at the red wound below his jaw. Else, he seemed not damaged; he seemed to have been killed tenderly, strange as such a thought should be. Shuddering, she leaned closer.

Could she yet breathe life into the still form?

Could she even bring herself to lower her lips to his, with that red wound open below?

Her face was grotesque with shock and horror, inhuman in her emotions, looking almost bestial—to eyes that looked for a beast.

Marisa had entered the church before she gathered the villagers and announced her child had disappeared. Perhaps she had gone to offer a prayer for him—or an act of contrition. Now, leading a grim-faced group, she brought them up the pathway and upon the foreign bride as Catherine hovered over the dead child, with her face so contorted.

Marisa screamed and her arm jerked out, forefinger pointing like a dagger.

"Oh, see! See! She has murdered Ivan!"

Behind her, they stared, jaws levered wide open, as if to gnaw at their own hearts, eyes drawn like iron filings to the magnetism of such evil. The baker was there, and his living son; the parents of Otto, and his cousins. Catherine looked up and her face was fraught with emotion, that face so foreign to them. Marisa was shrieking, the others silent. Catherine attempted to speak, but her vocal cords were too taut and she hissed wordlessly, and in an unknown tongue. She rose as they closed upon her, tall and fair and different. By the time that she screamed, it was with her final breath.

Xavier was met and told upon his return at dusk, mounted and they white faced in shadow. Had he been less wild, he would have seen the hesitation in their words, the wariness in their eyes, the furtiveness in their manner. But he was racked by sorrow and disbelief; his peasants had no cause to hate his bride; but his wife and the child had been murdered by the unknown fiend, he had no doubts. Stricken by his grief, he took some consolation in the knowledge that Catherine had been good, and brave, and had died as she went to the rescue of a child—a child she never knew as his own.

Ivan had been placed within the church; the body of Catherine had been left in the forecourt. Xavier did not think to question this, and carried her body within himself. She had not been of the religion. Nor did he notice that the icons were all turned to the wall this day; he was in no mind to notice, nor was he devout.

The killings stopped then, as abruptly as they had begun, and life went on. The children were no longer kept at home, the danger was seen as past. But life was not the same, and most of all for the lord of the manor. Xavier found he could not bear to dwell within those grey walls where his bride had brought colour and the child, unacknowledged, had still given him pleasure.

He arranged for a factor to manage his estates and, with Marisa, moved far away and abroad. In the days before departure, Marisa had become aloof and haughty once again. The townsfolk shrugged it off; Xavier had never known.

He never overcame his sorrow and it profoundly affected his judgement. Marisa, with grief of her own, consoled him. In a faraway land the customs were different, nor was Marisa known as his servant, for she behaved as his wife. It seemed quite ordinary that he should wed her, at her suggestion, for his life was in ruin and what did such a gesture matter?

But to Marisa, who was to give him many sons, it mattered greatly. The wedding absolved her of her guilt and soothed her remorse. It made things right, really, that ceremony—it made things as they should be. For her child had died a bastard but, with her marriage, he was legitimised and it was not hard to know it had been for his good and that Ivan would rest happier now in heaven as a child of lawful wedlock . . .

The Dead End

I

THE WAITER SPLASHED A LITTLE WINE in my glass and waited for me to taste it. Across the table, Susan was studiously avoiding my gaze. She was looking out of the leaded window at the blur of motorcars moving past in Marsham Street. The waiter stood, blank faced and discreet. This was a place where we had often been very happy, but we weren't happy now. I nodded and the waiter filled our glasses and moved away.

"Susan . . ."

She finally looked at me.

"I'm sorry."

Susan shrugged. She was very hurt and I was very sad. It is a sad thing to tell the woman you love that you aren't going to marry her, and I suppose I could have chosen a better place than this restaurant, but somehow I felt I needed a familiar place, where we could be alone but have other people surrounding us. A cowardly attitude, of course, and yet it had taken great courage to break the engagement. I wanted nothing more in the world than to marry Susan, and now it was impossible.

"I've been expecting it, Arthur. It wasn't really such a shock."

"Susan."

"I could tell, you know. It's been different. You've been different. Ever since you returned from South America, I've been expecting this. I expect you met someone else there . . ."

"No. Please believe that."

She gave a bitter little smile across the table.

"I love you, Susan. As much as ever. More. Now that I realize how much I'm losing, I want you more than ever."

"Arthur, you haven't even made love to me since you came back. How can I believe you?"

"I can't, Susan."

"Then tell me why."

121

I shook my head.

"You owe me that much, Arthur. At least that much. Some explanation. Whatever it is, I'll understand. If there's someone else, if you're tired of me, if you simply want your freedom, I'll understand. There'll be no bitterness. But you can't simply break it off like this, without even telling me why. It's inhuman."

And perhaps she would have understood. Susan, of all people, might have understood. But it was too horrible and I couldn't bring myself to tell her. I couldn't tell anyone. I didn't even tell the doctor who examined me what he was supposed to be looking for. It was a terrible secret, and I had to bear it alone.

"Susan, I can't tell you."

She looked towards the window again. The leaded panes distorted the outside world. I thought she was going to cry, then, but she didn't. Her lip trembled. Waiters moved efficiently past our table, and the other customers wined and dined and pursued their individual lives, while I sat there alone. Susan was there, but I was alone.

"If only you hadn't gone," she whispered.

Yes. If only I hadn't gone. If only a man could relive the past and undo what had been done. But I had gone, and I looked down at the wine shimmering in my glass and recalled how it had happened; recalled those monstrous things which had been, and could never be undone . . .

It is hard to believe that it was only two months since the director of the museum called me to his office on a grim London afternoon. I was excited and expectant about his summons, as I followed the echo of hollow footsteps through those hoary corridors to his office. I was well aware that Jeffries, the head of the anthropology department, planned to retire at the end of the year, and had hopes of being promoted to his position. I can recall the conflicting thoughts that bounded in my head, wondering if I wasn't too young to expect such promotion, counterbalancing this by mentally listing the well-received work I'd done since I'd been there, remembering that many of my views were opposed to the director's, but knowing him as a man who respected genuine disagreement and sought out subalterns who did not hesitate to put forth their own theories, and also, perhaps mainly, thinking how delighted Susan would be if I could tell her I'd been promoted and that we could change and hasten our plans in accordance with my new position. Susan wanted children, but was prepared to wait a few years until we could afford them; she wanted a house in the country but had agreed to move into my flat in town. Perhaps, now, we would not have to wait for these things. Visions of happiness and success danced in my head that afternoon, as they do when a man is young and hopeful.

I was only thirty-one years old that day, although I'm old now.

It was two months ago.

Doctor Smyth looked the part of a museum director, the template from which all men in that position should have been cut. He wore an ancient and immaculate double-breasted suit crossed with a gold watch chain, and reposed like a boulder behind a massive desk in his leather-bound den.

"Ah, Brookes. Sit down."

I sat and waited. It was difficult to feel so confident now that I faced him. He filled a blackened pipe carefully, pressing the tobacco down with his wide thumb.

"Those reports I sent on to you the other day," he said. He paused to touch a match to the tobacco, and I watched it uncurl in the flame. I was disappointed. I'd hoped this meeting would be far more momentous than that. A haze of smoke began to drift between us.

"You've studied them?"

"Yes, sir."

"What's your opinion?"

I was mildly surprised. I'd been surprised when he sent them to me. They were the sort of thing one usually takes with a grain of salt, various unsubstantiated reports from Tierra del Fuego concerning a strange creature that had been seen in the mountains; a creature that appeared vaguely manlike, but behaved like an animal. It was reported to be responsible for destroying a few sheep and frightening a few people. The museum receives a good many reports of this nature, usually either a hoax or desire for publicity or over-stimulated imagination. True, there had been several different accounts of this creature with no apparent connexion between the men who claimed to have seen it, but I thought myself too much a man of science to place much faith in rumours of this sort.

And yet Smyth seemed interested.

"Well, I don't really know. Some sort of primate, perhaps. If there is anything."

"Too large for a monkey."

"If it weren't South America, I'd think possibly an ape . . ."

"But it is South America, isn't it?"

I said nothing.

"You mentioned a primate. It isn't a monkey, and it can't very well be an ape. What does that leave?"

"Man, of course."

"Yes," he said.

He regarded me through the smoke.

I said: "Of course, the Indians in that area are very primitive. Possibly the most primitive men alive today. Darwin was certainly fascinated by them, running naked in that climate and eating raw mussels. This creature might well be a man, some hermit perhaps, or an aboriginal who has managed to avoid contact with civilization."

"And more power to him," Smyth said.

"I should think that's the answer."

"I doubt it, somehow."

"I don't see . . ."

"Several aboriginals have been known to have seen this creature. Surely they would have recognized him as a man like themselves."

"Perhaps. But there's certainly no proof to suggest it is something less than a man. I'd rate the plausibility of anything else well behind the Abominable Snowman, and you know my views on that."

Smyth smiled rather tolerantly. I had done some research on the Yeti which had been well received, but my conclusions had been strictly negative. Smyth was inclined to admit the possibility of such creatures, however.

"I thought much the same way, at first," he said.

"At first?"

"I've given it considerable thought. I was particularly impressed by the story that half-breed fellow told in Ushuaia. What was his name?"

"Gregorio?"

"Yes, that's the one. Hardly the sort of thing a man would imagine without some basis in truth, I should think. In fact, I sent a wire to a fellow I know there. Man named Gardiner. Used to be a manager with Explotadora, when the company was really big. Retired now, but he figured he was too old to start a new life in England and he stayed there. Splendid fellow, knows everyone. Helped us considerably the last time we had a field team out there. Anyway, he replied, and according to him this Gregorio is a fairly reliable sort. That got me wondering if there mightn't be more to this than I'd supposed. And then, there's another angle . . ."

His pipe had faltered. He spent several moments and several matches lighting it again.

"What do you know of Hubert Hodson?" he asked.

"Hodson? Is he still alive?"

"Hodson is several years younger than I," Smyth said, amused. "Yes, he's still very much alive."

"He was before my time. Not highly regarded these days, a bit outdated. I've read him, of course. A renegade with curious theories and an adamant attitude, but a first-class scientist. Some of his ideas caused quite a stir some twenty years ago."

Smyth nodded. He seemed pleased that I knew about Hodson.

"I'm rather vague on his work, actually. He specialized in the genetics of evolution, I believe. Not really my line."

"He specialized in many things. Spread himself too thin, perhaps. But he was a brilliant man." Smyth's eyes narrowed, he was recalling the past. "Hodson put forth many theories. Some nonsense, some perhaps not. He believed that the vocal cords were the predominant element in man's evolution, for instance—maintained that any animal, given man's power of communication, would in time have developed man's straight spine, man's thumb, even man's brain. That man's mind was no more than a by-product of assembled experience and thought unnecessary to development. A theory of enormous possibilities, of course, but Hodson, being the man he is, threw it down like a gauntlet, as a challenge to man's superior powers of reasoning. He presented it as though he preferred to cause consternation and opposition, rather than seeking acceptance.

"It was much the same with his mutation theory, when he claimed that evolution was not a gradual process, but moved in sudden forward spurts at various points in time, and that the time was different and dependent upon the place. Nothing wrong with these ideas, certainly, but his manner of presentation was such that the most harmless concepts would raise a hue and cry. I can remember him standing at the rostrum, pointing at the assembly with an accusing finger, his hair all wild, his eyes excited, shouting, 'Look at you! You think that you are the end product of evolution? I tell you, but for a freak Oligocene mutation, you would be no more than our distant cousins, the shrews. Do you think that you and I share a common ancestor? We share a common mutation, no more. And I, personally, find it regrettable.' You can imagine the reaction among the learned audience. Hodson merely smiled and said, 'Perhaps I chose my words rashly. Perhaps your relation to the shrews is not so distant after all.' Yes, I can remember that day clearly, and I must admit I was more amused than outraged."

Smyth smiled slightly around his pipe.

"The final insult to man came when he claimed all evolution had been through the female line. If I remember correctly, he stated that the male was no more than a catalyst, that man, being weaker, succumbed to these irregular mutations and in turn was merely the agent that caused the female to progress or change, was only necessary to inspire the female to evolve, so to speak. Men, even men of science, were hardly prepared to countenance that, naturally. Hodson was venomously attacked, both scientifically and emotionally, and, strangely enough, the attacks seemed to trouble him this time. He'd always delighted in the furore before, but this time he went into seclusion and finally disappeared entirely."

"You seem to know a great deal about him, sir," I said. "Considering he's rather obscure."

"I respected him."

"But how does this tie in with the reports from South America?"

"Hodson is there. That is where he went when he left the country twenty odd years ago, and he's been there ever since. That's why you've heard nothing from him for the last generation.

But God knows what he's doing there. He's published nothing, made no statements at all, and that's very unlike Hodson. He was always a man to make a statement simply for shock value, whether he really believed it or not."

"Perhaps he's retired."

"Not Hubert."

"And you believe that his presence is connected with those reports?"

"I have no idea. I just wonder. You see, no one knows exactly where he is—I don't expect anyone has tried to find out, actually—but he's located somewhere in the Chilean part of Tierra del Fuego, in the south-western section."

"And that's where the reports have come from," I said.

"Exactly. It just makes me wonder a bit."

We both pondered for a few minutes while he lighted his pipe again. Then I thought I saw a flaw.

"But if he's been there for twenty years . . . these reports have all been within the last six months. I don't see how that would tie in."

"Don't you?"

I didn't. He puffed away for a while.

"This creature which may, or may not, have been seen. It was as large as a man. Therefore, we may assume it to be full grown. Say, twenty years old, perhaps?"

"I see. You believe—I mean to say, you recognize the possibility—that Hodson may have heard something about this creature twenty years ago, and went to investigate. That he has been looking for it all this time."

"Or found it."

"Surely he wouldn't keep something of that enormity secret?"

"Hodson is a strange man. He resented the attacks that were mounted against his ideas. He might well be waiting until he has a complete documentation, beyond refutation—a life's work, all neatly tied up and proven. Perhaps he found this creature. Or creatures. We may safely assume that, if it exists, it had parents. Possibly siblings, as well. I think it more likely that Hodson would have discovered the parents and studied the offspring, or the whole tribe. Lived with them, even. That's the sort of thing he'd do."

"It seems—well, far-fetched, sir."

"Yes, it does, doesn't it? A science fiction idea. What did they used to call it? The missing link?" He chuckled. "The common ancestor is more accurate, I suppose."

"But you can't really believe that a creature like that could be alive now?"

"I admit it is most unlikely. But then, so was the coelacanth, before it was discovered alive."

"But that was in the sea. God knows what may exist there. We may never know. But on land, if a creature like that existed, it would have been discovered before now."

"It's a wild, barren place, Tierra del Fuego. Rough terrain and a sparse population. I say only that it is possible."

"You realize that the Indians of Tierra del Fuego are prehistoric, so to speak?" I said.

"Certainly."

"And yet you feel there is a chance this creature might be something other than one of them?"

"A possibility."

"And still a man?"

Smyth gestured with his pipe.

"Let us say, of the genus homo but not of the species sapiens."

I was astounded. I couldn't believe that Smyth was serious. I said, with what I thought admirable understatement, "It seems most unlikely."

Smyth looked almost embarrassed. When he spoke, it was as though he was offering an explanation. He said, "I mentioned that I have great respect for Hodson. And a great curiosity. He's not a man to forsake his science, and he's spent the last twenty odd years doing something on that island. That in itself is interesting. Hodson was primarily a laboratory man. He had little time for field work and believed that to be the proper task for men with less imagination and intelligence—believed that lesser men should gather the data for men of his own calibre to interpret. And then, quite suddenly, he disappears into the wilds. There has to be a reason, something to which he was willing to dedicate the rest of his life. And Hodson placed the highest possible value on his life, in the sense of what he could accomplish while he lived. It may have nothing whatsoever to do with these reports. Quite likely it doesn't. But whatever he is doing is definitely of interest. Whatever he has accomplished in twenty years is bound to be fascinating, whether it is right or wrong. I've often considered sending someone to locate him, but always put it off. Now seems the perfect time to kill two birds with one stone. Or, perhaps, the same bird."

I nodded, but I was in no way convinced.

"I expect you think I'm grasping at a straw," Smyth said, noticing my hesitation. "I knew Hodson. Not well, not as a friend, but I knew him. You'd have to know him to understand how I feel. I was one of the last people he spoke with before he vanished, and I've always remembered that conversation. He was exuberant and excited and confident. He told me that he was working on something new, something very big. He even admitted that the results might disprove some of his earlier theories, which was very impressive, coming from a man who had never in his life admitted he might be mistaken. And he said that this time no one would be able to scoff or doubt or disagree, because when he was finished he would have more than a theory—he would have concrete proof."

Smyth tapped the ash from his pipe. He seemed tired now.

"You've never been to South America, have you?" he asked.

"No."

"Would you like to?"

"Very much."

"I think I'd like to send you there."

Smyth opened a drawer and began thumbing through some papers. There were handwritten notes in the margins. He said, "The place to start will be Ushuaia. I'll wire Gardiner to expect you, he should be helpful. You can spend a few days there checking on the reports in person. Then try to locate Hodson. Gardiner might know where he is. He'll certainly know where he buys his supplies, so you should be able to work back from there."

"Are you sure he gets his supplies from Ushuaia?"

"He must. There's nowhere else anywhere near there."

Everything seemed to be moving very fast suddenly.

"Now, I'd better arrange a hotel for you," Smyth said, turning a sheet to read the margin. "The Albatross or the Gran Parque? Neither has hot water nor central heating, but a dedicated scientist shouldn't mind that."

I tossed a mental coin.

"The Albatross."

"How soon will you be able to leave?"

"Whenever you like."

"Tomorrow?"

I believe I blinked.

"If that's convenient," Smyth said.

"Yes, all right," I said, wondering what Susan would think about it with no time to get used to the idea.

"Fine," Smyth said, and the interview was over. I was amazed and sceptical, but if Smyth had respect for Hodson, I had respect for Smyth. And the prospect of field work is always exciting.

I rose to leave.

"Oh, Brookes?"

"Sir?"

I was at the door and turned. He was filling another pipe.

"You know that Jeffries is retiring at the end of the year?"

"I'd heard as much, sir."

"Yes. That's all," he said.

Then I was very excited.

Tierra del Fuego.

Delighted as I was at Smyth's open hint of promotion, I think I was even more excited about the opportunity to visit that fascinating archipelago. I suppose that every anthropologist since Darwin has been fascinated by the opportunities existing there to study primitive man. Separated from the South American mainland by the Straits of Magellan and divided between Argentina and Chile, Tierra del Fuego consists of the large island, five smaller islands, numerous islets, peninsulas, channels, bays and sounds crouched beneath the low clouds and fierce winds where the Andes stagger down, stumbling across the straits and limping out to fall, at Cape Horn, into the mists at the end of the world. There was little there to attract civilization, 27,500 square miles of rugged wilds with sheep, lumbering and fishing, a recent discovery of poor oil in the plains to the north-east—and the fascination of Stone Age man.

They were there when Magellan discovered the land in 1520, and named it the land of fire because of the signal fires that smouldered along the windy coast, a group of human beings that time and evolution had overlooked, leading their natural and prehistoric lives. And they are still there, diminished by contact with civilization and unable to cope with the fingertips of the modern world that have managed to grope even to this forsaken place, reduced to living in wretched hovels on the outskirts of the towns. There are few left. These creatures who could face the wind and snow without clothing could not face the advance of time.

But surely not all had succumbed. And this, I felt, would prove the answer to the rumours of a wild creature, that it would be an aborigine who had refused to give up his dignity and forsake his wild freedom, and still ran savage and naked through those mountains and canyons. It was a far more feasible solution than Smyth had put forward, and no little opportunity for study in its own right. I believed that was what Hodson had been doing all these years, but that Smyth, never a sceptic, was so overpowered by the force of this man that his imagination had run wild; that he could have believed anything in relation to Hodson.

Or was Smyth, perhaps, testing me in some fashion? Could he be inviting me to draw my own conclusions as the future head of my department?

It was an intriguing thought, and I was quite willing to stand the examination. I needed no unfounded rumours or vague speculation, the opportunities of Tierra del Fuego were enough in themselves.

I had only one reservation. What was Susan going to think of this immediate and prolonged parting? I knew that she would put forth no objections, she was not the sort of woman who would interfere with a man's work, but I knew she would be disappointed and disturbed at our separation. I wasn't happy at the thought of being away from her either, of course, but this feeling was tempered by my excitement. It is always harder for the one who stays behind.

We had never been apart before. We'd met some six months before and become engaged within a fortnight—one of those rare and remarkable meetings of mind and body that seem destined to be, a perfect agreement in all things and a blissful contentment when we were together. We were old enough to know that this was what we wanted, and all we wanted, with no doubts whatsoever about our future. I knew Susan would understand the necessity for the separation, and had no qualms about telling her; I worried only that she would be saddened.

Susan was preparing dinner at her place that evening. She had a small flat in South Kensington where she practised her culinary arts several times a week, not as the way to her man's heart, which she already had, but through a splendidly old-fashioned idea of being an ideal wife. I was still in an excited mood as I walked to her place through the late afternoon, scarcely noticing the steady drizzle as a discomfort, although possessed of a feeling that all my senses were alert, that I was aware of everything in the slightest detail. The sky was darkening and the street lamps had come on, pale and haloed. The traffic was heavy but strangely silent. Pedestrians hurried home from their work, collars up and heads lowered. They all seemed very dismal and drab to me, creatures of humdrum habit who could not but envy my life and future, my woman and my work, had they known. I would have liked to stop some passing stranger and tell him of my success, show him a photograph of Susan, not through vanity as much as a feeling of gratitude. It was the first time I could remember wanting to tell someone about myself. I had few friends and most of my acquaintances were professional, and had never felt the need before. But then, I had never felt this happy anticipation. I quickened my pace, anxious to be with Susan.

I had a key to her flat and let myself in at the front door, walked up the two flights to her floor and entered. The flat was warm and comfortable, the gramophone was playing a record of baroque harp and recorder and I could hear Susan manipulating utensils in the tiny kitchen. I stood in the doorway for a moment, appreciating the way Susan had decorated the room, with great care and taste and little expense, and feeling the contentment that always filled me when I was there. I realized then just how much I was going to long for Susan while I was away.

Susan heard the door close and came into the room. She was wearing a simple black dress of which I was exceptionally fond and her hair fell to her shoulders with all the tones and shades of a forest fire. She smiled as she crossed the room and we kissed. Then she must have seen something in my expression, because her forehead arched in query.

"You look thoughtful, darling."

"I was thinking."

"Oh?"

I moved to the couch. She didn't press her question.

"Dinner in fifteen minutes," she said. "Sherry?"

"Fine."

She poured the sherry from a cut-glass decanter and handed me a glass, then sat beside me on the couch, curling her long legs under her. I sipped the drink and the record ended and rejected. The Hebrides Overture began to play.

"What about?" she asked then.

"Two things, really. I was talking with Smyth today. He made a point of mentioning that Jeffries is retiring."

"But that's wonderful, Arthur."

"Oh, it's nothing definite. I mean, he didn't tell me I was in line for the position or anything."

"But he must have implied it."

"Yes, I suppose so."

"Oh, darling, I'm so pleased." She kissed me lightly. "I know you'd hoped for it. We should celebrate."

I smiled, not too cheerfully.

"Is anything wrong?"

"No, not really."

"You hardly seem elated."

"Well, there's another thing."

"Good?"

"In a way. It's just that—well, I don't know what you'll think about it."

She looked at me over the rim of her glass. Her eyes were green and lovely. She was very beautiful.

"Tell me," she said.

"I have to go to South America."

She blinked.

"Oh, not to live or anything. Just a field trip for the museum. A wonderful opportunity, really, except it will mean being away from you for a while."

"Did you expect me to object?"

"I knew better than that."

"How long will you be gone?"

I wasn't at all sure. I said, "Two or three months, I suppose."

"I'll miss you very much, darling. When will you have to leave?"

"Tomorrow."

"So sudden? But why?"

"Well, it's an idea Smyth has. I don't agree with him, but either way it's a marvellous opportunity. And my promotion might well rest on what I do there."

Susan pondered for a moment, then smiled. It was all right. She understood, as I'd known she would, and conflicting emotions struggled for only that moment before yielding to logic rare in a woman.

"I'm happy for you, darling. Really I am."

"It won't be long."

"You're very excited about it, aren't you?"

"Yes. It's a splendid opportunity. Except for being away from you."

She dismissed that with a gesture.

"Tell me about it."

I talked for a while, telling her about Tierra del Fuego, Hubert Hodson, the recent reports and my own ideas about them. Susan listened, interested because it interested me, and getting used to the idea of our separation, balancing it with the advantages that would follow my potential promotion. Presently we had dinner with candlelight and wine, and Susan was as lively and cheerful as ever. I loved her very much. I could already feel the pain of parting, the emotional tone of our last evening together and a touch of the thrill that would come when we were together again on my return.

We took our brandy out to the little terrace that ran around the side of the building and stood hand in hand at the railing, looking out across the dark canyons of the city. The lights of the West London Air Terminal loomed garish and gaudy above the rooftops. They reminded me of my flight, making the prospect more concrete and immediate, and perhaps they did the same for Susan. She became solemn, holding my hand tightly.

"God, I'll miss you so much," she said.

"Me too."

"No longer than you have to, darling?"

"No longer."

"I'll be awfully lonely."

"So will I."

She looked at me then, feigning a frown of deep concern.

"Not lonely enough to seek solace in the arms of another woman, I trust," she said. But she said it as a joke, to dispel the tension. Susan knew I wanted no one but her, and never would. I'd never imagined a time when I would place a woman ahead of my work, but if she had asked me not to go, I would have remained with her.

Ah, why didn't she?

II

I refilled my glass.

Susan hadn't touched her wine. I recalled how happy we'd been the night before I'd left, and the contrast made our sorrow worse. If it could possibly be worse. The waiter looked towards our table to see if we wanted anything and looked quickly away. A man dining alone across the room glanced appreciatively at Susan, admiring her long legs and amber hair, then lowered his gaze as I looked at him. Susan would have no trouble finding a new man whenever she wanted, and this bitter knowledge sent a chill down my backbone, all the colder because I knew she wanted no one but me, and because I could never marry her. My hand trembled with the weight of the bottle and my heart trembled with the weight of despair.

Susan looked up through her lashes, a glance that would have been flirtatious had her eyes not been dull with grief.

"What happened in Tierra del Fuego, Arthur?" she asked, pleading for an answer, a reason which might make her sorrow less through understanding.

I shook my head.

I couldn't tell her.

But I remembered . . .

*

I flew from Buenos Aires to Ushuaia.

In the footsteps of Darwin, the modern speed seemed wrong and disappointing. Darwin had been there on HMS *Beagle* from 1826 to 1836, exploring the channel on which Ushuaia was situated. It was called, appropriately enough, the Beagle Channel. But I flew in from Buenos Aires in five hours, seated next to a middle-aged American tourist and disturbed by the thought that there could be nothing left for discovery in a town with an airport and the beginnings of a tourist trade.

The tourist wanted to talk, and nothing short of direct impoliteness would have silenced him.

"Going to Ushuaia?" he asked.

I nodded.

"Me too."

That seemed obvious enough, since that was where the aeroplane was headed.

"Name's Jones. Clyde Jones."

He had a big, healthy face clamped around a huge cigar.

"Brookes."

Jones extended a wide hand. He wore a ruby ring on his little finger and an expensive camera on a sling around his neck. His grip was very firm. I suppose he was a pleasant enough fellow.

"You a Limey? I'm a Yank."

He hesitated, as though wondering if this required another handshake.

"You a tourist? I am. Travel a lot, you know. Since my wife died I travelled all over. Been in your country. Been all over Europe. Spent two months there last summer, saw it all. Except the communist parts, of course. I wouldn't want to go there and give them any foreign exchange."

"Quite right," I said.

"Did you know this Ushuaia is one of the southernmost communities in the world? I want to see this Ushuaia. Don't know why. 'Cause it's there, I guess. Like mountain climbers, hah? Ha ha."

I looked out the window. The flat tableland and glacial lakes of the north were behind, and the terrain was beginning to rise in rugged humps and twisting rivers, glimpsed through clouds as heavy and low as the smoke from Jones's cigar. It was exciting land, but I was depressed. Jones did not seem interested. I suppose he saw nothing that was not framed in his camera's lens. He chatted away amicably, and I was seized with a feeling that I had been born too late, that nothing new remained to be discovered, and that all one could do now was study the past.

And no man has ever been more wrong.

Everything seemed much brighter after we landed.

The airport was on the edge of the town, and Jones shared a taxi with me. He was staying at the Albatross, too. The taxi was a huge American model, as modern as a missile, but somehow this didn't trouble me, now that I was in contact with the land. It was as if the motorcar were out of time and place, not that the land had changed. Jones may have felt something of this anachronism, as well, for he became quiet and almost apprehensive, perhaps sensing that he didn't belong here, that the soul of this place had not yet been sucked into the tourists' cameras. I looked from the window and became excited once more as we jolted through the streets.

Ushuaia looked like a Swiss mountain village set on a Norwegian fiord. Sharp-spined wooden chalets leaned on the steep hills and a glacier mounted the hill behind, impressive and impassive. Farther to the west the high peaks of Darwin and Larmeinto rose into the low clouds. The taxi slowed suddenly, throwing me forwards on the seat. We had braked behind a man on horseback, sitting slumped in his poncho. The horse moved sedately up the middle of the road. The driver sounded the horn and the rider, if anything, slumped more and carried on at his own pace. The driver cursed, revving the monstrous engine in helpless frustration and moving his hands in wide gesticulation. I was pleased.

The taxi stopped at the Albatross and we got out. The wind was dipping and swirling through the streets. It was late afternoon. Jones insisted on paying the fare and waved away my protest, saying I could stand him a drink later. He was shivering in his Brooks Brothers suit. We had to carry our own bags in to the desk while we registered, and I walked up to my room while Jones looked about for a page boy or a lift. I was gratified for the chance to be alone, and pleased with my room. It was primitive and satisfying, although

I don't suppose Jones was too happy about such accommodation.

I washed and shaved with cold water and went to the window to look out. It would soon be dark, and I thought it too late to call on Gardiner that afternoon. This didn't displease me. I was far more anxious to pursue my own wanderings than Smyth's theory, and although I was certainly anxious to meet Hodson it was more because he was an eminent and interesting theorist in my own field than because he might provide a link in the implausible chain of Smyth's reasoning. I decided to spend what remained of the daylight in roaming about the town, getting the mood of Ushuaia as a fulcrum towards understanding the land.

I hoisted my suitcase to the bed and opened it, found a warmer coat and put it on, put a notepad and pencil in the pocket and left the room. I had to pass the entrance to the bar on the way out, and glanced in. Jones was already there, chatting in familiar tones with the barman. He didn't notice me. It was cold and damp in the street and the vortex of wind had straightened and came more steadily from the south. I turned my collar up and lighted a cigarette in the shelter of the building, then walked out to the street. The wind fanned the cigarette until it burned like a fuse, bouncing sparks as I turned my head.

I had a street map of the town, but didn't use it. I had no particular destination but walked in the general direction of the port, down steep streets lined with the trading companies that supplied the whole area, facing that powerful wind. Motorcars and horsecarts shared the streets with an assorted population of many nationalities and many backgrounds; English, Spanish, Yugoslavian, Italian, German—the racial mixture that invariably gathers at a frontier, colonialists and conquistadors, sailors and settlers, farmers and shepherds, the leftover dregs of the gold rush and the seepage from the oil fields in the north, men who had come to seek and men who had come where they would not be sought—and, of course, the few tourists looking disgruntled and uncomfortable and wondering what had possessed them to come here. This was a rich lode indeed for a social anthropologist, but that was not my field, and I had only a mild interest in observing the men who had come here. I wanted the men who had been here long before anyone came, and there were only a few natives in the town. They had been drawn towards this outpost of civilization but had not been integrated into its core; they had stopped and clustered at the outskirts.

Standing on the quay, I looked into the hard water of the Beagle Channel and the deserted islands in the mist beyond. The water ran in jagged lines of black and white, and a solitary hawk circled effortlessly in the air currents above. A man, almost invisible inside an ancient leather coat, led a loaded llama straight towards me, forcing me back from the water. He didn't notice me, although the beast turned a curious eye as he lumbered past.

I turned back up the incline. My heavy coat was proof against the cold, but the wind slid through the fabric and cascaded my hair over my brow. The sensation was not unpleasant, and I felt no urge to return to the hotel yet. I turned in the opposite direction and climbed away from the centre of the town.

Night was deepening the sky beneath the darkened clouds when I found myself at the end of the modern world—the outskirts of Ushuaia. I had a very concrete sense of standing at a barrier. Behind me electric and neon blanketed the town, the light confined within the limits. This was the point to which civilization had penetrated, although it lay in a thin veneer within the boundaries, its roots shallow and precarious, a transplant that had not yet taken a firm hold. Before me the land broke upwards and away, jagged and barren and dotted with clusters of sheet-metal shacks painted in the brightest tones, oranges and yellows and reds. The thin chimneys rattled bravely in the wind, and the smoke lay in thin, flat ribbons. Kerosene lamps cast futile pastel light in the doorways, and a few shadowed figures moved.

This, then, was where the natives lived. This was where they had been drawn, and then halted, those who had surrendered. And beyond this fringe, perhaps, were those who had refused to yield to the magnet of time.

I walked slowly back to the hotel, and slept well.

III

I awoke early in the sharp cold. The window framed a rectangle of bright and brittle light blocked on the opposite wall. I dressed quickly and went to the window, expecting to see the sun, but the light was filtered through a tissue of cloud, diffused throughout the sky. It left the streets strangely without shadow or contrast, and made the day seem even colder than it was. I put an extra sweater on before going down to the breakfast room. No one else was there yet. A fire had been lighted but hadn't yet taken the chill from the room, and I didn't dawdle over my coffee. I wanted to send a wire to Susan to let her know I had arrived safely, and then I had to contact Gardiner. I was just leaving when Jones came in, looking haggard and bleary. He smiled perfunctorily.

"You tried that pisco yet?" he asked.

I didn't know what pisco was.

"The local booze. Grape alcohol. Gives a man a wicked hangover, I'll tell you."

He shook his head and sank into a chair. He was calling for black coffee as I left. I wondered if he'd ever managed to get out of the hotel bar the night before. And yet, in his fashion, he would learn things about this town that I would never know.

I walked to the telegraph office and sent the wire to Susan, lighted my first cigarette of the day and started back toward the hotel. Three hawks were perched, evenly spaced, on the telegraph wires, and I wondered, whimsically, if they would be aware of my message darting beneath their talons. A taxi had pulled up at the hotel to let a passenger out, and I asked the driver if he knew where Gardiner lived. He did, and I got in the back seat, smoking and looking out of the windows. We drove out past the ancient Indian cemetery on the crisp morning road, with crackling tyres and white exhaust, on a day that made me feel very much alive.

Gardiner's big house was stuck against the glacier in two-dimensional silhouette. I walked up from the road and Gardiner opened the door before I had knocked. He wore a red wool dressing gown and held a gin and tonic.

"You must be Brookes."

I nodded.

"Smyth wired me to expect you. Thought you'd be here last night."

"I got in rather late."

He stepped back and let me in. He hadn't shaved yet, and had vaguely waved the gin in lieu of a handshake. We went into a large room curiously devoid of furnishings. A beautifully engraved shotgun hung on the wall and there was a sheepskin rug by the fire.

"I hope I'm no trouble," I said.

"Not at all. Glad to help if I can. Glad to have some company. Gin or brandy?"

"It's rather early."

"Nonsense."

He gave me gin and we sat by the fire.

"Smyth said you've been very helpful to us in the past," I said.

"I'm no scientist, but I expect I know as much about this place as anyone. Been here thirty-odd years. Not much to do here now. A little shooting and a lot of drinking. Used to be different in the old days, before the land reforms whittled the company away." He shook his head, not necessarily in disapproval. "But that won't interest you."

"Well, I'm more interested in the natives."

"Of course." He looked thoughtful, shaking his head again. "There were three tribes when the white man came here. The Alacalufs, the Yahgans, and the Onas." I knew all this, but was content to listen. "They were absolutely prehistoric, stark naked savages. Probably very happy, too. They didn't understand the white man and they didn't trust him. Good judges. They were even rash enough to steal a few of the white man's sheep, and the white man shot a few of them, of course. Did them a little harm. But then the enlightened white men came. The missionaries. They came burning with the fever of reform and saw these unfortunate lambs of God running about naked and indecent and, in the fashion of their kind, gave them blankets for warmth and modesty. The blankets hadn't been disinfected, so they also gave them plague. Killed off all the Onas and most of the others. But, oh well, we couldn't have them trotting about naked, could we?"

Gardiner sighed and poured another gin.

"Will you stay here?" he asked.

"I'm already at the hotel."

"Ah." I think he would have welcomed a guest. "Well, how can I help you, then?"

I told him about the rumours and reports, and what Smyth thought possible. Gardiner nodded. He'd heard them himself, of course.

"Would you think there was anything in it?" I asked.

"There must be something. All rumours have some basis in fact. But I doubt if it's anything very interesting. Nothing like Smyth suggests. I've never seen or heard of anything like that before, and if something did exist it surely would have been discovered before. Left some evidence of its existence, at least."

"That's what I thought."

"I should think perhaps a wild dog, or possibly a man—maybe even an escapee from the penal colony, living wild."

"That would account for the dead sheep. But what about this man who claims to have seen it? The one Smyth queried you about?"

"Gregorio. Yes. Of course, when I answered Smyth's wire, I didn't know what he was interested in Gregorio for. I thought he might be contemplating using him for a guide perhaps, and he's reliable enough for that sort of thing. But as far as his account of this strange creature—" he paused, as if giving it every consideration. "Well, I suppose he did see something that frightened the hell out of him, but I'm sure it wasn't what he thought it was. He's a superstitious, imaginative sort of fellow, and he certainly hasn't tried to capitalize on the story so I expect we can discount the possibility that he made it up. He hasn't said anything about it for some time."

"I'd like to talk to him."

"No harm in that."

"Do you know where I might find him?"

"Yes. He lives in a shack just west of town. Scrapes out a living as a freelance farmer and tourist guide, now that they have started to come." Gardiner shuddered at the idea of tourists. "Speaks English well enough. I shouldn't offer him much money, though, or he's liable to feel he owes you a good story and embellish it."

"Anyone else I should see?"

"You might have a chat with MacPherson. He has a small farm near here. Had a few sheep destroyed. He'll be more accurate than Gregorio."

MacPherson was one of the names I remembered from the reports Smyth had received.

"Where will I find him?"

"He's in town right now, matter of fact."

"That will be convenient. Where?"

Gardiner was pouring another drink.

"Where else?" he said, smiling. "At the bar of the Gran Parque. I'll drive you in and introduce you, if you like."

Gardiner drove an ancient Packard with considerable panache. I asked him about Hodson as we rumbled ponderously into town.

"Hodson? Haven't seen him in years."

"Smyth seemed certain he was still here."

"Oh, he's here. But he never comes into Ushuaia."

"Any idea where he lives?"

"Not really. He's an unsociable type." Gardiner seemed scornful of such behaviour. "He's out in the mountains somewhere. Graham might know more about it. He runs a trading company and I think Hodson gets his supplies there. But he never comes in himself."

"If you'll introduce me to Graham—"

"Certainly," Gardiner said, concentrating on the road with both hands on the wheel. He wore string-backed driving gloves and a flat tweed cap. We came over a sharp rise and there was a horse and rider blocking the road, slowly moving towards us. We seemed to be moving frightfully fast. I started to shout a warning but Gardiner was already moving, shifting down with a fluid sweep of the lever and letting the engine howl. He didn't bother with brakes or horn, and scarcely turned the steering wheel. The rider hauled the horse around in a rearing sidestep and the animal's flank flashed by my window. Remembering the taxi driver's difficulty, I decided that Gardiner must have a considerable reputation.

"Certainly I shall," he said.

The trading company was on our way and we pulled up in front. The old Packard ran considerably better than it stopped. It rocked to a halt like a weary steeplechaser refusing a jump. Gardiner led the way into a large building cluttered haphazardly with a catholic selection of goods and supplies. Graham was a dusty little man behind a dusty wooden counter, and when Gardiner introduced us, he said, "Baa."

I expect I looked startled.

"Local greeting," Gardiner said. "Has something to do with sheep, I assume."

"That's right," Graham said. "Baa."

"Baa," I said.

"Brookes is trying to get in touch with Hodson. Does he still trade with you?"

"That's right."

"Do you know where he lives?" I asked.

"Nope. Never see him. Haven't seen Hodson in three or four years."

"How does he have his supplies delivered?"

"He doesn't. Sends a man to fetch them."

"Well, do you know anyone who could take me to him?"

Graham scratched his head.

"Can't think of anyone offhand. Funny. I guess the best thing would be to wait for the man who fetches his supplies."

"That would do. If I could speak to him the next time he comes here."

"Can't speak to him."

"Oh?"

"Can't speak. He's a mute."

I felt rather frustrated. Gardiner was grinning. He asked, "Does he come frequently?"

"Yeah. Has to, pretty much. See, Hodson's camp or whatever it is, is up in the mountains. Probably over on the Chilean side. There aren't any roads up there, so he has to take the things on pack horses. Can't take very much stuff on horseback, so he has to come in every few weeks. Should be coming in any day now, matter of fact."

"Could you let me know when he does?"

"Guess so."

"I'm at the Albatross."

"Yep."

"I'll be glad to—"

"Not necessary," he said, foreseeing the offer of money. "If you need any supplies yourself, buy 'em here."

That was something I hadn't thought of.

"What will I need to reach Hodson's?"

"Hard to say, since I don't know where it is. You'll need a horse and pack. I can get something ready for you, if you want. Have it waiting when Hodson's man arrives."

"That will be fine."

I wasn't sure how fine it would be. I hadn't been on a horse for years, but some obscure pride rose up in a dubious battle against the urge to ask him to find me a docile animal. The pride won. I suppose I was already being affected by contact with these self-sufficient frontiersmen.

We went back to the car.

"It's a rather rough trek up those hills," Gardiner said, as he started the engine. He let it idle for a moment. Perhaps he'd seen my doubts mirrored in my expression. "I suppose you can handle a horse all right?"

"I've ridden," I said. "Not for some time."

"Best to let the horse pick his own way. Good, sure-footed animals here."

"Well, the worst I can do is fall off."

Gardiner looked horrified.

"A gentleman never falls off," he said. "He is thrown."

He was chuckling happily as we drove off.

MacPherson wasn't in the Gran Parque.

This distressed Gardiner, who hated to have people behave out of character, and hated to have his predictions proven wrong. We found him in the next bar down the street, however, so it wasn't too unjustifiable. MacPherson was classically sandy haired, proving that truth has less regard for triteness than literary convention. He was standing at the bar, talking with a villainous-looking man with a drooping moustache and splendidly hand-tooled boots.

Gardiner drew me to the bar at the far end.

"He's talking business. We'll wait here until he's finished."

"What a remarkable looking fellow."

"Mac?"

"The other one. Looks like a Mexican bandit."

Gardiner grinned. "He is rather traditional, isn't he? A Yugoslav. Free zone trader."

"What would that be?"

"A smuggler. Works from here up to Rio Grande through the Gortbaldi Pass. Quite a bit of that goes on. This fellow is very respected in his line, I understand. Not that I would have any dealings with him, of course." Gardiner looked amused. The Spanish barman came over, running a rag along the bar, and Gardiner ordered gin and tonics, after checking his wrist-watch to make sure it wasn't yet time to switch to the afternoon whiskies. I expect he lived by a rigid code in such matters. The barman set the drinks down and wiped his hands on the same rag he'd wiped the bar with.

Gardiner said "Cheers," and took a large swallow.

I was unaccustomed to drinking this much, and certainly not this early in the day, and sipped cautiously. Gardiner drank fast. I could see that Clyde Jones, in many ways, would fit into this society much more readily than I; that my first impression had been hasty and ungracious and single-minded. But I resisted the temptation to drink more quickly.

Presently the Yugoslav departed, walking very tall and proud with his spurs clanking, and we moved down the bar. Gardiner introduced us and I bought MacPherson a drink. He drank Scotch, but I expect his code was more accountable to nationality than chronometry. "Lived here long?" I asked.

"Too long," MacPherson said. Then he shrugged. "Still, it's not a bad life. It's all right."

"Brookes is interested in this thing that's been killing your sheep," Gardiner said.

"Oh?"

"Came all the way from London to investigate it."

"I don't suppose there are many natural predators here, are there?" I asked.

"Ah, there's the odd fox and the hawks and such. Never been anything like this before, though."

"It's a curious business, from what I've heard."

"It is that."

"What do you make of it?"

He considered for a few moments and a few swallows of Scotch, the skin on his brow like furrowed leather. "Well, it's not serious, really. Not enough damage been done to do me any financial harm. I guess I lost half a dozen sheep all told. But it's the way they were killed that bothers me."

"How was that?"

"Well, they were torn apart. Mutilated. Throats torn out and skulls crushed. Never saw anything quite like it. Whatever did it is not only powerful but vicious. And the strangest part is that my dogs seem helpless."

Gardiner signalled for another round of drinks, and MacPherson seemed to be thinking deeply while the barman brought them.

"Have you tried to find it?"

"Of course. I almost had it once. That was the strangest part of all. It was a month or so ago and I was sort of keeping an eye out for it. Had my gun with me, and four good dogs. Well, we found a sheep that had just been killed. Couldn't have been dead more than a few minutes. Torn to pieces. I put the dogs on to it and they started howling and growling and sniffing about, then they got the scent and took off after the thing. The land's rocky and I couldn't see a trail myself, but the dogs had it sure enough. I followed them and they tracked it a few hundred yards in to a ravine. I thought I had it then for sure. But when I was coming up behind, the dogs suddenly stopped dead and for no reason I could see, the whole pack started yelping and came running back with their tails between their legs. Made the hair stiffen on my neck, I'll tell you that. They came back so fast they almost knocked me down, and they all crowded around my legs, whimpering. Gave me a funny sensation, that. I kicked 'em and beat 'em but damned if I could make them go into that ravine. Even when I went up to the edge myself, they wouldn't follow. I looked around a little, walked along the edge for a little way, but it was rocky wasteland with heavy undergrowth all along the bottom and I had no chance of finding it without the dogs. But I was sure that it was in there, waiting."

He paused. He looked a little shaken.

"Matter of fact, I was scared to go in after it."

MacPherson didn't look the type to be afraid of much.

"Any trouble recently?" I asked.

"Oh, it's still there all right. Whatever the hell it is. I've tried setting traps for it and poisoned one of the carcasses, but it did no good. Cunning brute. I got the idea, you know the feeling, that it was watching me all the while I was putting the traps out."

"Could it be a wild dog or something of the sort?"

"I doubt that. No dog could have put the fear into my pack that way. And no dog could've crushed those sheep's skulls that way, either. No dog I ever saw."

"A man?"

"Maybe. I thought of that. Used to have a few sheep carried off by the Indians. But they always stole them to eat. This thing just mangles them and leaves them where they died. Maybe eats a mouthful or two, the carcasses are so shredded I can't really tell. But no more than that."

"Few animals kill purely for pleasure," I said. "Wolverine, leopard maybe . . . and man, of course."

"If it's a man, it's a madman."

MacPherson bought a round. I had a glass in my hand and two waiting on the bar now, and felt that I'd soon be in no condition to pursue any investigations.

"Would it be possible for me to stay at your place if I find it necessary to look for this thing?" I asked.

"Surely. I don't know if you can find it, but I'll give you every help I can. I'll have to take you out, though. You'd never find my place on your own. It's in the mountains west of here and there are no roads and only crude maps. I'm not even sure if I'm in Chile or Argentina."

"I have some other things to do first," I said. "I may not have to take advantage of your hospitality."

"I hope you get the bastard. What gun are you using?"

It took me a moment to comprehend that.

"I didn't come to shoot it," I said.

MacPherson blinked.

"Then what the hell are you going to do?"

"That depends on what it turns out to be."

MacPherson snorted. Then he looked serious. He said: "Well, it's none of my business, but if you're going to look for this thing, you'd better take a gun with you."

"Surely it wouldn't attack a man?"

MacPherson shrugged.

"You haven't seen those sheep, son. I have. Believe me, you better take a gun."

The way he said it was quite impressive.

It was past noon now, and Gardiner had switched to Scotch. MacPherson approved. We had not had lunch, and Gardiner and MacPherson both seemed content to spend the afternoon at the bar. I'd had more than enough to drink, and the barman brought me a coffee with the next round. A few more customers wandered in and stood at the bar, talking and drinking. I noticed them vaguely, my thoughts on what MacPherson had told me. It was virtually the same story that I'd read in the reports, but hearing it in person, and seeing the man who told it, was far more effective than reading it in the grey safety of London. I was far less sceptical, and ready to believe a great deal more. Perhaps the alcohol had stimulated my imagination; it had certainly fired my impatience to get to the bottom of the mystery. I was convinced now that something very strange indeed was roaming those all but inaccessible mountains, and much too excited to waste any more time in that bar.

"Would this be a good time to see Gregorio?" I asked.

"Good as any," Gardiner said.

"If you could direct me—"

"I'll drive you there. It's not far."

He looked a shade disappointed at the prospect of leaving the bar.

"That's not necessary. Actually, I could use some air to clear my head. I'll walk."

"Are you sure?"

"Absolutely. It'll give me an opportunity to look around a bit more, too. I couldn't see much at the speed you drive."

Gardiner laughed. He was possibly a certain degree in his cups by this time. MacPherson seemed absolutely impervious to intoxication. I took my note pad out to write down the address, but Gardiner laughed more at this, and when he'd given me the directions, I saw why. They were accurate but somewhat unusual. Gregorio lived in the third orange shack on the western approach to town. There was a grey horse in a tin shed beside the shack. The shed was green and the horse was gelded. It was surely a more exact method of location than street names and postal districts, as any stranger who has asked directions in London will know.

I finished my coffee.

"One last drink before you leave?" Gardiner asked.

"Not now, thanks. Will you be here?"

"Undoubtedly."

I turned to leave and Jones came walking down the bar. He was wearing a purple sports shirt and smiling. His hangover seemed to have been effectively reduced by drowning.

"Hello there, Brookes. Have a drink?"

"I can't just now. I have some business to attend to."

He looked disappointed. He had a very American friendliness, and was probably lonely. I introduced him to Gardiner and MacPherson and he shook hands eagerly.

"You fellas live here? Quite a place, this."

Jones bought drinks and merged easily into the group. I felt obliged to wait for a few minutes and not leave him with strangers, but it proved unnecessary. He was perfectly suited to the situation. When I left, Gardiner was telling him how the Explotadora company used to virtually rule the territory and give the governor his orders, and Jones was agreeing that government by private enterprise was vastly superior to Democrats and communism.

I walked out beyond the town.

The wind was stronger here, without the shelter of the sturdy buildings of the town. A *pasajero* rode past me, leading a pack horse burdened with all his possessions and trailed by a pack of mangy mongrels. There were shacks on both sides of the road, hideously bright and clattering metallically. Indians sat huddled in the doorways and on the crooked steps. Men of ancient leather and twisted cord, their eyes turned listlessly after me, not really interested but simply following a motion, the same way that they watched a ragged newspaper tumble before the wind; sullen and listless and uncomprehending, perhaps sensing their lives were changed and unnatural, but not recognizing their defeat. A few sheep grazed behind the shacks, facing away from the wind with splendid unconcern, placid and eternal, and forming perhaps the only bridge between the present and the past.

Gregorio was sitting on a gnarled log beside his door, smoking a hand-made pipe. God knows what he was smoking in it. He wore a poncho with a hood roughly sewn on and shadowing his eyes. His hands were strangely delicate, despite the horny calluses, the fingers long and mobile. He peered at me suspiciously. He'd had enough experience of civilization to be wary, unlike the Indians who had watched me walk past.

"Are you Gregorio?" I asked.

The head nodded under the hood.

"You speak English?"

He nodded again.

I squatted down beside him.

"My name is Brookes. I'd like to speak with you for a few moments if you can spare the time."

There was no reaction.

"I'll gladly pay you for your time."

He nodded again. I began to wonder if he actually did speak English.

"It's about the creature you claim ... the creature that you saw in the mountains."

Gregorio rustled within the poncho and the hood fell back from his head. He had hair like black wire and a face like a Cornish farmhouse, sombre, grey and grim. But his eyes were bright with intelligence and perhaps something else—perhaps it was fear.

"Bestia hombre," he said. His voice rasped. I felt certain then, looking into his face, that this man was not faking or pretending. He had seen something and that something was very terrible indeed.

I took a small bank note from my pocket and offered it to him. He took it without looking at it, with a vestige of pride long vanquished by necessity. He held it crumpled in his palm.

"Tell me what you saw."

He hesitated.

"Is that enough?"

He motioned with the hand holding the note, a scornful gesture. "It is enough," he said. His English was surprisingly clear, with a faint North American intonation. "It is not a good memory, Señor." He puffed on his pipe, his lean cheeks sinking inwards. I felt he was gathering more than his thoughts, and waited anxiously.

"When I tell them, they do not believe me," he said, turning his eyes toward the town. "They laugh. They think I see things that are not there."

"I believe you."

His eyes shifted back to me.

"I've come all the way from London to speak with you, and to find what you saw."

"You will look for this thing?" he said, incredulously. He couldn't believe that anyone would voluntarily seek the creature he had seen—or thought he'd seen. A curious mixture of disbelief and respect moved his expression.

"Yes. And I will find it, if you help me."

"Help you?"

"Tell me all you can remember."

"I will tell you, yes."

"When was it that you saw this thing?"

"It was some weeks ago." He shrugged. "I have no calendar."

"You were in the mountains?"

He nodded and looked westward. The land rose steadily away from us and the clouds seemed to tilt down to meet the far mountains. Gregorio stared into the distance. And, without looking at me, he began to speak. His voice moved musically over the foreign English words, but it was music without gaiety, a tragic overture introducing his sombre theme.

"I was looking for work on the sheep ranches. I had the horse and two dogs." He stabbed the stem of his pipe toward the green tin shack. "That is the horse. The dogs—" he hesitated, his face still turned away from me, and I saw the cords knot in his neck. "The dogs were running after me. They were happy to be away from this town, in the mountains. They were good dogs. One especially, a dog of great courage and strength. El Rojo he was called. His breeding one does not know, but his loyalty was firm. He was mine many years, although I had been offered much money for him." He paused again. His hands were restless. Then he seemed to shrug, although his shoulders did not actually move.

"We rode on a narrow trail through trees. The trees there lean and turn because of the great wind. The wind was very loud then, and the horse made great noise on the rock. It was becoming night. I do not know what hour, I have no clock. But it was time that I make camp, and I looked for a place. I went from the trail and was among dark trees. And then there was no noise. It was like a storm about to break, that silence. But there was no storm, the sky was clear. It was something else. I knew it was not good. The dogs also knew. The little dog cried and El Rojo had stiff hair over his neck. I felt the horse tremble between my knees. All up my legs I feel this, and the eyes are white, the nostrils wide. I kicked at the horse with my heels, but it did not walk."

Gregorio turned to face me then. His face was terrible. He was reliving those moments vividly, and perhaps this was how his face had appeared then. He seemed scarcely aware of me, his eyes turned on the past.

"Then I heard the sound of this thing. It was a snarl. Not like a dog. A warning, perhaps a challenge. I am not sure what it was. I turned to the sound and then I saw it. It was in a thicket, but I saw it plainly. I looked at it, and it looked at me. We regarded one another. I was unable to move and my throat would not work. My backbone was of ice.

"It was not tall. It bent forwards with long arms. Its chest was huge and shoulders heavy. There was much thick hair, and where there was not hair the skin was dark. For some time we do nothing, and it made the sound again. The hindquarters raise, as if it is stiffening its tail. But it has no tail. Something was beneath it. A sheep, I think. It was woolly and red with blood, and this thing was red at the mouth. Blood dropped heavily from the teeth. But they were teeth. They were not fangs of a beast, they were teeth. And the eyes are on me all this time. It has the eyes of a man . . ."

He was staring into my eyes as he said this. His pipe had burned out, but his teeth were clamped on the stem. I didn't move, afraid to break the memory that held him, and the belief that gripped me.

"I wished to run from this thing, but the horse was filled with fear. It would not run. And I, too, am frozen. Only El Rojo has sufficient courage. He feared nothing, that dog. He moved toward the thing. The other dog was not so brave. It ran. The movement makes the horse able to run, also, and he followed after the dog. The horse ran faster than he could run. Faster than I think any horse can run. I am a horseman. All my life I have ridden horses, and I knew this horse well. But Señor, I could no more stop this horse than stop the wind. And I did not want to."

He was aware of me again, and I thought the story was finished. But he lowered his face and spoke again, more softly.

"But I looked back," he said. "I could not look away from this thing. I saw the dog make a circle on stiff legs. The dog is snarling with bare fangs, and then the thing moved to the dog. The dog was not fast enough. Or the thing is too fast. They are together on the ground then, and I could see no more. But I can hear what happens. I can hear the cry of the dog, the sound of pain and death. It is loud, then it is not so loud, and when I can hear the dog no longer I hear the sound of this thing. It is not like before. It is more terrible. It is the worst sound a man has ever heard. There was nothing I could do. I could not stop the horse for a long ways, and when finally I did I was trembling more than the horse. I thought of the dog. I loved that dog. But I did not go back."

Gregorio lapsed into silence. He seemed sad and exhausted. The note was still clasped in his hand. I waited for several moments before he raised his head.

"That is what happened," he said.

"Do you have any idea what it was?"

He shrugged.

"Could it have been some animal? Some animal you have never seen before?"

"It was a man."

"It was dark you said . . ."

"The light was sufficient."

"A man then. An Indian?"

He shook his head patiently.

"A man and a beast," he said. "A beast-man. A man like no man ever was."

A man like no man ever was? Or is?

I left him then. I said that I might wish to talk with him again and he shrugged. He was filling his pipe again, and when I looked back from the road he was slumped on the log exactly as he'd been when I came. I was profoundly affected by his tale. I believed him. He might have been mistaken, but he had not deceived me. He had seen something much too terrible to be imagined, and the emotions of his memory were far too genuine to be feigned. Somewhere in those trackless and forsaken wastes, a creature existed. I did not know what it was, but I knew that I had to find it.

I thought of MacPherson's advice.

I did not like the idea of carrying a gun, but I decided that I should. There was another idea that I liked considerably less . . .

IV

I spent the next three days in Ushuaia.

It gave me the opportunity to observe these primitive people, as I'd wanted, but my interest in this pursuit had greatly waned. I regarded it now as something that had been done by others before me, interesting enough but hardly a challenge, compared to the possibilities of a new discovery. The tales I had heard from Gregorio and, to a lesser extent, MacPherson, had inflamed my imagination. I had never been a man to draw easy conclusions from incomplete data, and yet the same idea that had seemed absurd when Smyth presented it to me in his quiet, dark office, and the same statements I had passed over lightly in the objective reports that reached the museum, took on a new reality now, just as the clouded sky cast a new light over this land.

I was consumed by an impetuous urge to proceed with my investigations, and frustrated by the need to wait. But the first essential was still to locate Hodson. That was why Smyth had sent me, and it would have been foolish to follow another line of research until I'd seen him, and settled my mind one way or the other on that account. And it seemed there was no way to find Hodson until his man arrived for supplies.

I went to Graham's every morning to inquire, and be disappointed. Graham had prepared a knapsack and saddlebags for me, and arranged with the stables down the street to have a horse ready to be hired at any time. The knapsack contained a portable stove and foodstuffs in lightweight plastic containers, along with other articles which surprised me, but which Graham thought might possibly prove handy if not essential in traversing that rugged land: a small hatchet, a folding knife, several lengths of rope and cord— things of potential value in survival, rather than in comfort. There was also a sleeping bag and groundsheet. It hadn't occurred to me that I might be spending a night in the open, and I was grateful for Graham's foresight, although not so pleased by several tales he told me of men who had been lost in the mountains. With his guidance, I purchased a suitable outfit of clothing for the trek, heavy whipcord trousers, wool plaid shirt, quilted windbreaker with hood attached, and sturdy, treble-soled boots equally suited to riding and walking over broken land. I felt a certain satisfaction in being so well prepared which somewhat mollified my impatience.

In the meanwhile, I spent the days walking miles into the country on all sides. I wore my new clothing, getting accustomed to the freedom of this new manner of dress at the same time as I felt myself becoming acquainted with the land. I made no particular effort at observation, and made no entries in my notebook. Whatever I learned was simply absorbed without conscious effort, coming through the senses while my mind turned over manifold plans and possibilities. I didn't attempt to restrict my thoughts to what I knew, or could be proved. It was out of character for me, but I was out of the world I knew, and anxious to enter the world of which Gregorio had spoken.

There were aspects of his story that fascinated me, that had the solid ring of truth, fantastic as that truth might be. These were not the things that seemed to have affected Gregorio most, however. He had seemed most impressed by the creature's eyes, but I passed this over. Many animals have eyes that seem almost human in their intelligence, often the most loathsome creatures, rats and moray eels for instance. Gregorio could easily have been misled in this.

But he claimed it had teeth, not fangs, and referred to its forward
or upper limbs as arms, not the legs he would have attributed to
most animals—small points he had not pressed unduly, but which
convinced me. And, more than anything else, there was the action
he'd described—the raising of a non-existent tail. I have often
wondered why mankind emotionally resents the tail that his fore-
bears carried; why that is so frequently the point chosen when a
man without knowledge scorns the process of evolution. For the
same reason that he portrays the devil with a tail, perhaps? A feeling
of superiority for the misguided reason that man has lost a useful
and functional part of his anatomy. Surely a man like Gregorio
would have given a tail to a figment of his imagination, or added
one to a trick of light upon a superstitious nature. The tail is an inte-
gral part of bestial evil, and it seemed reasonable to assume that he
would have. But he hadn't. The thing had no tail, and moved as if
it had.

My mind danced back through the aeons, obscuring fact with
fancy and the present with the past, jamming two dimensions into
one space, in my readiness to believe almost anything. I built fantasies of unbelievable intricacy and detail, and was content not to
hinder the construction of this fragile architecture of the imagination. And, in this structure, there was the cornerstone of truth. For
somewhere, sometime there had existed a creature which was less
than man, and in many ways less than an ape, at some point where
the distant line forked and began to pursue constantly diverging
trails. It had happened once, at some point in time, and evolution
has a pattern we have not yet mapped, a stamp that surely may be
repeated in different places, when the time of those places is right.
I had always believed in the likeliness of simultaneous evolution,
finding it far more plausible than since-sunken land bridges and
fantastic ocean emigrations on crude rafts, to account for the
presence of mankind in the New World and the islands. The only
new concept was the timing, and this problem did not seem insur-
mountable now that I was at a place like this, a land untouched by
change as the world aged around it. Could the old pattern have
begun again, working here along the same old lines that had popu-
lated the rest of the world in forgotten ages? The same evolution, a
million years behind?

My wild musings surprised me, as I realized what I had been considering. And yet I didn't scoff at the thought.

On the evening of the third day I walked out beyond the new Italian colony and turned from the path to ascend a rocky incline. The stones were soft beneath the heavy soles of my boots, and I carried a stout walking stick, using it as a third leg against gravity. Some small creature scurried unseen through the brush as I scrambled on to the flattened top of the hillock. A solitary beech tree twisted up from the undergrowth, and an owl hooted from the line of trees fringing a ridge to the north. It was raining lightly, and the wind was drifting higher than usual. I stood beneath the tortured limbs of the tree and lit a cigarette, looking out towards the west. I could not see far in the darkening mist, but I knew that somewhere out there were the mountains and canyons, the unmarked Chilean frontier and, somewhere beyond that, the place where I would find Hodson. I wondered what chance I would have of finding him if I were to set off myself, and the thought tempted my impatience. But it would have been more than hopeless. I had to wait.

Presently, aided by my stick, I clambered back down the incline and walked back to town through the soft, dark rain.

I encountered Jones on the stairs the next morning, and we descended together. I had intended to go to the breakfast-room, but I saw that it was occupied by three widowed tourists who had arrived the day before amidst cackling disorder. They were calling for separate bills and debating over who had devoured the extra doughnut. I believe they were from Milwaukee. I turned into the bar with Jones.

We sat at the bar. Jones had Pernod with his black coffee.

"Women like that make me ashamed to be a tourist," he said. The nasal tones still reached us, although we felt quite sure the ladies wouldn't come into the bar. "That's the trouble with tourists. They get some place and then, instead of relaxing and enjoying themselves they rush about trying to see everything. Laden with guidebooks and preconceived ideas of what they must look at. Now me, first thing I do is find a nice sociable bar and have a drink. Get to meet some of the people. That's the way to be a tourist." He poured some water into his Pernod and admired the silicone effect as it clouded. "Course, you're lucky. You can travel without being a tourist. Gardiner was telling me how you were a famous scientist."

"Hardly famous."

"What's your line?"

"Anthropology. I'm on a field trip for the museum."

"You don't work on atom bombs and things, huh?" He looked vaguely disappointed.

"Decidedly not. My work lies towards discovering where mankind came from, before it is gone."

Jones nodded thoughtfully.

"Yeah. Still, I guess we got to have those atom bombs and things since the commies got 'em. Better if no one had 'em. You work for a museum, huh? I like museums, myself. Been in all the big museums all over the States and Europe. Not 'cause I think I got to, though. Just 'cause I like 'em. We got some fine museums in the States, you know. Ever thought of joining that brain drain? A scientist gets lots better money back home than you get over in England."

"I hadn't considered it, no."

"Ought to. I mean, science and all is fine, and that England's a great little island, but a guy's got to earn a decent living for himself, too. That's right, isn't it? You got to look after yourself first, before you can look after the rest of the world. That holds for science and politics and charity and everything."

"You have a point."

"Want something with that coffee?"

"No, thank you."

"I don't usually drink much at home, myself. But when I'm travelling, a little drink relaxes me. I like drinking in your country. Those pubs are fine things, 'cept they're never open when a guy's thirsty."

The barman refilled our cups, and poured Jones another Pernod.

"What you doing here, anyway?" Jones asked me.

I almost launched into a detailed explanation, but caught myself in time.

"Studying the natives, more or less," I said.

"That so? Ain't much to study, is there? I mean, they're sort of primitive."

"That's why I'm studying them."

"Oh," said Jones.

A boy was standing in the doorway, blinking. It was the boy from Graham's trading company. I raised a hand and he saw me and came down the bar.

"Mister Graham sent me over. Said to tell you that Hodson's man is here."

"I'll come with you," I told him.

"Want a drink before you go?" Jones asked.

"Sorry. I don't have time."

"Sure. Business before pleasure, huh?"

I left Jones at the bar and followed the boy out to the street. It was a bright morning, unusually warm. Half a dozen hawks were circling against the sun. I felt stimulated as we walked toward Graham's. This was what I'd been waiting for.

There were three horses tied in front of the trading post, and Graham was busily gathering the various supplies, referring to a handwritten list. He glanced up as I entered, and nodded toward the back of the room.

"There's your man," he said.

It was dark in the shadow of crates and shelves, and for a moment I didn't see him. Then, gradually, the outline took shape, and I believe my mouth may have gaped open. I don't know what I'd expected, but certainly not a man of such ferocious and terrifying aspect. He was gigantic. He must have stood closer to seven feet than six, a massive column of splendidly proportioned muscle and sinew, wearing a *caterino* over chest and back, leaving shoulders, arms and sides bare. He was standing completely motionless, huge arms crossed over his massive chest, and even in this relaxed position the definition of his muscles cleaved darkly against the brown skin. The man's countenance was in accord with his body, his features carved from mahogany with a blunt chisel. A dark rag was knotted across his wide forehead, just above the eyes, the ends of the knot hanging loose and frayed and his hair a ragged coil over the edge.

Graham was grinning.

"Quite a lad, eh?"

"Rather impressive. Any idea what tribe he could belong to? He doesn't look like any of the Indians I've seen around the town."

"No. I heard somewhere that Hodson brought him down from up north. The Amazon, I think. As his personal servant. Can't see why he'd want something like that around the house, though."

"And he can't speak, you say?"

"I never heard him make a sound. Dumb, I reckon. Brings a list of supplies and waits while I get it packed and loaded, then he's off again. Brings a cheque on Hodson's bank every few months to settle the account, but I don't think he knows what it is."

"Can you communicate with him?"

Graham shrugged.

"Sure. Sign language, same's I talk to any of them that can't understand English. Simple enough. Universal."

"Could you ask if I may accompany him?"

Graham frowned.

"Well, I can tell him you're going. Don't really know how I'd ask. No sense in it, anyway. He's got nothing to say about it. Can't tell you where you can go, and it wouldn't do to give him the idea he could. I'll just let him know you're going with him, and you'll have to do the rest. Keep up with him, I mean. Not that he might try to lose you, but I wouldn't be willing to bet he'd wait for you if you dropped behind. Probably wouldn't even notice."

"I see."

"You shouldn't have to worry about keeping up, since he's got two animals to lead. Can't go too fast. But he'll probably just keep right on going until he gets there, so it may be a long haul in the saddle."

"I'll manage."

"Sure. No worries."

Graham finished gathering the supplies into a pile by the door. The Indian paid no attention to either of us. He hadn't moved since I'd entered. I noticed that he carried a machete in his waistband and wore nothing on his feet. He fascinated me, and I could hardly take my eyes away from him.

"You can start loading these on the horse," Graham said to the boy. Then he held his hand up. "Wait. You better get Mister Brookes' horse over from the stables first. Get it saddled and ready to go before you load the pack horses." The boy went out. Graham went behind the counter and brought out my saddlebags and knapsack.

"Now we'll see what we can get across to him, eh?" he said. I followed him to the back of the room. The nearer I got, the bigger the Indian looked. I didn't actually get too near. Graham began making hand signs, simple symbols that I could have done as well myself. He pointed at me, at the Indian, and then out toward the horses. Then he made a few subtler movements. The Indian watched it all with absolutely no change of expression, no comprehension but also no disagreement, and it was impossible to know how much he understood.

"That's about all I can do," Graham said.

"Does he get the idea?"

"God knows."

"Should I offer him money?"

Graham frowned.

"I don't suppose he uses it. Probably doesn't know what it is. You might offer him something else, a present of some sort. Damned if I know what, though."

I rejected that idea as being too much like baubles and beads for the savages. Graham and I went back to the door. The Indian still hadn't moved. I looked out and saw the boy leading my horse around the side of the building. The animal wasn't too large and didn't appear frisky, walking with its head down. It had high withers and a long, arched neck.

"Not much to look at," Graham said. "You don't want a spirited animal on a trip like this. This one is placid and sure-footed, it should be just the thing."

"I'm sure it will be fine," I said, wondering if Gardiner might have influenced the decision. The horse stood with wide spread legs and drooping back while the boy saddled it, but it looked sturdy enough—more bored than aged or tired.

I put my knapsack on. It felt comfortable. The boy began carrying Hodson's supplies out to the pack animals and loading them with quick efficiency, while Graham and I watched from the doorway. I lighted a cigarette, feeling a nervous energy tightening in my belly, a core of anxiety wrapped in the spirit of adventure.

Graham motioned to the Indian. The horses were ready. The Indian moved past us and over us, and went down the steps. He tested the straps and balance of the packs, his biceps ballooning as he tugged. Then he gathered the leads into one and moved to his mount. There was a blanket over the horse's back, but no saddle, and the Indian was so tall that he virtually stepped on to the animal. He arched his back and the horse moved off at a walk, the pack animals following.

I mounted and settled. Graham came down the steps.

"Good luck," he said.

The anxiety was gone now. I felt fine. I felt like thundering out of town in a swirl of dust. But I heeled gently and we moved off at a walk, behind the pack animals, which was much more sensible.

V

The Indian paid no attention to me as I rode behind him. He seemed totally unaware of my presence, an eerie feeling once Ushuaia was behind us, and we were the only two people in sight. We went at a moderate pace and I kept about ten yards behind the pack horses, realizing again how much energy it takes to ride a horse over broken ground, even at such a slow gait. The Indian, however, seemed to use no energy. He rode with an easy grace, his long body relaxed and shifting to the horse's motion, a technique well suited to a long journey, functional rather than stylistic. Although his horse was of a good size, it looked more like a burro beneath this vast man, and his feet almost brushed the ground.

The sun was abnormally bright and I began to sweat in my heavy clothing, and down my temples. After a while I shrugged out of the knapsack and balanced it on the pommel while I took the quilted windbreaker off and stuffed it in the saddle-bags: slid into the knapsack again. During these gyrations I dropped farther behind, and had to urge the horse into a trot to catch up. The ground was firm and the gait jarred me. I knew I was going to be stiff and sore in a short time, but discomfort earned in such a genuine way didn't bother me; the slight ache of bones and joints lends a certain awareness of one's body and of being alive. It would be a dull existence without pain.

The landscape changed gradually.

We had passed the farthest point of my walks, and I observed this new terrain with interest. The contours were lunar. Large, smooth boulders loomed on all sides and our path wound around and between them. There were few marks of civilization here. Indeed, few signs of life. A few stunted trees grew between and above the rocks, dull moss covered the stony surface, the odd wild sheep peered at us from impossible perches, an ostrich raised its curious head and turned its long neck until it resembled one of the twisted trees. I had had some idea of making a rough map of our journey, but gave the idea up without attempting it. The landmarks were all of a sameness that made recognition difficult—impossible, with my limited knowledge of cartography and compass reading. I knew only that we were heading westward, but not directly. The trail, where there was a trail, curved and zigzagged, following the broken face of the land. We were climbing steadily, the land rising and falling in changing pattern, but always drawing higher in the end. The sun pursued us until it drew level to the north of us, following its eternal path over the equator, and our truncated shadows shifted away from it. The light caught blinding points in the rocks. Time lost objective meaning for me, I was dulled by the heat and the motion and the unchanging contours, and did not even refer to my wristwatch. I'd had no breakfast, and my stomach was empty, but the effort of opening my pack and eating in the saddle was too great. My throat was parched, but I did not raise the waterbag. I slumped in the high Spanish saddle and rode on.

And then, some time in the afternoon, I became aware that the land had changed. It had been an unnoticeable transition, but suddenly we had come into the genuine foothills, the rising plain was behind us and we were ascending into the mountains.

There was no longer even the semblance of a trail, and the going was more difficult, the trees thicker and the rocks higher. The Indian seemed to know the way without having to pay attention, turning and detouring for no apparent reason, but never pausing or backtracking. My horse was placidly confident of his footing. Loose rocks clattered from beneath his hooves, soft mud sucked at his legs between spaces of bare rock, but he never faltered; he lurched but recovered instantly and smoothly. Graham had made a wise selection.

The sun had outdistanced us. It slanted into my face now, hotter than before. I turned to look behind, and found that the plains were already hidden by the folding hills. I knew that I was lost; that I could never have retraced our path back to Ushuaia. I wondered whether we had yet crossed the frontier into Chile. There was no possible way to tell, and it didn't matter in the slightest. Time and distance had both become completely subjective, and my mood was almost stoic; eventually we would be at our destination, and what more did I need to know or concern myself with?

It was in this mood that I nearly rode past the Indian before I noticed he'd dismounted; I didn't, in fact, notice until my horse had the sense to stop. I slid stiffly from the saddle and stretched. It must have been mid-afternoon. Our steady pace had taken us quite a distance, but the path had been so devious that it was impossible to estimate how much actual progress had been made.

We were in the shadow of a large, flat-sided overhang of rock, and trees grew all around, draped with thick yellow moss and stretching down to the dense shrubbery of the undergrowth. The moss stirred restlessly, and cast tangled, shifting shadows. I started to ask my silent companion whether we were halting very long, and then realized the futility of that. He was squatting beside the horses, thigh muscles bunched as great in circumference as a normal man's torso. There was a leather pouch at his waistband and he drew some coarse bark from it and commenced to chew it. The aromatic fumes hung on the air: Winter's-bark, stimulant and tonic, and apparently all the nourishment that vast body needed for this tedious journey. I watched his jaws work methodically and opened my own pack. I had no idea if there would be time to prepare a meal, and had a hasty bite of dried meat and a bar of chocolate. I would have had time for nothing more. I had not even fastened my pack again before the Indian stood up and approached his horse, stooping under the overhanging limbs. My muscles throbbed as I hauled myself back into the saddle, but my seat was all right. The Spanish saddle was very comfortable with its high, square cantel. I pushed my horse up level with the Indian as he started off, and volunteered with obvious gestures to take my turn leading the pack horses. He didn't actually refuse. He simply failed to acknowledge the offer, and a moment later I was once more trailing along behind.

Some time later, we came to a shallow stream bordered by steep, soft banks, and moved along beside it for a while. The water ran in the opposite direction, strangely rapid for such slight depth and bursting over the rocks that lined the bed. Trees burrowed their roots down to the water and mossy limbs stretched over in an arch. We weaved through the foliage and the moss clung to my shoulders, the soft earth gripped the horses' hooves. The Indian had some difficulty leading the pack horses here, and had to move slower. I was closer behind him, wanting to make sure we followed in his exact footsteps, close enough to notice the long scar that ran diagonally over his naked ribs, down to his hip. It was an old scar and not very visible against his dark, dust-covered skin, but it must have been a hideous wound when it occurred, a deep gouge with lesser marks on either side, not clean enough to have been caused by a knife or bullet and yet following a straight course that seemed to imply a purpose to the infliction. Perhaps the talons of some powerful beast, I thought, and wondered what animal might have dared attack this giant.

We came to a break in the bank, where the land had cracked and folded back in a gully, and here the Indian urged his mount down, leaning back from the waist as the horse slid down on stiff legs. The pack horses followed him down reluctantly and my horse stopped, tossing his head nervously and looking for an alternative route. I tugged the reins and heeled to little effect. The Indian was already moving away, riding up the centre of the stream, and I felt a moment of panic thinking I might not be able to get the horse down and would be abandoned here; I heaved heavily on the reins, bringing the horse around and off balance. He sidestepped and missed the edge of the bank and we went down sideways, the horse snorting and kicking, and somehow managed to stay upright. I took a deep, relieved breath, and the horse shook his head, then started off again behind the others. The bed was strewn with rocks and the pack animals kicked spray up at me. It felt refreshing. We rode through the water for some time, perhaps an hour, and then ascended the far bank, lurching and heaving up through the slippery mud.

The land had changed once more on the far bank of the stream. We were traversing dense forest. The rocks and boulders were still there on all sides, but they were hidden and engulfed by the trees and shrubbery. The undergrowth was heavy, and I could not see the horse's legs beneath the knees, yet he carried on steadily enough on this invisible ground. Moss braided my shoulders and clung around my neck like Hawaiian leis. It was cooler here, the sun blocked out and the earth damp. I put my windbreaker on again. We passed through an open space and back into the shade, through patterns of light and shadow, moving chiaroscuro imprinted on the senses. I was still sweating, but the moisture was cold, and I was aware of my discomfort now, the blunted sensations of the hot afternoon sharpened unpleasantly. I became conscious of time again, hoping we had not far to go, and looked at my watch. It surprised me to find it was seven o'clock. We had been riding, virtually without pause, for ten hours. The Indian seemed as fresh as he had when we started, and who knew how long he'd ridden to reach Ushuaia that morning. It seemed impossible that anyone, even that extraordinary man, could have travelled through this terrain through the night, and yet we pushed on with no sign of a halt.

We emerged once more into an open space, a hill scarred with stumps. A waterfall sparkled from the ridge to the south and a fallen tree leaned like a buttress against the cliffs below. Halfway up the hill we passed a grave, an indented rectangle of earth and a weathered wooden cross lashed, leaning, against a stump. It amazed me. What solitary shepherd or recluse woodchopper had died in this forsaken place, and who had been here to bury him? Yet, in a way, this forlorn grave gave me a sense of security. I was not at the end of the world, man had been here before, if not civilized at least Christian, and they would be here again. In Ushuaia I had burned with the urge to get away from civilization and to explore undiscovered secrets in forgotten lands, but somewhere along this tedious journey those thoughts had modified and science had yielded to instinct. I would have been very happy indeed to have a drink with Clyde Jones at that moment . . .

We approached the top of the hill and yet another line of trees, silhouetted in tormented tangles against the darkening sky. Small birds watched from the safety of the limbs and butterflies waifed through the vines, catching the last sunlight in their brilliant wings. We drew near and I started at the sudden battering of wings, jerking around to look as a dark form rose up beside me, hovering for a moment and then rising slowly and heavily—a giant condor, a dozen feet between its wingtips, elevating from some disturbed feast. The Indian seemed as unaware of it as he was of me. I shivered and bent over the pommel. We brushed a tree, the rough surface scraping my cheek, but I was too exhausted to feel the pain, scarcely aware of the mountains ahead, capped with snow and fingers of white running down the slopes. They did not seem high, and then, dimly, I realized that we were high; that we had come to the peak of this range of hills, and a long valley was spread out before us.

I gripped the pommel and relaxed my aching knees, knowing I would be unable to go much farther, hoping we would be there soon, or that night would come and force a stop. It couldn't be long now, the mist was low and the light feeble. The horses were tiring, too, heads down and legs weary and uncertain. We were moving on level ground, crossing the flattened top of the hill towards the descent. A jagged arroyo yawned before us, we passed along the ridge and came out through a field of blasted and broken trees where the wind snarled. There was no shelter here, and the wind had conquered. It was moaning over us, and then, suddenly, it was raging and howling across the surface of the land. It struck without warning, nearly dragging me from the saddle. The horse whinnied and I clutched at mane and pommel and leaned far over. Even the Indian seemed to sway in the unexpected blast. Streamers of yellow moss ran over the ground and a dead tree cracked and splintered. This was not the swirling wind of Ushuaia, but a straight shot from beyond the shoulder of the world, hauling the clouds behind it.

Clinging tightly to the horse, I faced into the wind. I caught my breath. I was looking out beyond those last rocks that stumbled from the edge of the land and sank beneath the towering walls of clouds, looking over the edge of the earth. For an instant the view was clear, and then the rain whipped in and the mists blanketed the sea. It was, in the lapse of seconds, black night.

Even the Indian yielded to this storm. He turned the horses back to the treeline and dismounted in the scant shelter of a rock castle, towers and pillars and spires of ancient stone, stroked smooth on the southern side and harbouring tenacious moss on the north. The horses stood quietly, facing the rocks, their tails rippling as the wind curved around behind, while he unburdened them of their packs. This, obviously, was to be our home for the night, or the duration of the storm. I didn't know which; I didn't know if the Indian had intended to stop or if the storm had brought about the decision, and didn't care about the reason, so long as we had halted. I could scarcely slide from the saddle, every joint was stiffened and I ached through the length of my bones, as though the very marrow had petrified.

I unsaddled the horse and unpacked my sleeping bag and groundsheet, going through the motions mechanically. I hobbled the horse and put the feeding bag on as Graham had demonstrated, feeling hollow with hunger myself but much too weary to make the effort of eating. The horse shuffled off to join the others, dark outlines against the trees, grouped together. The Indian was wrapped in a blanket, lying close to the base of the rocks. I could barely see him. The end of his blanket was lifting as the wind tried to find us, curling around the edges and lashing through the columns, and then hurtling on to vent its fury in the trees.

I slid into the warmth of the sleeping bag, too numb to feel the hard ground under me, and looked up at the raging sky. Darts of rain stabbed my eyes and I turned toward the rocks. I thought for a moment of Susan, of the comfort of being with her in her flat, and decided I was mad to be here, as I drifted into sleep.

Some sound awakened me.

It was early and bright. The world was fresh and clean, and the wind had risen up above the clouds again. I sat up, all my muscles objecting, and saw that the Indian was already arranging the packs. I wondered if he would have ridden off and left me sleeping, and felt certain he would have, through indifference rather than maliciousness.

It was agony to slide from the sleeping bag, and I recalled my thoughts of the morning before—that I didn't object to genuinely earned discomfort—and decided that this principle could be taken too far. But necessity forced me on.

My horse stood patiently while I saddled him and removed the hobble. The Indian was already moving off through the broken trees as I painfully hauled myself into the saddle. My stomach muscles ached and my thighs throbbed as they gripped. I doubted that I could last through another day like the last, and yet there was no choice now. I couldn't turn back and I couldn't go on at my own pace. I had to follow the Indian at whatever speed he travelled, and pray we found Hodson before I collapsed.

Strangely enough, however, this second day was not so bad once it had started. We were descending now, and this threw new muscles and balance into use, fulcruming against the grain of the old stress, but my body was deadened and the pain was a dull constant which could be ignored. The muscles, being used, did not stiffen. I found it easier to keep my balance without conscious effort, and was able to eat dried meat and chocolate from my pack without slowing or faltering. Perhaps we travelled at a lesser pace, as well, for the horses must have been feeling the efforts of the long day before. Only the Indian seemed incapable of fatigue, and he was wise enough not to push the animals beyond their endurance.

At first I kept my mind from my discomfort by observing the landscape, and after a while my thoughts turned inward and dwelt on any number of unrelated subjects. When I came back to reality from these wanderings, I was surprised to discover how well my body was standing up to the rigours of the journey—far better than I would have thought myself capable of when I lurched painfully into the saddle that morning. There was a touch of pride and self-respect in this, and there might have been vanity as well, but for the example of the Indian riding on before me, relentless and enduring, and looking at him I felt that it was only luck that kept me going.

I had no idea how far we'd travelled when, in the late afternoon, we came to Hodson's.

VI

We came around a fold in the hills and Hodson's house was below us, in the basin of a narrow, converging valley. The sun was in the west. It lighted the surrounding hilltops but hadn't slanted down the valley, and the house was shrouded in gloom. It was a bleak structure, rough grey wooden walls and a corrugated iron roof, protected from the wind by the shoulders of land that rose on three sides and a sheer rock face towering behind.

I was surprised. I'd expected something more, or something less—either a rough field camp or a civilized home, perhaps even a laboratory. But this was a crude, makeshift building, sturdy enough but poorly finished. Still, it fitted in with what I knew of Hodson. He wasn't a man who needed or wanted the fringes and frills of modern convenience; perhaps, with no income I knew of and only his limited personal funds, he could afford nothing else.

We followed a hard dirt track down the incline, where two rises rolled together. As the angle of vision changed, I noticed that the house seemed connected with the rock face behind—not leaning against it for support, but actually protruding from the rock, making use of some natural crevice or cave.

We had reached the bottom of the descent and turned toward the house when a figure emerged and stood by the door, watching our progress. A stocky man, solid on wide-spread legs. I recognized Hubert Hodson, from photographs taken a generation before, a little heavier, a little greyer, but the same man, sturdy and imposing in woollen shirt and heavy boots. His face was windburnt and tanned, and his brow was as corrugated as the roof above him. He was watching me, and he didn't seem pleased.

We halted in front of the house and the Indian slid from his horse. I nodded to Hodson. He nodded back and turned to the Indian, his hands moving rapidly. The Indian replied in the same fashion, and glanced towards me. I believe it was the first time he'd actually looked at me. Hodson made a final, terminating gesture, and walked over to stand beside my horse. His shirt was open halfway down, his chest hard and matted with hair. He looked more like a lumberjack than a scientist, and his obvious strength would have impressed me, had such feelings not been overwhelmed by observing the giant Indian.

"You wanted to see me?" he asked.

The Indian had apparently understood that much.

"Yes, very much."

Hodson grunted. "Well, you had better come in. Leave your horse, the Indian will take care of it." I thought it curious that he referred to his servant that way, instead of by name. I dismounted and handed the reins to the man, and he led the horses around the side of the house. Hodson had gone to the door and I followed. He'd started to enter the house, then stepped back to let me go through first, a perfunctory politeness that seemed to show a determination to keep our meeting on a formal basis. Courtesy had never been associated with Hubert Hodson.

"I saw you coming," he said. "Thought you'd most likely been lost in the mountains. A mistaken idea, obviously. Always been a fault of mine, leaping to the hasty conclusion. Well, I'm usually right, anyway."

The interior was as bleak as the outside. We stood in a barren room with home-made furnishings and bare walls, one small window throwing insufficient light. Two doorways led out at the other side, hung with curtains of strung beads. There was one battered leather chair, the sole acquiescence to comfort.

"Who are you?"

"Brookes. Arthur Brookes."

"You know who I am," he said. He held his hand out, another surface politeness. His grip was unconsciously powerful. "Afraid I can't offer you much hospitality here. Have a seat."

I sat on a straight backed chair that wobbled on uneven legs.

"This is luxury after a night in those mountains."

"Perhaps."

"Your servant sets an inexorable pace. A remarkable man. I don't know his name—"

"I call him the Indian. I expect you did, too. Mentally, I mean. Anyway, he can't speak so there's little sense in giving him a name. Always better to classify than denominate. Avoid familiarity. Once you label a thing you begin to think you know what it is. Clouds the issue. Trouble with society, they designate instead of indicating. Give everything a name whether it's necessary or not. Etiquette. Confusion. Nonsense. But I expect I'd better give you a drink, for all that."

This brisk monologue pleased me. I saw he was still the same Hodson I'd been given to expect, the same iconoclast and rebel, and that seemed to indicate that he would still be carrying on with his work—and furthermore, that he might be willing to talk about it. That was a paradox in Hodson. He denied society and civilization, and yet burned with the need to express his ideas to his fellow men, needing the objects that he scorned.

"I've some brandy. Not much. Plenty of the local stuff, if you can take it."

"That will be fine."

Hodson clapped his hands loudly. He was watching me with an expectant expression. A movement caught my eye at the back of the room and I glanced that way. I saw a young woman come through one of the beaded curtains, started to look away and then found myself staring at her. She was coming towards us, and she was absolutely splendid.

I don't believe I've ever seen such a magnificent physical specimen, and there was little cause to doubt my perception because she was wearing no clothing whatsoever. Hodson looked at me and I looked at the girl. She was tall and lithe, her flesh burnished copper and her hair so black that it reflected no highlights at all, an absence of all colour. She smiled at me inquisitively, flashing teeth in a wide mouth and eyes as dark as her hair. It is extremely difficult to manage a polite smile of greeting in such circumstances, and Hodson was amused at my effort.

"This is Anna," he said.

I didn't know what to do.

"Anna speaks English. Anna, this is Mister Brookes. He has come to visit us."

"How do you do, Mister Brookes," she said. She held her hand out. Her English was flawless, her handshake correct if somewhat disturbing. "It is very nice to have a guest. I don't think we have had a guest before?" She looked at Hodson.

"Bring Mister Brookes a drink, my dear."

"Oh yes. Of course."

She smiled again as she turned away, her firm breasts in profile for an instant, and her buttocks inverted valentines rolling tautly together as she walked away. She left the same way she'd entered, moving through the beads with supple grace, not the acquired poise of a woman but the natural rhythm of some feline animal.

Hodson waited for me to comment.

"A charming young lady," I said.

"A trifle disconcerting, I suppose?"

"I must confess I was a bit taken aback. By her symmetry, of course, not her nakedness."

Hodson laughed.

"I wondered how you would—but no matter."

I felt I'd passed some examination, although I wasn't sure how he'd graded my reactions.

"She is an Indian?"

"Yes. Not a local, of course. From the Amazon. I found her there when she was just a baby—must be fifteen years ago or more. Bought her on a whim of the moment."

"Bought her?"

"Of course. What else? Surely you didn't think I stole her? Or does the idea of purchasing a human being offend your morality?"

I didn't like that.

"My morality is unequivocally subjective. But I notice you've given her a name. Unlike the Indian. Would that be significant, in any way?"

Hodson frowned and then grinned.

"It was necessary to the experiment. I had to give her an identity, in order to see how it developed. But, I must admit, it would be rather difficult to refer to Anna as, say, the subject under observation. Some matters defy even my principles."

Anna returned with two glasses, gave us each one and left the room again. Hodson pulled a chair over and sat facing me, balanced on the edge as though the interview would not be lasting very long.

"Now then. Why have you come here, Brookes?"

"I'm from the museum. You know Smyth, I believe. He sent me to find you."

"Smyth?" His face was blank for a moment. "Yes, I know Smyth. One of the more sensible men. Knows better than to scoff without comprehension. But why did he send you here?"

I took my cigarette case out and offered Hodson one. He declined. I wondered if a direct approach would be best. Hodson would certainly resent anything else; would slice through any oblique references with his sharp perception. It had to be direct. I lighted a cigarette and proceeded to tell him about the reports and Smyth's deductions. He listened with interest, hands resting over his knees, eyes shifting as though they reflected the thoughts behind them.

"And so I'm here," I said.

Hodson leaned back then, crossing his legs. "Well, I hardly started these rumours," he said. "I don't see any connection with my work."

"Just an idea of Smyth's."

"An erroneous idea."

"Surely you've heard these rumours yourself?"

"No reason to make that assumption. I am, as you can see, completely isolated here. My only contact with the world is through the Indian."

"Well, you've heard them now."

"What you've told me, yes."

"Don't they interest you?"

"Unfounded and fantastic."

"I thought so. Smyth didn't. And now that I've spoken with these people . . ."

He waved a hand.

"Genetics is my line. This wouldn't concern me, even if it were possible."

"Yes, I know your work. Tell me, what has kept you here for twenty years?"

"That same work. Research. Paper work, mostly. Some experimentation. I have a laboratory here, crude but sufficient. I stay here for the isolation and lack of distraction, no more. You were mistaken to assume that my research had any connection with the area in which I chose to pursue it." He drained his glass.

"You see, Brookes, I have the unfortunate trait of optimism. I overestimate my fellow man constantly. When I am surrounded by other men, I invariably try to give them the benefit of my work. It's disrupting, takes time and proves less than useless. That's why I'm here, alone, where my progress can continue peacefully and steadily. It's going well. You are, in point of fact, the first distraction I've suffered in years."

"I'm sorry if—"

He waved the apology away.

"I understand your interest," he said. "I've observed these people. Anna, for instance, is a fascinating study. One of the few people in the world who is completely natural and unspoiled. Been kept from the degrading influence of society. Not necessarily modern society, either. All society corrupts. If I hadn't bought her she'd be ruined already, filled with superstitions and legends and taboos and inhibitions. Sometimes I actually believe that the so-called primitive man is more degraded than civilized man; more governed by superstructure. She came from a savage tribe and has become a superb woman, both physically and emotionally. Her nakedness, for instance. She is as immune to the elements as she is to shame, as innocent of the wiles of a modern world as she is the sacrifices and bloody religion of her parents. If I had met a woman like Anna when I was a young man, Brookes, I might have—oh well, I suppose I was born a misogynist."

Hodson was becoming excited. He was a talker, denied the opportunity for twenty years, and although he might not have wanted to, he was talking.

"Or the Indian," he said. "The intellect and the instincts of an animal, and yet I have his total devotion and loyalty—not an acquired trait, like patriotism, hammered into the young by conditioning, but a natural loyalty such as a dog gives to his master. It doesn't matter if the master is kind or cruel, good or bad. That is irrelevant. A most interesting aspect of natural man."

"Then you are studying these people?" I said.

"What?" Hodson blinked. His face was flushed beneath the weathered skin. "No, not studying. A sideline. One can't help observing. It has nothing to do with my work."

"Will you tell me about that work?"

"No," he said. "I am not ready yet. Soon, perhaps. It's a new field, Brookes. Unrelated to the study of primitive peoples. I leave that to the social anthropologists, to the do-gooders and the missionaries. To you if you like. You're welcome to them."

"And these rumours?"

"I may have heard something. Perhaps an aborigine or two just trying to live their own lives. They'd be enough to shock anyone who saw them, and of course no one has ever told them it's wicked to kill sheep."

"That, too, would be of immense interest."

"Not to me."

"You surprise me."

"Do I? That's why I'm here, alone. Because I surprise people. But I have nothing for you, Brookes."

He waved towards the window. The sun was coming in now, as it settled into the western junction of the hills, blocking a shallow parallelogram on the floor.

"You may seek your wild man out there. But you'll find no clues here."

And that positive statement ended the initial phase of our conversation. We sat in uncomfortable silence for a time. I felt a sense of futility and annoyance that, after waiting so impatiently in Ushuaia and then undertaking that arduous trek through the mountains, it had all come to nothing. I blamed myself for expecting more than I reasonably should have, and felt irritated at Hodson, even while I admitted his right to resent my visit. Vexation does not depend on justice.

Hodson seemed to be pondering something that didn't concern me or, more likely, something he didn't wish me to be concerned with. My presence both pleased and disturbed him, and he seemed undecided whether to treat me as the conversational companion he'd been without for so long, or the disturbance he wished to avoid. I felt it best to refrain from intruding on his thoughts, and sat quietly watching the dust dance in the oblong of light beneath the window.

Presently he clapped his hands again. Anna must have expected this, for she appeared instantly with fresh drinks, flashing that searching smile at me, undoubtedly puzzled at my visit and, I think, enjoying the change in daily routine. She moved off reluctantly, looking back over her shoulder with interest that was innocent, because she'd never learned that it wasn't.

Hodson began to talk again. His mood had changed during those minutes of silence, and he wasn't expounding now. It became a mutual conversation. We talked in general terms, and Hodson was interested to hear of some of the latest theories which hadn't yet reached him here, although he expressed no opinions and no desire to go into them in depth. I referred to some of his own earlier work in this context, and he seemed pleased that I knew it, but passed that same work off as misguided and outdated. This turn of the conversation came naturally, and brought us back to his present work, from a new angle, and he had lost his reticence now.

"For the past twenty years or more," he said, "I have been mainly concerned with the replication processes of the nucleic acids. I believe—I know, in fact—that my work has progressed far beyond anything else done in this line. This is not conjecture. I have actually completed experiments which prove my theories. They are immutable laws."

He shot a quick glance at me, judging reactions with his old desire to shock.

"All I require now is time," he continued. "Time to apply my findings. There is no way to accelerate the application without affecting the results, of course. Another year or two and my initial application will be completed. After that—who knows?"

"Will you tell me something about these discoveries?"

He gave me a strange, suspicious look.

"In general terms, of course."

"Do you have any knowledge in this field?"

I wan't sure how much familiarity I should show here—how much interest would inspire him to continue without giving him reason to suspect I might be too formidable to be granted a hint of his secrets. But, in fact, my acquaintance with this branch of study was shallow. He was speaking of genetics, connected with anthropology only at the link of mutation and evolution, the point where the chains of two different sciences brushed together, invariably connected but pursuing separate paths.

I said: "Not very much. I know that nucleic acid determines and transmits inherited characteristics, of course. The name is used for either of two compounds, DNA and RNA. I believe latest thinking is that the DNA acts as a template or mould which passes the genetic code on to the RNA before it leaves the nucleus."

"That is roughly correct," Hodson said.

"Very roughly, I'm afraid."

"And what would result if the code were not transmitted correctly? If the template were bent, so to speak?"

"Mutation."

"Hmmm. Such an ugly word for such a necessary and elemental aspect of evolution. Tell me, Brookes. What causes mutation?"

I wasn't sure what line he was taking.

"Radiation can be responsible."

He made a quick gesture of dismissal.

"Forget that. What has been the cause of mutation since the beginning of life on this planet?"

"Who knows?"

"I do," he said, very simply and quietly, so that it took me a moment for it to register.

"Understand what I say, Brookes. I know how it works and why it works and what conditions are necessary for it to work. I know the chemistry of mutation. I can make it work."

I considered it. He watched me with bright eyes.

"You're telling me that you can cause mutation and predict the result beforehand?"

"Precisely."

"You aren't talking of selective breeding?"

"I am talking of an isolated reproductive act."

"But this is fantastic."

"This is truth."

His voice was soft and his eyes were hard. I saw how he was capable of inspiring such respect in Smyth. It would have been difficult to doubt him, in his presence.

"But—if you can do this—surely your work is complete—ready to be given to science?"

"The genetics are complete, yes. I can do, with a solitary organism's reproduction, what it takes generations for selective breeding to do—and do it far more accurately. But remember, I am not a geneticist. I'm an anthropologist. I have always maintained that the study of man's evolution could only be made properly through genetics—that basically it is a laboratory science. Now I have proved that, and I demand the right to apply my findings to my chosen field before giving them to the self-immured minds of the world. A selfish attitude, perhaps. But my attitude, nonetheless."

I said nothing, although he seemed to be awaiting my comments. I was considering what he'd told me, and trying to judge the truth of the statements and his purpose in revealing them, knowing his tendency to jump to conclusions and cause a deliberate sensation. And Hodson was peering at me, perhaps judging me in his own way, balancing my comprehension and my credulity.

I don't know which way his judgement went but, at any rate, he stood up suddenly and impulsively.

"Would you like to see my laboratory?" he asked.

"I would."

"Come on, then."

I followed his broad back to the far end of the room. The beaded curtains moved, almost as though someone had been standing behind them and moved away at our approach, but there was no one there when we pushed through. The room beyond was narrow and dark, and opened into a third room which was also separated by curtains instead of a door. The house was larger than it appeared from without. At the back of this third room there was a wooden door. It was bolted but not locked. Hodson drew the bolt and when he opened the door I saw why the house had appeared to project from the cliff behind. It was the simplest, if not the most obvious, reason. It actually did. We stepped from the room into a cave of naked rock. The house, at this part, at least, had no back wall and the iron roof extended a foot or two under the roof of the cave, fitting snugly against it.

"One of the reasons I chose this location," Hodson said. "It was convenient to make use of the natural resources in constructing a building in this remote area. If the house were to collapse, my laboratory would still be secure."

He took an electric torch from a wall holder and flooded the light before us. The passage was narrow and angular, a crack more than a cave, tapering at a rough point above our heads. The stone was damp and slimy with moss in the wash of light, and the air was heavy with decay. Hodson pointed the light on to the uneven floor and I followed him some ten yards along this aperture until it suddenly widened out on both sides. Hodson moved off and a moment later the place was lighted and a generator hummed. I looked in amazement at Hodson's extraordinary laboratory.

It was completely out of context, the contrast between chamber and contents startling. The room was no more than a natural vault in the rocks, an oval space with bare stone walls and arched roof, untouched and unchanged but for the stringing of lights at regular distances, so that the lighting was equal throughout this catacomb. There was no proper entranceway to the room, the narrow crevice through which we had passed simply widened out abruptly, forming a subterranean apartment carved from the mountain by some ancient upheaval of the earth. But in the centre of this cave had been established a modern and, as far as I could see, well-equipped, laboratory. The furnishings appeared much sturdier and more stable than those of the house, and on the various tables and cabinets were racks of test tubes and flasks and beakers of assorted shapes and sizes, empty and filled to various degrees. Files and folders were stacked here and there, just cluttered enough to suggest an efficient busyness. At the far side of the room there was a door fitted into the rock, the only alteration that seemed to have been made to the natural structure of the cave.

Hodson gestured with an open hand.

"This is where I work," he said. "The accumulation of years. I assure you this laboratory is as well equipped as any in the world, within the range of my work. Everything I need is here—all the equipment, plus the time."

He walked to the nearest table and lifted a test-tube. Some blood-red fluid caught a sluggish reflection within the glass and he held it up toward me like a beacon—a lighthouse of a man.

"The key to mankind," he said. His voice was impressive, the dark fluid shifted hypnotically. "The key to evolution is buried not in some Egyptian excavation, not in the remnants of ancient bones and fossils. The key to man lies within man, and here is where the locksmith will cut that key, and unlock that distant door."

His voice echoed from the bare rock. I found it difficult to turn my eyes from the test-tube. A genius he may well have been, but he definitely had a flair for presenting his belief. I understood the furore and antagonism he had aroused, more by his manner than his theories.

I looked around a bit, not understanding much of what I saw, wanting to read his notes and calculations but fairly certain he would object to that. Hodson had moved back to the entrance, impatient to leave now that I'd seen the laboratory, not wanting me to see beyond a surface impression.

I paused at the door on the opposite side of the chamber. I had thought it wooden, but closer observation showed it to be metal, painted a dull green.

"More equipment beyond?" I asked.

I turned the handle. It was locked.

"Just a storeroom," Hodson said. "There's nothing of interest there. Come along. Dinner will be ready by now."

It was curious, certainly, that a storeroom should be securely locked when the laboratory itself had no door, and when the entrance to the passageway was secured only by a key which hung readily available beside the door. But I didn't think it the proper time to comment on this. I followed Hodson back through the tunnel to the house.

A table had been set in the front room, where the initial conversation had taken place, and Anna served the food and then sat with us. The Indian was not present. Anna was still quite naked, and somehow this had ceased to be distracting. Her manner was so natural that even the absurd motions of placing her napkin over her bare thighs did not seem out of place; the paradox of the social graces and her natural state did not clash. The meal was foreign to me, spicy and aromatic with perhaps a hint of walnut flavouring. I asked Anna if she had prepared it, and she smiled artlessly and said she had, pleased when I complimented her and showing that modesty, false or otherwise, is a learned characteristic. Hodson was preoccupied with his thoughts again, eating quickly and without attention, and I chatted with Anna. She was completely charming. She knew virtually nothing outside the bounds of her existence in this isolated place, but this lack of knowledge was simple and beautiful. I understood full well what Hodson had meant when he'd suggested that, had he met a woman like this when he was young—was surprised to find my own thoughts moving along a similar line, thinking that if I had not met Susan—

I forced such thoughts to dissolve.

When the meal was finished, Anna began to clear the table.

"May I help?" I asked.

She looked blank.

"Why no, this is the work of the woman," she said, and I wondered what pattern or code Hodson had followed in educating her, what course halfway between the natural and the artificial he had chosen as the best of both worlds, and whether convenience or emotion or ratiocination had guided him in that selection.

When the table had been cleared, Anna brought coffee and brandy and a humidor of excellent Havana cigars, set them before us and departed, a set routine that Hodson obviously kept to, despite his avowed denials of social custom and mores. It was like a dinner in a London drawing-room, magically transferred to this crude home, and seeming if anything more graceful for the transference. I felt peaceful and relaxed. The cigar smoke hung above us and the brandy lingered warmly within. I would have liked to carry on the conversation with this intriguing man, but he quite suddenly shifted the mood.

He regarded me over the rim of his brandy glass, and said, "Well, now that you see I have no connection with these rumours, you'll be impatient to get away and pursue your investigations along other lines, I assume."

His tone left no doubts as to which of us was anxious for my departure. Now that his exuberance had been satisfied, he was disturbed again—a man of changing moods, fervour followed by depression—feeling, perhaps, that he'd once more fallen victim to his old fault, the paradox of talking too much and too soon, and regretting it directly after.

He looked at his watch.

"You'll have to stay the night, of course," he said. "Will you be able to find your way back?"

"I'm afraid not. I hate to be a bother, but—"

"Yes. Ah well, perhaps it's for the better. At least my location remains a secret. I mean no personal offence, but already you disrupt my work. The Indian assists me in certain ways and now he must take the time to guide you back through the mountains. I'll know better than to make that mistake again, however. It should have occurred to me before that I must instruct him to return alone from Ushuaia." He smiled. "I can think of few men who would disagree with the Indian, if it came to that."

He said all this with no trace of personal ill will, as if discussing someone not present, and I could take no exception to his tone, although the words were harsh.

"The Indian may well be one of the most powerful men alive," he said. "I've seen him do things, feats of strength, that defy belief

... all the more so in that it never occurs to him how remarkable these actions are. He's saved my life on three separate occasions, at great danger to himself and without hesitation. Have you noticed the scar on his side?"

"I did, yes."

"He suffered that in rescuing me."

"In what manner?"

Hodson frowned briefly, perhaps because he was recalling an unpleasant situation.

"It happened in the Amazon. I was attacked by a cat—a jaguar. He came to my assistance at the last possible moment. I don't fear death, but I should hate to die before my work is completed."

"I'd wondered about that scar. A jaguar, you say? Was the wound inflicted by fangs or claws?"

"I don't—it was a bit hectic, as you can well imagine. A blow of the front paw, I believe. But that was some time ago. Amazing to think that the Indian hasn't changed at all. He seems ageless. Invulnerable and invaluable to me, in such help that requires strength and endurance. He can go days without sleep or food under the most exhausting conditions."

"I learned that well enough."

"And you'll undoubtedly learn it again tomorrow," he said, with a smile, and poured more brandy.

We talked for the rest of the evening, but I could not lead him back to his work, and it was still quite early when he suggested that we retire, mentioned once more that I would want to get an early start in the morning. I could hardly disagree, and he clapped for Anna to show me to my room. He was still seated at the table when I followed her through one of the curtained doors at the back and on to the small cell where I was to spend the night. It was a narrow room with a cot along one wall and no other furnishings. There was no electricity and Anna lighted a candle and began to make the cot into a bed. This was disrupting again, not at all like the natural acceptance I'd felt at dinner, seeing her naked by candlelight, bending over a bed. The soft illumination played over the copper tones of her flesh, holding my eyes on the shifting shadows as they secreted and then moved on to reveal and highlight her body. She moved. The shadows flowed and her flesh rippled. Her firm breasts hung down like fruit ripe for the plucking, tempting and succulent. I had to tell myself that it would be a wicked thing to take advantage of her innocence, and think very firmly of Susan, waiting for me in London. I think man is naturally polygamous, although I don't know if this is necessarily a bad thing, and it took great resolution to force my thoughts away from the obvious.

She straightened, smiling. The bed was ready.

"Will you require anything else?" she asked.

"Nothing, thank you."

She nodded and left, and the room was stark and harsh with her departure.

I crawled into my crude bed.

I didn't sleep well.

It was still early and, although my body ached and protested from the rigours of the trek, my mind was active and alert. The thought of starting out again early in the morning was unpleasant, and I felt that very little had been accomplished by my efforts. Perhaps Hodson would tell the Indian to set a more leisurely pace, but I couldn't very well suggest this after he'd already mentioned how inconvenient it would be to have the Indian wasting time as my guide. It was a distasteful thought, added to the futility of the journey.

Presently I began to drift towards sleep, my body overruling my mind and drawing me into a state of half-consciousness, half thinking and half dreaming. A vision of Susan occupied my mind and then, as the dreams became more powerful than the thoughts and my subconscious mind rejected the restrictions of my will, it became a vision of the splendid Anna which I was unable or unwilling to reject. I yielded to this night-time prowling of the id, the transformation of thought to dream.

I was asleep.

I awoke in instant terror . . .

The sound awakened me.

There was no gradual surfacing from slumber, I was fully conscious in that instant, and I knew it was no dream . . . knew, even in that first moment, what the sound had been. Gregorio's haunted words flashed back to me—a sound like no man has ever heard—and I knew that this was that sound.

It was a cry, a deep rolling bellow, quavering at the end, a sound that only vocal cords could have made, but that no vocal cords I'd ever heard could possibly have made. It was indescribable and unforgettable, the howl of a creature in torment.

I lay, trembling and staring at the dark ceiling. The candle was out, and my fear was blacker than the room. It seemed impossible that a sound, any sound, could have rendered me helpless, and yet I was petrified. I've always considered myself as brave as the next man, but this sensation was far beyond human courage—beyond human conception. I wanted desperately to stay where I was, motionless and silent in the dark, but I knew I would never forgive such cowardice, and I forced myself to move, inch by agonizing inch, as though my bones grated harshly together.

My cigarette case and lighter were on the floor beside the cot, and I fumbled for the lighter and ignited the candle. Shadows leaped against the walls and I cringed away from their threatening shapes, waiting for reality to form. It was some seconds before I managed to stand up and pull my clothing over the ice and sweat of my skin. Then, holding the candle before me like a talisman to ward off evil, I moved to the door and pushed through the curtains.

The house was too quiet.

Surely no one could have slept through that sound, and yet there was no stir of awakening. It was as if everyone had been awake beforehand and anticipated the noise. It had been very near, loud and vibrating, as though echoing from close confines, and I thought of the cave behind the house; felt strangely certain the sound had come from there; moved quietly down the corridor to the front room and then through the second passage that led toward the cavern entrance. Although the sound was not repeated, the silence was terrifying in its own way, a silence formed from that sound or an effect of the sound. I was stiff with dread, my backbone tingling and my flesh rippling until it seemed that snakelike, I was trying to shed my skin. If all fear is emotional, this fear was primordial, linked more to instinct than conscious knowledge of danger. I wanted to locate the source of the sound, but the dread was far deeper than any conception of what I might find, a repulsion that lurked secretly within me in some atavistic remnants of the past, some hideous racial memory awakened.

I forced myself forwards, through the second room. The door opening within the cave was open, and the tunnel beyond was dark. Light showed at the end, where it widened into the chamber, but it failed to penetrate the passage, and stepping into the darkness was like plunging into cold liquid qualms of panic. I don't know what resolution drove me forwards, what reserves of willpower summoned the mechanical motions of advancing, but I held the candle before me and walked into the corridor.

The pale light circled before me, floating over the contorted rocks in evil designs, and wavering on to meet the electric light at the far end, fading against the great brilliance and recoiling over the stoves, over a bundle of rags that blocked my path.

Rags that moved.

I would have screamed, had my throat worked, but I was frozen into motionless silence as the rags shifted and took shape, and I found myself staring into a face, a face twisted and wrinkled and human, swathed in filthy shards, the eyes gleaming under the dark shelf of overhanging brow. It was a woman, ancient and bent and deformed. She had been coming toward me. Now she stopped and spread her arms wide, barring the way like some loathsome crucifix, the rags hanging from her elbows in folds that seemed part of her body, some membrane attaching her arms to her flanks.

She hissed, an exclamation, perhaps a word in some unknown language, rocking from side to side on crooked haunches, and another form loomed up behind her, brushed her aside and advanced on me. My heart stopped, then burst with a surge of blood that rocked my brain. I dropped the candle, and saw the Indian in the light that shot up from the floor, nostrils flaring and cheekbones casting oval shadows in the sockets of his eyes. His hand closed on my shoulder, the strength unbelievable, as if those terrible fingers could have closed effortlessly through my bones. I fully expected to die at that moment.

The grip relaxed then. I was dimly aware that Hodson had shouted something from the laboratory; I heard a dull clang as the metal door beyond was closed. Then the Indian had turned me and was pushing me before him, back the way I'd come. I offered no resistance, and he was not unduly rough, although those hands could never be gentle. He walked behind me until we were back

at my room, then pointed at the bed with all four fingers extended
and stood in the doorway, bending beneath the frame, until I had
crawled cringing on to the cot. When I turned he had left, the
beaded curtains whispered his departure, and I collapsed in a limp
reaction which it causes me no shame to recall.

It was some time before my mind was released from the emotions, and I was able to think. Then my thoughts came tumbling
in disorder. What had caused that sound? What had taken place in
the room beyond the laboratory? Who had the ancient crone been,
what was her function, what would the Indian have done to me
if Hodson had not shouted? Where was Anna? How on earth did
this household fit together, what purpose did the members fulfil
in whatever monstrous scheme was being conducted? I found no
answers, and I don't suppose that I wanted those answers, that I
was prepared to have such terrible knowledge etched on my mind,
with my shoulder still burning from the dreadful clutch of the giant
Indian, and that ghastly cry still vibrating in my memory.

Anna came to my room in the morning.

She acted as if nothing unusual had happened in the night, and
told me that breakfast was ready. I was still dressed, the sweat dried
on my clothing, but she didn't notice this, or comment on it. I got
up immediately and followed her to the front room, where Hodson
was already seated at the table. He looked tired and drawn. I sat
opposite him.

"Sleep well?" he asked.

I said nothing. Anna poured coffee from an earthenware jug.
Hodson's hands were steady enough as he drank.

"I found myself unable to sleep," he said, casually. "I often get up
in the middle of the night and do some work."

"Work? What work?"

"I beg your pardon?" he said. His annoyance and surprise at my
tone seemed genuine.

"What on earth caused that cry in the night?"

Hodson pondered for a few moments, probably not deciding
what to tell me as much as whether he should answer at all, rather
to satisfy my curiosity or castigate my impertinence.

"Oh, you mean just before you came to the laboratory?"

"Obviously."

"I wondered what brought you prowling about."

"And I wonder what caused that sound?"

"I heard it," he said. "Yes, now that I think of it, it's small wonder you should be curious. But it was merely the wind, you know. You've heard how it howls higher up in the mountains? Well, occasionally a blast finds a crevice in the rocks and comes down through the cave. It startled me the first time I heard it, too. I was tempted to find the fissure and have it sealed, but of course it's necessary for proper ventilation. Otherwise the laboratory would be as rank as the tunnel, you see."

"That was no wind."

"No wind you've ever heard before, Brookes. But this is a strange place, and that wind came from beyond where man has ever ventured."

I felt a slight doubt begin. I'd been positive before, but it was just possible that Hodson was telling the truth. I had noticed that the air in the laboratory was fresh, and couldn't doubt there were actually openings in the rock. But the doubt remained slight, with the sound still recent in my memory.

"I'm sorry if the Indian alarmed you," Hodson was saying. "I've instructed him never to allow anyone in the laboratory without me, you understand. He was just performing his duties."

"If you hadn't shouted—"

Hodson paused, his cup before his face.

"Would he have killed me?" I asked.

"For a scientist, you have a vivid imagination," he said. He shipped from the cup. "I'm no Frankenstein, you know. No mad scientist from a bad cinema film. Although, I must say, the mad scientists generally seem misunderstood by the clottish populace."

"Who was the old woman?"

"If it's any concern of yours, she's an old servant. Not actually so old, but these people age rapidly. She's past her usefulness now, but I let her stay. She has nowhere else to go. Surely you don't see evil implications in an ageing old woman, do you?"

His expression was scornful and angered me.

"Very decent of you to allow her to remain," I said. "And to supply her with such extraordinary garments."

His eyes reflected something that wasn't quite indignation.

"My affairs are my affairs," he said. "It's time for you to go, I believe. The Indian has your horse ready and is waiting for you."

At the door, I said, "I'm sorry for troubling you."

Hodson shrugged. Anna was standing beside him.

"No matter," he said. "Perhaps it did me good to talk with someone. And good luck with your investigations."

"Good-bye," Anna said.

We shook hands solemnly, as she must have thought a parting required. She remained in the doorway after Hodson had gone back inside. The Indian had led the horses around to the front of the house, and I saw they were both nervous, stamping and shying. When I placed my foot in the stirrup, my mount sidestepped away and I had to hop after him on one foot, holding mane and cantel, before I was able to get into the saddle. The horse had been very placid before. The Indian slipped on to his own horse and led the way up the track. I looked back and waved to Anna. She raised a hand rather timidly, possibly not acquainted with this gesture of farewell. Then she vanished into the house.

Well, that is that, I thought, as we wound up the track from the narrow valley. But I noticed one more thing. On the incline to the north a prominence of shrub jutted down toward the basin, and as we drew above it I saw that a strip, perhaps a yard wide, seemed to be broken and flattened, running from the top of the hill nearly to the apex of this growth, and where the strip ended some loose brush and limbs seemed to be stacked in a small mound, as if concealing something. A vague form, greyish in colour, was just visible through this tangled pile. It appeared that something had been dragged down from the rim of the hill and hastily covered. I couldn't quite make out what it was. As we reached the top of the trail, and the land levelled out before us, I saw two dark shapes circling and starting a cautious descent, thick necks poised attentively, lowering their sharp beaks below arched wings. These repulsive carrion eaters sank slowly down towards the northern slope, and then the land shouldered up and I could see no more.

VII

I must have looked in fine shape indeed, judging from Graham's expression when I halted the horse in front of his store, filthy and unshaven and brittle with exhaustion. I expect I looked no worse than I felt. The pace of the return journey had not been noticeably less than the first, and had followed too soon to allow my body to harden from that initial exertion. And that incredible Indian hadn't even paused before turning back. When finally we reached the hardened beginnings of the trail that led through the tablelands to Ushuaia, he'd pointed in that curious, four-fingered fashion, turned his horse sharply, and headed back into the hills.

Graham helped me to dismount.

"All right?" he asked.

"Yes. Just stiff and tired."

"You look like a wounded bandit who's been running in front of a posse for a week," he said.

I managed a smile, feeling the dirt crack along the creases of my face.

"Didn't expect you back so soon," he said. He looped the reins over the post and we went into the building.

"Neither did I. I wasn't particularly welcome at Hodson's, I'm afraid."

Graham frowned. Inhospitality is virtually unknown in frontier territories. He said, "I always thought there was something queer about Hodson. What's he doing out there?"

"I honestly don't know."

I began pacing back and forth over the wooden floor, loosening my muscles. The knots were firm. Graham called the boy to take my horse back to the stables.

"How far did you go?"

"God knows. How fast can a horse travel in those hills? We must have been actually riding more than twenty-four hours."

"Yeah, that's right. God knows. But I'll bet that Indian covered the greatest possible distance in the time. It's amazing how these people find the shortest routes. Can't understand that Hodson, though."

He reached behind the counter and came up with a bottle; he handed it to me and I drank from the neck. It was brandy, and it felt very good.

"Well, what now?" he asked.

"I don't know. First thing, I want to crawl into a hot bath. Then I'm going to sleep through until morning. I can't make any decisions in this state."

"Good judge," he said.

I thanked him for his help, told him I would see him the next day after deciding what further supplies or assistance I might need, and limped back to the hotel. The desk clerk raised a polite eyebrow when he saw the condition I was in, and I asked him to have the maid heat a bath. I think he concurred with that judgement, and he asked if I needed any help getting upstairs. I managed on my own, however, and as soon as I was in my room I stripped my grimy clothing off and put a bathrobe on, then sat down on the bed to wait for the bath to be readied. After a moment or two, I lay back and closed my eyes, just for a second.

I never heard the maid knock, and when I awoke it was morning . . .

I spent the day relaxing and writing two letters, seated at a table in the bar. Jones, despite his reluctance to follow in the paths of his fellow tourists, had succumbed to a chartered flight to Cape Horn, and there were no distractions, other than my own musings as to how he was getting along with the three widows, and an admission that I would rather have liked to see Cape Horn myself.

The first letter was to Smyth. I considered for some time before I began writing, and informed him in detail of my interviews with Gregorio and MacPherson and my visit to Hodson's, stressing, I fear, the devotion to duty which the latter entailed. I sketched the nature of Hodson's work briefly, from what the man had actually told me, and asked Smyth for his opinion of the possibilities of that, from general interest rather than in relation to my own investigations, and stressing that it was a theoretical point because Hodson would surely not welcome further concern on my part.

I mentioned the Indian and Anna in terms, respectively, of awe and admiration, and was surprised to find how greatly Anna had impressed me. My conclusion was that I considered further probing warranted, despite Hodson's avowed disinterest and lack of connection.

But I made no mention of that sound in the night.

Somehow, I found myself unable to express the feeling it had driven into me, and certainly there was no way to describe the sound itself, no comparisons whatsoever. And, now that I was back in the quiet hotel, I found myself almost willing to discount Hodson's connection with the rumours. There seemed to be no connection with his laboratory work, however advanced that might have been in its own right, and his explanation—the wind howling down the fissures—seemed reasonable enough, likely even, although it brought a chill to remember my certainty at the time. But it was far too subjective a feeling to symbolize by the written word, and I did not attempt it.

The second letter was to Susan. Before starting this, I re-read what I had written of Anna, and a sense of infidelity swept through me. I remembered how I had felt, watching her bend naked over the bed, with the candle light dancing over her flesh; how my loins had tightened with desire, and how close I had come to reaching out to her. I had never been unfaithful to Susan, and had never before felt the slightest urge or need, but there in the confines of that narrow cell, in that remote and forbidding land, I had struggled with an urgency so powerful—

Well. I had resisted, and I was very glad that I had, and I wrote to Susan with love.

VIII

My mind came back from that faraway place, through those eternal weeks. The waiter was taking the dishes away, concerned that we'd barely touched the food, but not mentioning it; aware that something was very wrong between us.

"Anything else, sir?" he asked, softly.

"A drink?"

"Yes. A strong drink," Susan said.

Susan had never drunk very much. I ordered large brandies, and she downed half of hers with the first swallow.

"I kept your letter," she said, as if she had somehow followed my thoughts. "The letter you wrote from Ushuaia. You still loved me when you wrote that, didn't you? Or was that a lie, too?"

"It was no lie. There is no lie, Susan. I love you now as much as then."

"Yes, whatever changed your mind must have happened after you wrote. I know there was love in that letter."

She drained the brandy.

"But I shan't ask you again."

"Another?"

"Yes," she said. She turned the empty glass in her hands. "No, never mind. I want to leave, Arthur."

"All right."

I signalled to the waiter.

"I want to leave alone, Arthur," Susan said.

"Susan. Darling—"

"Oh God. I can't stand this. I can't bear it. I'm going now."

She stood up and walked quickly towards the entrance. I pushed my chair back and started to rise, then collapsed back on to the seat. The waiter stood beside the table and Susan was getting her coat at the counter.

"The bill, sir?" the waiter asked.

I shook my head.

"No. Not yet. I'll have another brandy."

"Large, sir?"

"Yes," I said.

I'd been drinking a large brandy the day that Gregorio came into the bar at the Albatross, too. It was the second day since my return from Hodson's, and I'd sent the boy from Graham's store to fetch Gregorio, feeling that it might be to my advantage to put my proposition to him here at the hotel, rather than at his shack—to talk to him on my own ground, removed from the realities of Gregorio's life.

He stood in the doorway, beside the boy. I nodded and the boy pointed to me and went back out. Gregorio walked down the bar and stood beside me.

"Oh, it is you," he said. He didn't seem pleased. "I didn't remember the name." I had the impression that, had he remembered, he wouldn't have come.

"A drink?"

"Pisco," he said, shrugging. The barman poured the grape alcohol into a large tumbler. Gregorio was in no hurry to drink, and his feet shifted nervously.

"I've been looking for your Bestia Hombre," I said.

He nodded, expecting that. He lifted the glass.

"Pray God it doesn't look for you," he said.

"Will you help me, Gregorio?"

"I? How is that possible?"

"I'd like you to take me to the place where you saw it."

"No. I will not go there again." It was more a statement of unalterable fact than an assertion of refusal. He took his blackened pipe out and began to fill it with some exotic mixture from a rubber pouch.

"I'll pay well."

He looked balefully at me, struck a match and continued to regard me above the flame as he sucked the pipe into a haze of smoke. The contents blackened and curled above the bowl, and he pressed it back with a hardened thumb. A few shards escaped and drifted, smoking, to the floor.

"I need money," he said. "We all need money. But not to that place."

"You needn't do anything else. Just guide me there. What danger could there be?"

"Danger? Who knows? Perhaps none. But that place is ... it is not a good place. It has very bad memories. I am no longer young and no longer brave. The dog was brave."

He shrugged once more.

"Well, could you show me on a map?"

"A map?"

I thought he hadn't understood the word.

"Mapa," I said.

"Yes, I know this word. But what map? There is no map of that place. Not with detail."

"Could you make a map?"

"Of no use to you. I have lived all my life here, and I am not young. I know the land. But to make a map—what is there to show on this map? It is rocks and trees and hills. How are they different? To me, perhaps, for I know them. But on the map it is the same."

This was true, of course. It had been a thoughtless request. And, anyway, I needed a guide with me, a man who knew the land and, preferably, knew where Gregorio had seen the creature. And that was only Gregorio.

"I have already been out there," I said.

"Yes."

"I have heard the sound of the thing. Gregorio, I have heard it, and I know you told me the truth."

His eyes were wide. I wanted to shock him.

"I heard it in the dark of night," I said.

"And still you wish to find it?"

"Yes."

"You are very brave, Señor. Braver than I."

"That is because I know there will be no danger," I said. "I was frightened when I heard it, yes. But it is a living thing. It is no demon or spirit, whatever it is, it is alive, and we'll be well armed. It can't hurt us." I tried to look confident, almost nonchalant, and Gregorio seemed to weaken slightly. He took the pipe from his mouth and drank, replaced the pipe and drew, cheeks hollowed and a deep line etched between his eyebrows.

"I would have a gun, too?" he asked.

I nodded. I don't honestly know if I had intended to carry a weapon, against my principles, but I do know I was relieved that Gregorio's reluctance made it necessary.

"I would like to kill it," he said.

"Only in self defence—"

"I would very much like to avenge the dog, yes." His jaw tightened. "But the dog is dead. It would not help the dog. It is my Spanish blood that has the desire for revenge." He leaned against the bar with both hands, head down between his shoulders. His shoulder-blades were sharp beneath the canvas poncho, and his thoughts were sharp beneath his furrowed brow.

"I would be very much afraid," he said, without looking at me. The pipe bobbled in his teeth as he spoke.

"But you will show me?"

After a while he looked up.

"How much money will you pay me?" he asked.

But I knew that the money had very little to do with it.

We decided to leave in two days, which gave ample time to make preparations, and for me to recover from the physical effects of the last trek. Actually, I felt very well. I'd been exercising lightly since my return, so that my muscles hadn't stiffened much, and I felt that the exertion had hardened me sufficiently so that I didn't dread repeating the journey. Then too, this time I would be able to dictate the pace at which we travelled. Although I was eager to get to the area where Gregorio had seen the creature, I felt no need for haste now that definite arrangements were being made for departure, unlike the impatience I'd felt while waiting for Hodson's man to arrive without knowing when to expect him, when time and distance were unknown quantities. This time, we were able to plan accurately and take all the equipment and supplies necessary for a prolonged camp in the mountains.

Graham and Gregorio conferred on what we would need, and I left the decisions to them, with complete confidence in their judgements, hiring what I could and purchasing the rest according to their recommendations. For my own part, I bought only a change of clothing similar to what I'd worn on the first trek, and a pair of light sandals to alternate with the heavy boots. I'd paid so little attention to the rest that, on the night before our departure, I was surprised at the size of the pile that had accumulated.

We were taking two small Everest tents as well as sleeping bags, groundsheets and blankets for warmth and shelter; a large amount of food both for ourselves and the horses, along with cooking utensils which fitted neatly together when not in use, and a double burner Butane stove which Gregorio considered an unbelievable luxury, without disdaining it; a complete first aid kit and a spade and axe, both of which were hinged and could be folded to simplify transport and packing, and an ample supply of pisco which did treble duty as sustenance, warmth and medicine, and which I found myself growing rather fond of at a few shillings a bottle. Stacked together, these supplies made a considerable mass in one corner of Graham's storeroom, but he assured me that everything could quite easily be distributed between two pack horses and our own mounts.

He had already arranged for the hire of the pack animals and the same horse I'd ridden before, which I'd suggested, feeling confident in its reliability, and in my own ability to control it. Gregorio intended to use his own horse, the grey gelding, and I added the hire fee for one horse to what I was paying him as a guide.

Graham was dealing with a customer while I made the gesture of checking the supplies. Gregorio stood behind me.

"Well, we certainly seem to have everything we could possibly need," I said. "You've been very thorough."

Gregorio nodded, then frowned.

"What is it?"

"The guns?" he said.

I'd forgotten them, actually. I hesitated. I was afraid that Gregorio might do something rash out of hatred or fear or vengeance. But he was watching me expectantly, and I knew he couldn't be persuaded to go without a weapon. I didn't really blame him, either, and knew the idea of being able to defend ourselves would make us both feel better.

"Yes, I'll see about that now," I said.

Graham had finished with the customer, and I went over to the counter and inquired about hiring guns. Gregorio followed, as if he wanted to make sure.

"I never thought of that," Graham said. "I didn't know you'd be needing guns."

"I certainly trust we shan't."

"Well, I don't hire guns myself. All my regular customers have their own guns, and the tourists who want to do any shooting usually make arrangements through their travel companies."

Gregorio moved closer.

"There must be somewhere to hire them."

"Oh yes. But why don't you borrow a couple from Gardiner?" Possibly he resented the idea of sending me to a competitor. "Gardiner does some shooting and I know he has several spare guns. Want me to ask him?"

"I'll ask him," I said. It seemed a good idea, and I was certain he wouldn't object. "I'll go out to his place now."

Gregorio moved back towards the supplies, satisfied I was making an effort, and I went out to the street and found a taxi to take me to Gardiner's.

He seemed pleased, as usual, to have company, and gave me a drink while we discussed my trip to Hodson's and I told him a little about my plans for the second journey. When I'd finished, he asked if there was anything he could do to assist me. It was just the opening I needed, but somehow I felt rather ridiculous about the guns.

As casually as I could, I said, "I was wondering if I should take any weapons? What would you think?"

"Weapons?"

"Well, guns."

"For sport or food or protection?"

"Protection, I guess," I said, feeling foolish.

Gardiner smiled. "So you've come to believe those rumours, have you?"

"I don't know. I recognize the possibility."

He nodded thoughtfully, the smile gone.

"Might it be a good idea, anyway? There are foxes and such that might try to raid our supplies."

"A damn good idea, if you ask me," he said. "No harm in being safe. And, I must say, these rumours are a bit hair-raising, no matter what it is that's been killing Mac's sheep."

"What would you suggest I take?" I asked, feeling uncomfortable about asking a favour, and Gardiner saved me the necessity.

"I can lend you a gun, if you like," he suggested.

"I'd appreciate that, if it's no inconvenience."

"I've several spare guns. Not much to do these days but shoot, actually, and guns accumulate the same as golf clubs or tennis racquets or darts—whatever your game is, there's always a new piece of equipment that strikes your fancy. But I'm wondering what would be best for you? It's hard to decide when you have no idea what you might have to shoot." He seemed completely serious in considering this. "Shotgun or rifle, which would you prefer?"

"I'd be more comfortable with a shotgun, I think. But if you can spare two, Gregorio could carry the rifle."

"Sure. That solves that problem. Gregorio will probably be happier with a gun, too."

"Yes. He believes what he saw, whether I do or not."

Gardiner refilled our glasses and left the room; he returned in a moment with the firearms and handed me the shotgun. It was a superb gun, matched to the one hanging on the wall, hand engraved by some craftsman in Bilbao.

"Double twelve bore," he said. "Full choke on the left."

I admired the workmanship for a moment, then threw it into aim. I was roughly the same size as Gardiner and the balance suited me well.

"A splendid gun. This will do me."

"I suppose Gregorio can use this all right," he said, handing me the rifle. It was a .303 Savage, the lever action feather-weight model, light and efficient in rough, wooded country where a longer rifle might be cumbersome. "It hits hard and it's fast," Gardiner said. He looked at me gravely. I suppose he'd sensed something of my nervousness, and he was quite serious when he said, "Just in case."

"Yes. Just on the off chance, eh?"

"I'll give you cartridges and shells before you leave."

"I'll pay you, of course."

He gestured.

"On the museum, of course."

"Oh, well, all right then. Better yet, have Smyth send me half a dozen bottles of that fine brandy he keeps."

"Certainly," I said.

I'd never known that Smyth kept brandy, fine or otherwise. There were many things I didn't know.

Gregorio was sitting on the front steps at Graham's when I got out of the taxi with the guns. He nodded appreciatively and I handed him the rifle. He worked the lever a few times, then threw it to his shoulder in quick aim. I could see he'd used a rifle before. He nodded again, satisfied.

"'This is good. I will carry this?"

"That's right. But, Gregorio, you must promise me that you won't use it unless it's absolutely necessary."

"Necessary?"

"To our safety."

He smiled. His teeth flashed.

"Yes, I will promise that," he said. "But, if we find this thing, I think it will be most necessary . . ."

IX

We left early in the morning. It was raining and the dark clouds were torn by wind, strung long across the sky. Gregorio led the pack horses and I rode beside him, just stiff enough so that my muscles welcomed further exertion. Gregorio rode much the same as the Indian, although he used a saddle and boots, slumped slightly forward and relaxed. We both had our hoods pulled up against the rain and didn't speak much. I was concentrating on our route, and knew that we were following the same trail the Indian had taken from town, apparently the shortest or the only trail to the hills, such as it was. I was able to spot several landmarks I'd passed before, unusual rock formations and abnormally formed trees, the same impossible perch from which, perhaps, the same placid wild sheep observed our passage. We travelled slowly and steadily, and stopped for lunch before we'd reached the foothills; we rested for a few minutes and then pressed on again. Gregorio had lighted his pipe and the battered bowl jutted from his cowl, spluttering as the rain damped the burning mixture. The sky was dark, the weather foul. Where the low clouds were shredded by the wind darker clouds covered the gap from above. It looked as if it might rain for days.

When we reached the foothills and began to climb, everything seemed familiar, unlike the outstanding landmarks of the rising tableland, and I realized this was because everything was the same, curious and unusual formations repeated many times over until they became commonplace. I had no idea now whether we were still following the path the Indian had taken. Gregorio undoubtedly knew the land, but lacked the Indian's infallible sense of direction or familiarity, and he had to stop from time to time to get his bearings, relying on a visual knowledge which the Indian hadn't needed. We made frequent mistakes, and had to turn or backtrack, but they were not serious and our progress wasn't greatly hindered. Several times we stopped to stretch and sample the grape alcohol. The rain continued and it grew colder; the reins were slippery and the damp began to seep through my windbreaker, adding the unpleasant sensation and scent of wet wool to my discomfort. I was quite satisfied when Gregorio suggested we stop for the night, although I knew we had not made nearly as much progress as I'd made on the first day following the Indian.

We made a campfire, not bothering with the Butane stove or the tents until we'd reached a more permanent camping place, but sheltering against the rocks in our sleeping bags, talking for a while and then lapsing into silence. Gregorio's pipe glowed for a while longer and then we slept.

It was still raining in the morning. The fire was out and we had to relight it to make coffee. We ate our breakfast from tins while the horses watched with drooping ears. Progress was slower on this second day, as we climbed higher and the forest thickened around us. It was necessary to move in single file now, and I dropped to the back of the line. We had been travelling for several hours when we came to a stream. It was impossible to tell if this was the same stream I'd crossed behind the Indian, when I'd noticed that scar on his side, but if it was the same water, we had certainly come to it at a different place. The banks were shallow and we had no trouble fording it. I thought it was probably the same stream, but that we were farther to the north. On the opposite bank the land rose more sharply, and I began to anticipate reaching the top of the range— the same distance, roughly, as I'd made in the first long haul of some twelve or thirteen hours behind the Indian. But as we continued to rise higher and the land did not begin to level off, it strengthened my belief that our path lay farther north, where the mountain range extended towards the Pacific. Either that, or we were travelling much slower and more circuitously than I hoped.

In the late afternoon we came to the highest point of this slope, and the land lay below us on all sides. There were further moun-

tains to the west, hazy and unreal in the rain. I asked how far we'd
come and Gregorio told me we were more than halfway there. This
was encouraging, but inspired no great desire to press on more rapidly. We went on a few miles beyond the top, to gain the shelter of
the trees and hills, and made our second camp.

Sitting beside the fire, after dinner, Gregorio broke open the box
of cartridges and silently began to load his rifle. He put the safety
catch on but kept the gun beside him. The shotgun was in my pack,
stock and barrels separated and carefully wrapped. I felt no urge to
get it out. My foreboding had diminished, and the land no longer
seemed so wild and savage on this second trek, at a slower pace and
with a guide to whom I could speak. But I thought Gregorio might
prefer me to be armed.

"Shall I get my gun out?" I asked.

He shrugged. "We are not very close," he said. "It is just that I am
nervous. I have never before been in the mountains without a dog
to awaken me if there is danger. I left my dog with a friend . . ."

I wondered if he still had the same dog that had fled when El
Rojo died. But I didn't ask him.

We descended gradually throughout the morning of the third day.
The rain had slackened somewhat, although the sky remained dark,
gunmetal streaked with black. Progress was good and, although the
land still lay below us north and south, looking back I could see
we had come a considerable distance from the peaks. The land was
fairly open and I was able to ride abreast of Gregorio, but he seemed
in a solemn mood. He had the rifle slung across his back and looked
like a Hollywood Hemingway bandit. We stopped late for lunch,
and he didn't seem interested in the food but drank rather more
pisco than usual to wash it down, then forfeited his after-lunch pipe
in his impatience to get under way again.

A mile or so from where we had halted, he turned from the
obvious flat route and led the way along an inclining shelf towards
the north. Trees grew in a curiously straight line on our right, their
limbs drooping wearily under the weight of hanging moss and
pressing rain, and the ridge on our left dropped away sharply in
layered rock. Presently, the incline became more gradual and then
disappeared as the land rose to meet it in a triangle. I realized it had

been a long canyon, and we had come to the end of it. Gregorio pushed his hood back, and the wind rippled his stiff hair. He was looking about, alert and concerned, and I wondered if we were lost.

Then he reined up, slipped the rifle from his back and held it across the pommel. The grey gelding pawed the ground.

"What is it?" I asked.

"We are there."

"Where?"

He pointed towards the trees at the head of the canyon.

"That is where I saw it," he said.

I nodded and dismounted. Gregorio looked down at me for a moment, then swung from the saddle.

"Will you show me?" I asked.

"I came here. I am not very brave about this, but neither am I a coward. I will show you."

He looked very Spanish suddenly, arrogant and proud. We tied the horses to a leaning tree and walked towards the trees. I remembered the darkness and silence he'd told me about, but didn't feel that sensation. It didn't seem a frightening place. Gregorio pushed through the brush, the short rifle held before him, and I followed. The trees inclined towards us and we were in an open glade. There was nothing there. Gregorio moved across the space, his boots sinking into the soft earth, head lowered and moving from side to side.

Suddenly he stopped very quickly. I came up beside him. His knuckles were white on the rifle, his teeth were white as he drew his lips back, and when he moved the toe of his boot I saw something else flash white on the ground. I knelt, and felt a sudden beat of sympathetic pain. It was the broken skull of a dog. A brave dog.

I wanted to say something, but one doesn't express those things. Gregorio stared at the skull for a moment, stone faced, and then he shrugged.

"It is done," he said.

There was nothing else there. He walked silently back to the horses.

X

We made our permanent camp some distance from that glade. That was our focal point and I didn't want to go too far from it, but Gregorio wouldn't have wanted to be too close to the scene so horrible in his memory, although there was certainly nothing there now. I'd searched methodically for footprints or patches of hair that might have been torn out on the thorns, but found nothing except a few more bones, scattered and picked clean. The scavengers had made a thorough job of their grisly feast.

Physically, the spot where we made camp was far more gloomy than the glade. Gregorio had chosen it for maximum shelter and convenience rather than scenic grandeur, although there was a certain unreal and eerie enchantment about the place. A brooding, timeless, unchanging mood clung to the rocks and trees, a smell of arrested decay that had begun but would go no further, as though a primordial swamp had been suddenly frozen for eternity.

It was an area enclosed by a rough oval of rocks and trees a dozen yards wide at the narrowest segment of the ring. The rocks were of all shapes and sizes, from boulders to stones, and the trees grew from all angles between them and around them, twisting to conform with the immovable rocks and bowing away from the constant winds. Several trees had grown together, joining at the trunks and limbs while boulders separated their roots; others had split around narrower rocks so that two trees shared the same roots. The stones were covered with slimy moss and fungus and sallow creepers dripped from the limbs.

I held the horses while Gregorio scrambled over the rocks, vanishing behind a curtain of swaying vines. He returned shortly, satisfied that the interior of that oval would be the ideal place to make our camp. It was enclosed from the wind, the trees arched into a roof overhead, and best of all a narrow stream ran through the space, appearing in a spurt of fresh water from between the rocks.

It was difficult to get the horses inside. They were reluctant to cross the barrier of rock and we had to lead them one at a time, clattering and sliding, but once they were inside they were safe and we didn't have to worry about them. They wouldn't cross the rocks voluntarily and it eliminated the need to tie or hobble them, as well as the effort of carrying water from the stream across the treacherous footing, as would have been necessary had we left them outside.

I erected the tents while Gregorio fashioned an interior barrier of rock and dead trees to keep the horses out of the living quarters of our strange dwelling, and used the folding axe to hollow a log into a feeding trough. Then I set up the stove and attached the Butane bottle while he built a circle of rocks in front of the tents to serve as a fireplace. The stove was adequate for cooking, but we needed a fire for warmth and light. Together we unpacked the rest of the supplies and covered them with a tarpaulin. Our camp was made, crude but adequate, and it was time to decide what the next step should be. I lit a cigarette and considered the prospects. Gregorio was gathering whatever dry wood he could find. Now that the destination had been reached, I felt a sense of futility. We were here, but had anything other than distance been accomplished? I don't know what spectacular clue I'd hoped to find, but there had been nothing, no sign of the creature's presence in the area and no reason to suppose he was still there. All I could do was wait and observe and hope, and that seemed a passive and remote approach. I decided to confer with Gregorio and waited while he used a chemical fire lighter to start the camp fire, and brought water for coffee.

The smell of coffee boiling in the open air is sufficient to raise the lowest spirits, and the prospect of lacing it with grape alcohol was even better. Gregorio seemed to have shaken off his depression by the time we sat huddled at the fire, tin cups steaming in the damp air. I felt peaceful again. It was the end of the day, but nightfall was not a definite thing under that overcast sky. The raindrops battered at the fuscous forest surrounding us, seeking entrance through the foliage and falling like moths to the firelight. It was dark and sombre, a scene from a nightmare world. The little stream splattered from the rocks in peaceful contrast to the wind calling overhead, and the pungent odour of Gregorio's pipe drifted sharply through the scent of sodden vegetation and mouldy earth.

Presently, feeling that I should do something constructive, I took out my map case and unfolded the best map obtainable of the area.

It was sadly lacking in detail, with frequent gaps, indicating nothing more than approximate altitude. I asked Gregorio where we were, and he frowned over the map. A raindrop bounced heavily from the Straits of Magellan.

"Here. Somewhere here."

He stuck a forefinger in the centre of one of the blank areas. It told me nothing except that we were over 5,000 feet above sea level.

"Well, are there any landmarks, anything to get an approximate bearing from?"

Gregorio thought for a moment, his finger moving over the map. "MacPherson's ranch is nearest," he said. His finger strayed northwards a vague distance but remained within the confines of the blank space. "Somewhere here. It was there I was travelling when I looked for work. When I saw it."

That was encouraging, and I kicked myself mentally for not finding out sooner where MacPherson's place was. The creature had been there several times, at least once since Gregorio had seen it, and this knowledge increased my hope that it still frequented this area. I modified my self-castigation by realizing I couldn't have found MacPherson's on this map, anyway, and hadn't known Gregorio was headed there, but decided I'd better tie up the other possibility into this framework.

"Do you know where Hodson's is?"

Gregorio shook his head. "I don't know that name. Is it a ranch?"

"No. Just a house. In a valley."

He smiled. "There are many valleys," he said. "I know of no house. Not north, I think. I know what is north from here, that is where I sometimes work."

I folded the map carefully and slid it back in the case.

"How shall I go about finding the creature?"

He shrugged, looking into the fire. The light danced off his face like sunbeams off granite.

"Wait," he said. "You must wait."

"But why should it come here?"

"Perhaps for two reasons," he said. He was smiling again, but it was a strange, tight smile. "One is the water." He nodded towards the stream. "It is the only water to drink on this side of the mountain. There are small streams that come and go and ponds that grow stagnant, but this is the only constant fresh water in some miles. It begins only a little way from here, and it ends just beyond. So, if this thing must drink, I think it will drink near here."

This revelation delighted me, although I felt very much the amateur for not thinking of such a simple aspect of the search, and I was grateful for Gregorio's good sense. He was still smiling into the fire.

"And the other reason?" I asked.

"Because we are here," he said.

It took a moment to understand what he meant. The fire was hot on my face, but a definite chill inched up my spine. Gregorio stood up and walked over to the supplies and packs, then returned with the shotgun and handed it to me. I saw his point. I bolted it together and kept it in my tent.

In the morning I set out to trace the stream to its source. Gregorio assured me it wasn't far, and that it emerged from a subterranean course through the mountains. I wore my heavy boots for scrambling over rocks and carried the shotgun. Gregorio volunteered to accompany me, but I didn't think it necessary since I was going to follow the stream and couldn't very well become lost since I could easily follow it back again.

The stream burst into the camp in a miniature waterfall, tumbling from a narrow opening in the rocks and falling a few inches with comical fury, a Niagara in the insect world. It was impossible to follow the winding stream around and under the rocks but that wasn't necessary. I crossed the barrier at the easiest point and walked back along the perimeter until I came to the spot where the water flowed into the circle. It was just a shallow flow there, and I saw that it must have been compressed and confined as it ventured through the rocks, to break out in such Lilliputian ferocity at the other side. But on this open ground it wandered through marshland with little direction, and it wasn't easy to follow its main course. Several times I found that I'd gone a few yards along a side branch which diminished and then vanished, seeping into the ground. There was still no danger of losing my way, however, since I was moving upwards and could still see the trees surrounding the camp, and as I walked farther the stream became wider and deeper.

I had been walking for ten or fifteen minutes when I heard the rumbling ahead, and knew I must be approaching the source. I was almost at the crest of the hill, and behind it a high cliff towered against the sky. The stream was much larger here, and when I came to the top I saw the waterfall, still above me on the next hill. It was an exact replica of the cascade in the camp, magnified many times over. The water surged from a long gash in the cliff and pounded down, defying the wind, in a torrent at the foot of the unassailable rock wall. The avalanche had worn the land away and formed a turbid pool at the base of the cataract, and this in turn spilled the overflow out to form the stream.

I hurried on until I was standing beside the pool. The spray dashed over me and the sound roared in my ears. It was a natural waterhole which any large animal would use in preference to the shallow stream, and I immediately saw traces of those animals. I recognized the tracks of fox, muskrat and wild sheep, and saw various other unidentifiable prints.

I moved around the bank to the other side.

And there, quite distinctly, I found a print that was almost human. I stared at it for some time, hardly believing I'd discovered it so easily and so soon. But there it was. It wasn't quite the print of a barefoot man. The toes were too long and the big toe was set at a wider angle than normal. But it was without doubt the footprint of a primate, and a large primate at that. My heart pounding, I searched for further evidence, but there was only the one print. From that point, the creature that made it could have easily leaped to the nearest rocks, however, and it was all the evidence I needed to convince me I was in the right place, and that all I needed now was patience. If I waited, concealed near the waterhole, sooner or later the creature would appear.

But that suddenly posed another problem, one I'd been deliberately ignoring until the time came. If and when I did find the creature, what would I do? Or what would it do? My problem was based on not knowing what it was, whether it was man or beast or both. If there was any chance it was a man, I couldn't very well trap it or use force to capture it. It was a tricky moral judgement, and one I was hardly qualified to make before I'd seen it, and decided, tentatively at least, what it might be.

I returned to the camp, excited and anxious to tell Gregorio what I'd found. As I slid down from the rocks, I thought for a second that he wasn't there, and then I saw him by the horses. He had the rifle in his hands, pointing at the ground, but I had seen a blur of motion from the side of my eye, and wondered if he'd been waiting with the rifle aimed at the sound of my approach. Once again I felt a fore-boding that he might act rashly; I knew, without doubt, that if it had been the creature that had just scrambled into the camp, Gregorio would have used his weapon with no hesitation.

I didn't tell him about the footprint. I told him I'd been to the waterhole, however, and that I intended to wait there in conceal-ment.

"When will you wait?" he asked.

"As soon as possible. Tonight."

"At night?" he asked, his tone not quite incredulous—more as though he couldn't comprehend such a thing than that he disagreed with it.

"I think the chance of seeing it would be better at night. And it will certainly be easier to conceal myself in the dark."

"Yes. Those things are true," he said, as if other things were also true. But he offered no discouragement, in the same way that one doesn't argue with a madman.

XI

There was a moon above the clouds and long shadows drifted across the land in skeletal fingers. By day that desolate cataract had been eerie enough, but in the moonlight the rocks seemed to take on a life of their own, grotesquely carved monsters that writhed and rolled in confused contortions, and would have been more in place on that moon which lighted them than on earth.

I lay face down in the forest, watching the water leap in silver spray from the pool. The shotgun was beside me and I kept one hand on the stock, the other on my electric torch. I lay very still, hardly daring to breathe, conscious of the soft ground and wet grass, the night noises cutting through the dull roar of the water, and my own heartbeats. I had no way of knowing how long I'd been there. My watch had a luminous dial, and I'd left it back at the camp, taking no chances with my concealment.

A sudden sound stiffened me. There was a scurrying in the brush beside me as some small creature passed by, not a dozen feet from my right hand, and emerged beside the pool a moment later. I relaxed, letting my breath out quietly. It was a fox, only a fox. It looked about, cautious and alert, and then began to drink. An owl peered down from a nearby tree, then turned round yellow eyes away, seeking a less formidable meal. I judged it to be about three o'clock and my eyes were heavy. I was about to concede that my first night's vigil would be ended without results, although I intended to stay there until dawn. A large cloud spun out across the moon, black with frosted edges, and all the long shadows merged over the pool. Then, whipped on by the wind, the cloud disintegrated and the light glided back.

I was instantly alert.

The fox had stopped drinking. It stood, poised and tense, pointed ears quivering. I had heard nothing, and felt certain I'd made no sound, but there was something in the animal's bearing that implied caution or fear. The owl had vanished, the fox stood silhouetted against the waterfall for several minutes. Then suddenly it darted to the side, toward the undergrowth, halted abruptly and changed course. There was a louder stir in the trees as the fox disappeared. I rolled to my side, trying to follow the animal's flight without using the torch. Just above the spot where it had gone into the brush, a tree limb swayed, a heavy limb, moving as though it had just been relieved of a weight.

I pushed the shotgun out in front of me, thinking even as I did how I'd feared Gregorio might act rashly, and how that fear could well be extended to myself. And then there was time for thought.

The limb moved again, bending farther down and slowly rising until it merged with the limb above at one wide point. The point moved toward the trunk, blocking the light. There was something on that limb, something heavy and large, crouching. Then it was gone, the limb swayed, unburdened, and something moved through the dark trees, away from the clearing. The sound grew faint, and left only the wind and water to throb against the silence.

I did nothing. For a long while I lay perfectly still, waiting, hoping it would return and, at the same time, feeling relief that it had gone. Whatever it was, it had arrived with a stealth that had defeated my senses; I'd heard nothing and seen nothing, and was quite aware that it could just as easily have been in the tree above me. I rolled on to my back and looked upwards at the thought. But the tree was empty, the barren limbs crossed against the sky, and whatever had come, had gone. I didn't go after it.

Dawn came damp and cold. I got to my feet and stamped, then stretched, feeling a stiffness far more unpleasant than that caused by exertion. I lighted a cigarette and walked out of the trees. I could see the marks the fox had left beside the pool, and bent down to scoop some water and drink; I splashed my face and washed my hands. The second part of my vigil had passed very rapidly, and I can't begin to recall the inter-mingled profusion of thoughts that had occupied my mind.

Then I walked back along the route the fox had taken to the trees, looking at the ground and not knowing what I expected to find. A patch of undergrowth seemed to have been broken and I leaned over it. There was nothing on the ground. As I straightened up a drop hit me on the cheek, too heavy for rain, and when I wiped it my hand came away red. I thought I'd cut myself on a branch, and rubbed my cheek, then took my hand away and held it out, palm upwards, to see if there was blood. There wasn't.

And then, as I was watching, there was. A drop fell directly into my palm, thick and red.

I jerked back and looked up, but the tree was empty. The blood was dripping, slowly, from a small dark blot on the lowest limb. I couldn't quite make out what it was, although I felt a cold certainty that I knew. I broke a branch from the thicket and reached up, lifted the object and let it fall to the ground. I felt sick. It was the hindquarters of a fox, blood-matted tail attached, torn away from the rest of the body.

I searched, but not too thoroughly, and I didn't find the rest.

Gregorio was squatting by the fire. He held a mug of coffee out to me as I walked over from the rocks. My hand shook as I drank and he remarked on how pale I was. It wasn't surprising. I'd spent a night without shelter on the cold, damp ground. I took the coffee into my tent and changed into dry clothing. I felt very cold now and drew a blanket over my shoulders, lighted a cigarette but found that it tasted foul and stubbed it out. Gregorio pulled the flap back and handed me a bottle of pisco. He seemed to want to talk, but saw I didn't feel like it. He didn't ask if I'd discovered anything, assuming perhaps that I would have mentioned it or, possibly, that I wouldn't mention it anyway. I drank the pisco and coffee alternately, my mind dull. The rain was smacking against the canvas without rhythm, a drop, a pause, two drops, three drops, another pause, and I found myself concentrating on the irregular tempo, a form of self-imposed Chinese water torture subconsciously devised to occupy my mind and avoid making conclusions and decisions. I shook my head, driving the stupor away and forcing my mind back into focus.

There had been something in that tree. That was one certainty, perhaps the only one. It had seemed large and bulky but the moonlight was tricky and I couldn't be sure of that. Just something. A large bird? I knew better and wondered why I was seeking alternatives to what I should have welcomed. I knew damn well what it had been, what I should have been overjoyed to know, and no amount of sceptical ratiocination was going to change that knowledge. Even had I logically thought differently, I still would have believed with the force of emotion.

I drank some more pisco and followed my thoughts.

Whatever it had been, it was powerful enough to tear that unfortunate fox apart. There were no marks of fang or claw, the fox hadn't been cut or bitten apart. It had been pulled in two with enormous strength. There had been no sound, save the rustling of the trees, no death howl or struggle. Either the fox had been stifled or destroyed so quickly that it could make no cry.

That struck a discord somewhere. I remembered the terrible sound I'd heard from Hodson's laboratory, and the sound, the same sound I felt sure, that the creature had made after it killed El Rojo. Why had it been silent last night? Had it heard me, detected my presence in some way and been frightened off? Or was a fox too insignificant a victim to warrant a victory cry? If it had sensed my presence, would it return? I might have missed my only opportunity. Why hadn't I used my torch? Was it caution or fear or . . .

Gregorio was shaking me.

I opened my eyes and was startled to realize I'd been half-conscious, between thought and nightmare. My teeth were clicking together, my stomach turned over, my forehead was burning. Fever laced me. Gregorio put his long, delicate hand on my brow and nodded thoughtfully. His concerned face drew near and then receded, swelled like a balloon and then shrunk away again. I observed everything through a haze, an unequal fog that parted on reality and then closed over again. I was only dimly aware of Gregorio's strong hands as he helped me into my sleeping bag, and then quite distinctly knew I was taking two of the small white pills Graham had recommended, could feel their roundness in my throat and taste the bitterness on my tongue. Reality paled once more, and yet my mind was alert on a different level and I wondered with lucid objectiveness whether I'd fallen prey to some exotic fever or merely succumbed to the wet cold of the night. Then I fell into disturbed sleep.

When I awoke it was evening. The campfire turned the canvas burnished gold. I watched the rough texture glow, aware of the minute details of colour and grain on that clear, disinterested level of consciousness. Presently the flap parted and Gregorio looked in.

"Feel better?" he asked.

"I don't know." I didn't. "What's wrong with me?"

"Fever. Chill. Who knows? Not serious, I think. You must rest and be warm for a few days."

"What time is it?"

"I have no clock," he said.

My own watch was on the crate I'd used as a table. I nodded towards it and Gregorio handed it to me. It was ten o'clock.

"I intended to go back to the waterhole tonight."

He shrugged.

"That is not possible now."

"No, I guess not," I said. I felt relieved about it. After I was feeling well would be time enough; I would be unable to observe properly in this weakened condition and would undoubtedly become more seriously ill. And, perhaps feeling a need for more justification than my own physical failure, I told myself that the creature might well have sensed my presence and be wary. It was far wiser to wait.

I took two more pills, drank a glass of water, and slept more soundly.

I felt better in the morning. I still had a slight fever, but my head was clear, the curious dichotomy of muddled reality and sharply focused details had ceased. I was able to walk around a bit in the afternoon and force down some food in the evening, and decided I had fallen to a chill rather than some disease. But I was still weak and dizzy, and there was no question of returning to the vigil that night. Gregorio saw that the delay disturbed me.

"I could keep watch," he said, dubiously.

"No. That wouldn't do any good. I'll have to see this creature myself; you've already seen it."

"That is so," he said, and celebrated his reprieve with a mug of pisco.

I went to bed early and read, but found the strain of the kerosene lantern painful, the words blurred. I turned the light out and closed my eyes. I didn't feel sleepy, but sleep crept over me in modulated waves. I remember feeling annoyed that I was wasting this opportunity, and blaming my weakness for hindering the investigation; telling myself that I had to find the creature while it was in the area, that there might never be another chance to find it. I was determined to return to the waterhole the next night.

There was no need. It found us.

XII

I was awake and something was snarling outside the tent. It was the second time I'd been awakened by a sound in the night, but this time I didn't hesitate—this snarling did not petrify me as that other terrible cry. I slid from the sleeping bag and grabbed the shotgun. My eyes felt too large for their sockets, my mouth was dry. The snarl came again and I could hear the horses screaming. I pushed the flap open and let the gun precede me from the tent. The fire was burning low, and it was dark beyond. Gregorio came from his tent standing straight, the rifle at his shoulder, his eyes wild in the glow of the fire. He turned toward the horses.

The horses had gone mad. They were frantically milling about their enclosure. I moved to the side, to get a line of vision beyond the fire, and one of the horses leaped the rocks Gregorio had piled up. It was the grey. It charged towards me blindly and I flung myself to the side, heard the horse tear into my tent, saw the canvas flapping as I scrambled to my feet again. Another horse had attempted to leap the wide outer barrier and I heard its hooves clattering desperately for a footing, then saw it go down between the rocks, struggling to rise again. The other two horses were running in a mad circle around the enclosure, one after the other, following the circle. The second horse flashed past and I could see into the centre of the corral.

Something crouched there.

The firelight barely reached it, outlining it dimly against the barrier. It stood on four legs, but the shoulders were higher than the haunches, its weight on the hindquarters as it circled, turning with the horses. As I watched, it drew its arms upwards and coiled.

"Something's in with the horses!" I cried.

And it moved. One arm swept out wide, hooking at a horse's flank. The horse reared, forelegs pawing the air as it rose, rose too high and toppled over backwards. It blocked the creature from my sight. I had the shotgun up and, man or beast, I would have fired. But I couldn't shoot without hitting the horse. Gregorio was frozen in position, the rifle levelled, his face grotesque. The horse flailed the air, fighting to get up, but the creature was on it, rending and tearing, its snarls muffled against the horse's flesh.

The shotgun boomed. It sounded unbelievably loud to my inflamed senses. I had discharged it into the air, whether by accident or design or instinct I don't know, and the hollow blast bounced from the surrounding rocks as the pellets laced through the trees.

The horse was up, bucking and rearing, and the creature turned toward me, squat and square, poised motionless for an instant. Then its long arms swung, knuckles brushing the ground, and I brought the shotgun down; for a moment I was looking at the creature down the barrels, my finger on the second trigger. I could have shot it then, but I was looking at its eyes. And it looked back at me, savage and fierce but also curious and startled by the sound. I couldn't pull the trigger. The creature wheeled about, its great bulk pivoting with amazing speed, and moved toward the rock barrier. I followed it with the gun; saw it leap into the shadows; heard the report of Gregorio's .303, sharp and crackling in contrast to the shotgun.

The creature went down, howling, twisting in pain. Then it lunged up again. Gregorio worked the lever, the spent shell sparkled, spinning through the firelight. The creature was in the trees when he fired again, and I heard the slug smack against solid rock. We looked at each other. The creature was gone.

Gregorio was holding the grey, one arm around its neck. He spoke softly and the horse lowered his head, trembling. The horse that had been attacked was dashing about the corral, white foam pouring from his mouth, lips curled back from square teeth. A great hunk had been torn from its flank and long gashes were open over its ribs. I saw that it was my horse, the one I'd ridden and become attached to, and felt my jaws tighten.

I moved back to the wreckage of my tent. The poles were snapped, the canvas spread over the ground. I found my trousers amidst the debris and pulled them on. The horse that had fallen on the barrier was still struggling to rise, wedged between two smooth boulders, whimpering in pain.

"Now you have seen it," Gregorio said.

I nodded.

"That was how the dog died," he said, with far more sadness than hatred. The grey's head came up, ears pricked, and he whispered soothingly. The fourth horse moved toward him uncertainly, head turned, looking at his injured companion. I pulled the canvas from our supplies and found the box of shot-gun shells, broke the gun open and reloaded the right barrel, then stuffed shells in the pockets of my windbreaker. I felt no fear now. Action had dispensed with dread. I felt determined and angry, and had no doubts that I'd use the gun if I had to. I knew that, whatever the creature was, it was not human enough to command human rights. I was not much of a scientist at that moment, but perhaps more a man. The smell of gunpowder was sharp on the thick air, a few leaves fluttered down from the blasted branches overhead. I walked over to Gregorio.

"You will go after it?" he asked.

"Yes."

"It is wounded."

I nodded. Gregorio had hit it once, and there are few animals a .303 won't bring down. I had no doubts that I could find it now.

"Someone should stay with the horses," Gregorio said.

"Yes. You must stay."

"It may be waiting for you."

"I'll be all right."

Gregorio regarded me with Indian eyes. He wanted to be brave, and he was brave. The grey gelding was still trembling under his arm and he nodded. That was right, someone had to stay with the horses. But he lowered his head and didn't watch me leave the camp.

I could hear the horse screaming in the rocks behind me. When I'd passed, he turned a wide eye upwards. His foreleg was snapped and he was lodged helplessly, looking for help we could not give. I called Gregorio and went on. The crack of his rifle came through the trees and the horse stopped screaming. I felt a cruel satisfaction when I found a smear of blood marking the creature's passage. It was large and dark in the light from my electric torch, and I didn't think he'd be moving very fast.

He wasn't. When I had crossed the rocks I saw him lurching up the hill that led to the waterfall. When he'd attacked the horse, he had uncoiled like a steel spring, fast and fluid, but he moved with a rolling, drunken gait now. His legs were short and crooked and he used his long arms for support as he ran. Perhaps his peculiar gait was not suited to travelling on open ground at the best of times, and the bullet had taken its toll of his strength.

I moved to the right, towards the trees, so that I would be able to cut off any attempt to disappear into the bush where he could move so much more silently and faster than I. But he didn't attempt that. He was following a straight course up the hill, as though not merely fleeing but moving towards a definite destination. I had the torch in my left hand and the shotgun cradled on my right arm. There was no need for stealth or caution as long as I kept him in sight, and I followed quickly. He was only three or four hundred yards in front of me, and I drew closer without great effort.

He reached the top of the hill and paused, then turned and looked back at me. He was silhouetted against the sky and his eyes gathered the moonlight. I knew he had the vision of a night animal, and was thankful for my torch. He watched me for a few seconds, his heavy head turning from side to side, then wheeled and vanished over the crest. I began to run, wanting to keep him in sight, but not worried. I was familiar with this terrain, and knew that the second hill stretched on for a long distance, that he couldn't possibly ascend it before I was over the first hill. I was breathing hard now, the soft earth sucking at my boots and slipping from under me, but I ran on and topped the rise.

The creature was not in sight. There was a small pool of blood where he had paused and looked back, and a few scattered dark patches beyond, heading toward the waterfall. But he had vanished. The far hill stretched away, smooth and rolling, with no concealment. The trees to the right had been in sight as I climbed. Behind the waterfall, the cliff rose sheer and unscalable. There was nowhere he could have gone except to the waterfall, and I moved down, walking slowly and cautiously now, my thumb on the torch switch and my finger on the triggers.

I came to the soft mud surrounding the pool and switched the torch on. A point of light reflected back from the cliff and I tensed, thinking it was those night-creature eyes, but it was only a smooth stone, polished by the waterfall. The beam played over the reeds and found nothing; then, at my feet, I found his prints. They were distinct and deep, moisture just beginning to seep in, the feet with wide angled toes and the impressions of his knuckles on either side. The tracks moved to the edge of the pool. I turned the light on the water, but the broken surface revealed nothing. Very slowly, I walked around the bank to the far side and inspected the ground. There were no prints emerging from there. The creature had gone into the pool and had not come out. And yet, it was not in the water. There could be only one explanation, and I let the light flood over the tumbling cataract. The cliff was perpendicular, grey stone, the water sparkled down, and there, just where they met, a narrow rim of blackness defied illumination.

I walked up to the cliff, the water lapping at my feet, the gun level at my hip, and there I found the cave. It opened behind the waterfall, an aperture some three feet high, completely hidden in the light of day unless one stood against the cliff face. The pool was slightly higher than the cave floor, and the water ran inwards, several inches deep. There was a smear of red against the angle of rock.

I had found far more than the creature's waterhole, when I'd come to this cascade. I'd found its home.

Did it take a greater courage than I'd ever known I possessed to enter that black cavern, or were my senses and emotions too numbed with fever and excitement to feel fear? I know that I went into the Stygian darkness without hesitation, and that I felt very little at all. I simply did it, without thought or doubt. The only sensation I was conscious of was the water rivetting my neck and back as I stopped under it, and then I was kneeling in the cave. The floor rose and the water penetrated only for a few yards. I shone the torch before me. It flowed well into the tunnel, but the blackness stretched on in the distance. It seemed interminable, and I had the sudden fear that it emerged again at some point and that the creature would escape me. The thought forced me on. I had to crawl for a few yards and then found it high enough to stand, crouching. It was narrow, my arms brushed against the sides, and it was straight. There was little danger. I had the torch and the gun and the creature could only come at me from the front. If I was forced to kill it, I would be able to. I didn't want to, however. My anger at seeing my horse's agony had lessened, I was more the scientist than the hunter once more. I determined that I would make every effort not to kill it; if I was forced to fire, my first blast would be aimed at its legs. But perhaps it was already dying, had crawled home to suffer its death throes alone. If that were true, it seemed brutal to pursue it, but there was no way to know, and I moved forward following the beam of light.

The walls were slimy with greenish moss, cracked with numerous narrow fissures where the mountain had moved in ages past. It was very quiet. My heavy soled boots made no sound on the stone, and the drops of blood underfoot became fewer and farther apart. The cave widened gradually as I moved into the depths, fantastic formations of broken rock emerged from the walls, pillars and trellises jutted up and hung down from floor and ceiling. I approached

them warily, but there was nothing waiting behind. The tunnel continued to follow a straight course and it seemed I'd been walking a
long time.

And then the light hit rock ahead, spreading out fluidly to both
sides. I thought for an instant that I had come to a dead end, and
then saw that the tunnel turned at right angles, a natural geomet-
ric angle following a fault in the solid stone. I approached the turning very slowly. If the creature were waiting for me, it would be
here.

I stopped a few feet from the turn; held the torch under the stock
so that I had both hands on the gun and the light followed the line
of the barrels, took a deep breath, braced myself, and stepped out
wide of the corner in one long stride.

I stopped dead.

The creature was not waiting there. There was nothing there.
Nothing but a green metal door . . .

The door swung open, heavy on its hinges. Hubert Hodson said:
"I expect you'd better come in."

XIII

Hodson took the shotgun from me. I was too staggered to resist.
I realized I'd passed completely under the mountain, and that
we had inadvertently made our camp directly opposite Hodson's
house, separated by the unscalable cliff but connected via the
tunnel through the rock; that the door he'd claimed led to a storeroom actually opened into the tunnel. I followed Hodson through
the door, expecting to enter the laboratory, but in that respect
I was wrong. There was a connecting chamber between, a small
poorly lighted room with another green door in the opposite wall.
That door was open and I could see the brightly illuminated laboratory beyond. Hodson closed the door behind us and turned the
key. Heavy tumblers fell into place. He pushed me ahead of him,
towards the laboratory.

A low snarl sounded beside me. I wheeled about, pushing Hodson's hand from my shoulder, tensed and then froze. The creature
was in that room. It crouched in the corner, behind heavy steel

bars, watching me with comprehension and hatred. All the details instantly impressed themselves on my consciousness as a whole, a single, startling tableau. The bars fitted into the wall on one side, and were hinged so that they could be swung open and closed again, forming a cage with three solid rock walls. The creature was in the cage, only a few feet from me, a grotesque caricature of man. Its chest was rounded, its shoulders stooped and heavy, its arms long. Short, coarse hair bristled on its body, but its face was smooth and brown, wide nostrils flaring and small eyes burning beneath a thick, ridged brow. I saw a dark, damp patch on its side, a few spatters of blood on the floor, and standing between us, one hand on the bars, stood the old crone. She had turned to look at me, and her eyes glowed with malevolence, with a hatred more intense and inhuman than that of the creature itself.

The creature lunged at me. One huge hand tore at the bars and the steel sang with vibration. I started to shout a warning to the old woman, but it was not after her. It ignored her. It reached out, groping for me through the bars, snarling with broad lips drawn back. I backed away and Hodson touched my shoulder.

"Come. We mustn't stay here. He knows you injured him and I wouldn't trust even those steel bars if he goes berserk."

"The old woman—"

"She will be all right," he said.

He pushed me toward the laboratory. The snarling became less violent and I heard the old woman speaking in some strange language—speaking to the creature. And the second metal door clanged shut behind us.

Hodson took me to the front room, motioned to a chair and began searching through a drawer. I saw him slip a hypodermic needle in his pocket.

"You aren't going to use that on it?" I asked.

He nodded and brought out a large box of medicinal supplies.

"A tranquillizer," he said.

"But it'll tear you apart if you get near."

"The woman can manage it," he said. "Wait here. I'll be back when I've repaired the damage you've done." He went back through the curtains. I sat down and waited.

Hodson returned, his shirt sleeves rolled up, poured two large drinks and handed me one.

"It wasn't a serious wound," he said. "He will live."

I nodded. Hodson sat down opposite me. The drink tasted strange on my dry tongue, and my fever was returning. There were so many things I wanted to ask, but I waited for Hodson to speak first.

"So this is the proper study of man? To shoot man?"

"Is it man?"

"Assuredly."

"It attacked my camp. It was killing one of the horses. We had no choice."

He nodded.

"Quite so," he said. "That is man's nature. To kill and to have no choice." He shook his head wearily, then suddenly laughed. "Well, you've found my secret. Now what?"

"I don't know. It's still a secret. I'd like a chance to examine the creature."

"No. That isn't possible."

"You've already examined it completely, I suppose?"

"Physically?" He shrugged. "I'm more interested in studying his behaviour. That's why I've allowed him to run wild and unrestricted."

"And yet it returns here? It comes back to a cage of its own choice?"

He laughed again.

"I told you. It is man's nature to have no choice. It returns because it is man, and man goes home. That is a basic instinct. Territorial possessiveness."

"You're certain it is human?"

"Hominid. Yes. Absolutely."

"Will you tell me about it?"

"It's a bit late for secrets."

"How can you be sure it's human? Hominid? As opposed, say, to some new form of ape? What is the definition, what criteria are you using?"

"Criteria? There is so much you fail to understand. There is only one definition of man. I used the absolute criteria."

I waited, but he didn't clarify. He sipped his drink; he seemed to be waiting for my questions.

"You discovered it here, I take it?"

"In a sense, yes."

"How long have you known about it?"

"For a generation."

"Are there others?"

"Not at the moment."

This was telling me nothing. I said: "Why have you waited so long, why keep this secret? What have you gained by your silence?"

"Time. I told you once before. Time is essential. I'm studying him as a man, not as a curiosity. Naturally I had to have time for him to mature. Who can gauge man's behaviour by studying a child?"

"Then you found it when it was very young?"

"Yes. Very young indeed."

He smiled strangely.

"And when did you determine it was human?"

"Before I . . . found him."

"You aren't making sense," I said. "Why give me riddles at this stage? What is your definition of man?"

"I need no definition," he said. He was enjoying this. He wanted to tell me, his irresistible urge to dumbfound his fellow scientists returned, his countenance livened.

"I didn't exactly discover him, you see," he said. "I know he is man because I created him."

He regarded me through a long silence.

"You mean it's a mutation?"

"A very special form of mutation. It is not a variation, but a regression. What little I told you on your last uninvited visit was true, but it wasn't all the truth. I told you I'd discovered how to control mutation, but this went much further. In mastering mutation, I found it was the key to cellular memory—that the law of mutation can be applied to unlock the forgotten replications."

He finished his drink. His face was flushed.

"You see, cells forget. That is why we grow old, for instance. Our cells forget how to replicate youth. But this knowledge, although forgotten, is still there, in the same way that things a man forgets exist in his subconscious mind. Exactly the same, on a different level. And as subconscious knowledge can be remembered under hypnosis, so the cells can be induced to remember by chemical treatment. And this, Brookes, is the very root of life. It may, among other things, be the key to immortality. We can teach our cells not to forget the replication of youth." He shrugged. "But man, as he is, isn't worthy of immortality, and I'm not interested in giving it to him. It will come. I am interested in man's evolution, and I've applied my knowledge in that field. I am the first and only man who has seen evolution as it occurs. Brookes, I am the creator of my ancestor!"

There was more than enthusiasm in his face. There was something akin to madness.

"But how—"

"Don't you understand yet? I treated the parents, chemically affecting their genes so that they carried a recessed heredity. The offspring, the creature you have seen, is regressed back through aeons of time—carries the traits our cells have long since forgotten. I could possibly have taken it even further, back to the first forms of life, the single cellular creatures that existed in the dawn of life. But that, too, is of no interest to me. I limit myself to man."

He took my glass, crossed the room and refilled it.

"How do you classify this creature?" I asked.

He sat down again, frowning.

"I'm not sure. The ancestor of a branch of modern man. Not our branch, perhaps, but a parallel line. Man as he may have been ten million years ago. Or five million years. Time is essential but indefinite."

"And it was actually born of parents living today?"

"The father is dead. I'm afraid that his offspring—or his ancestor, whichever you prefer—tore his throat out several years ago." He said this with clinical detachment. "The mother—did you wonder why the old woman could control it? Why it came back here when it was hurt? She is the mother."

After a while I said, "Good God."

"Shocked or surprised?" Hodson asked.

"Surely it can't be right to create something so unnatural?"

He stared scornfully at me.

"Are you a scientist? Or a moralist? Surely, you know that science is all that matters. What does that old crone matter? What are a few dead sheep? Or a few dead men, for that matter? I have seen the behaviour of one of man's ancestors, and isn't that worth any amount of suffering?" He was talking rapidly, gesturing with both hands, his eyes boring into me.

"And the further possibilities are countless. Perhaps, with time to work in peace, I will learn to reverse the process. Even that. Perhaps I will be able to progress cellular memory. To sidestep evolution. The knowledge must already be there, the cells simply haven't learned it yet; they learn it gradually as they forget the old knowledge. But it's there, Brookes. It was there when the first life crawled out of the sea. The future and the past, side by side. Think of it! To create man as he will be a million years from now!"

I was in two minds, on two levels. I didn't know whether to believe him or not on the superficial scale, but deeper, where I couldn't help but believe, magnetized by his voice, my reactions were divided again. The fact, and the possibilities, were wonderful beyond comprehension, but the details were appalling, the use of human beings in this experiment grotesque. To think of a living woman giving birth to that monstrosity in the cage was abhorrent. Perhaps, in some ways, I was a moralist, and certainly scientific interest struggled against a surge of repulsion.

"Think of it!" Hodson repeated, his eyes turned inwards now as he thought of it himself. His knuckles were white, tightening on his glass. He had been profoundly affected by this opportunity to speak of his discoveries, the overpowering urge to break the silence of twenty years. We had been talking for some time. A grey early light blocked the window; a bird was singing outside. In the surrounding hills day was breaking, day creatures awoke and night creatures slunk back to their warrens and dens, following the ways of nature, oblivious to the ways of science. But science was overtaking nature. I lighted a cigarette and drew the harsh smoke deeply into my lungs. I knew it wasn't a good thing, and it went far deeper than outraged morality.

"It can't be right, Hodson. Preying on these primitive people who don't understand what you are doing to them. That old woman—"

Surprisingly, he nodded in agreement. But not for the same reasons.

"Yes, that was a mistake. I'd misjudged the potency of my process and, more important and less forgivable, I failed to consider the
theory of parallel evolution. This creature wasn't my first attempt,
but it was the first to survive. The others didn't bear up to the strain,
although the post-mortems proved most enlightening. But we
learn from our blunders, and I have at least proved that all modern
man did not descend from the same common ancestor. I suppose
that was a worthwhile discovery. Evolution in the New World, at
least in this part of South America, developed without connection
to the rest of the world and, more surprisingly, at a different time
in history." He had been talking softly, rather wearily, but now his
oratorical tone returned, his eyes lighted once more.

"Twenty million years ago, sometime in the late Cenozoic era,
and somewhere in Asia, the ancient primates divided into two
branches. One branch led to modern apes, the other to creatures
which became increasingly human. One million years ago, these
creatures became *Homo*. Forty thousand years ago, they became
sapiens. And they are our ancestors, Brookes. Yours and mine.
But these men did not come to this part of the world. The same
process of division occurred here, in much the same way and for
much the same reason, but countless ages later in pre-history. The
humans who developed here, like the New World monkeys, were
different in many respects. Less advanced on the hereditary scale,
because they emerged at a later point, and had to survive harsher
conditions in some respects. The climate was the greatest factor
responsible for the differences. The hominids developed in relation
to this hostile climate, they became much tougher and resistant to
extremes, able to exist naked in freezing wind and water. In that
way they advanced faster, beyond our branch. But there were fewer
natural enemies here, they were the predominant life form, and
survival was gauged only against nature. While our branch of mankind developed tools, thumbs, uncurved spines, vocal cords and,
finally, superior brains to enable them to exist against the powerful
predators, these people had no need to advance along similar lines.
Quite naturally, they did not. The physically stronger lived to breed
and pass on those traits, while the intelligent, with no advantages
in survival, succumbed to the evolutionary laws and advanced at
a much slower rate. These creatures were as different from their

Asian and European counterparts as llamas from camels, capuchin from rhesus.

"Who knows? Perhaps this branch was superior; given time they might well have developed into supermen. But they didn't have that time. Our branch had a head start and developed too quickly. We became travellers. We ventured down here from the north and the natives could not survive against us, or beside us. They died out. Perhaps we killed them, perhaps we brought disease unknown to them, perhaps our superior brains succeeded in acquiring all the available food. At any rate, they did not survive. But there was some interbreeding. That was selective and the offspring retained the qualities of both branches—the mind of one, the strength of the other. They were remarkably adaptable to life. The native branch ceased to exist, but the crossbreeds survived alongside the new branch. God knows how long ago this cross-breeding took place, perhaps fifty thousand years. They were still here when Darwin came, I know that. But, little by little, the native traits had weakened in the individuals. Although they may have been predominant at first, they were bred out by sheer weight of numbers, until only the odd throwback possessed them."

He paused, choosing his words, while I waited in dumb fascination.

"The old woman is one of those atavisms, as far as I know the last and only living human to bear a prepotency of the vanishing characteristics. That was why I selected her for my experiment. Her genes were closer to the past, the memory was not buried so deeply, and the ancient traits were predominant. That was why I selected her, and that was where I blundered.

"Do you begin to understand?" he asked.

Behind him, the window had silvered as the sun began to slant down the hills. I was burning with fever, and a different fever had set my mind alight. I nodded.

"The experiment succeeded too well," he continued. "The result —you have seen the result. It is human, because it was born of woman, but it is not human as we know the word. It is fascinating and fabulous, certainly the living ancestor of an extinct branch of mankind, but not our ancestor. Not yours or mine and only partially the old woman's. And thus it is a dead end, a creature whose offspring are already extinct. There is much to be gained by studying it, but little to be learned of man. I have formulated the theoretical descent of a being that no longer exists, but it is not much different to tracing the remote ancestry of the passenger pigeon or the dodo. You can understand the frustration of that?"

"But my God, what an opportunity—"

"Perhaps. But it is not my field. I will give it to the world when I have applied it to my own pursuits. Another experiment, eliminating the error. If only I can live long enough to see it through. With what I have already learned from this creature—from watching it grow and mature, with strictly clinical interest—" His mind seemed to be wandering now, his thoughts confused, divided between acquired knowledge and the further knowledge he anticipated. "It killed its father when it was twelve years old. It developed much more rapidly than man. I judge its lifespan to be a mere thirty years, certainly not more. But it will not grow old. This branch could not survive an old age, it will retain its physical powers until it has attained its normal lifespan and then it will die. And with it will die its genus. Perhaps the post-mortem will be interesting. The study of its life has been frustrating. It can't speak. It has vocal cords but they aren't capable of mastering more than bestial sounds. That was the greatest disappointment. Think of being able to converse, in your own language, with prehistoric man! Its cranial capacity is about 1,550 cubic centimetres—roughly the average of Neanderthal man, but its brain is relatively free of convolutions. Its branch did not need a mind, it needed strength and endurance. Did you see its eyes glow in the dark? The inner wall of the eye is coated with guanin, like most night creatures. Perhaps that is more valuable than thought to the creature. It hardly thinks at all. It feels, it acts by instinct. Its basic instinct seems to be to kill. Only the old woman has any control over it now. The Indian used to manage it by his great strength, but soon it became too powerful and vicious even for him to handle. It attacked me one day. That was where the Indian acquired that scar, of course. He saved my life, but even he fears it now. Only the old crone—it shows the basic instinct of mother-love—it killed its father, but obeys its mother without needing to understand her . . ."

I shuddered. There was something terrible in this regard of a beast for a human, and even more terrible knowing that the pitiful old woman regarded that monstrous creation as her child. I wondered, with absolute horror, if she had given it a name. I closed my eyes, uselessly. The horror was behind them.

Hodson stood up and took my glass. He brought it back refilled and I took a long swallow.

"You intend to continue this experiment? To create another creature like that?"

"Of course. Not like that, however. The next one must be our ancestor. The same process, with parents of our branch of mankind. It is only necessary to treat the male, although the regressed mutation occurs in the female. The Indian might be an ideal specimen, in fact."

"You can't," I said.

Hodson's eyes widened, amused.

"It's fiendish!"

"Ah, the moralist again. Do you consider the creature evil? Brookes, if you had been born a million years in the future—how would your behaviour seem to the men of that distant time?"

"I don't know," I said, very slowly. I had trouble forming the words. Something seemed to weigh my tongue down, and the same weight pressed on my eyes. Hodson's eyes burned at me, and then they began to dull. The fire had left him, extinguished in his revelations, and he became solemn, perhaps knowing he had once again succumbed to his old fault; he had told me too much.

"Do you believe me?" he asked, smiling.

"I don't know," I repeated. I moved my head from side to side. It swivelled beneath a great burden, my neck faltered under the heaviness and my head dropped. I was staring at the floor. I could hear Hodson speaking, far away.

"It wouldn't have taken much imagination to think of these things," he said. "But it would have taken fantastic discoveries to actually do them. Perhaps I have merely been toying with you, Brookes. You know how I have always taken pleasure in shocking people. Perhaps this is all simply a hoax, eh? What do you think, moralist? Have I been deceiving you?"

I tried to shake my head again. It hung down, lower, my knees seemed to be rising to meet my face. The chair receded from under me. I fought under this enormous gravity, struggled upwards and stood before Hodson. He was still smiling. The room whirled and spun, his face was the only fixed point in my focus, my eyes were held on his grinning teeth.

"You're not well, Brookes?" he asked.

"I ... dizzy ... I ..."

The empty glass was still in my hand. I looked at it, saw the points of light reflected along the rim; saw the tiny flakes of white powder in the bottom ... Saw nothing.

XIV

I floated back through planes of awareness and Hodson's face floated over me, lighted from beneath with weird effect. I wondered, vaguely, why he had stopped grinning, then realized I was no longer in the front room, that I'd been unconscious for some time. I was dressed, but my boots were off. They were on the floor beside the candle that shot dancing light upwards, sweeping Hodson's countenance and fading out weakly in the corners of the room. It was the room I'd slept in on my last stay, and I was lying on my back on the cot.

"Ah. You are awake," Hodson said.

I blinked. I felt all right.

"What happened to me?"

"You fainted. You have a fever, apparently you've been ill. I didn't realize that, or I wouldn't have deliberately shocked you so outrageously. I'm sorry."

"That drink—you drugged me."

"Nonsense. You simply fainted. In your feverish state my little amusement was too much for you. Your perceptions were inflamed. Why, for a few minutes, I believe you actually thought it was the truth."

"You told me ... those things ..."

"Were all pure fabrication. Oh, there was a basis in fact; I have indeed experimented along those lines, but without success. I'm afraid I simply couldn't resist the opportunity to—pull your leg shall we say? Of course, had you been thinking clearly you would have seen the impossibility of such a tale."

"But I saw the creature."

"An ape. I assure you it was merely an ape. A curious cross-breeding of Old and New World primates, resulting from one of my experiments in controlled mutation. Unsuccessful, from my point of view, actually, since it's merely a hybrid, not actually a mutation—far less a regression." He chuckled at the absurdity of such a concept.

"I don't believe you."

Hodson shrugged.

"As you like. Your opinions cease to interest me, now that I've had my little game."

"Will you allow me to examine it then? There can be no harm in that, if it's just an ape."

"That, I regret to say, is impossible. The wound you inflicted upon it was more serious than it appeared. There were internal complications and my surgical skill is paltry. I'm afraid that the ape has expired."

"An examination of the body will satisfy me."

"I have no desire to satisfy you. If it weren't for you, the ape would still be alive. At any rate, the remains have already been dissected and disposed of."

"Already?"

"You have been sleeping for—" he regarded his watch, "some ten hours. Sufficient time to derive whatever scientific benefit can be found in examining a deceased hybrid. You may see my notes, if you like."

"Everything you told me was a lie?"

"Not a lie. What is a lie? A study in man's gullibility, perhaps. An objective observation of the effect of the absurd upon the credulous. You have undoubtedly heard how I used to enjoy shocking people with unfounded theories? My pleasure was not so much in the outraged reception of my statements, as in observing a man's reaction afterwards. This, in its way, was also a study of mankind. And that, Brookes, is my field, in all its manifold aspects."

I shook my head. It should have been so much easier to believe him now than it had been before. But, somehow, I couldn't quite do so. His tone lacked that enthusiasm and excitement it had carried before—an enthusiasm derived from success and pride in his accomplishments. And yet, I had not been thinking clearly, I'd been feverish and weak and susceptible to suggestion, and Hodson was a master of deliberate deception. I tried to reason, but my thoughts came helter skelter, my mind whirled, touching on valid points and then spinning on before I could follow a line of reasoning.

"Rest now," Hodson said, far away again. "You'll be able to laugh at yourself in the morning."

He took the candle with him. The room was black, and a sympathetic blackness began to nudge me towards sleep, a blank space growing larger in my brain.

The light had returned when I opened my eyes again.

Anna stood beside the bed, holding the candle. The curtains swayed behind her, the house was very quiet. She smiled down at me, looking concerned.

"You are all right?" she asked.

I nodded.

"I was worried for you."

She hovered over me uncertainly. She wasn't embarrassed, because she knew nothing of propriety or shame, but she seemed undecided.

"May I sit beside you?" she asked.

"Of course."

I slid over. Anna sat on the edge of the cot. I was still wearing my shirt and trousers and she was still naked. She curled one leg beneath her and placed the candle on the floor, stared at it for a moment and then moved it a few needless inches. Her smile was shy, although she did not know what shyness was. She placed a cool hand on my brow. My fever seemed to have left me now, but that cool palm felt very good and I placed my hand over hers. She leaned slightly toward me and her firm breast brushed against my forearm. I remembered how much I had wanted her the last time we were together in this little cell; realized that desire was stronger now than before; wondered if she knew, if she understood, if she had come to me because she felt the same way.

"I don't disturb you?" she asked.

"You do. Very much."

"Shall I leave?"

"No. Stay here."

It wasn't the playful teasing of a woman, she meant exactly what she said, honest and artless.

"You are not yet well—"

I moved my hand to her hip. Her flesh was silken warmth, her hair so black it seemed a hole in space, falling over her shoulders and absorbing the candlelight completely, without gloss or shine. My hand moved, stroking her thigh, and my mind avoided all thoughts of right and wrong.

"Shall I lie down?" she asked.

I pulled her to me and the length of our bodies pressed together. I could feel her smooth heat through my rough clothing, and her lips parted willingly against my mouth.

"I don't know how to do it," she said.

"You've never made love?"

"No. You will show me how?"

"Do you want me to?"

"Very much," she said. Her arms clung to me, timidly but firmly. I shifted, rising above her, and she lay back, watching and waiting for me. Her passion showed only in her eyes, and was all the more inspiring because she did not know the accepted motions of manifesting desire.

"Really? You never have?" I asked.

My hand moved on her gently.

"Never. There has been no one to teach me."

It cut sharply through my fascination. She hadn't come because she wanted me, but simply because I was the first man available to her. My hand stopped moving on her flat belly, she frowned, looking into my face.

"What is wrong?" she asked.

Another thought was toying with the edge of perception, a vague uneasiness that had seized its foothold in that moment of diminished desire. I wasn't quite sure what it was . . .

"Does Hodson know you've come to me?" I asked.

"Yes."

"He doesn't mind?"

"Why should he mind?"

"I don't—Anna, when I was unconscious—did Hodson do anything to me?"

"He fixed you. Made you well."

"What did he do?"

My heart was thundering, pumping icebergs through my
arteries.

"What is wrong? Why have you stopped loving me?"

"What did he do?"

"I don't know. He made you well. He took you to his laboratory
and fixed you so that you would be all right for me to come to . . ."

She said this as though it were the most natural thing in the
world. The icebergs melted in my blood.

"Why have you stopped?" she asked. "Am I no good for making
love?"

My mind erupted in horror.

I stood beside the bed, my boots in my hand. I didn't remember getting up. Anna was staring at me, hurt and disappointed, unable to
understand how she had failed—a child punished without reason.
But what reason could I give her? She was of a different world and
there was nothing I could say. My breath came hard, but not with
desire now. I wanted only one thing, to escape from that fiendish
place, and Anna's graceful body had become loathsome to me.

I moved to the door. Anna watched me all the while. I couldn't
even say farewell to her, couldn't even beg her not to give the alarm.
She was still staring as I passed through the curtains and they closed
between us. It was more than those curtains that stood between us.
I went down the hallway to the front room. The house was silent,
Anna made no sound behind me. The front room was empty and
I moved quietly on bare feet. I didn't know what Hodson would
resort to if he found me, didn't know if he would force me to stay,
even if he might not kill me. But I felt no fear of this. The numb
horror of the situation was too great to share its place with any
other emotion, too great to be realized; and my mind froze in self
preservation.

I crossed the room and went out of the door, started walking
calmly across the narrow basin of the valley, almost sluggish in
my determination. The night was black and cold, my body felt

like a heated rod passing through the absolute zero of space, my course preordained and no friction to halt me. The ground rose and I began an angled ascent of the hills; I noticed objectively that I was climbing the same hill where the vultures had dropped down to feast the last time I departed from Hodson's. But this made no impression. Everything was external, my breath hung before me and the clouded sky was low, blanketing the hills as I climbed up to meet it.

My thoughts were superficial and purely functional, my mind rejecting the horror of the situation and concentrating on the task at hand, plotting the logical course. I had to ascend the hills, keeping in a north-eastern direction which would bring me out east of the sheer cliffs which housed the tunnel, then descend the opposite side towards the north-west, compensating for the angle and coming out somewhere near the waterfall. The high, unscalable cliffs would be visible for miles as I walked down, and I felt certain I could find them, and find the camp in relation to them. I told myself I was safe now; there was no way that Hodson could find me.

Halfway up the incline I paused to catch my breath and realized I still carried my boots in my hand. I sat down and pulled them on, looking back toward the house as I tied the laces. The house was dark and quiet. Perhaps Anna was still waiting and wondering in that little room, or perhaps Hodson knew that pursuit would prove futile. The night was very dark, and there was no way he could follow me over that rocky land. Even the extraordinary Indian would not be able to track a man at night through such terrain. Hodson had no dog to follow by scent, no way to know what direction I'd fled in, no way to—

My fingers snapped the laces.

There was one way.

There was one being behind me with the senses and instincts of the hunting carnivore—one creature capable of silently tracking me through the blackest night—one creature whose eyes glowed with night vision and seethed with hatred—

I ran, mad with fear.

I ran. The broken laces slapped at my ankle, loose stones slid beneath my feet, trees loomed up suddenly before me and I crashed through in wild flight. I stumbled and fell, leaped up to fall again, banging against rocks and trees, tearing my finger-nails at the roots as I heaved myself over boulders and caught at sapling limbs, crushing my shins and elbows without feeling pain. My mind was outside my body; I watched myself scramble through dark confusion; saw my forehead collide solidly with a rocky overhang and a line of blood seep down my temple; saw my balance tilt as I overstepped a ridge and tumbled down, legs still churning—and, all the time, apart from my body, my mind screamed that Hodson would have no qualms, that Hodson had no regard for human life, that Hodson would release the creature—

And then my mind was back inside my throbbing head, and I leaned exhausted against a mangled tree at the top of the mountain. I'd run for hours and for miles, or for minutes and for yards, it was all the same. My chest heaved so violently that it seemed the tree was vibrating and the land was running beneath my feet. I looked back. All the trees were vibrating. A razorback of land humped up in the centre and crumbled at the edges, a solid wave of earth skimmed over the rock toward me, uprooting brush and trees in its wake, and the earth itself groaned in agony. Far away a deep rumble sounded for a moment, and then died out. The movement ceased and the moaning faded. The land looked different, the contours shifted and altered, but the same wind cried above and the same blood pounded through my bursting veins.

XV

Gregorio found me in the morning.

I was still walking, following some natural instinct toward the camp, the long night a blurred memory behind me, highlights and shadows in contorted chiaroscuro and strained awareness. My panic had left with the dawn, I was walking on calmly and steadily, placing one foot before the other in studied concentration. From time to time I looked up, but I couldn't see the cliffs; lowered my head and watched my feet; noticed that the broken lace was still flaying at my ankle but didn't think to tie it. Then I looked up again and there was Gregorio. He was on the grey, staring at me, his mouth open, and I saw him through the red-rimmed frame of hollow eyes.

He moved forward on the horse and I leaned against his knee.

"Thank God," he said.

He swung from the saddle.

"How did you find me?" I asked.

"I rode this way. I didn't know. I thought that I had killed you."

That made no sense, but I didn't want sense. I collapsed against him.

I was in Gregorio's tent. My own tent was still spread over the ground. Gregorio gave me a tin mug of water and I gulped it down, feeling it trickle over my chin.

"You are all right now?"

"Yes."

"I thought that I killed you."

"I don't understand. How—"

"When you did not return in the morning—when it was light—I followed your tracks. And the tracks of the creature. I followed to the waterhole and saw where you had gone into the cave behind the water. There were no tracks coming out. I called to you and there was no answer. I did not dare to enter and I returned to the camp. But I felt very bad because of this. I waited all day and felt bad because I had not gone in the cave. I drank pisco and waited and when it was night again and the pisco was gone I was not so afraid. I went back to the waterfall, pretending that I was brave and that it was shameful I had not gone into the cave. I called again and then I went past the water and stood inside the tunnel. I stood in the entrance but I had no courage to go farther. I could not see the sky and I had no torch. I called more but there were only echoes. I thought you were dead. Then I thought that perhaps you were injured and were too far away to hear me call, and so I fired the rifle three times so that you would hear."

He paused, his hands moving expressively and frowned as he sought the words.

"The noise of the gun and the echoes—they caused something. The noise inside the mountain. It caused the mountain to move. I ran out just in time. I saw the cave close, the rocks came together and the cliffs moved backwards so that the top slid down. But it slid on the other side, not on me. I thought you were inside, maybe you were injured, and that I had buried you. Thank God it was not so."

I nodded. "The vibrations. There were faults in the rock. I felt the mountain move last night, but I thought it was my imagination. Did it move very far?"

"I think far. I could not tell, it moved on the other side. To the south."

"Perhaps it is just as well," I said.

"If the creature was inside—" Gregorio began.

"Perhaps there are things that man should not know," I told him. And then I suddenly understood the full import of that, the full extent of what I did not know. Hodson's words sounded in my mind . . .

"It is only necessary to treat the male . . ."

Gregorio looked at me with concern. He thought I was sick again, because I was very pale.

Two days later I was well—as well as I will ever be. We rode back along the path of my flight, in the early morning. My horse was as placid as ever, despite the gruesome wound on its flank. It was a good horse, and I was glad it had survived. Gregorio was curious as to why I should insist on this journey, but there was nothing I could tell him. There was nothing I could tell anyone, and when we rode over the top of the hills my last hopes vanished. It was what I had expected, what I had known with terrible anticipation.

The narrow valley was no longer there. The sheer cliffs at the apex had slid back at a gentler angle, forming the Tarpeian Rock from which my hopes were hurled to their death, and the base spread out in broken rock and upheaved earth in a shallow triangle where the valley had been. There was no sign whatsoever of Hodson's house or the cave beyond. I looked down from the hills, but hadn't the heart to descend. There was nothing to be found amidst that wreckage that would help me, no way to discover which of Hodson's stories had been deception. After all, it might have been an ape . . .

It might have been. Perhaps he had done nothing to me in that laboratory. Perhaps.

There was only one way to tell, and the method was too horrible to contemplate; it shared a common path with madness.

"Shall we go down?" Gregorio asked.

I had a fleeting thought of Anna, innocent and helpless within the framework Hodson had built around her life, buried somewhere beneath those countless tons of stone. Had she still been waiting in my bed? It didn't seem to matter. I had no sorrow to spare.

"Shall we go down?" Gregorio asked again.

"It won't be necessary."

"This is all you wished to look for?"

"This is all there is, my friend."

Gregorio blinked. He didn't understand. We rode back toward the camp, and he watched me nervously, wondering why I would not look at him. But it had nothing to do with him.

It was raining, but there was sunlight above the clouds. A flock of geese passed overhead, flying in precise formation toward the horizon, following a call they did not understand. Birds were singing in the trees and small animals avoided our path. The world was moving on at its own slow pace, with its own inexorable momentum, and nature avoided us and ignored us. Perhaps, for a few moments while the land was rumbling, nature had acted in outrage and defence, but now it was quiet once more; now it would survive.

We broke camp and headed back to Ushuaia.

There was a letter from Susan waiting at the hotel, telling how much she loved me, and Jones told me how Cape Horn looked from the air . . .

The restaurant was closing.

The late diners had departed, the waiters had gathered in the corner, waiting for me to leave. Susan had gone. My glass was empty and I was alone. I signalled and the waiter came over quickly with the bill. He thought I was drunk. I over-tipped him and went out to the street. It was late; only a few people hurried past. They were strangers, and I was a stranger. I began walking home, slowly and thoughtfully, accompanied by whatever horror I may, or may not, bear in my loins. I will never know.

There are some things it is better not to know.

THE DEAD HAND THAT CRAWLS, KILLS AND LIVES!!!

AND NOW THE Screaming Starts

for them and for you!

CINERAMA RELEASING PRESENTS
AN AMICUS PRODUCTION
AND NOW THE SCREAMING STARTS Starring PETER CUSHING/HERBERT LOM/PATRICK MAGEE/IAN OGILVY/STEPHANIE BEACHAM

Produced by MAX J. ROSENBERG AND MILTON SUBOTSKY / Directed by ROY WARD BAKER / Screenplay by ROGER MARSHALL

R RESTRICTED   IN COLOR

73/100

"AND NOW THE SCREAMING STARTS"

AFTERWORD

—And Now the Screaming Starts!

T HE 1973 PAN BOOKS PAPERBACK *And Now The Screaming Starts...* reprints David Case's story "Fengriffen" from his 1971 collection *Fengriffen and Other Stories*, with a "Now filmed by Amicus Productions" label and a remarkably lurid still of Geoffrey Whitehead with gory empty eye-sockets (strictly, a spoiler for the end of the movie) tilted at a ninety-degree angle, so that a corpse lying on the floor seems to be standing up and looming over someone.

In the early 1970s, there was quite a hook-up between the British horror film industry and paperback publishing. The indefatigable John Burke's *Hammer Horror Omnibus* books were back in print and there were novelizations of Hammer's more recent (and more lurid) *Countess Dracula* (by Michel Parry), *Lust for a Vampire* (by William Hughes) and *Scars of Dracula* (by Angus Hall) out from Sphere Books. Even *Virgin Witch* (1970) got a paperback tie-in, and reissues of J. Sheridan Le Fanu and R. Chetwynd-Hayes collections had covers using stills from Hammer's *The Vampire Lovers* (1970) and Amicus' *From Beyond the Grave* (1974), respectively.

Hammer Films cut their horror teeth on hand-me-down literary adaptations—though their *The Curse of Frankenstein* (1957), *Dracula* (1958), *The Two Faces of Dr Jekyll* (1960) and *The Phantom of the Opera* (1963) might have been scripted by writers who'd barely skimmed the source novels. They didn't reckon much to contemporary writers—their three-film relationship with Dennis Wheatley came about through Christopher Lee knowing the author, and somehow *The Devil Rides Out* (1967) seemed more of the era of Stoker and Stevenson than Richard Matheson (who scripted Hammer's film) and Robert Bloch.

Amicus Productions, Hammer's chief rival, was different. Milton Subotsky—talented producer and iffy screenwriter—was a genuine horror fan. He kept up with what was published in the 1950s, '60s and '70s rather than rely on the state of the written genre circa 1897 as Hammer did. Because the company came to specialize in anthology movies, Amicus tore through material.

Their big literary gun was Robert Bloch, still riding high on the source novel for *Psycho* (1960)—Bloch stories were spun into *The Skull* (1965), *Torture Garden* (1967), *Asylum* (1970) and *The House That Dripped Blood* (1970), and he also scripted the original *The Psychopath* (1966) and *The Deadly Bees* (1966), the latter a sadly inadequate version of H. F. Heard's brilliant novel *A Taste for Honey*.

Amicus' *They Came From Beyond Space* (1967), *The Terrornauts* (1967), *The Mind of Mr. Soames* (1969), *Scream and Scream Again* (1969), *What Became of Jack and Jill?* (1972) and *Madhouse* (1974) are all based on novels—by Joseph Millard (a huge paperback name in the UK because he novelized and then sequelized the "Man With No Name" Westerns), Murray Leinster, Charles Eric Maine, Peter Saxon, Laurence Moody and Angus Hall, respectively. Even *The Beast Must Die* (1974) is based on James Blish's werewolf novella "There Shall Be No Darkness". Subotsky also looked to the EC horror comics of the 1950s and started in on the contributors to the Pan and Fontana books of horror and ghost stories.

Eventually, he'd option Guy N. Smith's "Crabs" books which, after the rights were passed on, evolved into *Island Claws* (1980), and pick up cheap options on some Stephen King stories from the *Night Shift* collection, which were eventually acquired by Dino de Laurentiis and earned Subotsky producer credits on *Cat's Eye* (1985), *Maximum Overdrive* (1986), *Sometimes They Come Back* (1991) and *The Lawnmower Man* (1992).

In all this reading, Subotsky hit on David Case's "Fengriffen"— one of the few of the writer's novellas *not* to be reprinted by Herbert van Thal in *The Pan Book of Horror Stories*.

Objectively, it's not a very Amicus sort of horror subject. The studio distinguished itself from Hammer—and from then-busy competitors like Tigon and the British arm of American International—by concentrating on contemporary settings, with killer creeping vines in the suburbs and voodoo curses in Soho jazz clubs in *Dr. Terror's House of Horrors* (1965). "Fengriffen" was an 18th century subject, with the sort of costumes and carriages seen in

The Black Torment (1964) and a flashback instance of aristocrat-on-peasant rape and mutilation reminiscent of Hammer's *The Hound of the Baskervilles* (1958).

It even uses the familiar environs of Oakley Court, near Windsor, as Fengriffen Hall, revisiting a location seen in many Hammer films (starting with *The Man in Black*, 1950) and also featured in *The House in Nightmare Park* (1973) and *The Rocky Horror Picture Show* (1975).

Amicus' only period horror to date had been Stephen Weeks's *I Monster* (1970), an unhappy stab at Jekyll and Hyde with Christopher Lee, Peter Cushing and a 3-D process which never worked.

Also, "Fengriffen" is all about sex . . . and Amicus (specifically, Subotsky) was surprisingly prudish, especially when set beside all the cleavage and neck-nibbling shown over at Hammer, not to mention the increased emphasis on wenches being raped in the likes of Tigon's *Matthew Hopkins—Witchfinder General* (1968) and *The Blood on Satan's Claw* (1971).

With Roy Ward Baker—who had unleashed the bosoms of Ingrid Pitt and Madeleine Smith in *The Vampire Lovers*—on board as director and Stephanie Beacham, who had (as the tabloids had it) romped nude with Marlon Brando in Michael Winner's *The Night-comers* (1971), as the leading lady in very tight, very low-cut gowns, *—And Now the Screaming Starts!* might have been expected to be steamier than it is.

British folk-horror of the early 1970s could be nasty *and* sexy at the same time, but this just manages the nastiness. An odd parallel with *Witchfinder General* is that the climaxes of both involve Ian Ogilvy dementedly hacking at the person he holds responsible for his wife's rape, and the abused heroine going so mad that the film fades on her beginning to scream.

Roger Marshall, a TV veteran with many episodes of *The Avengers* to his credit, had scripted a minor UK horror film (*Theatre of Death*, 1967) and come up with the story for *Twisted Nerve* (1968). He arrived at Amicus to write *What Became of Jack and Jill?*, fresh from the ITV horror series *Shades of Darkness*, and stuck around to wrestle with a script that was first called *Bride of Fengriffen*.

Subotsky and partner Max J. Rosenberg wanted to call the film *I Have No Mouth But I Must Scream*—the title of an unrelated (and very well-known) Harlan Ellison short story—and went so far as to ask about rights, but Ellison's righteous fury squashed that idea. Subotsky then came up with the meaningless —*And Now the Screaming Starts!*, perhaps on the grounds that the equally contrived *Scream and Scream Again* (a re-titling of *The Disorientated Man*) had done well (though that at least had a great Amen Corner title song to justify it). Subotsky didn't abandon this peculiar title-poaching practice—for his werewolf whodunit, he used the title of Nicholas Blake's brilliant (and well-noted) novel *The Beast Must Die*. This time, he didn't tell anyone's agent first and got away with it.

A problem with the plot of "Fengriffen" loomed large for audiences in the swinging early 1970s. Everyone in the cheap seats realized the curse upon the house could handily be averted by Charles (Ian Ogilvy) having sex with his new bride Catherine (Beacham) between the marriage ceremony and arrival at the great house (a quickie in a lay-by in the coach would settle the ghost's hash). Ogilvy and Baker suggested that Charles could be either gay or impotent (though it's important to the plot that he does at least think he's impregnated his wife) to explain this, but the very crowded film—full of character actors and jump-scares—doesn't find the time to pursue either interpretation.

The novella is narrated by Dr. Pope, the rational proto-psychologist played by Peter Cushing in the film. Case's character assumes the haunting is all in the mind, but gradually comes to suspect there's something genuinely supernatural going on, allowing for a pastiche of the Gothic lady-in-peril narrative of Ann Radcliffe which turns the conventional plot (in which ghosts are plotters in disguise) on end. This theme was quite a commonplace in the early 1970s—Christopher Wicking's original script for *Demons of the Mind* (1972) takes the same route, with Patrick Magee (the regular doctor in —*And Now the Screaming Starts!*) as a pre-Freudian head-shrinker. Amicus' *Asylum* has *several* psychoanalysts (including Magee again) presented with supernatural events they are forced—usually too late—to believe in.

However, Marshall's script unpacks Case's plot and tells it in chronological order, so that Dr. Pope shows up half-way through, after we've seen a crawling severed hand (the impressive leftover prop from *Dr. Terror's House of Horrors*) all over the house and guest stars Guy Rolfe, Gillian Lind and Rosalie Crutchley have been killed by it.

A few apparitions of the ghostly Silas (Geoffrey Whitehead) *might* be the hallucinations of the high-strung Catherine—whose very tight stays could be contributing to her discomfort—but much of the supernatural business is shown by Baker in privileged shots—only the audience sees the spectral hand fade in and out of existence, establishing the objective reality of the spook. Therefore, poor old Dr. Pope has to catch up with what we already know, and all Cushing gets to do in the film is listen to Charles explain what a dastard his wicked grandfather (Herbert Lom) was in abusing the original Silas.

There are one or two genuine shocks—the bloody-hand-through-the-picture gambit—and some touches of poetry, though the last *Rosemary's Baby* riff is just silly: you can accept the baby inheriting Silas-Son-of-Silas' facial birthmark, but how can a severed hand be hereditary?

Incoherent it might be, but the film *looks* terrific—Denys Coop's camera prowls fluidly through Tony Curtis's multi-leveled mansion set, the costumes and set-dressing are up to British bodice-ripping standards, and Douglas Gamley's score is splendid. Everyone emotes with high seriousness—Lom, against all the odds, brings a touch of subtlety (wicked Sir Henry knows he's doing wrong even as his mates egg him on, and starts regretting his rape-and-mutilation spree even before it's over), and the buxom Beacham trembles and clutches her night-gown beautifully, even as it seems her screaming will never stop.

—*And Now the Screaming Starts!* went round the UK cinema circuits as the top half of a double-bill with the silly, likeable US horror movie *Doctor Death Seeker of Souls* (1973). For me, its greatest achievement might have been inspiring Pan Books to issue a paperback with David Case's name—and those blasted-out bloody eye-sockets—on the cover.

Kim Newman
London
September 2015

DAVID F. CASE was born in upstate New York in 1937. Since the early 1960s he has lived in London, as well as spending time in Greece and Spain. His acclaimed collection *The Cell: Three Tales of Horror* appeared in 1969, and it was followed by the novels *Fengriffen: A Chilling Tale*, *Wolf Tracks* and *The Third Grave*. His other collections include *Brotherly Love and Other Tales of Trust and Knowledge*, *Pelican Cay & Other Disquieting Tales*, and an omnibus volume in the *Masters of the Weird Tale* series from Centipede Press. A regular contributor to the legendary *Pan Book of Horror Stories* during the early 1970s, his powerful zombie novella "Pelican Cay" in *Dark Terrors 5* was nominated for a World Fantasy Award in 2001.

STEPHEN JONES lives in London, England. A Hugo Award nominee, he is the winner of three World Fantasy Awards, three International Horror Guild Awards, four Bram Stoker Awards, twenty-one British Fantasy Awards and a Lifetime Achievement Award from the Horror Writers Association. One of Britain's most acclaimed horror and dark fantasy writers and editors, he has more than 135 books to his credit, including *The Art of Horror: An Illustrated History*, *Horrorology: The Lexicon of Fear*, the *Zombie Apocalypse!* series and twenty-six volumes of *Best New Horror*. You can visit his website at www.stephenjoneseditor.com or follow him on Facebook at Stephen Jones–Editor.

KIM NEWMAN is a novelist, critic and broadcaster. His most recent publications include the non-fiction studies *Kim Newman's Movie Dungeon* and *Quatermass and the Pit*, the mini-series *Witchfinder: The Mysteries of Unland* (a spin-off from Mike Mignola's *Hellboy* series with Maura McHugh) for Dark Horse Comics, the expanded reissues of his acclaimed *Anno Dracula* series, and his latest novel, *Secrets of Drearcliff Grange School*. He is a contributing editor to *Sight & Sound* and *Empire* magazines, has written and broadcast widely, and scripted radio and television documentaries. His official website is at www.johnnyalucard.com and he is on Twitter as @AnnoDracula.

CPSIA information can be obtained
at www.ICGtesting.com
Printed in the USA
BVHW080358180322
631650BV00010B/1599